Mystery Novels by Laurie R. King

Mary Russell Novels

THE BEEKEEPER'S APPRENTICE
A MONSTROUS REGIMENT OF WOMEN
A LETTER OF MARY
THE MOOR
O JERUSALEM

Kate Martinelli Novels

A GRAVE TALENT
TO PLAY THE FOOL
WITH CHILD
NIGHT WORK

A DARKER PLACE

And coming soon in hardcover:
FOLLY

Night Work

Raves for Laurie R. King

"One of the most original talents to emerge in the '90s."
—*Kirkus Reviews*

"King's prose is immensely readable and her characters [are] complex and interesting. King is a damned fine prose-smith . . . too good a writer not to read."
Mystery News

"King is a talent to be reckoned with."
—*Feminist Bookstore News*

"King always writes well, and her stories sweep along with an inexorable force that comes from a power greater than mere skillful plotting."
—*The Boston Globe*

. . . And Kate Martinelli

"Laurie King knows how to keep a plot boiling, and her crusty, sharp-tongued Kate is appealingly vulnerable."
—*The Philadelphia Inquirer*

"Laurie R. King manages to create from Page 1 of every book the feeling that the reader will be in good hands. Martinelli is the kind of person you'd like to know and talk with over many lunches; a smart and tough woman."
—*Chicago Tribune*

NIGHT WORK

"Kate's passion, and King's, brings new urgency to a familiar story about merging personal conviction with professional duty."
—*Kirkus Reviews*

"A solid choice for those who like tough female cops."
—*Booklist*

WITH CHILD

"Smart, thoughtful . . . Ms. King has a way with children . . . warm characterizations . . . searching insights . . . This detective has a mind that is always on the move."
—*The New York Times Book Review*

TO PLAY THE FOOL

"Beautifully written, with clearly defined and engaging characters."
—*The Boston Globe*

A GRAVE TALENT
Winner of the Edgar and Creasey Awards for Best First Crime Novel

"If there is a new P. D. James lurking in this stack of books, I would put my money on Laurie R. King, whose *A Grave Talent* kept me reading deep into the night."
—*The Boston Globe*

"An amazing first novel with intelligence, intrigue, and intricacy . . . This work exhibits strong psychological undertones, compelling urgency, and dramatic action."
—*Library Journal*

And Laurie R. King's stand-alone novel
A DARKER PLACE

"A nail-biter thriller."
—*The New York Times Book Review*

"Laurie R. King delivers a story that . . . casts a spell of psychological terror more visceral than any serial killer melodrama and that, for the thoughtful reader, offers intellectual rewards as well."
—*The San Diego Union-Tribune*

A KATE MARTINELLI MYSTERY

by

Laurie R. King

BANTAM BOOKS
NEW YORK   TORONTO   LONDON   SYDNEY   AUCKLAND

NIGHT WORK

A Bantam Book

PUBLISHING HISTORY
Bantam hardcover edition published February 2000
Bantam mass market edition / December 2000

ISBN: 0-553-57825-1

Published simultaneously in the United States and Canada

Bantam Books are published by Bantam Books, a division of Random
House, Inc. Its trademark, consisting of the words "Bantam Books"
and the portrayal of a rooster, is Registered in U.S. Patent and
Trademark Office and in other countries. Marca Registrada. Bantam
Books, 1540 Broadway, New York, New York 10036.

To Linda Allen,
friend and agent,
who believed

With thanks to Gretchen Tom, who deciphers the King hieroglyphs better than their creator does, and to Bob Pori, for sharing his pharmacological expertise.

And with deep gratitude to the members of the San Francisco Police Department, especially Captain Kevin Dillon, Inspector Holly Pera of the Homicide Detail, and Inspector Pamela Hofsass, who took pity on a poor novelist and tried their best to inject a little reality into the following story. They are not to be held responsible for the stubborn insistence of a weaver of fiction, who values the textures of storytelling over the actualities of on-call schedules and promotion priorities.

But I got the gun right.

INTRODUCTION

The kingdom of Kali is within us deep.
The built-in destroyer, the savage goddess,
Wakes in the dark and takes away our sleep.
She moves through the blood to poison gentleness.

The image on the wall was enough to give a man nightmares. It showed a woman of sorts, but a woman who would have made a playboy shrivel, given pause to the most ardent feminist, and had Freud scrambling to retract his plaintive query concerning what women wanted.

What this lady wanted was blood.

Her skin was dark, so deep a blue it seemed black against the crisp, bright, bloodred waves that splashed against her muscular calves. Around her hips she wore a belt strung with human hands that had been hacked off at the wrist; her neck was looped with a necklace of skulls. Her wild black hair made a matted tangle from which serpents peeped, and from her right ear hung a cluster of dry bones. Four arms emerged from her strong shoulders, in the manner of Hindu deities and the half-joking fantasy of busy mothers the world around, and all twenty of her dagger-long fingernails were red, the same bloodred as the sea around her. In her lower right hand she held a cast-iron skillet, wielding it like a weapon; her upper left grasped the freshly severed head of a man.

The expression on the lady's face was at once beautiful and terrible, the Mona Lisa's evil sister. Her stance and the set of her shoulders shouted out her triumph and exultation as she showed her tongue and bared her sharp white teeth in pleasure, glorying at the clear blue sky above her, at the pensive vulture in a nearby tree, at the curling smoke from the pyres of the cremation grounds on the hill nearby, at the drained, bearded, staring object swinging from the end of her arm.

She looked drunk on the pleasure of killing, burning with ecstasy at the deep hot lake of shed blood she was wading through.

And she looked far from finished with the slaughter.

She was Kali, whose name means black, the Indian goddess of destruction and creation. Kali, who kills in joy and in rage, Kali the undefeatable, Kali the mother who turns on her faithless children, Kali the destroyer, Kali the creator, whose slaughter brings life, whose energies stimulate Shiva to perform his final dance, a dance that will bring about the end of all creation, all time, all life.

1

It is a place of skulls, a deathly place
Where we confront our violence and feel,
Before that broken and self-ravaged face,
The murderers we are, brought here to kneel.

Kate Martinelli sat in her uncomfortable metal folding chair and watched the world come to an end.

It ended quite nicely, in fact, considering the resources at hand and the skill of the participants, with an eye-searing flash and a startling crack, a swirl of colors, then abrupt darkness.

And giggles.

The lights went up again, parents and friends rose to applaud wildly, and twenty-three brightly costumed and painted children gathered on the stage to receive their praise.

The reason for Kate's presence stood third from the end, a mop-headed child with skin the color of milky coffee, a smile that lacked a pair of front teeth, and black eyes that glittered with excitement and pride.

Kate leaned over to speak into the ear of the woman at her side. "Your goddaughter makes a fine monkey."

Lee Cooper laughed. "Mina's been driving Roz and Maj nuts practicing her part—she wore one tail out completely and broke a leg off the sofa jumping onto it. Last week she decided she wasn't going to eat anything but bananas, until Roz got a book that listed what monkeys actually eat."

"I hope she didn't then go around picking bugs out of tree trunks."

"I think Roz read selectively."

"Never trust a minister. Do you know—" Kate stopped, her face changing. She reached into her pocket and pulled out a vibrating pager, looked up at Lee, and shrugged in apology before digging the cell phone out of her pocket and beginning to push her way toward the exit and relative quiet. She was back in a couple of minutes, slipping the phone away as she walked up to the man who had been sitting on her other side during the performance and who was now standing at Lee's elbow, watchful and ready to offer a supporting hand in the crowd. Lee's caregiver spoke before Kate could open her mouth.

"What a pity, you're going to miss the fruit punch and cookies."

She rolled her eyes and said low into Jon's ear, "Why it couldn't have come an hour ago . . ."

"Poor dear," he said, sounding not in the least sympathetic. " 'A policeman's lot is not a happy one.' "

"If I find you a ride, would you take her home?"

"Happy to. I'll be going out later, though."

"She'll be fine." Now for the difficult part. "Lee," Kate began. "Sweetheart?" but groveling did not prove necessary.

"You're off, then?"

"I'm sorry."

"Liar," said Lee cheerfully. "But you've been a very brave honorary godmother, so now you can go and play with your friends. That was Al, I assume?"

Kate and her partner, Al Hawkin, were on call tonight, and in a city the size of San Francisco, a homicide was no rare thing. She nodded, hesitated, and kissed Lee briefly on the cheek. Lee looked more pleased than surprised, which Kate took as a sign that she was doing something right, and Kate in turn felt gratified beyond the scope of her lover's reaction—their relationship had been more than a little touchy in recent months, and small signs loomed large. She stepped away carefully, looking down to be sure she didn't knock into Lee's cuffed crutches, and walked around the arranged folding chairs to congratulate Mina's adoptive parents. They were surrounded by others bent on the same purpose—or rather, Roz was surrounded by a circle of admirers, this tall, brown-haired, slightly freckled woman who was glowing and laughing and giving off warmth like (as one article in the Sunday *Chronicle* had put it) a fireplace of the soul.

When she had read that phrase, Kate had wondered to herself if the reporter really meant that Roz was hot. She was, in fact, one of the most unconsciously sexy women Kate knew.

Kate hadn't seen Roz in a couple of weeks, but she knew just looking at her, the way she gestured and leaned toward her audience, the way her laugh came and her eyes flashed, that Roz was involved in some passionate quest or other: She seemed to have grown a couple of inches and lost ten years, a look Kate had seen her wear often enough. Or it could have been from the fulsome praise being heaped on her by the other parents—all of whom, it seemed, had seen a television program Roz had been on the night before and were eager to tell her how great it had been, how great she had been. Roz threw one arm around the school principal and laughed with honest self-deprecation, and while Kate waited to get a word in, she studied the side of that animated face with the slightly uncomfortable affection a person invariably feels toward someone in whose debt she is and always will be, an ever-so-slightly servile discomfort that in Kate's case was magnified by the knowledge that her own lover had once slept with this woman. She liked Roz (how could she not?) and respected her enormously, but she could never be completely comfortable with her.

Roz's partner, Maj Freiling, stood slightly to one side, taking all this in while she spoke with a woman Kate vaguely remembered having met at one of their parties. Maj was short, black-haired, and—incongruously—Swedish; her name therefore was pronounced "my," forming the source of endless puns from Roz. Most people who knew Roz assumed that her quiet partner was a nonentity whose job was to keep house, to produce brilliant meals at the drop of Roz's hat, and to laugh politely at Roz's jokes. Most people were wrong. Just because Maj spoke little did not mean she had nothing to say. She was the holder of several degrees in an area of brain research so arcane only half a dozen people in San Francisco had ever heard of it, and they in turn were not of the sort to be found in Roz's company of politicians and reformers. It seemed to Kate a case of complete incompatibility leading to a rock-solid marriage, just one more thing she didn't understand about Roz Hall.

Kate looked from one woman to the other, and gave up on the attempt to reach Roz. Maj smiled at Kate in complicity as Kate approached. Kate found herself grinning in return as she reached out to squeeze Maj's arm.

"Thanks for inviting me," she said. "I was going to come to the party afterward, but I got a call, and have to go. Sorry. Be sure to tell Mina she was the best monkey I've ever seen."

"I will tell her. And don't worry, your avoidance of our potluck desserts is in good company." Maj glanced over Kate's shoulder toward the door. Kate turned and saw a distinctively tailored and hatted figure sweeping out of the school cafeteria. The moment the door swung shut behind him, someone's voice rose above the babble with a remark about the Ladies of Perpetual Disgruntlement, the group of feminist vigilantes who had in recent weeks set the city on its ear with a series of creative and, Kate had to admit privately, funny acts of revenge. Just that morning the mayor had issued a statement to the press saying, in effect, "We are not amused."

Kate smiled absently at the overheard remark and turned back to Maj. "That was the mayor, wasn't it?"

Maj shrugged and gave her a crooked smile as if to apologize for a flashy display.

"I wondered whose car that was. Very impressive,"

Kate told her. "Look, Maj, could you find someone who might be able to take Lee and Jon home? We only brought the one car."

"We, on the other hand, always bring two, because Roz invariably finds someone she just has to talk to. I'd be happy to give them a ride, if they don't mind waiting for Mina to stuff herself with cookies first."

"I'm sure they won't mind. Jon secretly adores Oreo cookies and—what are those Jell-O things called?"

"Jigglers," Maj pronounced with fastidious disapproval, giving the word three syllables. Kate laughed and reached out again to pat Maj's shoulder in thanks, waved to Lee, and hurried out of the school hall in the footsteps of Hizzoner to her own, lesser vehicle.

The western sky was still faintly light ahead of her as Kate drove down Lombard Street in the recently acquired and thoroughly broken-in Honda, which on the first warm day she owned it had declared itself to be the former property of a pizza delivery boy. She rolled down the window to let in the air of this April evening, clear and sweet after the drizzle earlier in the day, and wished she hadn't let Lee bully her into giving up the motorcycle.

Kate loved San Francisco best at night. During the day it was an interesting city, decorative and lively and every bit as anonymous as a villain, or a cop, could ask for. But at night the city closed in and became intimate, a cluster of hills and valleys with the sea curled up against three sides of it. Sometimes, beneath the stars and the hum of traffic and the collective breathing of three-quarters of a million people, Kate imagined she could hear the city's song.

The imagined song was a flight of fancy unlike Kate—or rather, unlike the image Kate had of herself—and a thing she had never mentioned to anyone, even to Lee. (Perhaps especially not Lee, an analytical therapist who tended to read far too much into small imaginings.) Like an old tune that had been recorded in a hundred ways, the song of the City could be smooth and sexy from the throat of a torch singer or ornate in *a cappella,* coolly instrumental or raunchy in rock. The city's complex melody was never the same on two nights or in two places: Here it had a salsa beat, there the drive of rap held it, elsewhere it was transformed by the plink and slither of Chinese instruments and harmonies, in another part of town it had the raga complexity of Indian music. During those "only in San Francisco" times when the latest outrageous excess of the City by the Bay made the final, tongue-in-cheek segment on the national news—since the Ladies of Perpetual Disgruntlement had come on the scene, for example—the song occasionally took on comic overtones, like a movie score preparing the audience for a pratfall. No matter the setting, though, it was the same song, the night song of the City of St. Francis, and it kept Kate Martinelli company as she crossed its streets to the scene of a crime.

Lombard Street's garish blast of motel and cocktail lounge lights cut off abruptly at the wide gate that marked the entrance to the Presidio, and the clutter of buildings and phone lines gave way to trees and dignified officers' housing. The Army was in the process of withdrawing from the base it had built here, the most gorgeous piece of open land left in San Francisco, but so far the untidy life of civilian San Francisco had been kept at bay, and Kate's headlights picked out neatly trimmed lawn and ranks of dark barracks. Following the directions she had been given, she kept to the right. The road passed along the edge of a parking lot so huge it might have been a parade grounds, with three cars in it, before narrowing further to become a single lane between a wooden building and the madly busy but oddly removed freeway that led to the Golden Gate Bridge, and then Kate saw the gates to the military cemetery and a police car across the adjoining road, turning cars back. She showed the uniform her identification and drove on, headlights playing now across rows of gleaming white gravestones that stretched up the hill to her left, and then the City's song took on a discordant note, like the warning of a minor chord in a suspense movie, with the appearance of a brilliant blue-white light thrown against the undersides of the trees around the next turn.

The stark glare rising before her in the night made Kate slow to a crawl before rounding the corner. What looked like two hundred people were scattered up the road before her, although she knew it could not be more than thirty at the most, and that included the reporters, who had come here on foot, dragging their equipment with them, from where they had been forced to leave their vans on the other side of the cemetery. She pulled to one side and parked among a wild assortment of official vehicles—park police and SFPD cruisers, ambulance and coroner's van, half a dozen unmarked police cars—and a few small cars from personnel who had been called from home. Further along the curve of the road, kept at a distance by uniforms but making full use of their long-range lenses, television vans were already in attendance, hoping for a lead story for the eleven o'clock news. A uniformed patrolman was still in the process of wrapping yellow tape around the perimeter of the crime scene, using trees, a fence post, and a convenient street sign. Kate nodded at familiar faces among the cops, ignored the questions of the reporters on this side of the scene, and ducked under the restraining tape.

Al Hawkin was standing with his hands in his pockets watching the medical examiner at work, homicide bag on the ground at his feet. He turned when he felt his partner at his side.

"So much for an evening off," he said by way of greeting.

"If you'd called an hour earlier you'd have saved me from the whole play."

"Which one was that?"

"A school play, if you can believe it. You know Roz Hall?" He nodded; half the people in the City knew Roz Hall, to their pleasure or their fury, and occasionally both at once. "Well, she and her partner, Maj, adopted Maj's niece last year, and asked Lee to be the godmother. The kid—her name's Mina—goes to a private school that's big on ethnic celebrations, and this was some complicated Indian story about gods and wars. Mina played a monkey. The mayor himself was there." Hawkin's eyebrows went up. "So, what do we have here?"

"The ME beat me here, so I haven't had a chance to look. Called in by a jogger just after six-thirty—there's a uniformed at the guy's house. Seems to be a white male, no obvious signs of violence that the jogger could see, but then he only looked close enough to pass on the CPR before heading home for a phone. I'd say the vic looks to be about twenty-four hours old."

"Funny place to have a heart attack," Kate remarked. "And he wasn't exactly dressed for jogging." What they could see of the body, half hidden by the bushes at the side of the paving, was clothed in heavy, stained work boots and some sort of khaki pants. "And why on earth didn't anyone spot it during the day? This is a pretty heavily used road."

"Not as many people on foot as usual, because of the rain. It was getting dark, so the guy who found him figured it was safe to stop and have a pee, happened to stop here."

There was a certain humor in the picture, which Kate turned over in her mind as they waited to be allowed access to the body. Al broke into her thoughts with a question.

"Why do you suppose he was dropped here? Other than it's dark and you can see cars coming?"

Kate looked around, and she had to admit that it was not the first place she would have chosen for easy disposal of an inconvenient corpse. "If it'd been me, I'd have gone on down there," she told her partner, nodding toward a cluster of dark buildings in the hollow of the hill. "There's no gate across the access road, is there?"

"Nope. And the park guys say there wasn't anything going on there last night, shouldn't have been any traffic down there at all."

Kate turned and looked in the other direction, up the

hill. On the other side of the road, some brambles and
trees rose up, then the fence that surrounded the cemetery. "You suppose they were aiming for the cemetery
but missed? Maybe there were people in there, scared
the perps off." She herself had run through the Presidio
when she was feeling ambitious, and knew the cemetery
for a closed-in area with limited access and regular visitors, too likely to get trapped in there, and hard to
explain a dead body missing its casket and mortuary
van.

Eventually, the ME stood away and she and Hawkin
moved into the glare of the portable floodlights to get a
closer look at their dead white male.

Dead he clearly was, and Kate agreed that trying
CPR on that darkened face with that swollen, froth-
covered tongue protruding was not a cheering prospect.

"Strangled," she said, pointing out the obvious.

"With something other than hands," Al added as he
lifted back the collar of the man's plaid shirt. Something had torn into the soft skin of the throat, chafing it
raw as it did its work.

The man had blunt features, cropped hair, and the
coarse bloom of long-term alcohol use in his nose. His
belly was big and soft although his chest and upper
arms appeared muscular where his shirt had been
pulled away by the paramedics. He wore a jeans jacket
but cotton-polyester uniform trousers, and a belt with a
buckle declaring the man's loyalty to Coors beer.

"Are his hands tied?"

Al tugged at the inert shoulder, which showed signs
that rigor mortis was passing off, to reveal the man's
thick wrists. They wore a pair of regulation police
handcuffs identical to those in Kate's bag. Neither of
them commented on the cuffs, but Al held the man's
torso off the ground until Kate had removed a fat wallet
from the hip pocket of the pants, then eased the body
back down until it was lying as it had been when Kate
arrived on the scene.

"Not robbery." It was Al's turn to point out the obvious. A gold band dug deep into the flesh of the man's

meaty ring finger, and in his wallet were eighty-two dollars, a stack of membership cards to video rental parlors, a credit card, and a California driver's license that identified the corpse as one James Larsen, with an address in the bedroom community of South San Francisco. A working man's address to match his clothes and his hands, and somewhat out of the ordinary for a San Francisco homicide victim.

They patted down James Larsen's pockets with care, since the rubber gloves both detectives wore gave no protection against the myriad of sharp and potentially lethal objects people carried around. Kate found a ticket stub to an action movie dated three days before, six coins, a used handkerchief, and the wrapper from a stick of beef jerky. No keys. Al slid a hand into Larsen's left-side jacket pocket and pulled out three cellophane-wrapped pieces of candy: a lump of hard butterscotch, a flattened square of striped coconut chew, and a squashed wad of something red and soft. Mr. James Larsen, it would appear, had had a sweet tooth.

Hawkin dropped the candies into an evidence bag and stood up to let the rest of the team move in. The photographer took a few close-ups to go with his earlier shots of the crime scene as it had appeared before anyone went near the body, and the Crime Scene officers bent to their labors. Kate and Hawkin walked over to where the techs were leaning against their van, the smoke from their cigarettes mingling with the tang of eucalyptus in the cool night air. All four city employees ignored the calls of the gathered news media as if it had been the noise of so many plaintive seagulls.

"Any idea when the autopsy'll be?" Al asked them.

"Might be tomorrow, more likely the next day. The morgue's pretty crowded."

"Let me know."

"But I can tell you now what they'll find," the man continued.

"Clogged arteries, a bad liver, and strangulation," Hawkin offered.

"A taser."

"What?"

"A stun gun, taser, whatever you call it. One of those things women carry. It wouldn't have killed him, but whoever did this used one to put him down." The tech threw his cigarette on the pavement and ground it under his heel, blithely contaminating the periphery of a crime scene, then led the two detectives over to the body. He squatted and pulled the plaid shirt back again from Larsen's strong chest. "That's a taser burn," he asserted, pointing to a small red area, and looked up to catch their reaction.

There was none. Both detectives kept their faces empty, and Al merely said, "I suggest you keep that theory to yourself," casting a quick glance over his shoulder at the waiting reporters, and allowed the process of removing the body to go on.

Still, Kate made a note of what the tech had said before she followed Al over to where they had parked their cars.

"It looked more like a bruise to me," she said firmly, as if saying so would make a bit of difference. Her partner grunted. "And really, even if it is a taser—"

"We'll know soon enough," Al remarked, and walked over to give the reporters what little he could. Or would.

The taser, if the mark on James Larsen's chest was not bruise, birthmark, pimple, or the growth of some exotic contagion, would create a problem, because that was how the Ladies of Perpetual Disgruntlement, that source of sly jokes at school parties and embarrassment to mayors and cops, began life: with a taser.

The reign of the Ladies (quickly shortened by an admiring public to the LOPD, although they referred to themselves as merely the Ladies) had begun back in late January, when a lowlife named Barry Doyle was acquitted of statutory rape. Belinda Matheson, aged fifteen years and ten months, had gone cruising with some friends with a borrowed ID that looked very like her (hardly unusual, since it belonged to her older sister) and declared her to be twenty-one. Doyle was twice her age, although his boyish features had a vague resemblance to Leonardo DiCaprio, and the combination of his cute face, his clever flattery, and his illicit booze had landed the teenager in Doyle's bed. Her parents, apoplectic with worry by the time Belinda dragged herself home the next afternoon, furiously pressed charges, but Doyle had a good lawyer and drew an inexperienced prosecutor who allowed a jury that was predominantly male and exclusively unmarried or divorced. The combination of testimony—that Doyle had been seen to check Belinda's ID, reassuring himself that she was no minor; that she had looked to be the person on the license (this bolstered by a blowup photo of Belinda in adult makeup and upswept hair); and most damaging of all, that she was by no means an innocent (this last from an ex-boyfriend who showed great promise for stepping into Barry Doyle's sleaze-covered shoes)—conspired to produce a verdict that had Doyle, owner of six adult video parlors and a topless bar that the jury knew nothing about, crowing his victory over the forces of "disgruntled feminists and other human rights fascists" right there on the courthouse steps—and announcing that he was in turn suing the Matheson family for the "emotional, financial, and professional damage" he had suffered through their "cold-blooded deception." He ended his impromptu press conference by looking straight into the nearest television camera and declaring, "Fair's fair, Belinda."

Shortly before midnight that same day, following a wild celebratory dinner, Doyle vanished somewhere between his car and his front door. He was discovered eight hours later by morning commuters, quite alive if spitting with rage, stark naked and spread-eagled across the window of a building under renovation. His genitals had been dyed purple (as could be seen from the cars that were soon at a complete halt on the freeway) and the duct tape that suspended him from the window frame ripped most of the hair off his wrists, ankles, and face, but most shocking (and delicious) of all was the revelation that underneath the purple dye, he had been tattooed. The phrase I SCREW CHILDREN was now an indelible part of Barry Doyle's equipment, until such time as he was driven to submit to the pain of eradication, and the note duct-taped to his backside put the cap on the episode:

FAIR'S FAIR, DICK.
—The Ladies of Perpetual Disgruntlement

Oh joy, oh ecstasy, on the part of all the world that had never flirted with the idea of bedding an underage girl. And oh the discomfort, oh the uneasy shriveling felt by all society's members (so to speak) who had. A thousand duct-tape jokes bloomed on late-night television, the color purple took on a whole new significance, tattoo artists became the heroes (and the suspects) of the hour. The Ladies instantly overtook their predecessors in the Only-in-San Francisco category, the gay/lesbian/bi/and-a-few-straights protest group called the Sisters of Perpetual Indulgence. In three days the Ladies had half a dozen fan Web sites, twenty designs of T-shirts for sale around the city's tourist sites (all of them purple), and a hundred jokes about how many Ladies it took to tattoo a man. (A representative answer: None at all, if he's a true Dick.) Even Doyle's friends began to forget that his name was Barry.

Since then, the Ladies had struck twice more. Their most visible action was when a billboard went up, again overlooking the freeway and this time only five hundred yards from police headquarters, showing the face of a prominent local politician superimposed on a male with a naked child in his lap (the politician took an immediate extended vacation, considered by all a sure admission of guilt). Taped to the billboard's access ladder was a note saying:

NAUGHTY BOY.
—the Ladies

Their third strike was against a chronic flasher out in the Sunset, overcome by a taser-wielding duo and duct-taped, naked and face-forward, to embrace a metal lamppost on a very cold night. The note taped to his anatomy read:

BIT DRAFTY?
—*the Ladies*

The official Departmental line, of course, was that vigilante actions of this sort were wrong, dangerous, and not to be tolerated. But there were as many cracks about frostbite within the walls of the Justice building as there were outside, and a cop only had to murmur the words "duct tape" to have the room convulsed.

Other actions had been attributed to the Ladies of Perpetual Disgruntlement, both in the Bay Area and across the state, but none were certain, since they lacked the hallmark humor. The police had no more idea who the Ladies were (or even if they were actually women) than they had in January. The obvious suggestion, that some of the "nuns" of the Sisters of Perpetual Indulgence had decided to grow teeth, was investigated, but no links were found beyond the middle words in the two names and their clear common regard for irreverence. No fingerprints had been found on the duct tape, no identifiable evidence recovered from the crime scenes, the three notes were on paper sold by the ream in chain stores and generated by software and a computer and printer that half of the state could own. Even the billboard, as public an act as could be imagined, had been a fast strike involving prepainted sheets and wallpaper glue. All the police knew was that the Ladies struck at night, and that two of their actions had involved tasers.

And now a man with a possible taser burn on his chest lay dead.

Crime Scene agreed that, particularly as the rain seemed to have stopped for the night, it would be far better to leave the site until morning. Al arranged for the road to remain closed off and for the scene to be guarded from the depredations of the cameras, before the two detectives went to interview their only witness.

The jogger who had come across the body seemed to be just that, not the murderer returned to the scene to "discover" his victim. He even produced the stub from an airline boarding pass to prove that he had only returned that morning from a business trip. They thanked him and left, and then set off to the Larsen home, to make the announcement and see what they could see.

The Larsen address was in South San Francisco, half an hour down the peninsula from the city and a different world. The big white letters on the hillside declared South San Francisco to be THE INDUSTRIAL CITY, a place dominated by San Francisco International and all the freight, crated and human, that the airport moved.

The Larsen house proved to be one of a thousand cramped stucco boxes thrown up after the war. Even in the inadequate illumination from their flashlights and one dim street lamp, the house showed every year of its half century. Weeds grew in the cracks of the walkway, the cover of the porch light had broken and been removed, and the paint was dull and beginning to peel. Al put his thumb on the bell, and after a minute of no response pounded on the door, but the house remained dark. A trip around the building with flashlights at the windows showed them merely the untidy interior of a tract house, so they split up, heading in opposite directions along the street to stop in at every house where lights still showed. When they met up again to compare notes, the information each had gleaned from the neighbors amounted to the same thing.

The Larsen family had lived here for at least ten years. James worked as a baggage handler at the airport, his wife, Emily, kept house. Their two kids were grown and moved away. His wife had recently left him, and the across-the-street neighbor he went bowling with, the only one who might possibly know where

Larsen's wife or kids were, was away on vacation, due back in three or four days. The one piece of information Kate could add concerned the Larsen car, a six-year-old Chevrolet sedan. DMV gave her the license number, and as they sat in the front seat of Kate's car to write up their field notes, she put out a bulletin for the car. Then, since there was not a great deal more they could do at that time of night, and since there seemed to be no immediate reason to roust a judge out of bed to sign a search warrant, they went their separate ways through the dark and drowsing peninsula, and were both in their beds not so much after midnight.

A deceptively ordinary beginning to a far from ordinary case.

2

There are times when
I think only of killing
The voracious animal
Who is my perpetual shame.

One of the medical techs had talked. Either that, or the *Chronicle* reporter had a contact within SFPD who had heard the rumor, because the front page of the paper that Kate fetched from the flower bed the following morning had the story of the body found in the Presidio, an indistinct picture of Al Hawkin walking away from it, and the clear speculation that the death was linked with the Ladies of Perpetual Disgruntlement. Kate cursed, told Lee that she wouldn't be having breakfast, and while Hawkin was out checking on the progress of the crime scene search, Kate set off to hunt down the history of a victim.

James Larsen had a lengthy arrest record, though only two convictions: one for drunk-and-disorderly at the age of nineteen, and one five years before his death, for assaulting his wife. In the twenty-five years between those two convictions, Emily Larsen had been a regular visitor to the hospital emergency room, but had consistently refused to press charges. Only in recent years, when the law was changed to make spousal cooperation unnecessary for domestic violence prosecution, had Larsen been vulnerable.

Since then he had been careful. The police still came to his house every six or eight months, but they had not arrested him again until the end of February, when the beer binge that he had begun the day before fed into resentments real and imagined and was topped off by his anger over his favorite team's defeat, leaving Emily bleeding onto the floor of the emergency room. He had been arrested and charged with attempted murder, and bail was placed too high for him to reach. Three weeks later the charges were reduced, to battery and assault, and a tired judge had sentenced him to time served, a year of probation, a hundred hours of community service, and marriage counseling. He then turned Larsen loose. Two weeks after that, a pair of SFPD homicide detectives were standing over his corpse.

Just before his release from jail, according to the neighbors, Emily had packed her bags and been driven off by a woman in a Mercedes; she had not been seen since. Or heard from: Emily's few acquaintances did not know where she was, her sister in Fresno hadn't spoken with her since early March, and their father, in a rest home near Fresno, neither knew nor was he interested.

When Emily Larsen had not shown up at her house the following morning, Kate had asked the phone company to preserve the records of the incoming calls for a few days, and then made out a request for a search warrant on the records for the Larsen phone. It was the previous month's phone bill that gave the missing woman away. Four days before her husband was released from jail, Emily had made a telephone call to a lawyer's office in San Francisco. Kate, working her way through the calls, heard the greeting "Law offices" and knew she'd found the wife. She identified herself, asked to speak with the partner who was representing one Emily Larsen, declined to be called back, and settled in with her heels on the desk to wait. She listened to the piano music of call-holding coming through the receiver, understanding that legal dignity required that a cop be made to wait. She'd done the same herself to lawyers. With the phone tucked under her chin, she sat tight and glanced through a stack of memos and Daily

Incident Recaps that had been accumulating on her desk. The recaps, in addition to the usual list of attempted robberies, hit-and-runs, and sexual assaults, included the laconic description of assault by a chronic urinator who was proving a nuisance to passersby— particularly those on bicycles. The memos included one decree (what Kate reckoned was the thirtieth such issued) that department personnel were not, under any circumstances, to make jokes about the Ladies of Perpetual Disgruntlement, or duct tape, or the color purple. Another memo was the announcement that an unknown group had been plastering up flyers seeming to advocate the extermination of all male children, which caused Kate to read it more closely and shake her head. She was looking at a third memo bearing a stern reminder concerning the cost to local supermarkets of the oversized plastic shopping carts favored by the homeless, when the music in her ear cut off abruptly and a woman's voice spoke in her ear.

"Inspector Kate Martinelli?"

"That's right."

"Carla Lomax here. I believe we've met, at a fundraiser for the teen shelter. I certainly know your name."

And reputation, Kate thought. In fact, she'd counted on it. "Good, then you'll know I'm not the bad guy here. I'm trying to reach one of your clients, Emily Larsen."

"What makes you think—"

"She called this number on March sixteenth, a few days before her abusive husband was freed from jail. A day or two later, some woman came to the house and drove Emily Larsen away. Her husband has died. I need to talk with her."

"What happy news."

"I beg your pardon?"

"That the bastard is dead. It makes my job a lot easier, and Emily's life. Not that she will see it that way, poor thing, but truth to tell she would have gone back to him eventually, and eventually he would have killed her. Much better this way."

"Um." In Kate's experience, lawyers did not speak so frankly, certainly not to a cop. "Right. You are representing her, then? May I have her address, please?"

"I am representing her, yes, and I think it would be better if I continued to do so by asking you to come here to interview her in my presence. She's living in a shelter, and it's better if the residents don't feel invaded. I could bring her to you, if you'd prefer, Inspector."

Kate reflected for a moment before deciding that if the much-abused Emily Larsen had nothing to do with her husband's death, it would not help matters to drag her downtown, whereas if she did, keeping the first interview away from police territory would give the woman a false sense of security that might come in useful later.

"I'll come there," she said. "What time?"

They agreed to two o'clock at Lomax's law offices south of Market Street. Kate took her heels off her desk, brought the paperwork for that report and a couple of others up to date, and went home for lunch, a rare occurrence.

At two o'clock, while Al Hawkin was bracing himself for the first cut of the pathologist's knife into the body of James Larsen, Kate rang the bell at the entrance of the anonymous building. As Kate thoughtfully eyed the dents and bashes in the surface of the stout metal door, the speaker set over the bell crackled to life, and the same secretarial voice she had heard before declared, "Law offices."

"Inspector Kate Martinelli to see Ms. Lomax." She lifted her face to the camera lens concealed in the reaches of the entranceway, and was buzzed in.

Half a mile north of this address, law offices meant marble, polished oak, smoked mirrors, abstract art, and a size-five receptionist with a daily manicure. Here it meant industrial-quality carpeting, white walls in need of a touch-up, museum posters in drugstore frames, and a size-sixteen secretary with short, unpainted nails on her skilled hands. She also had a waist-length braid keeping her graying brown hair in order, no makeup to speak of, skin too pale to have spent time out of doors, and a large basket of toys next to her desk. The woman fixed Kate with a gaze that had seen it all.

"Have a seat," she offered, though it sounded more like an order. "Carla will be here in a minute."

"That's a good security setup," Kate commented, remaining on her feet. "Do you have a lot of problems here?" SoMa was not the most crime-free part of town by any means, and that door had been the victim of at least one determined assault.

"It's because we have security that we haven't had problems."

"Angry husbands?"

"And boyfriends and fathers. They pound away until the cops get here, making fools of themselves for the camera." She glanced at the monitors with amused but slightly bitter satisfaction, and Kate, reflecting that the odds were high the woman had once needed the services of a women's advocate lawyer herself, moved around the desk as if the glance had been an invitation. Peering over the secretary's shoulder, she saw the displays of four security cameras. Two showed a small parking area; as Kate watched, a light-colored, boxy Mercedes sedan at least ten years old pulled through an opening gate on one screen and parked on one of a half-dozen spaces shown on the next. From the car stepped two women, the driver sorting through her keys as she approached the building until the all-seeing secretary pressed a button and freed the door.

Kate walked up and down for a few minutes, trying to get an impression of the law offices. Casual seemed to be the unifying decorative theme, beginning with the untidy forest of objects on the receptionist's desk (two spindly plants; a flowered frame with the picture of a young girl; a delicate terra-cotta Virgin and Child; a figurine of an Indian goddess with a black face and golden crown; a three-inch-tall carved box representing a heap of cheerfully intertwined cats; a sprig of redwood cones; and a chipped coffee mug, stuffed with a handful of pens and pencils, that proclaimed "When

God created man, She was only joking"). The works of art on the walls were similarly eclectic, with museum posters (Monet and Van Gogh) adjoining framed crayon studies (stick figures and box houses) and one competent and very original tempera study of a woman and two children, done with a deft hand in pleasing tones of green and blue. In the corner were the initials P W, and Kate was just thinking that Lee would like this when Carla Lomax came into the room to shake Kate's hand and lead her back into the building. As Kate followed, she glanced into the other rooms. There looked to be a couple of other partners in the firm, neither of them at their desks. Between two unoccupied offices was a meeting room with a large round wooden table that took up so much of the floor space, it must have been assembled in the room. On the wall a striking black and white poster caught Kate's eye, the blown-up photograph of a woman with a swollen mouth and two black eyes, a bandage on her scalp, and a cast on one hand, gazing tiredly at the camera. Underneath her image were printed the words, *But he loves me.* Kate wasn't sure if it was meant to be a joke; if so, it was a bleak one.

Carla Lomax stepped into the next office, sat behind her desk, and waved Kate at a chair across from her. Again Kate remained on her feet. Two could play games in the world of legal give-and-take.

"I thought we might have a word before I bring Emily in," Lomax told her. "Just so we're in agreement here."

"What is there to agree about?" Kate asked, half turned away from Lomax to study an attractive arrangement of framed photographs of the City at night, gaudy North Beach, Chinatown shimmering in the rain.

"Emily Larsen has just lost her husband. She does not need to be harassed."

Kate took a step over to the next display of photos, an assortment of scenes from foreign countries: a woman in a market, brilliant colors in her shawl and a bowler hat on her head; three thin but laughing children playing in a street with a bicycle rickshaw behind them; a woman seated at a backstrap loom, a weaving of vibrant oranges, pinks, and greens emerging from the threads.

"These are nice," Kate commented. "Where are they from?"

"Bolivia, India, and Guatemala."

"Did you take them?"

"Yes," the lawyer said. "Inspector Martinelli—"

"Ms. Lomax, how much criminal law have you done since you passed your exams?"

"Not a lot."

"Mostly family law, right?"

"I know my law," Lomax said, offended.

"I'm sure you do. But please, rest assured that so do I, and I don't go around screwing with family members; it jeopardizes both my job and my cases. Let's just bring Mrs. Larsen in and let me talk with her, and then I'll let you both be."

As Kate had suspected, Carla Lomax was more at home with the intricacies of divorce, child custody, and restraining orders than she was with Miranda rights and criminal investigations. The lawyer hesitated, but in the end she stood up and went to fetch Emily Larsen.

Kate continued to wander around the room, moving from the photos to a display of ethnic dolls and trucks on a low shelf (the better to distract the children of clients?), an impressive bookshelf of legal and psychological tomes, and finally a glass case containing female figures from all over—a grimacing Aztec goddess giving birth to the sun, a multiple-breasted female who looked vaguely Mediterranean next to a woman in wide skirts holding a pair of snakes, the Polish Black Virgin, and the Mexican Virgin of Guadalupe. Prominently displayed in front was a crude dark-skinned figure six inches tall, with many arms, bare breasts, and a protruding tongue: wild-eyed and wild-haired, the figure wore a necklace of grinning skulls and held a decapitated head in one of her hands. Kate, nonplussed, could only wonder what Carla Lomax's troubled clients made of their lawyer's art collection.

The door opened and Carla came in with Emily Larsen, and Kate shook her hand and introduced herself, sitting down with the two women in a group of chairs and making remarks about the weather and traffic to put Emily at ease.

In fact, though, Kate was always uncomfortable around victims of chronic spousal abuse, those walking reminders of the vulnerability of women—particularly those weighed down with children. Intellectually, professionally, she fully understood that a person's willingness to put up with abuse had its roots deep in childhood, when a groundwork of self-contempt and a deep sense of worthlessness was laid down, feelings that made it nearly impossible to stand up to bullying. As a person, however, as a woman, Kate felt primarily frustration and impatience, and even a tinge of completely unfounded revulsion, at their weakness, their willingness to crawl back like beaten dogs to lick the hand of their tormentor. When confronted by a woman who persisted in an abusive relationship, Kate inevitably found herself stifling the question, Why hadn't the woman just hauled off and brained her husband with a skillet?

But then again, maybe this one had.

Everything about the recent widow in front of Kate was apologetic and unassuming, from her limp handshake to her slumped shoulders. The heavy frames of her cheap glasses nearly hid the washed-out brown of her eyes, her face was a pale contrast to the flat black of hair that showed gray at the roots, and the drab cotton dress that hung over her dumpy figure had been washed to the point of colorlessness. Kate began by expressing her sympathies over the loss of her husband; Emily Larsen responded by wincing, her eyes filling. Kate sighed quietly to herself.

"Ms. Larsen . . . Emily. I believe that Ms. Lomax has told you that your husband was killed, on Monday night or Tuesday morning? That he was murdered?"

Kate waited for a response from the woman before she went on, expecting either a meek nod or silent tears. What she saw instead made her sit back sharply, the usual string of questions cut short. A small grimace had puckered up Emily Larsen's mouth—brief, but clear. Why on earth would the woman react to Kate's words with *disapproval*? But what else looked like that? Could it have been an objection to the tasteless word "murder"? Kate wondered. She wished Al were here. With all her instincts set to quivering by that involuntary moue across the woman's face, she would have to proceed very carefully.

"Were you and James separated, Mrs. Larsen?"

"A trial separation," Emily admitted in a small voice.

"Your husband had a history of abusing you. Was that the main reason?"

"I was . . . yes."

"You were afraid of him, I do understand. He hit you, didn't he?"

Emily glanced at Carla, mouth open as if to protest, but she subsided and only nodded.

"Did he hit your kids as well?"

The woman looked up quickly. "Never. He wouldn't. Jimmy's—Jimmy was a good man. He loved us, he really did. He just . . . lost control sometimes."

"When he was drinking."

Another nod.

"Did you ever get the feeling that your husband was involved with someone outside the home?"

"Involved? You mean, like with another woman?" The very idea was enough to shake Emily Larsen in a way nothing else had.

Kate hastened to reassure her that her loving husband hadn't been taking it elsewhere, so far as she knew.

"Not necessarily a woman. Gambling, maybe, going to the races, perhaps something mildly illegal that he wouldn't have wanted you to find out about?"

"I really don't know. There's nothing I can think of,

and Jimmy never went away much except to work and
bowling and stuff. And someone having . . . you
know, an affair, they always say they're working over-
time, don't they?"

"Did your husband ever have money that wasn't explained by his salary?"

"No," Emily replied, reassured that Kate wasn't
about to spring a rival on her, but obviously bewildered
by the questions. Kate let it go. A baggage handler behind the scenes at a busy airport might have opportunity for crime, but if Larsen had indulged in smuggling
or rifling bags, he had kept it from his wife. Kate would
try another tack.

"Mrs. Larsen, did your husband come up to San
Francisco a lot?"

"No. He never did."

"Never?"

"Except for the airport, of course, and to Candle-
stick or whatever they're calling it now. He mostly liked
football, but he'd go to baseball games if he could get
cheap tickets. And if he was going to Oakland, he'd go
through the City even if he came back around the Bay.
To save on the bridge fare, you know? Jimmy hated to
pay the fare." Toll on the Bay's various bridges was
collected only one way, although as far as Kate knew, it
was cheaper to pay it than to drive clear around the
Bay. James Larsen may have been one who resented the
fare enough to spend the gas money, and an hour
longer on the road, to avoid paying it.

"So you have no idea what he was doing in the Presidio on Monday night?"

Emily shook her head, as much in wonder as to indicate a negative. "It seems a strange place for Jimmy to
go."

"Was he a golfer?" Kate asked desperately, thinking
of the Presidio golf course—although Larsen had not
been dressed for golf any more than he had been for
jogging. Emily looked as if Kate had suggested nude
sunbathing or jai alai, and told her no.

No drugs on the body, no unexplained cash, no extramarital entertainment on the side. Larsen's death was proving more and more enigmatic. "Mrs. Larsen," Kate said finally, "do you have any idea why someone would have wanted to kill your husband?" she asked, and for the second time Emily Larsen's answer gave Kate a jolt. This time the woman looked directly into Kate's face, her eyes theatrically wide.

"No. Of course not," she said. "Who would want to kill Jimmy?"

She had all the guile of a child, her lie so blatant Kate couldn't help glancing at the lawyer. Carla Lomax was sitting motionless in her chair, working hard at not reacting to her client's words, but Kate had the distinct impression that the lawyer was as dismayed by Emily's response as Kate was.

At that juncture Kate had two choices. She could press Emily Larsen until the woman came clean or broke down—or, more likely, until Lomax put a halt to it. If Kate knew what was going on, if she even had a clear suspicion of what lay behind Emily's odd evasiveness, she would not hesitate to push, but there were times when it was better to pull away and go do some research, and all Kate's instincts were telling her this was one of them. Find out who Emily Larsen was and what pushed her levers, and with that weapon in hand, come back and pin her to the wall.

Kate arranged an expression of openness on her face, and nodded as if in acceptance of the answer. "When was the last time you talked to Jimmy?"

"About, oh, a week ago?" She looked at Carla Lomax, who knew better than to give her an answer. "It was—oh right, it was last Tuesday. I called to let him know I was okay, and not to forget that the gas man was coming the next day to check a leak I'd smelled. We didn't talk much. I asked him how he was and told him I was okay, and he said when was I coming home and I said I wasn't, and then he started getting mad and so I just hung up on him," she said proudly, and then spoiled the effect by letting out a sad, deflating little sigh halfway to being a whimper, and adding parenthetically, "I don't even know if he stayed home to let the gas man in."

"So you didn't call your husband on Monday?"

"Oh no, I sure didn't."

"And you didn't talk to anyone else who might have told him where you were? A neighbor, maybe? Or a friend you saw in the street?"

"I didn't see anyone, no."

"Where were you on Monday night, Mrs. Larsen?" Kate slipped the question in as if it had no more weight than the others, and Emily answered it before her lawyer could stir in her chair.

"I was staying at a shelter that Carla set up for me. I'm still there."

"And did you leave at all, any time after, say, six on Monday night?"

"No, I don't think so. No, I'm sure I didn't—there was a meeting and then I stayed up talking to some people until, golly, near midnight."

Kate slapped her notebook shut before Carla Lomax could voice an objection.

"We'd like to borrow the keys to your house, Mrs. Larsen. We need to do a search, to see if your husband may have had visitors or something. We won't disturb anything, and we'll be out of the way before you get back."

Carla Lomax automatically began to protest Kate's need for a warrant, but Emily, in a rare gesture of assertiveness, overrode her. "I really don't mind, Carla. I think I'd rather they were in and out before I got there. Instead of standing there watching them go through his stuff, you know."

Another indicator that Emily was more than she appeared, this ready grasp of the intrusiveness of a police search. Kate studied her thoughtfully as Emily took a set of keys out of her purse and handed the whole ring over to Kate. Kate wrote out a receipt for them and stood up to go.

"I'll phone you later this afternoon," Kate told the woman, "to make arrangements to get these back to you and let you know how things are going. Will you be at the shelter?"

"Oh. Well, I suppose I could meet you at the house, when you're finished, if I can get a ride. There's no reason not to go home now, is there?"

Looking at Emily Larsen's bleak attempt at a smile, despite the woman's deceptions Kate could have sworn that she was only now coming to realize that her husband was out of her life. "We have no objection to your returning there, if that's what you're asking, and I would be happy to arrange a ride if it would help. Thank you, Mrs. Larsen. Here's my card, let me know if I can do anything for you. Ms. Lomax, could I have a word, please?"

Carla Lomax followed Kate out to the hallway, shutting the office door behind them.

"I'd rather not tell you the location of the shelter," she began immediately, but Kate put up a hand to stop her.

"I wasn't going to ask you, although I probably know already. What I wanted to say, Carla," she said mildly, letting her gaze stray to a child's drawing of a purple cat on the opposite wall, "is that your client seems to know more about her husband's death than she was willing to say, and it might be a good idea for you to have a little discussion with her on the difference between not answering a question and obstructing justice. Before we get into the realm of actual perjury, that is."

Kate gave her a smile as insincere as Emily Larsen's declaration of ignorance, and left.

Back at the Hall of Justice, Kate handed the Larsen keys over to Crime Scene, booted up her computer, and got to work. Hawkin came in an hour later sucking at a peppermint, his thinning hair giving off the aura of the lemon shampoo he habitually used after witnessing an autopsy. She asked him what the pathologist had found.

"Rigor might have been delayed by fat, might have been speeded by a struggle, but the internal temp confirmed time of death between nine-thirty and eleven-thirty Monday night. Cause of death strangulation. No obvious sign of drug use. So far absolutely zilch at the crime scene. Not even a tire track. Oh, and the tech was right, that was a taser burn on Larsen's chest. Person or persons zapped him, cuffed him, tied a red cotton scarf around his neck, and pulled it tight. Exit one wife-beater."

The lab work—blood, organs, fibers, and fingernail scrapings—would take days; there was no need for him to tell her that.

"Speaking of the wife," Kate told him, "I think there's something hinky about her."

"Hinky?" Hawkin had gone to the coffeepot and paused in the act of holding the carafe up to the light to judge its drinkability. "What's 'hinky' mean, anyway?"

"Odd. Strange. Out of whack. You know."

"I don't know. You've been watching that TV cop show again, haven't you? You're worse than Jules."

"What's wrong with the way Jules talks?" Hawkin's brilliant teenaged stepdaughter was undeniably a handful, but Kate was very fond of her.

"Nothing, unless you want English. So, Ms. Larsen's hinky. Would you care to elaborate?"

"I was about to, until you started going hinky on me. She looks like a typical Betsy Homemaker whose husband liked to slap her around on Friday nights, but she's hiding something about the murder itself. I mean, I'd say she's honestly sorry about his death, God knows why, but she's more annoyed by the actual murder than horrified or in denial or any of the usual reactions. Plus that, when I asked if she knew who did it, she suddenly went all big-eyed and innocent. Even her lawyer thought it was weird."

"Big-eyed and innocent like she did it, or like she knows who did?"

"I think she knows, or suspects anyway. She herself has an alibi—there was a meeting Monday night at the shelter, and after it broke up she sat around until nearly midnight talking. I've been trying to find out about her, but there's not much there. She's never been arrested, never even had a traffic violation."

"People close to her?"

"I was just getting started on tracking down her family, but she doesn't seem to have had any real friends. Not among the neighbors we talked to, anyway."

"Doesn't sound like the kind to know a couple of guys who'd be willing to bash the hubby for three hundred bucks. Still, you never know. See what you can find, and then tomorrow we can go back down and talk to the neighbors again. Those people across the street should be back by then."

"So should Emily Larsen."

"We can talk to her, too."

They settled in for a session of keyboards and telephones. Hawkin was on the phone to James Larsen's supervisor at the airport when he heard a sharp exclamation from Kate's desk, and looked up to see a triumphant expression on her face. He finished the call and hung up.

"Was that a 'bingo' I heard?" he asked, scribbling a note to himself.

"My Catholic upbringing showing. Emily Larsen's brother is one of your basic bad boys. Name's Cash Strickland. In and out of trouble since juvy, just got out of prison in January for aggravated assault. The original charge was murder one, but he got off with a hung jury, and the DA took a plea instead of working through a retrial on the murder rap. Strickland's on parole in San Jose."

"Nice and close. Want to go talk with him tonight?"

Kate glanced at her watch. "The traffic will be hell, and I wanted to be home for an early dinner. Roz Hall and her partner, Maj, are coming over."

"The minister and the monkey's mother."

"Right. In fact, I'd bet Roz knows about women's shelters. Maybe I'll pick her brains over dinner, see what she knows about one Carla Lomax, attorney-at-law."

"Now, that ought to make Lee happy," Al said dryly.

"Some casual, general conversation, that's all."

"Sure. Tomorrow, then. We can do Larsen's neighbors on the way back. Want me to call Strickland's parole officer?"

"I'll do it—he's a guy I knew when I worked down there. What do you think—make an appointment with Strickland, or sneak up on him?"

"I'd say talk to the PO, find out what he thinks. Of course, if you make a date with Strickland and he bolts, that tells us something, too."

"True. What did the airport supervisor say?"

"He gave Larsen back his job when he got out, and Larsen lasted exactly one week before showing up drunk. The supervisor fired him."

"All in all, not a great month for Jimmy Larsen," Kate commented, and picked up the phone to call the parole officer assigned to Emily Larsen's brother with the violent past, the brother whose life went far to explain his sister's easy familiarity with arrest proceedings and the terminology of alibi and search.

3

For a long time we shall have only to listen,
Not argue or defend, but listen to each other.
Let curses fall without intercession,
Let those fires burn we have tried to smother.

The reappearance of a witness to one of Kate's other cases delayed her, and in the end she was late anyway to Lee's dinner party. Only a little, though, and by cutting the interview short and dodging through traffic in a manner that would have had Lee pale, she pulled up in her driveway only half an hour after she had said she would be home. Roz's car was parked down the block, a bashed-up red Jeep Cherokee that still showed the signs of the rock face that her assistant pastor had misjudged the previous summer, driving through Yosemite with the youth group on a camping trip. Roz had no doubt found better use for the insurance check than paint repair.

Kate let herself in, settled for a quick scrub of the hands in lieu of a shower and a change of clothes, and slipped into the empty chair while the entrée was still on the table. She glanced uneasily at Lee, and decided to opt for humor: She seized her spoon and twisted her face into a parody of winsomeness.

"Please, Mum, may I have some, too?"

Lee was not amused, but she relented enough to take Kate's plate and fill it. Kate said hello to Roz and Maj, asked after Mina-the-monkey (who was two doors down the street at the moment, dining with a friend from school on the forbidden fare of fish sticks and chocolate cupcakes) and the baby (a seven-month lump under Maj's dress, which a recent sonogram had revealed was to be another female addition to the all-woman household). She then dutifully turned to the other two places to greet Jon and his companion, a long-ago lover turned friend named Geoff DeRosa.

Kate had lived under the same roof as Jon for almost two years, and was occasionally struck dumb with wonder that in all that time she hadn't murdered him. Yet. Jon had been a client of Lee's in her previous life, before they had all become tied together by the bullet that nicked Lee's spine, and he had expiated his guilt feelings over the minor role he played in leading a killer to her door by turning the tables and becoming, over Kate's profound misgivings, his therapist's caregiver. He was strong for his size, a necessary consideration in the early days of Lee's care, and he worked cheap, an even more necessary factor. And if he drove Kate crazy with his continual presence, his endlessly mercurial relationships, and his deep devotion to bad music, he amused Lee, and in the end that was the most important consideration of all. Kate had grown to tolerate him, as she would have an irritating lapdog snuffling around the rugs; they occasionally even had moments of honest connection. Brief moments.

"I thought you were going to be out tonight," she said to him, and then hoped she hadn't sounded too disappointed. Jon took the question at face value.

"Later. Geoff has tickets for the opening of *Song*."

"A new play?" she asked around a mouthful of still-warm scalloped potatoes.

"You haven't heard of it?" Jon sat back in amazement, an emotion every bit as real as the one manufactured by Emily Larsen. Kate chewed politely and waited for the rest. "You will hear about it soon—the Bible bashers are up in arms. It's bound to be in the paper in the morning. Probably even the TV news."

"And why is that?" she prompted obligingly.

"Because it's from the Good Book itself. They've taken the Song of Songs and set it to music and dance."

Light began to dawn. "I suppose it's X-rated?"

"What else would be the purpose?" Jon answered, fluttering his eyelashes and murmuring in a dramatically throaty voice, " 'Oh, comfort me with apples.' " Geoff giggled in appreciation.

"You know," Roz broke in, "there's actually a long tradition of using the Song of Songs for what you might call bawdy purposes. The early rabbis had to pass an injunction against singing it in alehouses. It *is* pretty dirty."

"I don't remember it as being dirty," Kate objected. Her own childhood Catholicism was long lapsed, but the idea of using the Bible to make a smutty play tweaked some vestigial nerve, leaving her mildly affronted. Roz took her objection as a request for further enlightenment, and went on with her lesson in Bible studies.

"The Song is generally regarded as symbolic of God's love for His people, but in fact it's probably an adaptation from a royal marriage-slash-battle ritual. Capture your bride and then screw her."

"Ooh," Jon trilled. "Kinky."

Lee ignored him, and asked Roz, "Are you serious?" It was not always easy to tell with Roz, but the woman shrugged.

"It's part of what I'm working on in my thesis," she said, a trifle defensive—as Lee had once commented, Roz tended to hide her academic side like a dirty secret. She had been working on a Ph.D. for the last few years, in addition to being a full-time ordained minister in an alternative church composed mostly of gay and lesbian parishioners and spending long hours as unpaid advocate for a long list of causes. Maj referred to these, half despairingly, as her partner's Campaigns.

"I have heard that the production is gorgeous," Maj commented, since the academic discussion seemed to have reached a dead end. Geoff, it seemed, knew one of the costume designers, which was how he got opening-night tickets and an invitation to the party afterward. Roz, hearing this, declared that she had been looking for someone to help out with a church play, and before anyone quite knew how, she had bullied Geoff into bringing his designer friend by the church the next day to talk about some volunteer work, and then Maj stepped in even more firmly and diverted the conversation into a discussion of the various ethnic dance techniques and costumes used in *Song*, while Kate dedicated herself to her plate; both enterprises ran empty more or less simultaneously.

Kate cleared the plates, set some coffee to brew, brought in the glistening fruit tarts Lee had made for dessert, laughed at jokes and told one of her own, and began to feel a part of her relax a fraction under the sheer normality of an evening spent among friends. Maybe she wouldn't ask Roz about Carla Lomax after all.

When the tarts had been reduced to a few crumbs and Jon and Geoff had left for *Song*, Kate laid a fire in the fireplace. The four women took their cups (herbal tea for Maj) and moved to the sofas. Kate carried Lee's cup, waited until her lover had settled herself and tucked the cuffed arm crutches out of the way, and then handed Lee the coffee and sat down beside her. Maj eased herself into the overstuffed cushions across from them, and sat back into Roz's encircling arm, just as Lee was settling back against Kate, giving a little sigh of satisfaction that sent a brief electrical shiver up Kate's spine that was as powerful as lust, but more cerebral: hope, perhaps.

"Do you mind if I put my feet up on the table?" Maj asked. "I know it's rude, but my midwife tells me it helps my circulation."

"Of course not," Lee said. "Can we get you a pillow or something?"

"No, this is fine." Maj reached out and turned a magazine facedown before she threaded her bare feet, covered in thick black stockings that reminded Kate of rest homes, out over the low table and onto the magazine. She balanced her cup and saucer on her protruding belly, and grimaced self-consciously. "It's not all fun," she commented. Indeed, once Kate focused on her, Maj did not appear her normal collected self. She looked pale, even wan, and had not had her usual appetite at dinner.

"Seven more weeks," Roz said, rubbing her partner's arm by way of encouragement; Maj appeared more depressed by the remaining time than encouraged.

"I was very impressed to see the mayor the other night," Kate told Roz. "Don't tell me you have him making points?"

"God, no. It's part of his PR, going to school things. Keeping in touch with the community and all that. Someone suggested this because of the school's high test scores and great ethnic balance, that's all."

Kate could well guess who that someone had been, and she wouldn't have been surprised if points had indeed entered the mind of that savvy politician. Of both savvy politicians—Roz was well on her way to becoming a force to be reckoned with, and beyond the borders of the city, or even the state. She looked to be the gay equivalent of what Cecil Williams had become for the African-American community, a charismatic voice, reasonable yet devoutly committed, San Francisco's representative lesbian.

Roz simply had everything going for her. She was articulate, deeply committed, passionate in her causes but capable of choosing reason over rhetoric, communication over in-your-face confrontation. Despite her relatively moderate public stance and her willingness to compromise, there was no doubt whatsoever where she stood. Even the most radical of gay rights advocates admitted her to their fold, and she had been instrumental over the last few years in engineering seemingly impossible agreements between opposing sides. Enormous of heart, possessed of a cutting intelligence, charismatic, articulate, and tireless, Roz was, in a word, compelling, and Kate was no more immune to her charm than anyone else. Including the mayor, who had once called Roz the nicest woman he'd ever been stabbed by.

Kate had only met Roz a year before, in the course of an investigation that took her to Berkeley's so-called "holy hill," the site of a number of theological seminaries. Roz had been wearing her clerical collar and her guise as a late-blooming grad student, and only some months later did Kate discover that Roz and Lee had, as they say, history.

Lee had known Rosalyn Hall for years, since grad school at UC Berkeley, in fact, where Roz was doing a master's degree and Lee a Ph.D., both in psychology. The two had worked together, discovered a shared passion for Eastern religion, and had taken off to India and Nepal for six weeks, during which trip they had been, briefly, lovers. Two such dominant personalities were not a comfortable match, however, and they had parted—as friends, although from what Lee did not say about that parting, and her manner when she did not say it, Kate had the impression that some dark happening lay at the parting's roots. Roz was not all cleverness and light.

Long years later, when Kate came across the cleric and Lee was still struggling against the bullet's shattering effects, Kate, thinking only that a minor resumption of Lee's counseling work might be therapeutic, had all unknowing encouraged Roz to reach out to the injured woman. By the time Lee told her of the old relationship with Roz, Kate (who was not a detective for nothing) was not too surprised. Nor was she too worried, since she could also read the signs that the affair was long over.

Besides, everyone she knew was in love with Roz, even those who were not in lust with her. Even straight people—hell, even those who hated Roz loved her. She was not only charismatic, she was even good to look at; although she was hardly fashionably slim, her tall, voluptuous shape and wide shoulders gave the impression of a serious swimmer gone slightly to seed (actually, she had never been much of a swimmer). Her shiny brown

hair had just enough wave in it to overcome Maj's amateur haircuts, her dark eyes were large and long-lashed
enough to compensate for her habitual avoidance of
makeup. Increasingly in recent months, when television
broadcasts needed a spokesperson for a gay perspective,
they had begun to call on Roz; when the papers printed
a shot of the opening of a center for gay, lesbian, and
bisexual teenagers or the ground breaking of a crisis
center, Roz's face looked out at the reader; when the
governor put together a task force on lesbian and gay
parenting, Roz was on it. That the mayor of San Francisco had appeared at Mina's school play was no mere
happenstance.

So no, Kate was not jealous—or rather, she was honest. Jealous, yes, a little. But hell, if Roz Hall had asked
her to bed, she'd probably have gone too.

Roz had not asked. Instead, when Kate had been
injured during a case the previous winter, while Lee and
Jon were both away, it was Roz's concerned face Kate
saw from her hospital bed, Roz's red Jeep that drove
her home at her release, and Roz's longtime partner,
Maj, who brought Kate food and comfort and just the
right amount of companionship to keep her going. The
two women were now family, closer to Kate than any
of her blood relatives, and if Kate sometimes felt like a
poor relation bobbing in the wake of a glamorous star,
well, Roz had a way of making one feel that even poor
relations were good things to be. After all, even presi-
dents had blue-collar cousins.

Kate relaxed back against the soft sofa pillows, looking with affection at their guests. The talk had circled
back to Mina and her seven-weeks-to-go sister-to-be,
and half of her attention was on that. The other half
drifted back to the Larsen murder, which seemed to be
progressing on as straightforward a path as investigations ever did, but which nonetheless niggled at the
back of her mind.

One of the things she had to find out, she decided,
was what Larsen was doing in the Presidio parklands at
that hour. Emily had not been able to think of anything

that would have taken her husband there, and neither could Kate. A trap, maybe. Perhaps Crime Scene'll come up with something in the Larsen house, she thought, and then woke to the fact that Roz was talking to her.

"Sorry," she said, sitting upright to demonstrate her attentiveness. "I was miles away."

"Difficult case?"

"Puzzling," she conceded. Good manners required that she answer, but she could hardly go into the details of an active case. This was a problem she'd faced countless times over the years, however, and she had become skilled at the diversionary side-step in conversation. "I was thinking about this interview I had today with an abused woman. I just . . . it continually amazes me, what women will put up with for the sake of security."

"Oh, that's not fair," Lee protested. "It's not even true, to call it security. They often live in a constant state of fear."

"So why do it? Because the known, however awful, is better than the great unknown?"

"Sometimes it is," Roz broke in. "Especially when there are children, and no other family or friend to lean on. We're a terribly solitary culture, you know. It's not easy to find a support network in modern society, especially if you're a woman who already feels humiliated by being someone's punching bag. Self-respect is a luxury, and sometimes all these women can afford is pride, that they won't admit failure."

There was nothing in Roz's face or voice to show that her words were anything but general; nonetheless, Kate eyed her with the uneasy sensation that there was some underlying message there for her alone. Roz's next words confirmed it, and the evenness of her gaze.

"We all do this, to some degree, even if we're not in an actively abusive relationship. We let ourselves be shoved into a corner, humiliated, used, and abandoned, and then when our partner turns back to us, in the joy of reunion we forgive."

A memory swept into the room, so vivid in the space

between Roz and Kate that it seemed to quiver visibly in the air.

It was a scene from the previous December, a few days after Kate's release from the hospital to her cold and empty house. The morning had been taken up by one of her blinding headaches, legacy of a suspect's eighteen-inch length of galvanized pipe. In the afternoon Kate had wakened from a drugged sleep, stumbled into the bedroom she and Lee had shared until Lee's cruel and abrupt departure in August, and at the sight of the antique Wedding Rings patchwork quilt on the bed, she was seized by a rage so powerful it felt as if the spasm of migraine had finally invaded her mind.

She had not heard Roz letting herself in downstairs. She only became aware of her visitor when Roz was standing in the doorway, looking down at Kate where she sat on the floor, surrounded by the ten thousand shreds of faded cotton fabric and cotton batting that had been a quilt. Kate paused in her methodical and heavily symbolic destruction, saw in Roz's face the full, calm knowledge of precisely what she was doing, and then erupted into tears, wracked by hard, painful sobs of fury and despair that were wrenched out of her abandonment and betrayal. Her headache reawoke and her eyes and throat were seared raw, but Roz held her and rocked her, more maternal and comforting than Kate would have imagined possible.

They had never spoken of it after that day, and Kate had occasionally wondered if Roz had told Lee, but at that moment, sitting in front of the fireplace with their coffee cups and their partners, Kate saw that Roz had said nothing to anyone about the depths of the despair that Lee's leaving had visited on Kate. The sanctity of confession held, Roz's eyes said, even for the pastor of a church without confessionals.

The memory, and the knowledge, flashed between them in the blink of an eye, an instant of complete communication that Kate had only ever known in the intimacy of an interrogation room, with a suspect on the edge of a very different sort of confession, or a bare handful of times with Lee. The memory puffed away and vanished, leaving Kate disconcerted, and depressingly aware that she was even more deeply indebted to Roz Hall than she had thought. She cleared her throat and reached back urgently for the tag end of the conversation they had been having.

"Forgive, sure," she said. "But only so many times. These women, though, their forgiveness is pathological."

Roz, still holding Kate's eyes, nodded. "True. We are told to turn the other cheek in offering up our humility. We are not told to go on doing it indefinitely."

"Or told to put a club into the hand that slaps us. There was this picture on the wall in one of the law offices, that showed a woman who'd had the crap beaten out of her, all black-and-blue and bandages, with the caption 'But he loves me.' And you know, that's exactly what the woman I was interviewing said, that the husband who'd been beating her for years and years was, I quote, 'a good man' who 'loved us.' " To Kate's relief, Roz's attention finally shifted.

"Love and rage," Roz said thoughtfully. "They're never that far apart, are they?"

This time, the brief reaction that shot through the room reached across the other diagonal: Lee and Maj both twitched, almost imperceptibly. A faintly ironic smile played briefly over Maj's mouth before she wiped it away with a sip of her tea. Roz did not seem to notice anything, since she was now exploring an idea, a frown of thought between her eyebrows.

"That's more or less what I've been doing in the thesis, looking at how in the Old Testament you see God as creator, nurturer, loving mother/father, and protector, yet also as judge and executioner, enraged at a wayward people and on the verge of destroying them completely."

"Is it linked with the male/female imagery?" Lee asked her. Anyone who had been in Roz's circle for more than a few days was made quickly aware of the Bible's references to God's femininity, the metaphors of childbirth and child rearing used to describe the Divine. The God known by Roz Hall both begot and gave birth, and Roz was not about to let anyone forget it. Even a certain homicide cop was familiar with that bit of theological interpretation.

"You'd think it would be, wouldn't you?" Roz answered. "That in the passages referring to childbirth, God would be the loving mother, and in the God-the-father passages there would be judgment and wrath, but it's not that simple. The two go hand in hand, just like the ancient Near Eastern goddess figures that switch between love and destruction at the drop of a hat. It may have something to do with agricultural fertility—that floods bring destruction and life at the same time, that fruit and grain ripen at a time of year that appears dead."

They had gone far indeed from the subject of Emily Larsen, and all three of Roz's unwilling audience cast around desperately for a diversion. Kate got there first.

"Still, I doubt that someone like the woman I talked to today thinks of her husband as particularly divine. I think she's too busy praying that he comes home in a good mood."

It took Roz precisely two seconds to pause, blink, and make the shift from academic theoretician to pastoral counselor.

"Most of what I do in the group sessions is to drive home a dose of hard reality. I teach these women to say to themselves, 'My partner won't change; it's up to me.' But I make sure they add, 'I have the support of my friends.' "

"Sounds like a mantra," Lee said. " 'Every day in every way I'm getting freer and freer.' "

"Change your mind, change your life," Roz agreed.

"If their husbands don't catch up with them first," Kate added darkly.

"There is that. And sometimes it's so obvious they're in danger, and they're so oblivious, it's all I can do not to take them by the collar and try and shake some sense into them."

"You might be talking about Emily Larsen. I don't suppose you've met a woman by that name at one of the shelters?"

Roz reflected for a moment. "There is a client named Emily in the one on West Small Street, but I don't know what her last name is. We don't use surnames in group sessions, or even in one-to-one counseling, so unless I'm involved with the paperwork, I usually don't know their full names."

"Her husband's name was James, or Jimmy."

"Was?"

"He's dead."

"Oh dear. That's her. Black hair, glasses? She'll be crushed, I'm afraid. She must have said his name fifty times during the session on Monday. Classic. I must go see her."

"So you were at the shelter on Monday night?" Kate asked, trying to sound casual but aware of Al Hawkin's sarcasm, and of Lee at her side.

"Leading a group therapy session. I'm there two or three times a week. The director's a good friend."

Half the city was Roz's good friend. "How late—I'm sorry, Roz, it's not very nice to ask you for dinner and then question you, but the woman's husband was killed on Monday and it would save me having to hunt you down tomorrow to ask these questions. Can you tell me how late you were there?"

"I don't know. Fairly late."

"You got home at five after twelve," Maj offered with mild disapproval.

"So I must have left the shelter about eleven-forty-five. The group session is from seven until about nine, and I stayed on to talk with Emily for maybe an hour before I left. Are you looking for an alibi?"

"Oh, Emily Larsen's clear," Kate told her—the literal truth, if skipping over some of the details. "We're just looking for information, filling in the gaps, you know? Was she with you the whole time, then?"

"Not the whole time, no. When the session ended I had to talk with someone who was needing advice

fairly urgently for a friend, a neighbor I think, who's in
an ugly situation—the neighbor's an Indian girl, from
India, I mean, barely more than a child by the sound of
it, who was brought here in an arranged marriage—can
you believe it? In San Francisco in this day and age?
The child's in-laws disapprove of her, and it's beginning
to escalate into physical abuse. The woman who came
to me is worried, and I had to talk to her about the
girl's options, whether or not to just call the police, or
to turn it over to Child Protective Services, who would
involve the school district and a dozen other agencies.
Anyway, I was with her for about half an hour, forty-
five minutes, and then I went back to Emily."

"So you were inside the whole time?" Kate asked,
her voice as casual as if she were asking for the cream.
Lee was not fooled, however, and shot her partner a
hard look. Roz looked slightly uncomfortable, which
was a hidden satisfaction to Kate, but she answered
readily.

"No, not inside. We were outside in Amanda's car."

"Did you see anybody leave after the group session?"

Roz saw where the questions were going, and relaxed a degree. "A couple of people left, sure. Carla
Lomax and her secretary, Phoebe, and a woman named
Nikki. There might've been someone else, I can't remember."

"If you think of anyone, let me know. What about
Carla Lomax, Emily's lawyer? Do you know her? I
gather she got Emily into the shelter in the first place."

"We've worked together from time to time, but I
can't say I know Carla well. Good woman, very committed."

Lee sat forward on the sofa and firmly nudged the
conversation away from Kate's professional interest in
Emily and James Larsen. "What about that Indian girl?
Is there anything you can do about her, unless she's
underage? The Indian community tends to be pretty
closed to outsiders, doesn't it?"

"Even more than the Russians, and I thought *they*

were tight-lipped. You're right, I can't do anything direct, but there are people who can, and it's just a matter of digging them out and tightening the screws." She looked, for a moment, oddly fatigued, and her laugh was a bitter one, full of long experience of hopeless causes. "You wouldn't believe how Machiavellian I can be if I have to. I listen to the right-wingers and then to the left, and I agree with all the extremists to their faces. I eat shit and ask sweetly for the recipe. I even learned how to bat my eyelashes at men, if you can imagine that."

Kate glanced at Lee, to see what she was making of this, and saw a look of wary compassion on her lover's face.

"And when she has eaten the shit," Maj added in her slight, precise Scandinavian accent, "she comes home and breaks the furniture in a rage."

"I do not!" Roz protested.

"Only once," Maj allowed. "And I hated that chair anyway."

"God, it must be exhausting," Lee broke in. "Conflict resolution's the hardest job in the world."

"Isn't it just?" Roz agreed. "You know, more than once when I've been sitting in a room with two people, each of whom thinks the other is a monster of depravity, I've found myself fantasizing about just cracking their skulls together, or locking the two of them up together until they promised to treat each other like human beings. They wouldn't even have to agree with each other, just be polite and listen."

Kate was reminded of the notice that she had read while she was sitting with the phone under her chin, waiting for Carla Lomax to come on the line. "Have any of you seen that flyer somebody's been putting up on phone poles, suggesting that mothers should be required to insert a poison capsule under their sons' skin at birth?"

"What?" Lee said, shocked.

"Yeah. The idea is, if the boy gets out of hand as an adult, society could just trigger the capsule and deal with him. Shut him down." It was not, she realized belatedly, a topic a pregnant woman might be eager to discuss. Maj didn't wince, exactly, but she seemed to retreat slightly into herself. Lee, of course, caught it and moved to soothe, but before she could knock Kate's comment out of the air with a remark about the weather, Roz picked up on it.

"God, people are nuts," she was saying. "We have this friend whose lover left her because the baby she was carrying turned out to be a boy, and she couldn't take the conflict of raising a male child. I mean, men are half the human race. Who better to change the way they do things than lesbian mothers?"

"Nurture overcoming nature," Lee said in agreement.

"The irony is painful, isn't it?" Roz went on. "In developing countries they're aborting thousands of fetuses every month because they're girls and amnio followed by abortion is cheaper than coming up with a dowry, while at the same time in the West women are aborting babies because they're males and they don't want to deal with the problem of raising a male feminist. I mean, I'm all for the right to choose, but not over something petty. It's . . . obscene."

"Abortion has to be chosen with care," Lee agreed, uneasily going along with a topic she was interested in but keeping one eye on Maj. "There are always consequences. Sometimes it takes years for them to manifest, but they're there, and it's irresponsible to pretend they're not."

"You know," Maj said, going back to Kate's original remark to show that it did not bother her fragile, hormonally ravaged pregnant self, "the whole anti-male paranoia just gets to me. I wouldn't mind if this baby were a boy. You can't just say that men are violent, period. It isn't their sex that condemns men to brutality, it's their history."

"It's not men I mind," Lee noted. "It's mankind I can't stand."

"Hey," Kate objected, straight-faced. "Some of my best friends are males."

Their laughter was interrupted by the doorbell, and Kate went to let in Mina, being dropped off by the neighboring friend's mother. While the mothers chatted briefly, Lee got out an antique globe puzzle that had belonged to a great-aunt and showed Mina how it worked. When the mother left and with Mina in the room, the evening's talk slid on to less loaded matters than abortions and the iniquity of men.

Before long, however, Mina abandoned her attempt at reassembling the various layers of the globe. She wandered over to sit on the sofa beside Maj, who put out an arm and drew the child in to her. Almost instantly, Mina's eyelids began to droop, and her thumb went briefly into her mouth before she remembered that she was too old to suck her thumb.

"You tired, sweet thing?" Maj asked her. Mina's head nodded against her adoptive mother's shoulder. "Me too," Maj said. "Can you help your fatty ma up?" With Mina pulling (and Roz behind her adding an affectionate but only half-joking shove), Maj maneuvered herself upright and waddled off to use the toilet for the fourth time that evening. Roz bent down and picked up Mina, who snuggled happily into her other mother's arms and fitted the top of her head into the hollow of Roz's chin. Roz's arms went around the child with fierce affection, and by the time Maj came out of the bathroom, Mina's legs were limp in sleep.

Lee watched the family leave with envy in her eyes.

4

What Hell have we made of the subtle weaving
Of nerve with brain, that all centers tear?
We live in a dark complex of rage and grieving.
The machine grates, grates, whatever we are.

Lee locked up behind their guests and came back to the living room, moving in the careful rhythm of footsteps alternating with the tap of the rubber crutch ends that was such a contrast to her brisk, firm step of two years before. Kate was already seated at the dining table, pulling folders out of her briefcase, and Lee hesitated.

"Will it bother you if I watch the tape of that TV program Roz was on? I didn't get a chance to see it earlier."

" 'Course not. This is just paperwork, to keep me from getting too far behind. Was there any coffee left?" she asked, pushing back her chair.

"I think so. You want me to—?"

"You sit. You must be tired from cooking. Can I put that in for you?" Kate gestured to the tape sitting on top of the television set. At Lee's thanks, she fed it into the player, carried the controls across to Lee, and stooped down to gather up the scattered pieces of the globe puzzle that Mina had abandoned, putting them on the low table in front of the sofa. When she came back from the kitchen with her coffee, Lee was on the sofa putting the world together and Roz was on the television preparing to set it aright.

The program was a panel discussion on, according to

the sign in front of the moderator, WOMEN AND RELIGION IN THE 21ST CENTURY. Kate had missed the introductions of the first two women, a nun with Hispanic features and light blue habit followed by a tall woman with long blond dreadlocks and a patchwork blouse. Roz was the third (Roz in a navy jacket and green shirt, with the white square of her pastor's collar dominating her image). The fourth was a black Lutheran pastor, also in a collar, and the last panelist was described as a "neopagan follower of the goddess."

"Any particular goddess?" Kate asked.

"All of them," Lee explained.

"Who is the second woman?"

"A practitioner of wicca."

"What's that?"

"She's a witch."

"Oh. Right." Kate watched for a minute, then settled down determinedly at the table with those two staples of a cop's life, coffee and paperwork. She listened with half an ear to the far-ranging discussion, which ran the gamut from child care to radical feminist theology and from counseling a congregation's menfolk to raising the inner Feminine. This last exercise seemed to be the prime interest of the witch and the goddess worshiper, and their descriptions of the empowering energies— which they called "raising *shakti*"—by chanting the name of Kali or Durga during the act of sex had Roz looking interested, the nun looking fastidious, and the poor Lutheran minister looking as if she might stand up and flee. Lee chortled at the moderator's attempts to keep the subject a little closer to the audience's sense of reality, until finally Roz took pity on the woman and stepped in to bring the topic back to a more manageable track.

"I think what my colleagues are saying is that women have an immense source of inner power, a strength and energy we rarely tap into, because from childhood we are taught to keep it closed inside, even to deny its very existence." This was not at all what her colleagues had been saying, and Roz knew it, but she ruthlessly overrode their attempts to interrupt; Roz had the ball now, and she intended to run with it. "Because the energy—the *shakti*—is so tightly repressed, when it does find an outlet, it tends to blow, to erupt as rage. Come to think of it, that's exactly what happens in the Indian stories about the goddess Durga—or Kali, who personifies Durga's wrath: she gets drunk on battle, goes insane when she is finally released to shed blood. Which should, as myths are meant to do, make us stop and think: If we as women ever decided to stop being patient and forgiving and nurturing, to decide that it's time to begin with a clean slate, it might well feel to men as if Kali had been loosed. It's been said that if womankind ever truly sets her mind to freeing the *shakti* within, the blast of accumulated rage will scorch the earth."

She was good, Kate had to admit, mixing together lessons in women's psychology and Eastern theology but in a tone of light conversation, and managing to subtly correct the goddess worshiper at the same time. "Do you suppose that last remark of hers was actually a quote?" she wondered aloud.

Lee shook her head. "Not for a minute. That's a patented Roz Hall trademark, issuing a pronouncement as if it's some sage's wisdom. You've got to love the woman."

The moderator certainly did, and the Lutheran pastor. The nun stepped smoothly in when Roz paused for breath and made a remark about pacifism and Christian forgiveness, and the discussion rapidly shot off onto the question of whether a feminist could be a Christian, and vice versa.

Kate pulled her attention away from Roz Hall's passionate espousal of the cause of feminist churchgoers and stuck her nose back into her reports, and although the tape ended before her work did, she had enough of her paperwork out of the way to feel justified in putting it back into her briefcase and turning off the lights as soon as Lee's going-to-bed noises had died away in a last gurgle of water through the old pipes.

But the evening stayed with her, and behind the televised discussion of women's rage lay that look Roz had given her, a look that said none of them were all that far from being an Emily Larsen.

Not even Kate.

The next morning Kate was in the kitchen with the morning *Chronicle* gathering crumbs beneath her plate, bent over a review of *Song* that was tied (as Jon had predicted) to a front-page report on the right-wing Christian protest outside the theater, when she heard the sound of a key in the front door, and looked up to see Jon breezing through. He was singing, some cheery and inane song of an early sixties girl group, and Kate's heart sank. The door to his basement apartment closed on his chirpy lyrics, and Lee came in, her eyebrows up into her hair.

"Was that what I thought it was?"

"I'm afraid so," Kate answered.

Jon was in love again.

Every three or four months during the entire time he had lived with them, Jon would meet The One. For a couple of weeks he would drive his housemates crazy with golden-oldie love songs, long murmuring telephone conversations rising from his rooms in the basement, and a return to girlish giggles and dramatic bouts of despair over his appearance, his clothes, and his lack of a future. More than once Kate had longed to shoot him.

The aftermath of these great passions would almost have been a relief, had he not been so pathetic and their guilt over feeling relieved so strong. He faded before their eyes into a small man with a brave mustache, who dove back into his increasingly unnecessary labors for Lee, cooking elaborate meals, urging his charge out so he could drive her all over creation, redoubling his efforts in the men's choir and the gym and the volunteer work in the hospice.

No, all in all, Jon Samson singing love songs was not

a sound guaranteed to gladden the hearts of his house-mates.

Kate kept her mouth firmly shut. Lee was the one who bore the brunt of Jon's moods, since she was around him all day and Kate was not. And Lee was the one who had to decide if and when she was ready to do without his services, not Kate. So Kate said nothing, just stuck her coffee mug in the dishwasher, kissed Lee goodbye, and strapped on her gun to go to work.

When Emily Larsen opened the door to Kate and Al Hawkin two hours later, Kate almost did not recognize her. Her hair, though still a dull black, had been profes-sionally styled and the gray roots were gone. She also wore a defiant if amateurish splash of makeup on eyes and mouth, and her caricature housekeeper dress had been exchanged for slimming khakis and a flowered blouse. More than exterior changes, however, were the set of her shoulders and spine and the way her eyes met theirs without flinching. She stepped back to invite them inside, and was speaking before she had shut the door behind them.

"I'm really glad you came by this morning. Here, come on back to the kitchen, I've got some coffee on." The house was tidier than it had been when they had shone their flashlights through its windows on Tuesday night, although Emily had not been able to do anything about the wear on the shag carpeting and flowered up-holstery. The design sense of the residents leaned more to framed photos of children than to paintings, the liv-ing room had no fewer than three large arrangements of fake flowers, and one corner was haunted by a four-foot-long black ceramic panther with a chipped ear. The dust of print powder still lay over everything, and the house smelled unoccupied. "Can I take your jack-ets?" Emily was saying. "No? Well, sit down, I've got a confession to make."

To a police officer, the word *confession* has a fairly specific meaning, but the lighthearted way Emily Larsen said it did not encourage Kate to reach for her notebook to take down her words, and Al showed no sign of wanting to stop the woman and read her her Miranda rights. Instead they sat with their coffee cups on the Formica table in front of them and waited.

"I wasn't very up-front with you yesterday, Inspector Martinelli. You knew that, didn't you? Carla told me what you said, but I had to, well, mislead you, like, until I was sure what was goin' on.

"You see, I've got this brother, he's three years older than me, and he has this really bad temper, you know? And I was scared that he'd gotten piss—that he'd gotten PO'd with Jimmy and . . . done it to him. I couldn't reach Cash until last night—that's my brother's name, Cash—I couldn't get ahold of him to ask him if he'd . . . had anything to do with Jimmy's death. I didn't really think he did, you know, but he has a record, and he and Jimmy had a . . . an argument a while back, so I knew you'd think . . . well, not you personally, but the police, you know? But anyway, I talked with him and he told me it wasn't him. And he has a good alibi, too. He was in an AA meeting until eleven. So that's okay, then. I mean, Cash has done some really stupid things in his life, but at least this isn't one of them."

"We'll have to speak with him, though, Ms. Larsen," Al told her.

"Of course, he said you would. He works for a company, they clean offices at night. He said he'd be home in another hour, if you want to see him. Do you want his address? He lives down in San Jose."

"Thank you. However," Al continued, "the fact remains that someone killed your husband, and did so not in his usual surroundings. Someone either kidnapped your husband and took him to San Francisco, or else arranged for him to be there. The phone company's tracking down the last incoming call he had, but we also need to have a word with your postman about any mail he might have delivered."

"Oh. Sure. I mean, would you like me to ask him about it?"

"That's okay, Ms. Larsen," Al told her gently. "We'll take care of it."

For some reason, Kate had been anticipating a hulking bruiser of an ex-con, a younger, fitter version of James Larsen, but the man who opened Cash Strickland's door and invited them inside was not even as tall as his sister, and equally round-shouldered. The man's explosions of temper must be rooted in his resentment at the world's treatment of him rather than in any habitual aggressiveness; from his hangdog look, he might as well have been wearing a HIT ME sign pinned to his back.

Still, alcohol combined with chronic resentment made for a volatile mix, and both detectives kept one eye firmly on the ex-con as they introduced themselves and entered his apartment. Their free eyes flicked over the sparsely furnished room, and Al stuck his head into the adjoining rooms to be sure there were no unfriendlies waiting behind the shower curtains. Strickland knew what Al was doing, and waited politely until Al had made his reconnaissance before offering them seats on the thrift-store sofa and plastic chairs. A well-thumbed Bible lay on the coffee table beside a couple of folded newspapers. On one wall hung what Kate had seen advertised as a "sofa-sized oil" depicting a tree-shrouded lake; on another Strickland had thumbtacked up the poster of a mewing kitten on a tree branch, with the inspirational caption "All God's Creatures Need a Hand."

"You're here about Jimmy, aren't you?" he asked them.

"That's right, Cash," said Hawkin.

"Em told me you'd been askin' her questions. I hope to God you don't think she had anything to do with it. She wouldn't hurt a fly."

"No, she has an alibi for Monday night. She seems to think you do, too."

"I was at my AA meeting. Had dinner with my sponsor, helped set up the chairs at about seven-thirty, maybe seven-forty-five, stayed at the meeting until it finished about ten. I helped clean up afterward. Came back here, changed my clothes, got to work at eleven."

"Anybody see you come home?" Hawkin asked. Not that Strickland could have driven to San Francisco and back in an hour, but leave no stone criminal unturned was Hawkin's motto.

"Couple of my neighbors were sitting outside havin' a smoke and a brew. Guy in two-thirty-four—his wife won't let him smoke inside 'cause of the kid," he explained.

"Tell me about your brother-in-law," Al requested.

"Jimmy?" Strickland said, surprised that the questions about his alibi were over already. "What do you want to know?"

"What kind of a person was he?"

"He was a—" The reformed convict caught himself. "He was an awful man. Real horrible to my sister. More times than I can count I told her to leave him, take the kids and get away, but she wouldn't do it. I mean, any man that'd do that to a woman. You know he used to hit her?"

"We are aware of that. And that your sister finally left him just before he got out of jail this last time."

"None too soon."

"Do you know who would want to kill him?"

"I will admit to you that it passed through my mind, a couple of times when I was a drinking man. Not now, though. But I don't know enough about him to know who else there might be. Somebody he punched in a bar, maybe?"

"Did he get into fights, then?"

"No, not really. Saved it for his wife. Only time I saw him get into a fight with someone his own size was when he was giving Emily a hard time in a restaurant and this other drunk started callin' him names. Coward and stuff. So Jimmy punched him, they both fell over each other, and that was the end of it. Kinda funny, at the time. Now I have to say it was just pathetic."

Strickland's self-consciously pious remarks should have struck a note somewhere between comical and suspicious, but for some reason they sounded more dignified than anything else, perhaps even a touch brave. Kate was surprised to find herself hoping that Strickland was one reformed drunk who stayed that way, and even Hawkin's final questions were more gentle than a cop normally put to a recent ex-con.

Strickland gave them his sponsor's name and phone number, telling them that the man was expecting their call. When they were through, he showed them to the door.

"I hope you catch whoever did it," Strickland admitted reluctantly. "Jimmy was a no good—well. But Emily loved him, and if he'd got sober, who knows?"

Kate wished Cash Strickland luck when they left, and Hawkin shook his hand.

Strickland's AA sponsor and alibi provider was an undeniably upright citizen. He even owned his own insurance business, and although he freely admitted that he had a record for drunk driving, he had been sober now for twelve years and four months, and had acted as sponsor for Cash since the man had asked him at a meeting back in early February.

Cash Strickland's alibi stood, as did that of his sister, Emily, leaving Kate and Al with empty hands and facing the fact that they would have to begin from scratch, as if the days between the murder and walking out of the San Jose insurance office counted for nothing.

Until, that is, the phone company came across with the address for the final call to have reached the Larsen telephone.

It had been placed from a phone located on the wall of a laundromat six blocks from Carla Lomax's law offices.

And two blocks from the women's shelter that had given refuge to Emily Larsen.

5

*There are times when
I think only of how to do away
With this brute power
That cannot be tamed.*

"I could just arrive on their doorstep," Kate said to Carla Lomax over the phone, "I do know where the shelter is. I'm trying to be cooperative about this and talk to the director first, but if the only choice you give me is between waiting until I can dig up the name and phone number on my own or just driving over there and asking, then I'm sorry, I'd rather not waste my time."

"These women are in a very fragile state, Insp—"

"Carla, look. I'm not unsympathetic; I'm prepared to keep my voice down; I'm even willing to leave my male partner out of it. But it's going to happen, with or without your help. I have a job to do."

"Okay. Let me have your number. I'll ask her to call you."

"I'll give her five minutes, and then I'm going to leave this phone and climb in my car. You have my number."

A sigh came over the earpiece as the lawyer admitted defeat. "The director's name is Diana Lomax."

"A relative?"

"Cousin. She'll call you."

They both hung up at the same time.

Kate sat reading departmental memos for three and a half minutes before her phone rang.

"This is Diana Lomax," said a hoarse voice at the other end. "Carla tells me you want to come to the shelter and interview the residents."

"Anyone who was there on Monday night, yes."

"Carla said you have the address. Just don't come in a marked police car."

"I won't," Kate assured her, but the phone had already gone dead.

The building that housed the temporary residence for abused women and their children might have been chosen by the same eye that picked out the Lomax law offices. It, too, was anonymously like its neighbors, in a street busy enough that a few more cars would go unremarked but not so filled with traffic that a stranger would go unnoticed. Its hedges were trimmed back, the walkway had strong lights, the front door was solid and fitted with a sturdy dead bolt lock, and the glass on the ground floor was shatterproof, just in case.

The woman who opened to Kate's knock was enough like Carla Lomax in stature and the color of her skin and hair that Kate knew it had to be the lawyer's cousin, but whether or not the two women had once resembled each other could no longer be determined, for the face this woman wore was not the one she had been born with. Her nose had been comprehensively flattened and badly reset, a scar bisected her left eyebrow, and the two halves of her lower face were asymmetrical. Long ago something had bashed her face in, breaking her jawbone, knocking out teeth, and leaving her with the rasping voice Kate had heard on the telephone. Put together with her chosen employment as director of a women's shelter, it seemed unlikely that an industrial accident or car crash had been responsible for so brutally rearranging her features.

Kate put out her hand instead of her badge, and after a brief hesitation, the woman took it. Once inside the door Kate flipped out her identification. Diana Lomax glanced at it, then led Kate toward the back of the house.

"We had six women in residence on Monday night," she told Kate without preliminary, speaking over her shoulder. "Four of them are still here. Of the two who left, one went back to her husband, down near Salinas, the other—but of course you know about Emily."

The walls of the narrow hallway they had been passing through were broken by four doors, all closed, each with its own hand-lettered sign: CHAPEL and OFFICE on the right two, MEETING ROOM followed by TRAINING on the left. At the back of the house the hall opened up into a light, cheerful room the width of the house, a combination kitchen and dining room that was obviously the center of the shelter. Half a dozen children sat at a table along one wall with homework or crayons, washed in the sweet light of the low, late-afternoon sun, while three women were preparing a meal at the counter space under a window at the back and two adolescent girls laid plates and silverware at another table. Kate's stomach growled at the scents of dinner.

Diana went over to where the women were working and spoke quietly to a woman chopping tomatoes. The woman looked up at Kate, her face going pinched with a deep-rooted, habitual fear. Diana rested her hand on the woman's arm and said something else. The woman nodded, dried her hands, and followed in Diana's comforting shadow.

Going back through the central hallway, Diana opened the door marked OFFICE, standing back to encourage her charge to go in, and let Kate bring up the rear. Kate was not surprised to find Carla Lomax already sitting in the room, dressed in a gray-blue suit and looking every inch the lawyer.

"Crystal," Diana said, "this is Kate Martinelli. She's with the police department, and she's looking into a death that took place Monday night. It's nothing to do with you, and you don't have to talk with her if you're not comfortable with it, but she would appreciate it if you could help her with a few questions. Kate, this is Crystal Navarro."

Kate wondered if the director spoke to all the residents as if they were rather slow children, or if Crystal was simply a bit stupid. Perhaps she'd better keep her own words basic, just in case.

"Hello, Crystal, good to meet you. Sorry to interrupt your dinner. This'll only take a few minutes."

Crystal did not respond, except to hunch her head more deeply between her shoulders.

"Let's sit down," Kate suggested. Crystal looked less like a threatened turtle when she was seated, but her thin hands began twisting each other, over and over.

"There was a meeting here Monday night, Crystal. A group therapy session, do you remember?" The woman nodded. "Do you know what time it ended?"

Crystal shot a glance at Diana Lomax, then at Carla, to see if this might be a trick question. When neither of them reacted, she sat up a little straighter and said, addressing her hands, " 'Bout nine." The words were said with a strong Southern twang.

"Do you remember who was here?"

Again the nervous consultation, and again she spoke to her twisting fingers, frowning slightly. "There was about ten of us, I think. Me and Tina, Joanne, Emily, Carmelita, and Sunny. Then there was you two." Her gaze came up to touch on the Lomax cousins. "And Roz, of course. And I think Phoebe might've been here, but I'm not sure. And wasn't there someone else? Oh, right, Nikki was here for a while and then she had to go."

Without drawing attention to the notebook in her hands, Kate made surreptitious note of the names while asking the next question; she would ask Diana about them later.

"What were you talking about?"

"Just stuff, you know? I told 'em about looking for a job—I'm a dental assistant, or I used to be, once 'pon a time. And the others talked about this 'n that. Like, Tina's boy was acting up in school, and somepin' he said to her sounded just like it might've come out of his daddy's mouth and she was all in a bother, thinkin' that he was gonna come out like his daddy, and she didn't know if she wanted to shoot herself or shoot him. And then somebody said somepin' about just tyin' him up with duck tape and everbody laughed and joked for a while. You know, about them Ladies who're goin' around duck-tapin' naked guys to phone poles and stuff?" Kate nodded to indicate that she knew who the Ladies were, and that the joke was getting a bit tired. "Well, anyway. And then Emily talked a whole bunch—I remember that, 'cause it was the first time she'd said more'n two words. And Joanne. She was having problems with her ADC checks."

"What did Emily talk about?"

"Her husband. He sounds a real shit house, pardon my French, but she said she was thinkin' about giving him another chance. Stupid, really stupid."

"Was it?"

"Oh, God." Crystal went so far as to raise her eyes to Kate for a moment. "I mean, look. One thing we know here are men. Talk about denial—she figured he was gonna change, just because she'd moved out for a couple of weeks. Men like that never change. They just wait."

It was a voice of experience speaking, and Kate had seen enough domestic violence, had in her uniform days separated enough bloody, screaming couples, not to argue with her assessment of the Larsen situation. As Carla Lomax had said, James Larsen would have gotten his wife back, and he would have put her in the hospital, if not the morgue.

"So you finished around nine. Did everyone leave then?"

"Oh, no. Nikki, like I said, she was gone, and Carla. And yeah, Phoebe must've been here, 'cause I remember she left with Carla. But the rest of us had a cuppa tea in the kitchen and made the kids' lunches for the next day. Roz was around, with somebody who came in at the end—I didn't know her. That Roz," she said wistfully, "she's really somepin', isn't she? Has a knack for makin' you feel good about yourself. Like you're bigger'n you really are. Important, almost. But anyway, then that woman left and Roz came back in and sat in the meeting room with Emily. They were still there when I went off to bed."

"What time was that?"

"Maybe ten-thirty? I had a bath and I was in bed before eleven, so yeah, 'bout ten-thirty."

"You said Roz came back in. She had left for a while then, with this woman?" The Lomax cousins stirred simultaneously, the inevitable response to that question from the police, but Crystal did not see any import in it, and after a moment's consideration, she answered.

"I think so. I think the two of 'em just went outside to talk, in the woman's car maybe. It's sometimes hard to get much privacy here. Which is fine," she hastened to add, looking at the shelter director. "I like havin' company, and it's sure great for the kids. But if you're wantin' to have a quiet talk with someone, it's best to step outside."

Kate nodded her understanding. "How long were they out there?"

"Oh, I dunno. Half an hour maybe? By the time Roz came back in, all the cups'd been washed and put away. She joked about havin' good timin'."

Kate consulted her notes. "So other than Roz and her friend, and Nikki, Carla, and Phoebe" (Phoebe; wasn't that the name of Carla's secretary?), "did anyone else leave the house, even for a little while? Maybe disappear and then come back a while later?"

"They could've, I guess," Crystal said doubtfully. "People was comin' and goin'—they always are. Emily I know was in the kitchen till Roz came and got her, and the rest of us were there. Joanne may have gone up to check on her kids—she usually does—but I think I'd've heard if someone went out. But I'm not real sure. Sorry."

"Oh no, don't be sorry. That's very helpful."

"Was that all you wanted, then? I should go get my kids ready for bed."

"Yes, thank you. If you think of anything else, give me a call, here's my card. And—good luck with the job hunt."

When Crystal had left, Kate turned to the Lomax cousins. "Do you know who this woman was who came and got Roz?"

"No," Diana said, "but it was someone she knew. Roz is— Do you know Roz, Roz Hall?"

"I do, yes. She told me she'd been here, in fact."

"I should have guessed," Diana said. "Everyone knows Roz. Anyway, this woman stuck her head in the door and Roz spotted her, and told her she'd be out in a bit."

"Did you get the impression that this was a prearranged visit, that Roz was expecting her?"

"No, she was surprised to see her."

"Can you tell me about the other women Crystal was talking about?"

"Tina, Joanne, and Sunny are still here, you can talk with them if you like. Carmelita Rosario is the one who went back to her husband. You know the word *marianismo*? The woman's half of *machismo*, submission to the man's superiority. Remove *marianismo* and the man—but that isn't what you want to know," she interrupted herself, causing Kate to wonder what it was about this case that seemed to demand that everyone involved make speeches. Perhaps Roz was contagious? Diana went on. "Carmelita went home. Nikki Fletcher was a resident for about five weeks until she found an apartment and moved out last Wednesday. She drops in almost every day, just to stay in touch and to have us tell her that she can do it. Was that all?"

Kate looked over her notes and came up with another name. "Phoebe?"

Carla answered this time. "You met Phoebe at my office—Phoebe Weatherman. She's my secretary."

"Was she once a resident here?" Kate asked. That

might explain the woman's deep respect for security measures.

"Not this one, but she was in a shelter for a while, yes."

"She seems very competent."

"Not everyone who ends up in a shelter is from the unemployable dregs, Inspector," Diana said coldly.

"I didn't think they were," Kate told her, unintimidated. "Still, women with marketable skills tend to have more options than those without. And often savings accounts as well."

"Some women who come here do need more time than others," Diana admitted. "We give them training and help them with anything from bus schedules to taxes. And true, others find jobs quickly and move out. But any woman can find herself a victim, Inspector Martinelli. It only takes one bad turn to end up in an ugly place."

"Roz Hall," Kate asked in an abrupt return to the earlier topic. "How often does she come here?"

"It depends. She used to be here all the time when we first opened up, but since then she's been appointed to a couple of commissions and she can't get free as much. And then she's trying to finish her Ph.D. thesis, and leave a little space for Maj. You know her partner, Maj?"

"Well enough to have dreams about her tiramisu."

At that both Lomax cousins laughed. Diana said, "How many potluck dinners have been planned just because of Maj's desserts? God knows how either of them are going to have time for their baby. But they'll manage. Especially Roz. She always does—though I don't know where that woman gets her energy." Kate smiled, having wondered the same thing herself. "Anyway, some weeks Roz is only here two or three times, sometimes half a dozen. She does come regularly on Mondays and Thursdays for the group sessions, but other than that, it's whenever we need her. Or if she happens to be nearby, she'll stop in for a few minutes, have a cup of coffee, see how things are going."

"Fine. Can we see one of the other residents now? Tina?"

"She'll be with her kids. How about Sunny?"

"Sunny will do."

But Kate learned nothing from any of the other three residents, nothing but the details of life as a woman struggling not to be a victim. Joanne was gay and her abuser a woman, but the language of violence was the same for all, and by the time she finished her interviews, Kate felt the need for a strong drink. Instead she dropped her notebook into her pocket and rubbed her face.

"Don't you just despair sometimes?" she asked, more a rhetorical musing than a question, but Diana eyed her from her broken face, and then she nodded.

"All the time, Inspector Martinelli. All the time."

Kate drove the department unmarked car through streets thick with freeway-bound traffic to the Hall of Justice. As the light faded outside and the honks and squeals of frustrated commuters drew to its peak, she typed up the report of the interviews, found them every bit as unsatisfying as she had thought at the time, and went looking for Al Hawkin. Sometimes it helped to toss around ideas. This time it didn't. They went home, to try for a fresh view of things in the morning.

Things in the morning began with the news that the Ladies had struck again overnight, in another park, this time with a middle-aged drunk who was giving his girlfriend hell for some imagined infraction involving their neighbor. He had slapped her, hard; she had set out for a friend's house a few blocks away with him on her heels, shouting and threatening. When she got to the friend's house, she realized gratefully that he had dropped off her trail. In the morning it was found that he had dropped out of the world for a few hours.

Taser, again; duct tape, again, against a splintery tree this time rather than a frigid metal light post. And they had added a twist: the note was attached to his bare buttocks with Superglue. The emergency room told him the glue should wear off in a few weeks. Before they scrubbed the paper portion off him, the police had photographed the note in situ. It read:

BE NICE. OR ELSE.
—the Ladies

When Kate reached her desk, she found a note saying that James Larsen's car had been found, parked on a street in the Mission and stripped down to its chassis. She rounded up Hawkin and they went out to look at it. The old Chevy sedan hadn't been much to look at to begin with, and it had sat on the street for four days; no one had seen who left it; there were no keys and a million prints, most of which no doubt belonged to the kids who had liberated the car's radio, battery, and the rest. They arranged to have it towed off for closer examination, on the stray chance that Larsen had been transporting drugs in the trunk or had himself made his final journey inside it, and spent a few fruitless hours asking questions in the neighborhood, but it was a community of blind people when it came to seeing who had driven up and abandoned the car there with its doors unlocked.

They then set off on the entertaining task of trying to trace the cuffs that had been used to restrain Larsen. The number of shops selling that particular brand of regulation police handcuffs in San Francisco was astonishing, even to Kate, who thought she had seen it all. In each of the shops she ended up going through the same ritual, fending off the shopkeeper and customers who found the idea of an actual live, badge-wielding cop on the premises too titillating for words. She was only grateful that she wasn't wearing a uniform, or she might never have been allowed to escape without putting half the city in cuffs, for their own entertainment.

Aside from the car and the cuffs, the investigation

had become simple slog, contacting those of Larsen's family and acquaintances whom they had not reached earlier and going back over the phone bills and financial records. The preliminary lab report came through during the afternoon, telling them that Larsen's last meal had been two or three hours before his death and had probably been a fast-food bacon-cheeseburger and fries. There was no trace of drugs on his clothes, in his blood, or in his history. Emily Larsen showed no signs of making a run for it, no one else in sight had any particular reason to kill him, and there had been no whiff of connections to shady business deals, outright crime, sleeping with someone's wife, or any of the other customary reasons for knocking someone off.

This one looked to sit on the shelf gathering dust for a long time, Kate thought. Al agreed.

"One thing might be worth doing, though," he suggested.

"That phone in the laundromat?"

"Yeah, but it'll have to be about the same time the call was placed in order to do any good."

"You weren't doing anything tonight, were you, Al?"

"I'm already too late for dinner. I should probably call Jani and let her know not to wait up."

While Al made his worn apologies to his new wife and stepdaughter, Kate phoned Lee and agreed to bring home mu shu pork and kung pao shrimp. The three of them ate in the dining room of the old house on Russian Hill, looking out over the squat presence of Alcatraz and the ferries going to and from Sausalito, and with the descent of night, the long string of white lights stretching the length of the Bay Bridge. They had some coffee and talked of nothing in particular, and at eight-thirty Kate and Al returned to the car and pulled away from the curb to nose their way back into the city.

Kate parked across the street from the laundromat. On the back wall of the brightly lighted space, between a dryer the size of a compact car and a machine that dispensed tiny cartons of soap powder and fabric softener, there stood a telephone, a call from which may have brought James Larsen out to his death. The laundromat stood in the middle of a busy block. Next door was a bustling Mexican restaurant that seemed to do as much take-away business as table service. Across the street was a record store, a coffeehouse, a late-night bookstore, and a Chinese restaurant. Plenty of people around to witness a person making a call, standing beneath the harsh blue light of a couple dozen fluorescent strips, but no one to notice.

No patron of the laundry admitted to having washed her clothes there on Monday night. The woman in charge of watching the machines snapped irritably that she was too busy folding clothes in the back for the drop-off trade, and that the damn phone was a pain in the neck, she and her husband were thinking of having it pulled out or replaced with one of those new models that people couldn't call in on, and no, her husband had not been there on Monday. The two detectives thanked her and went back onto the street.

The staff in the Mexican restaurant, most of whom had been working Monday night, had also been too busy to notice any particular individual going in or out of the laundromat. The bookstore owner had seen a bearded Rastafarian using the phone for quite a while on Monday, in a conversation of escalating anger that ended with the man bashing the receiver down, kicking a wheeled laundry cart in passing, knocking over a menu board for the restaurant next door, and shouting his way down the street, though the bookseller thought it happened closer to ten, and Kate, while dutifully noting the story, could not summon much enthusiasm for the theory that a furious dreadlocked African-American had tempted James Larsen to drive from his home to San Francisco on Monday evening.

At ten o'clock, the businesses started shutting and the patrons of the laundromat staggered off with their bulging plastic sacks of clean clothes. The Mexican place seemed prepared to go on dishing up menudo and enchiladas until dawn, and at eleven, a pair of weary detectives went in and ordered bowls of soup at one of the back tables.

"Well, gee," said Kate. "That was sure fun."

"Lots of hot leads," Al agreed glumly.

There had been nothing of the sort, merely blank looks accompanying shakes of the head alternating with polite (or not-so-polite) incredulity that they might be expected to remember a person (male or female? white, black, brown, or striped?) making a telephone call from the back of a busy laundromat five days before.

It had been worth doing, but neither of them was surprised at the lack of results. That was how the job went.

Which meant turning back to the victim and his wife, looking for some little thing that wasn't right. Tomorrow.

"How's Jani?" Kate asked him. "And Jules?"

"Jules is great. Maddening, but great." Hawkin stirred the vegetables in his soup with close attention, and then his mouth twitched in a crooked smile. "Jani's even greater. She's pregnant."

"Al! How fantastic. When is she due?"

"November sometime. We just found out the other day."

"I'm so happy for you, Al. You are happy, I take it?"

"Oh, yeah. Nervous, I guess—I'll be retired by the time he's playing high school football. Or she."

"All the more free time to volunteer as a coach. You don't know what it is yet?"

"Jani doesn't want to."

"How did Jules react?"

"She's been great. Embarrassed a little, I guess—I mean, parents don't go around making babies, how gross. But underneath that, she's excited too."

"I must call her, see if she wants to go bowling or something. God, Al, you're a lucky man."

"Don't I know it. Has Lee said anything—"

His question was cut short by the insistent beeping of the pager in his pocket, followed seconds later by

Kate's. Al went into the empty laundromat to use the telephone that had been the cause of the outing, while Kate paid the bill and took advantage of the restaurant's toilet. When she came out of the restaurant Hawkin was leaning against the side of the car.

"Seems to be our week for dumped bodies," Al told her. "This one's out near the Legion of Honor."

Anonymously dumped bodies were the hardest of all murders to solve. They were usually drug-related, there were rarely any witnesses around, and the forensic evidence was generally scarce—most often the victim's pockets were empty, which made identification hard and in some cases impossible. No detective liked a John Doe, but there were any number of them on the books, going back years. Some would never be solved.

Again Kate's car took her from city lights into treeshrouded darkness. This time the lights were along Geary Boulevard, and the dark set in more gradually, eased by the orange glow of the parking area across from the Legion of Honor and the cool lights that turned the museum's pillars into a sort of strippeddown Versailles. The stone lions watched the playing fountain and preserved the facade of civilization; then the road turned downhill and the night closed in.

High fog rode the treetops and obscured the upper reaches of the world's most famous bridge, transforming it into a mere string of lights held up by stubby towers. A clot of fog settled across the roadway and then swept on, and when it lifted, they saw the cluster of official vehicles.

The coat Kate had worn for the relatively mild night down in the center of town was completely inadequate against the damp gale rising up from the sea. The yammer of voices and radios could not drown out the heavy pounding of the surf and the noise of the wind ripping through the cypress and pine trees. A foghorn groaned on and off; a nearby eucalyptus crackled with the brisk passage of air. Kate could also hear a noise like sobbing—but it *was* sobbing, from the backseat of a cruiser where a pair of teenagers huddled. Al went over to the car and had a brief word with them, which caused a brief renewal of wailing that died down again as the boy did his best to comfort his increasingly tiresome girlfriend. Love, Kate reflected, never did run smooth.

Fortunately, this body hadn't been stripped. The victim, like James Larsen, even had his wallet. At first glance, it was about the only thing the two men had in common. At first glance.

Matthew Banderas had been a fit and successful thirty-two-year-old man who had given a lot of attention to his appearance. Now he was lying in a heap at the side of the road like a sack of discarded garbage, down the hill from the Legion of Honor museum, where he had been found by the two teenagers out to enjoy the solitude, the lights of the bridge, and each other. Matthew Banderas wore a suit that had cost more than James Larsen made in a month, with another month's salary on his feet. Two years' worth of Larsen salary was parked a short distance up the road, with a vanity plate reading MATMAN. There was not even any physical resemblance between the two men: Banderas was little more than half Larsen's age, and had it not been for his surname, Kate would have taken him for Italian or perhaps half-Greek, for his skin was only faintly swarthy, his expensively styled hair thick and Mediterranean black. Nothing at all like Larsen.

Except that Matthew Banderas had a pair of police handcuffs on his wrists.

And a taser had left its mark on his flat stomach, just below the rib cage.

And he had been strangled to death.

In the left-hand pocket of his expensive jacket Kate found a wrapped chocolate bar, still soft with the fading warmth of Banderas's body. She dropped it into an evidence bag, and held it up thoughtfully.

Hawkin watched as Banderas was loaded up into the van, and rubbed his chin unhappily. "This is not good," he said. "This is really not good."

Kate could only nod. The moment she had seen the handcuffs she knew they were in grave trouble. They were now dealing with a serial killer, which aside from its own urgency would mean complicated, painstaking work under the full cacophony and glare of a media circus. She stood and shivered as she looked out over the Golden Gate, at the dark sea that lay between the heights occupied by the museum and the Marin headlands on the northern shore, and she became aware of the first gathering of news reporters on the crest of the road behind them.

"I'm surprised the TV cameras aren't here already," she said bitterly. "Guess it's too late for the eleven o'clock news."

Hawkin heard the dread in her voice, and knew all too well the reason for it. From the day they had been made partners, he new to the City and she new to the job, they had been faced with one high-profile case after another: the world-famous artist Vaun Adams, the renowned lesbian radical Raven Morningstar, Al's own stepdaughter's kidnapping—all made national, even international headlines. By now the press had only to hear the name Martinelli and they came baying. More than once she had thought about changing her name, coloring her hair, and going back into uniform for a nice anonymous foot patrol beat. She figured, though, that if she did she would be sure to stumble on Jimmy Hoffa's skeleton, or the president of the United States shooting up in an alley.

"Look," Hawkin said abruptly. "You don't need this. Let me get one of the others in on it."

It was tempting, very tempting, but after a minute Kate shook her head. "It's too late. I'm already involved—they won't leave me alone."

"Sure they will. I can ask—"

"Al? Leave it. I can't let them rule my life."

"Okay," he said. Both of them knew he had enough authority to shift her off the case; both knew he would do so if things got too crazy. He signaled that the techs could bag up the body and take it away. As he and Kate turned to look at the two teenagers in the back of the police cruiser, the boy trying to act manly as he comforted his girlfriend, whose endless whimpering was getting on everyone's nerves, Hawkin said, half to himself, "I don't know whether to hope this guy Banderas has a history of wife beating, or hope he doesn't."

Matthew Banderas did not have a history of spousal abuse.

Matthew Banderas had a history of rape.

6

The violent one
Whose raging demands
Break down peace and shelter
Like a peacock's scream.

The murder made the papers in the morning, but although the articles speculated on the possible links between this victim, James Larsen, and the lighter pranks of the LOPD, they did not yet have the key link of the criminal history of the two murdered men. It would only be a matter of time, however, and with that knowledge riding on their necks, the two detectives threw themselves at the case. Early on Saturday morning they met up in the Hall of Justice, to get the search warrants under way and to track down their latest victim's past.

Banderas had only been arrested once, shortly after his twenty-sixth birthday. For that he had stood trial, been found guilty, and served just under three years. The light sentence had been a result of his plausibility on the stand, and was further reduced by his spotless behavior in the low-security prison. Still, neither detective believed that the one rape was his only instance of aberrant behavior.

"How many rapists do you know who started when they were in their mid-twenties?" Kate asked Al skeptically, and indeed, when they began to dig, they found that Banderas had been closely investigated for three other rapes since his eighteenth birthday, all of them let go by a lack of evidence the district attorney found adequate enough for conviction. The one time he had been caught was seven and a half years before.

Hawkin shook his head. "He was a very clever boy. He took souvenirs—the victim's underwear—but he either destroyed them or hid each one. Assuming he was behind all of these."

In addition to the three for which Banderas was chief suspect, there was a whole string of unsolved rapes, three of them clearly related by place, time, and technique, two others with more tenuous links. Eight times over the last seventeen years some unidentified predator had waited for a lone woman to come out of a convenience store at night, forced himself into her car at gunpoint, driven to some dark place, raped her, and left her naked, bound, and missing her underwear. He always wore a mask and gloves.

None of the series had taken place while Banderas was incarcerated.

"Why didn't anyone catch this bastard?" Kate asked incredulously.

"No forensic evidence, and you can't lock a guy up on a similar MO. The one conviction, the woman bit him on the face and the mask came off. She identified him at the trial. But because he didn't finish up like he usually did—he dumped her out in the hills, didn't take a souvenir, didn't tie her up—there wasn't much point in going for the whole series. And he wore a condom, so there wasn't even any DNA."

Only two of the unsolved rapes had taken place since Banderas came out of prison. As Hawkin had said, the man was cautious.

"He never hurt any of the women beyond the rape. Though that's bad enough," he hastened to say, "but even a couple of the victims said he was 'polite.' Seems to me a strange way to describe a guy who's just raped you."

"Do you suppose he'd have let the next woman to see his face go free?" Kate asked him.

"Not if it cost him another spell in prison. But someone has taken that choice out of his hands and put the problem on our desk."

"So you think there's someone out there taking care of the bad guys?"

"Doesn't it look like that to you?"

"No chance of a copycat?"

"The taser and cuffs were described in the paper, but they all just said 'strangled' without giving details. And they certainly don't have the candy in the victim's pockets. I wouldn't have even thought of it as evidence with Larsen, but with this victim, it looks like it is."

"Banderas didn't really look the sort to carry a chocolate bar in the pocket of an expensive suit, true, but I don't know that I'd count it as a clear mark of a serial."

"We'll see."

"Christ, I hope not," Kate said fervently. Two was quite enough, and she'd just as soon leave a question rather than have a third body to confirm Al's theory. However, the question was further complicated just before noon when the preliminary results from the Banderas car search came up with an empty insulin pen, found in the back of the glove compartment, with no name on it of either patient or pharmacy. They had planned on searching the Banderas apartment later that afternoon, but with the possibility that a diabetic had been found in the possession of a chocolate bar, they called Marin to let them know that the SFPD was serving a search warrant in their jurisdiction, put on their coats, and left.

Banderas had lived in a condominium north of Mill Valley, a modern apartment complex filled with successful young singles and childless couples where both partners worked. Parking was in a three-story garage connected to the buildings by walkways, not outside the apartment doors, and the Banderas apartment was near the complex's entrance; none of his neighbors would ever know when he was home or not.

His apartment was unrevealing, the living quarters of a bachelor who ate out a lot and brought work and women home. There was an assortment of exotic condoms in the table beside the bed, a stack of the classier kinds of frozen dinners in the freezer, and a set of copper cookware that looked as if it had never been used. He wore expensive clothing, with a flashy taste in suit lapels, shirt collars, and neckties, and owned five more pairs of shoes as expensive as those he had died in, plus an assortment of loafers and athletic shoes. The paintings on the wall were splashes of bright color that did not mean much of anything except that he knew walls needed to have them, a painting in the bedroom showed a well-endowed naked blond woman either making love with or struggling beneath a clothed man, and he owned a lot of very hard-core pornographic videos, some of them violent, with one player in the living room and another in the bedroom. The room did not have a mirror on the ceiling, but the place looked as if Banderas might have thought of it.

Kate stood with a copy of a video entitled *She Really Wants It* in her hand and called to her partner in the next room, "Al, do we have to like this guy?"

"No, Martinelli. So far as I know there's no law yet that says we have to like our victims."

"Good thing," she told him, and went back to work.

The most interesting discoveries, however, were those the search team had already found in the bathroom. Two different discoveries, actually, although the detectives could have predicted the presence of a pouch of fragrant leaves and a small vial of white powder, with the attendant paraphernalia for marijuana and cocaine. The other find was even more interesting: a small machine for testing blood sugar, used by diabetics, and two disposable needles in the wastebasket. There was also a multi-use insulin pen like that found in the car, only this one was half full and had Banderas's name on the pharmacist's label.

Matthew Banderas had indeed been a diabetic; a diabetic who died with a candy bar in his pocket.

Professionally, Banderas was a computer man, in software sales. Going by the bank statements in his desk drawer, he was good at his job. Kate copied down the telephone number for the company, and its Santa Rosa address.

The last incoming call had been from a woman, who had left a message on the answering machine. A series of messages, in fact. Her name was Melanie, and she had started out teasingly inquiring where he was and ended up, five messages and six hours later, just plain mad. "Damn it, Matty, where are you?" her voice demanded, and the phone went dead. Hers were the only calls, beginning at 8:32 Friday night, ending at 3:14 Saturday morning. By the last one, Melanie had been more than a little drunk.

One of the apartment's two bedrooms had been made over into an office, with boxes of forms and sample disks, three computers, and two filled filing cabinets. Kate flipped open the man's laptop, Al pulled a chair over to the filing cabinets, and silence fell.

Half an hour later they were startled by a deep male voice in the next room saying in a plummy English accent, "There is a visitor at the door, sir." Kate was out of her chair with her gun in her hand before she realized what she was doing; Al was on his feet almost as quickly. They both stared at the door expectantly, and Al said in a loud voice, "We are the police; please identify yourself."

There was no response, not even the sound of startled movement. Kate held her gun up and edged toward the study door, where she popped her head out briefly for a cautious glance at the living room. There was no one visible. She opened her mouth to make her own demand, and another voice came, this time that of a woman, sultry and slow.

"Open up the door, you sweet thing, you."

Puzzled now, Kate looked at Al, and the two of them made their way cautiously into the living room, checking out every nook and broom closet in the intervening space. Bedroom, bath, and kitchen were cleared, and they stood in the living room between the black leather sofa and the huge gilt-framed mirror, waiting. When a voice came for the third time—this one a smarmy-sounding male with a heavy French accent declaring, "Eh, beeg boy, you have a fren' at ze door"—Kate whirled and nearly shot out the speaker next to the front door before she finally registered the mechanical quality of the sound. A fourth voice sounded immediately on the heels of the stage Frenchman (this one a Southern belle drawling "Hey there, honeybun, there's somebody here to see y'all"), and then a fifth, which was the same English butler's voice they had first heard. The pounding started as the person with a finger on the voice-doorbell got tired of waiting.

"Matty," a woman's voice called. "Matty, come on! I know you're home, your lights are on. And don't tell me you've got them on some kind of timing device, I'm just going to stand here with my thumb on the bell until you get sick of these goddamn voices and—"

It wouldn't take long to get sick of the cycle of announcements, Kate thought. Under the repetition of the four voices, coming from a box next to the door where clever-boy Banderas had adapted the normal chimes to a high-tech version of a doorbell, Kate slid her gun away and pulled open the door, to find herself face-to-face with a gorgeous, polished young woman who could have been a fashion model, dressed in skintight jeans, a low-cut and extremely well-filled top that did not quite reach a very shapely navel with a gold ring in it, a black leather bomber jacket, and shiny high-heeled boots that she might well have bought from one of the shops that Kate had gone into inquiring about recreational handcuffs. All she needed was a whip in her hand, but in truth, she seemed quite unconscious of the dominatrix overtones in her attire. She might have been a six-year-old dressing up in net stockings, makeup, and a miniskirt for Halloween, having not the faintest idea why it was incongruous.

As this was going through Kate's mind, the woman was in turn staring at her, looking surprised at first, then suspicious and resentful until finally, taking a closer look at Kate's undistinguished form and uninspired trousers and shirt, surprise again took precedence.

"Where's Matty?" she demanded.

"Matthew Banderas?"

"Yeah. Of course Matthew Banderas, this is his house. Who the hell are you?"

Kate pulled her ID out of her pocket and showed it to the young dominatrix. "You're a friend of Mr. Banderas?" she asked.

"Yes, I am. Where is he?"

"Come in please, Ms., um—?"

"Melanie Gilbert. Where's Matty? What's happened to him?"

"I'm very sorry, Ms. Gilbert, but Mr. Banderas was killed last night in San Francisco."

"What? Oh, no." The woman gaped at Kate, looking astonished but not teary. She scarcely noticed Kate's hand on her elbow, gently but firmly drawing her inside to the leather sofa. "Oh, poor, poor Matty. I can't believe it. What happened?"

As soon as she was safely inside and the door shut behind her, Kate let go of the slim, leather-jacketed arm. Gilbert was not exactly devastated to hear of her friend's death, Kate was relieved to see. Telling loved ones was hard; telling friends and acquaintances, once they were past the initial shock of it, often led to interesting pieces of information being shaken out of the tree of knowledge.

"Can I get you a glass of water, Ms. Gilbert?" Kate asked. She had never known why this was the traditional means of offering support; the times she had received shocks the only drink she'd wanted was alcoholic and preferably bottomless. Still, it did give the woman a chance to gather herself together, while allowing Kate to look as if she cared, and in this case let Al Hawkin sit down beside Matthew Banderas's girlfriend with the heaving breasts and the demure navel ring. This was one female who would respond more readily to the masculine touch. At which Al Hawkin was an expert.

Al gave the young woman a minute to sip her glass of room-temperature, chlorinated water before asking her in a gentle voice, "Ms. Gilbert, can you tell me how you know Matthew?" Formality combined with the intimacy of the victim's first name, Kate noted, and the emphasis on the relationship, not (yet) the more pertinent facts such as time and place.

"I'm an actress," she told them. "I met Matty when I was doing a job for his company last year, acting in a piece of film that they wanted to use in their software. I'm really not sure how they do it, something about feeding the film into their computers and using it from there. I think they were using it to demonstrate some editing software they were developing, or something. Anyway," she continued, relieved that these technical details were out of the way without any questions from her audience, "that's when I met Matty, when he came by the set one day to watch. We went out to dinner afterward, and, well, you know."

"What was your relationship with Matthew?"

"My relationship? I loved Matty, or at least I more or less did; anyway, I liked him a lot. I slept with him, if that's what you mean, but we never lived together."

Hawkin considered his next question carefully before deciding to ask it. "Did you know that Matthew spent three years in prison for raping a woman?"

"Matthew?" Her pretty face twisted in disbelief. "No, you've got the wrong man. In fact, you probably have the wrong man entirely—Jesus, Matty's gonna flip when he gets home and finds you here."

"Ms. Gilbert, I'm sorry. Unless Matthew had a twin brother who was carrying Matthew's ID, your friend is dead."

Melanie Gilbert pulled back from the edge of the hysterical thoughts she had been about to succumb to, and studied Hawkin's craggy features. She gave a small sigh, and slumped down into the black sofa. One melodramatic tear ran slowly down her cheek, and her chest heaved impressively.

"Matty? A rapist? God. You really are sure?"

"Yes."

"Oh," she said, and then in a different voice, one that suddenly recognized the implications, she said, "Oh. Oh my God. Rape? Did he hurt her? I mean—"

"No. Kidnapping and rape, but not battery."

"But still. Shit, I was sleeping with a *rapist*. How could I not—jeez, that's so creepy. I feel like throwing up."

Kate suddenly had enough of the sexy young actress's attempt to find out how she ought to be feeling, and stood up to go to the kitchen and find the coffeemaker. She suddenly realized that they hadn't stopped for lunch, that she was tired, hungry, edgy, and depressed, and was fed up with this young airhead with the twinkle of gold in her navel who was trying to talk herself into being shocked when she was really more than half titillated. Al Hawkin's voice went on as Kate found a gleaming gold French press coffeemaker, a bag of Italian roast coffee (pre-ground, for which Lee would have deducted points), and instead of a kettle, an attachment on the sink that dispensed near-boiling water. Kate spooned grounds into the coffeemaker and ran steaming water on top, and while she waited the requisite couple of minutes for the grounds to subside, she leaned against the tiled counter listening to the conversation in the next room.

"Ms. Gilbert, did you ever hear Matthew say anything about being harassed or threatened, either here or at work? Receiving letters or phone calls, anything like that?"

"No, I don't think so. Matty never talked much about work, though I know that his new boss is a real bitch. And, hey—somebody at work keyed his car back near Christmas, left a really nasty scratch. And there was somebody here in the apartments that kept stealing his parking place, but since they're not really assigned or anything, he couldn't do much about it."

"He never found who scratched his car?" Gilbert shook her head. "What about the argument over the parking place? Did it ever escalate? Did the two of them ever have words about it?" Scratched paint, territorial disputes—murders were committed every day for even stupider reasons.

"I don't think so," Gilbert repeated. Still, Hawkin dutifully got from her what little she knew about the intrusive neighbor, which was little more than he, she, or it drove a red Porsche (she pronounced it *Porsh*, and said that Banderas had pointed it out to her) and lived somewhere upstairs (which she had gathered by a rude gesture Banderas once made in the vague direction of the offender's apartment).

"So he knew whose car it was?"

"Oh yeah. I mean, he never told me her name, but he knew who she was." Then Gilbert added thoughtfully, "But you know, they might of had a fight after all, 'cause the last couple weeks the Porsche hasn't been in his spot, and when I said something about it to Matty, he just kind of nodded his head but he seemed, like, satisfied. You know?"

The coffee, pre-ground or not, smelled intoxicating, so Kate shoved down the handle, poured three cups, and carried the tray back into the living room. Melanie declined, saying virtuously that she had given up coffee, which was bad for the skin.

Kate nodded, took a large and satisfying swallow from her cup, and asked where Banderas bought his coke.

The actress blushed and tugged her cropped shirt down, covering a fraction more of her admirably flat stomach and revealing a little more of her round breasts. (Implants, or one of those push-up bras? Kate speculated. Or could those possibly be natural?) "What do you mean?" Gilbert said, trying for innocence.

"We found the cocaine in the bathroom cabinet. I wondered if you knew where he got it, if he was in the habit of buying it in San Francisco. We're not interested in prosecuting him for it, and I'm sure you had nothing to do with it. I just wondered if you happened to know if he bought it locally, or in the City?"

"Um. Should I, you know, talk with a lawyer or something?" asked this child of the television age.

"We're not interested in your drug use, Ms. Gilbert, or even Matthew's. Only in knowing if there might have been some drug-related reason for his being out near the Legion of Honor last night."

"Where's that?"

"You know that art museum on the cliff out near the ocean?" Kate offered. "Lots of high school classes go there."

The pretty face cleared. "Oh yeah, I remember that place. Sculptures and things, I think."

"That's the place."

"And that's where Matty was? At the museum?" From the sound of her voice, it was not a place she connected with her boyfriend's lifestyle.

"Nearby. The museum itself was shut."

She shook her head. "I don't know. Unless he was meeting someone there. But I wouldn't have thought he went there to score. He usually—that is, I think there's someone, um, local."

In the apartment complex, Kate interpreted; what a surprise.

Melanie Gilbert had nothing much more to add to their scant pool of knowledge. She had never seen another face to Banderas, never glimpsed a brutal or violent side to him: he had always been polite to her, even when drinking or doing coke. She confirmed that he was a diabetic, with "all kinds of things" he couldn't eat, and that she had never known him to consume anything as sweet as a bar of chocolate, even when he had been smoking dope. She did not know the names of any of Banderas's previous girlfriends, and thought his family was in Southern California somewhere, though she had never met any of them.

Hawkin then circled back to the topic of the Banderas rape charge, asking as delicately as possible about the man's sex habits. The young woman protested that there had been nothing at all kinky about Matty, but the vehemence of her denials indicated that some questioning note had sounded in the back of that pretty head, and she was beginning to doubt herself. It was something that needed going into more closely, but not, thankfully, by two visiting SFPD homicide investigators. Hawkin had reached the same conclusion, and let the topic go, to Melanie's obvious relief.

"And you're sure, Ms. Gilbert, that Matthew wasn't receiving any threatening phone calls or letters, anything like that?"

"No. Well, he did have a few wrong numbers, rude people in the middle of the night, things like that. Who doesn't?"

"Recently?"

"Last week. Do you think that could have been . . . whoever?"

"We'll try to find out, Ms. Gilbert. Well, I don't know that we need to keep you any longer today. Could we have a phone number, in case we need to ask you anything else?"

She gave them a list of numbers: her home number and her cell phone, her agent's number and his cell phone, and was trying to think of anyone else besides her sister and her ex-husband when Al plucked the paper from her fingers and shooed her out the door. When it had closed behind her, the two detectives looked at each other.

"Whew," said Al.

"That woman's in the wrong business," Kate agreed. "She'd make a fortune with a whip in her hand. Those boots alone would have a masochist squirming."

"You think she . . . does?"

"I strongly doubt it. Her face looks like a schoolgirl's. Mixed signals, you know? I think it's just her idea of fashion."

"Don't sound so disappointed, Martinelli."

"Not my kind of thing, Al," she said evenly. Still, as she turned back to the Banderas files, she couldn't help wondering how Lee would look with a ring in her navel. . . .

One day proved to be all they had before media hell broke loose. Sundays were generally a slack day for news, but the morning paper had the Banderas murder screaming across the front page:

SECOND SEX PREDATOR KILLED

The article beneath the headline reviewed the full details of the Larsen and Banderas murders, only this time the reporters had both men's history of crimes against women. The use of tasers to overcome the two men underscored the possible link with the "feminist vigilante group," the LOPD, with which tasers were now firmly linked in the popular imagination. An adjacent article bore the eye-catching heading HATE CRIMES CLASSIFICATION ASKED, and Kate read with growing amazement that a delegation of "prominent businessmen" had been to see the mayor the previous afternoon, asserting that since the Ladies' attacks and the two murders had all been aimed exclusively at heterosexual males with light skin, the attacks should be classified as hate crimes and pursued with all the commitment that the City had come to demonstrate in its prosecution of gay bashing.

Kate put the paper on the kitchen table for Lee's bemusement and left for the Hall of Justice, where she finished filling out as best she could the highly detailed VICAP forms for the FBI, asking if they had any crimes on the books that fit the profile of abusers, tasers, handcuffs, and including the possible link of candy. As Kate was reading it over, wondering if there were any more blank spaces she could fill, the telephone rang.

"Seen the paper?" Hawkin asked without preliminary.

"It tells everything except who done it," she noted. "Why didn't they call and ask for a comment?" It was the usual way reporters notified the cops that a story was coming, in the recognition that cooperation worked better in the long run, but there had been no such message waiting for them when they stopped in at the Hall of Justice the night before.

"New girl," Hawkin answered. "Gung ho. We'd better get up to the condos early before the place is under siege. Meet you at the Hall, or at your place?"

"Why don't you swing by here? Give me a chance to answer some of the messages."

"Fine. See you in a bit."

The messages were mostly from the media, and a few clearing up details in the Larsen case. Kate placed another call to the desk sergeant in Marin, suggesting that someone from the department might want to join them for an exchange of notes before the news reporters added "lack of interdepartmental communication" to their string of gibes. She left various numbers for the Marin detective to call her back, then trotted for the elevator.

The Marin detective rang them back when they were halfway across the Golden Gate Bridge.

"Inspector Martinelli?" the voice said. "Sergeant Martina Wiley here."

"Hello Sergeant, thanks for calling me back."

"I can guess what you want to talk about. I'm over here talking to a woman who lives upstairs from the Banderas apartment. I think you might want to join me."

"Er. Do you have any idea what kind of car she drives?" Kate asked. There was silence for a minute as Wiley gave this odd question her consideration, then Kate heard the receiver being half muffled and through the barrier Wiley's voice asking, "What kind of car do you have?" Kate could not hear the answer, but Wiley supplied it. "A red Porsche."

"Okay," said Kate with satisfaction. "What apartment are you in, Sergeant?"

"Number three-fourteen."

"We'll be there in twenty minutes."

The woman in apartment 314 did not look the type to drive a flashy car. Nor did the modern furnishings fit with the small woman dressed in jeans, a vastly oversized sweatshirt, fuzzy slippers, and plaster. The last item covered her left arm from knuckle to elbow, and half a dozen stitches had recently been removed from the still-swollen cut on her left eyebrow. That whole side of her face was yellow-green with fading bruises and she held herself stiffly, either from fear of causing pain, or from fear itself.

Kate and Al introduced themselves to Martina Wiley, who had answered the door with the air of a family friend and then took them across to the breakfast nook to meet the woman.

"This is Rachel Curtis," she said. "Rachel, these are two detectives from San Francisco, Kate Martinelli and her partner, Al Hawkin. They're investigating the murder of your neighbor Matthew Banderas."

Rachel Curtis flicked a glance at Kate and then Al, but kept her attention on the woman who had taken on the role of savior. Kate was distracted for a moment by the contrast between the cop and the victim, who might have been handpicked to illustrate the word *opposites*. Wiley was big, black, strong, and bristling with intelligence and energy. Curtis was about five feet tall and thin to the point of anorexia, with dark brown chin-length hair, pasty white skin, glasses, and no more energy than yesterday's pasta.

Kate shook herself mentally, and sat down in a chair across from the battered woman.

"Rachel was beaten and raped eleven days ago," Wiley told them bluntly. "She never saw her attacker, didn't recognize his voice. She was stopped in a parking lot by a man with a gun and a mask, who put a pillowcase over her head and drove her away. He raped her, dragged her out of the car, kicked her four or five times, and walked off."

Kate and Al looked at each other, and Kate cleared her throat. "Did he say anything at all?" she asked the woman. Slow tears had begun to dribble down Rachel's battered face, which Kate imagined had happened more or less continuously for the last week and a half.

"He said, 'Hold it' when I got to my car and then,

'Get in the passenger seat.' And then later, when he'd . . . Afterward, he told me not to move. Then he smashed the windows of the car and banged it with something hard, and after that it went quiet. I was lying on some rocks or sticks that were hurting me, and it was cold, so when nothing happened for five or ten minutes I figured he'd gone so I started to sit up and pull the thing off my head and then he was there shouting and kicking me. I curled up again and put my arms around my head, and he stopped, and then after a minute he told me not to move at all, and if I did he'd kill me. And then he said something about nothing being mine, and that was all. I must've laid there for at least an hour, but when I finally pulled off that pillowcase he was gone and my car was there. The tires were flat and all the glass was gone and the body smashed up, but he left the key and I could get one of the doors open, so I drove to the nearest road and found a gas station and a phone."

"What do you think he meant by nothing being yours, Ms. Curtis?" Al Hawkin asked. He had taken care to remain, literally and figuratively, in the background. Some rape victims could not stand being around men for a while, others found men more comforting than their possibly judgmental sisters. Rachel Curtis seemed oblivious of pretty much everything outside of her misery and Martina Wiley, and looked at him uncomprehendingly. Al tried again. "Can you try and remember his exact words?"

"They were, 'You don't own anything,' or, 'You don't own everything.' Yes, I think it was that: 'You don't own everything, you bitch.' And then I heard glass break again. I think he was smashing the headlights."

"I see," Hawkin said, and he did. They thanked the woman, apologized for bothering her, and walked with Martina Wiley out onto the third-floor covered walkway, where they could talk away from the victim's ears.

"Sounds like Banderas?" the sergeant asked them. "I looked up his sheet after I saw the paper this morning."

"Or a close copycat," Kate agreed.

"So what was that question about the car?"

"It would appear that Ms. Curtis had the nerve to park in Matthew's favorite though officially unreserved spot. His girlfriend said that he and Rachel may have had an argument over it about two weeks ago, after which he seemed to be, in her words, 'like, satisfied.'"

"Some argument," Wiley mused, looking down three floors at the unimaginative condominium garden. "And now Banderas is dead. Are you thinking Rachel could've pulled it off? Because I can't see what she has to do with your other case, assuming there is a link. And besides, look at her, she's a basket case. I mean, she might've shot him if you'd put a gun in her hand, or run him down if she saw him walking down the street, but from what I heard, it wasn't exactly like that, was it?"

"It certainly was not," Kate told her. "If—and we don't have any evidence so far except the record both victims have of crimes against women—if this killing is related to the murder of James Larsen, then this woman couldn't have done it. Not with that arm and those injuries."

"So you've maybe got somebody picking off the bad guys. Well, honey, better you than me. Personally, I'd be real tempted to look in the other direction for a while, maybe even offer a few names and addresses of my own, you know? Hey," she said more seriously, "that was a joke. Let me know if I can do anything to help."

But it had not been completely a joke, all three of them knew that, because any cop who had held a badge for more than a few months well understood the urge for a more simple and direct form of justice than the law could provide. Retribution, vigilante justice, call it what you would, it was a deep and powerful temptation, every so often when a known villain was finding a crack to fall through.

Well, here were two men who had run out of hiding places. And two detectives who had the job of finding the person or persons who had taken on the role of judge and executioner.

They talked for a few minutes with Wiley, the easy cop talk of a shared language and similar view of the world.

Wiley was more than interested to hear of Melanie Gilbert's reticence over her lover's bedroom habits, and promised to pass on the word to their sex crimes detail that an interview there might be of value. Sure, Banderas was dead, but clearance rates were law enforcement's bottom line, and the statute of limitations on that string of rapes was by no means expired.

Two young women carrying expensive tennis rackets came out of a door on the other side of the courtyard, talking loudly and happily until they glanced over and saw the three police detectives. Kate wondered idly if Rachel Curtis had been a happy tennis player two weeks ago.

Martina Wiley seemed to read her mind. "Rachel will be all right. She's a strong person who's been knocked for a loop by this, but I think she'll find her anger in a couple more days, and that'll help. I worked sex crimes down south before coming here," she explained. "You get to have a feel for how people will react."

"I hope you're right," Kate told her.

"We'll see. Good to meet you two. I'll be talking to you soon." They shook hands and, thus dismissed, Kate and Al made their way down the stairs, dodging a man with a bicycle coming up, a man with a dog going down, and the postman with an Express Mail envelope, special Sunday delivery, also heading up the stairs.

They let themselves back into the Banderas apartment. It smelled unoccupied already, of dust and stale air despite the lingering scent of yesterday's coffee, and would in a few days be cleared for removal of the victim's effects by his family. Kate had wanted to check a couple of the files in his laptop, but before she had gotten any further than booting it up, someone pounded on the door, bypassing the winsome-voiced doorbell for the sake of directness.

Kate opened it to Martina Wiley. She was holding an opened Express Mail envelope in her rubber-gloved hands, the envelope they had seen in the postman's hand five minutes before.

"It's for you," said Wiley. She carried it over to the dining table and, using the tips of her gloved fingers, she turned the envelope over above the table to allow a folded piece of paper to fall out. Touching only the extreme corners, she pulled it open, and they read:

Be strong, Rachel Curtis, it was not your fault. He will bother no woman again.

—a friend

"Oh, shit," said Kate.

Al Hawkin, looking over her shoulder, could only agree.

7

We have to reckon with Kali for better or worse,
The angry tongue that lashes us with flame
As long-held hope turns bitter and men curse,
"Burn, baby, burn" in the goddess' name.

Investigating the life of the dead man took up the rest of that day and several of the following. The department in Los Angeles sent someone to notify the Banderas family of the death, and on Sunday evening a brother flew up to identify the body and make funeral arrangements, and to begin the process of clearing out the apartment. The brother was a devout and conservative born-again Christian, a lay preacher in his church, and was so offended by his black-sheep brother's video collection that he had to arrange for the complex's gardener to come in and remove it from the premises. Some of them were a little rough even for the gardener.

The videos offered them a tentative and theoretical link with the Ladies of Perpetual Disgruntlement, since the group's first victim, Barry Doyle, sold several of the same titles, but credit card receipts at catalogues and video places closer to home accounted for most of them, and the frail link dissolved.

The note received by Rachel Curtis was duly transported to the lab, which told them precisely nothing: dropped in a mailbox in Oakland, the stamp wetted by bottled water rather than someone's revealing saliva, by a person wearing gloves, on paper produced by the ton, both paper and printer different from that used by the

Ladies on their victims. They spent a fruitless hour debating why, if the two murders were linked, Emily Larsen had not received a note, telling her that she was safe. Was the murderer's technique becoming more refined? Or was it simply that Emily knew who her abuser was, and would know that she was now safe, but Rachel, who had known only a faceless rapist, did not?

They did not find what had called Banderas away from his date with Melanie to end up at the Palace of the Legion of Honor. He had crossed the Golden Gate Bridge just at dusk, when the tollkeeper took his money and reminded him cheerfully to turn on his headlights, and he flipped her the finger before laying rubber in his acceleration. Not that he seemed to be in a rush; he was just being a jerk, she said, adding philosophically, people were, some of them.

Two people might have seen Banderas enter the park around the Legion. One elderly woman, cursed with failing night vision and hurrying to get home before full dark, thought she might have seen the flashy Banderas car parked next to a light car, white or tan, but it was neither of the two makes she knew—Volkswagen and Volvo—although it was closer to a Volvo sedan in shape. And it might have been light blue, or that metallic gray.

The search went on, their steps continually dogged, or preceded, by reporters covering the same ground.

It was all very frustrating and grueling and normal, and Kate dragged herself home each night worn-out but unable to sleep. Finally on Tuesday, trudging through the front door to yet another warmed-up meal, Lee met her in the front hallway with a pair of running shoes in her hand.

"You going jogging, love?" Kate asked, dredging up a joke.

"No, you are."

Kate moved around Lee and began to unload herself of what felt like a hundred pounds of briefcase, handbag, Beretta with its holster and two magazines, handcuffs, and assorted loose folders, heaping them precariously on the small many-drawered desk next to the stairs. "Not tonight, Lee. I'm tired."

Lee had somehow moved around to block Kate from the rest of the house. She held out the shoes, practically shoved them into Kate's chest, and said, "Go."

"Oh Christ, Lee, don't do—"

"Go. Now."

Kate glared at her determined lover, slapped the drawer shut on her holstered gun, snatched the shoes out of Lee's hand, and stormed angrily upstairs to change into shorts and sweatshirt. Several slammed drawers and loud curses later she pounded resentfully down to the main level and out of the house into the cold night air. The crash of the heavy front door was probably felt by the next-door neighbors.

Red-faced and too worked up to bother stretching, Kate shot down the precipitous side of Russian Hill, in and out of the illumination from the streetlights, moving at a rate that risked a mighty fall. With the luck of the mad, her feet managed to miss the patches of loose gravel and the raised edges of paving stones, the passing cars were always just through the crossings or else down the block, and the clots of people and the dog-walkers were always on the other side of the street.

Gradually, as her resentment cooled and her muscles warmed, she found her pace, and in the end she ran a lot farther than the original spiteful six blocks she had intended. She circled around the base of Russian Hill and came up the steep wooden stairs of Macondray Lane, at the top of which she stopped, bent over with her hands on her thighs to catch her breath. She cooled off by jogging slowly down Green Street and doing some belated stretches, and when she reached her front door, she was considerably more rested than when she had started out.

She paused in front of her door to pick a frail pansy from Jon's windowbox, carried it through to the kitchen, presented it wordlessly to Lee, and then put her arms around her partner. The two women stood in the silent embrace, wrapped up in each other, restored. It was Lee who moved first to break it off, by murmuring Kate's name with a question attached to it.

"Yes?" Kate responded into the hollow of Lee's throat.

"My love, you really, really stink."

"I know," Kate said. "I know," and she went off to luxuriate in a long, hot shower.

Dinner was not reheated leftovers. Dinner was a more or less vegetarian stroganoff with red wine, eaten by candlelight. Kate had not realized how starved she was until her plate was empty—for the second time. She drained her glass, sat back in her chair, and closed her eyes, feeling the hum of satisfaction running through her very bones.

Of course, she was fully aware that underlying the entire string of events from the moment she had come in the door was that ominous little phrase, "Honey, we need to talk." She had been neglecting Lee, and at a time when there were issues standing between them, issues that would rapidly calcify if left to themselves, requiring major demolition efforts later.

But Lee was right, and Lee was good, and Kate would not force Lee to do it all herself. Besides which, she did want to talk to Lee.

Talking to Lee had become a high priority in Kate's life, ever since the long, lonely months of fall and winter when she had feared she was losing her beloved. Talking, and laughing and loving and just being with her, and if it cut into the hours Kate could spend working a case, it also seemed to make her more rested, more what Lee would call "centered," and with that came increased efficiency in her working hours. So Kate told herself, at any rate, and so she would believe.

It had been eight months before, at the end of summer, when Lee had left her, pushing Kate away in a particularly brutal manner. Kate thought it final. Instead, with the new year came a glimmer of hope, shining through a hellish and highly personal case involving the kidnapping of Al's stepdaughter Jules, and when that case came to an end, miraculously Lee was still there.

A new Lee, a different Lee from the wounded, angry, and confused person who had fled north to her aunt's island on the Canadian border. This was closer to the strong and purposeful woman Kate had first met, but with a depth and stability that only the profoundly damaged attain. Lee had all but died, and then over the next two years she had been reborn. Kate did not yet know just what her lover had become, or what their relationship would become. All she knew was that Lee still chose to be with her; the rest of it would find its way.

"God, that was good," Kate said with a sigh. "Would you marry me?"

"I'm already married to you," Lee pointed out.

"Would you marry me again, then? Maybe if we do it twice, you won't need to do anything drastic like running off to your Aunt Agatha's to get my boneheaded attention."

"That isn't exactly why I did it," Lee protested.

"No, but that was one of the results." Kate pulled her napkin off her lap and dropped it onto the table, pushing her chair back and walking slowly around the table toward Lee. "You have my attention, my complete attention, and nothing but my attention." At the last word she reached Lee. Bending down, she slipped one arm behind her lover's back and one under her knees, and picked her up. The romance of the gesture was undermined by the involuntary grunt of effort she let out and the way she staggered across the room, accompanied by Lee's giggling shrieks of alarm and protest. At the sofa, Kate stumbled and, although Lee did end up on the cushions, Kate fell on top of her in a tangle of limbs and a brief crack of skulls.

They disentangled themselves and sat for a minute, rubbing their heads and recovering their breath.

"So much for romance," Kate grumbled. "I think I have a hernia or a slipped disk or something."

"Poor dear," Lee cooed, and took Kate's head in her

hands to kiss her bruise. The kiss lingered, and moved down to the lips, and suddenly Kate sat up.

"This is where Jon comes in," she said warily. "Where is he?"

"I told him if he didn't take the night off and go away, I'd fire him."

Kate reflected ungratefully that if he did walk in now, the momentary embarrassment would be well worth the result, and then Lee was kissing her and she thought no more for some time.

When they lay still beneath the inadequate cover of the sofa's throw blanket and the candles on the table were beginning to gutter out, Lee asked Kate, "What was that glance that went between you and Roz the other night?"

"Ah. I should have known you'd see it. It's kind of embarrassing. You know that quilt of yours I said the dry cleaner's ruined? It wasn't them, it was me. One day during the winter I was just sitting there and I . . . I just felt this tremendous . . . anger rise up. I just felt so pissed off at you, so I . . . destroyed it. Childish, I know, and stupid. I'm really sorry—it was such a beautiful thing, and I know how you loved it. But the point is that Roz happened to walk in on me."

"I see," Lee said, and from the way she said it, she truly did. "I'm sorry."

"No apologies," Kate said firmly. "It happened, it was both our faults, it's over."

The last candle flared wildly a handful of times and went out, leaving them in the dim light filtering in from the kitchen.

"And you," Kate said. "What was that look that went between you and Maj?"

Lee shifted, would have sat up but Kate held her, and she subsided stiffly, then relaxed again.

"It was something Roz had just said about love and rage. Roz had a terrible childhood, I think. She never told me directly, but from things she said in passing over the years, I gather that she had one of those mothers who enjoys ill health while manipulating everyone with her weakness, coupled with an emotionally destructive and often absent father. Both of them alcoholics, and Roz an only child. So although she has built herself a gorgeous, strong, competent persona, when it slips, there's a lot of pain and anger underneath. Maj and I are two of the few people who have seen it."

Much as Kate would have enjoyed hearing the gritty details of the golden girl's dark side, she had no right to ask, and Lee would very probably not tell her if she did. So Kate just pulled Lee to her feet, handed her the crutches, and gathered up their discarded items of clothing so as not to give Jon evidence of their activities when he came in.

Mind and body now restored to an equal state of tiredness and satisfaction, Kate followed her partner's slow progress up to their bedroom, where she slept very well indeed.

On the surface, the murders of James Larsen and Matthew Banderas were linked, by method and by the glaring fact that both men had been multiple offenders—Larsen against his wife, Banderas against a number of women. Still, surface links were often misleading. Which meant that nothing could be assumed, that painstaking detective work was the only option, both now in looking for someone to arrest as well as far down the line when court testimony loomed.

Every neighbor in the condo complex was interviewed, briefly or in depth. The members of the health club Banderas belonged to, his co-workers, his brother, the guys at the bar he frequented, all were noted, all were asked the necessary questions. On Monday morning, Kate tried to track down Banderas's "real bitch" of a boss, but she was out of town, at a conference in Cincinnati until Wednesday. Kate left her number, and turned to the other interviews on her schedule.

Wednesday morning Janice Popper surfaced, back from Cincinnati but pleading a burden of accumulated work too deep to fit in an interview with the police. She suggested Friday, Kate countered with some very mild hints about the possibility that the police were capable of just showing up that afternoon regardless of Popper's work, and in the end they compromised on Thursday afternoon. Popper's voice came over the line as brisk to the point of coldness. She made no pretense at being upset over her employee's death; made no bones about the fact that she had neither liked nor much respected him.

"Frankly," she told Kate, "I think he would've quit before too much longer. Either that, or I'd have been forced to fire him. Oh, he was good enough at his job, but he was one of those men who just can't deal with having a woman giving him orders. He'd alternate between trying to flirt and trying to treat me as one of the guys—you know, a dirty joke to see what you'll do and then getting all righteous if you don't laugh. I didn't know about his history until I'd been here a couple of weeks, and it made sense. It also made me very nervous, wondering what he'd do if he got angry at me. I know that if he'd shown up at my house one night, I sure as hell wouldn't have let him in. Look, I've got to go. I'll talk with you tomorrow."

Kate thanked the woman for calling back, and went back to typing up the endless reams of reports and interviews that constitute investigative work. Half an hour later, her phone rang. She picked it up, thinking it would be another reporter wanting a quote (although interest was beginning to wane, thank God).

"Martinelli," she said brusquely.

"Kate? Oh, God, I'm glad I—oh, Kate, I don't know what—"

"Who is this?" Kate demanded. Her voice cut through the woman's panic like a knife.

"Roz. This is Roz. Oh, Kate, look. I really need you. Need to talk to you, I mean. Can you—"

"Roz, what is it? Has something happened to Maj—or the baby?"

"No, no," she snapped impatiently, as if Kate were

being rather stupid. The cool annoyance made a startling contrast to her agonized voice an instant before. "It's really too much to go into on the phone. Can you come here?"

"Now? Where are you?"

"At the church. Kate, can you come?"

Kate stifled a sigh.

"Okay, Roz. Let me just finish what I'm doing and I'll be there within an hour."

"Thanks," she said, and hung up. Kate stared at the phone, wondering what would reduce calm, competent Rosalyn Hall to a state of gibbering rudeness.

It was not panic—Kate saw that the instant she walked into the church office fifty minutes later. She had never before seen Roz Hall consumed by fury, so she did not at first recognize the body language of the people in the outside office as fearful, merely seeing the tension in their faces and the apprehension in the white-eyed glances they cast at the closed door. A raised voice in monologue came from Roz's office, and Kate paused to ask the young man sitting at the desk marked (humorously, Kate hoped) SECRETARY if she could go in.

"If you really want to," he said ominously.

"What's happened?"

"Oh, she'll tell you," he replied.

One of the cluster of women in the other corner muttered, "You mean there's someone in the City who hasn't heard yet?" The comment sparked a flare of nervous and quickly damped-down laughter. Kate marched over to the closed door, rapped on it briskly and, without waiting for permission, turned the knob and walked in.

Roz Hall stood bent over the telephone on her old wooden desk, wearing her clerical collar, a suit that meant business, and a clenched look of absolute rage. She jerked upright at Kate's unceremonious entrance, dragged her fingers through her hair, and barked into the phone, "Never mind. I'll take care of it myself," before slamming it down on the base.

Roz glared down at the quivering phone for several

intense seconds. Then, with an enormous effort, she gathered up the energies that were racing through her and turned them on Kate—who very nearly stepped back under the impact of Roz's concentrated outrage until the minister suddenly and unexpectedly smiled, and all the murderous antagonism in the room flipped back on itself and slipped away into its box. Kate even caught herself smiling back, and wondered at the ease with which Roz had switched off the stream of fury in full spate to invite Kate instead to join her in a little self-deprecating humor.

Machiavellian, Roz had described herself? Oh, no— Machiavelli had nothing on Roz Hall.

But still Kate smiled, in uncomprehending but true sympathy, and Roz shook her head at herself and said, "What time is it? Not even four? God, I need a drink. Join me?"

"No thanks."

"Coffee then. Grab a seat." She circled her desk, reaching out in passing to give Kate's arm a quick squeeze that managed to express apology, affection, and gratitude all at once, and walked out the door. Kate pulled a chair away from the desk, and as she was lowering herself into it, she glanced out into the next room and saw Roz with her arms around the "secketary," wrapping him in a long hug. After a long minute, she released him and went to the others, giving each of them the benediction of her embrace. The level of tension in the building plummeted, the faces started to beam again.

When each person had been given a hug, Roz stood back. "I'm sorry, everyone. I'm a bitch and I don't deserve your help. Look—why don't you all go out and have something to eat? I don't know if it's lunchtime or dinnertime, but you must need something after the kind of day I've put you through. Just stick the answering machine on and get out of here. And Jory, would you be a dear and put on a fresh pot of coffee before you go? Thanks. All of you."

She hit just the right note to let her acolytes know

that she was okay, that they were safe, and that whatever problems they had been facing would resolve themselves. Tight mutters gave way to relieved chatter, and Roz came back in and walked over to a cabinet.

"Have a seat, Kate. You sure you don't want something stronger than coffee?"

Kate shook her head at the proffered bottle. Roz splashed a generous amber inch in the bottom of a glass, tipped it down her throat in a single gulp, and shuddered as it hit. After a moment she poured another inch in the glass, capped the bottle and put it away, and took her drink over to the three tall filing cabinets that stood shoulder to shoulder against the wall. With a minimum of searching she pulled out a well-filled manila folder, handed it over to Kate, and then dropped into a comfortable chair across from her guest, who sat waiting for an explanation before committing herself to the folder.

Roz took a sip from her drink, put it on the low table between them, and reached up irritably to peel off the stiff clerical collar. She dropped the curling tongue-depressor shape of white plastic onto the table, loosened the collar of the shirt itself, and sat back with a sigh, rubbing her throat with her eyes shut. It was all done so naturally, Kate couldn't tell if Roz even knew it was deliberate, this clear declaration that although the lesser beings in the outer office could be given a pat and dismissed as the worshipers they were, Kate was to be considered a near-equal.

A near-equal she wanted something from.

"Do you remember last week I told you about an Indian girl?" Roz asked.

Kate thought back; a week ago at dinner, it seemed like a lot longer. "Someone came to talk to you about the situation while you were at the women's shelter," she remembered. "Amanda something."

"Yes. The Indian girl died last night. They're treating it like an accident, although her husband has a history of violent behavior."

"Roz, what are you talking about?" Kate asked sharply.

"He burned the child to death," Roz said, her face as bleak as her voice. "It's done all the time in India, and now they've done it here. Look at the file, Kate. It's all there."

Now Kate looked at the folder, which bore the label *Bride Burning*. It consisted of clippings from newspapers and magazines, most of them foreign, and a number of journal reprints and articles downloaded from the Internet. Kate picked out one at random and read the brief account, written in oddly stilted English, of a sixteen-year-old bride from the Punjab district of India who brought to her marriage a dowry of what to American eyes seemed a peculiar assortment of goods, including a color television, a sewing machine, and a motor scooter. She went to live with her new husband's family two hundred miles from her village, under the same roof as his parents, his brother's family, two unmarried brothers, and a younger sister.

Eight months later the bride was showing no signs of pregnancy, the television was on the blink, and her in-laws were demanding that the dowry be increased by three hundred rupees and a refrigerator. The girl's parents had gone heavily into debt to pay for the wedding and the agreed-to dowry; they would be very lucky to pay off what they already owed before they died, and could afford no more.

Shortly after her first anniversary, the bride was dead in a "kitchen accident" involving spilled fuel from the cook stove and a match. The groom's parents were arrested, tried, and found not guilty due to lack of evidence.

That was not the end of the story, either. In a final, macabre twist that, had Kate not been a cop she might not have believed, two years later the groom was offered his dead bride's younger sister in marriage. The girl's family was forever "besmirched" (the article's evocative word) by their daughter's death, and could not hope to find a clean husband for the girl who remained. The groom was reported to be thinking it over while the prospective new wife's family decided if its dowry might stretch to a refrigerator.

The whole story sounded fantastic to the point of absurdity, from the motor scooter dowry to the blithe assumption that the dead woman's own sister might be willing to walk into this nightmare. Kate had been a cop long enough to have seen a little of everything, but this tale stretched credibility.

However, there were other such stories in the file—a dozen, fifteen, twenty-five sets of names, places, and "accidents," Hindu, Muslim, Christian, and otherwise, from lower-, middle-, and upper-class families. It was appalling.

"Jesus," Kate said finally. "This sounds like something out of the Dark Ages."

"It's terrifying, isn't it? An indication of the complete and utter insignificance of women, just a burden to everyone. And the frightful irony of women oppressing women. But you know, I do honestly love India. I've been there half a dozen times and I'm only beginning to see the country. I love the place, the people, the way it opens my eyes and my heart to go there. Is your coffee okay?"

Kate hadn't even noticed its arrival. She picked up her mug obediently and took a swallow. It was not hot, but it helped take the taste of those articles out of her mouth.

"And I detest the country as well," Roz went on. "The people can be so incredibly rude, and gracious at the same time. They can be cruel and hateful, greedy and so affectionate.

"They call India the meeting place of opposites, and it's true—extreme opposites, too, not the watered-down sorts of contrast we have in this country. There are the Jains, who wear masks and sweep ahead of themselves as they walk so they don't cause harm to so much as an ant, while at the other extreme there're these robbers who live in the hills and come down to murder and pillage, and they make movies about them, have fan clubs, everything. And of course every so often there's a paroxysm of religious-slash-cultural hatred and a few thousand people are slaughtered.

"God, don't get me started on India," she said, although in truth Kate had been wondering how to get her stopped. "The ironies would make you howl. A people that worships a warrior-goddess, a religion that clearly says the main god is completely helpless without feminine energy, a country that has had a woman prime minister when we can't even get one as a vice president, at the same time allows children of seven and eight to be married off, aborts female fetuses right and left, and sees six or eight thousand dowry deaths a year. Ten thousand? More—who knows?

"I'm sorry, Kate—you're wondering what on earth I'm rattling on about. What I'm trying to say here is that we now have a bride burning in the city of San Francisco, a city you have sworn to protect. What are you, as a police officer, going to do about it?"

Kate was tired, overworked, and unconvinced, and she had no desire to sit at the receiving end of Roz Hall's histrionic ire.

"Roz, enough with the drama, okay?" she chided. "I don't work at City Hall. If you have evidence of a homicide—evidence, not suspicion—let me see it, and I'll pass it on to whoever's in charge of the case."

Roz's head snapped up and she fixed Kate with a look that for an instant had the hardened cop beginning to quail, just as the church members in the other room had done. Roz was a woman magnificent in her rage, her eyes glittering with it, her hair seeming to crackle around her head. Kate half expected sparks to come from her fingertips and smoke from her ears, and she moved quickly to placate this particular warrior-goddess.

"Roz, my friend, please. I'm just a cop. If someone killed a girl in this city then, as you said, it's my job to put them behind bars. Ninety-nine percent of the time, if someone is murdered, there's evidence. If this death is being dismissed as an accident, then of course I'll ask for a closer look. But I do need to know why you think this girl was killed. Other than the fact that a lot of women on the other side of the world are killed by their husbands' families," she added.

Reason succeeded where honest emotion would have had Roz reaching for her Rolodex to summon lawyers and tame media moguls into battle. The waves of brute energy subsided, helped by the slowing effects of the drink. "Right," said Roz, making an effort. "So, what do you need to know?"

Kate reached into her pocket and drew out her notebook and pen. "We could start with her name," she suggested.

8

We are asked to bear it, to take in the whole,
The long indifferent beating down of soul.

The girl had been born Pramilla Barot a little less than sixteen years before in a small village on the border of Rajasthan and Gujerat, the disastrous third daughter of a struggling farmer and his hardworking but increasingly ill wife. When Pramilla was seven, her mother died giving birth to a son. The farmer, although he had been very fond of his wife, considered it a fair trade.

His first daughter made a successful and gloriously inexpensive marriage to a young schoolteacher with radical ideas, who declared himself willing to take the girl with only the bare minimum of dowry, and that to stay in the hands of his new wife. None of the wedding guests actually approved of this bizarre notion (although in truth it was closer to ancient dowry traditions than it was to the modern interpretation of dowry as little more than payment to any family willing to take a daughter off her father's hands). Secretly, however, all the fathers were more than a little envious of how easily Barot had gotten off, and all the mothers were more than a little softhearted at the romance of the thing.

So it was that Barot embarked on the marriage arrangements of his second daughter with mixed feelings, knowing how easy it could be, but fearing that karma would come around and kick him in the teeth.

It did so, with a vengeance. The young man identified by the astrologer as an ideal match looked good enough on paper, as it were (although Barot was not exactly literate), but when his family got into the act, Barot felt as if he'd clasped a basket of boa constrictors to his chest.

They squeezed. Oh, not at first—oh no. Only when arrangements were in their final stages, when the first gifts had been exchanged and everyone knew the chosen date, did the boy's harping mother flex her muscles and bare her teeth. The television chosen was not big enough for her fine son. The kitchen stove Barot was providing was inadequate. The rupees must be increased to cover the expenses they were incurring.

Pulling out was impossible. The girl would be marked as having been tried and found wanting, rejected by one man and therefore of questionable value to the rest. Barot's future in-laws were careful never to drive their demands so high he was forced to withdraw entirely, but they upped the ante in stages that made him gulp, and tear his hair, but in the end submit.

The alternative, after all, was to be burdened forever with an unmarriageable daughter.

The marriage took place, the demands continued after the wedding parties returned to their homes, but by vast good fortune (and a vast number of expensive *pujas* at the temple) the bride quickly became pregnant, and to the joy of everyone except perhaps the groom's mother (who had had her eye on a video player), she gave birth to a son.

Demands ceased, Barot took a deep breath at last— and looked at his fourteen-year-old Pramilla.

There was simply no money for her to get married. If Barot managed to raise it, he and his noble young son would starve. She was a pretty little thing, to be sure, and as bright and as helpful to her menfolk as a father could ask, but there was still no money.

There were offers, yes. A neighbor with an unfortunate facial deformity that made his speech nearly impossible to comprehend was willing to take the girl with only a small dowry. And a farmer in the next village was looking for a pretty young wife, but he was of a lower caste, and besides, Barot had heard talk about the man, and was too fond of his third daughter to feel easy about handing her over to a man who had not only gone through three wives already (all of whom had died of unfortunate accidents) but was older than Barot himself.

So Barot went to see his cousin and the cousin's wife, who between them seemed to know everything and everyone between Jaipur and Delhi. It was the wife who came up with the idea of the advertisement in the Delhi *Post*. When Barot saw the sorts of advertisements the marriage column offered, he despaired, as it was full of girls with university degrees and professional training, but his cousin pointed out that he had little choice, and it was worth the investment as a gamble. The three of them together decided on the wording.

> *Pretty young light-skinned village girl, hardworking, traditional, and respectful, no dowry but ideal for the right man.*

Barot could see that even his cousin's wife had grave doubts about the chances of a response, but she had to admit that the advert was honest, and that in a market bristling with nursing certificates and BA hon degrees, it had the advantage of its own simplicity. And Pramilla did have skin as light as a farmer's daughter could hope for. Maybe, just maybe, there was a rich man out there (or another schoolteacher with radical ideas) who valued a cowlike, hardworking girl of a respectable caste over an educated potential troublemaker with her own money.

There was.

To everyone's astonishment, three weeks later a letter came, on a piece of paper with a letterhead engraved on it, bearing a stamp from the United States of America.

They read it at the house of Barot's cousin. The cousin's wife read it to them, stumbling over the more unfamiliar English words and translating tentatively as she went.

The letter in its magnificent crisp typescript was from a man who called himself Peter Mehta. He was the Chief Executive Officer (a vastly impressive phrase) of a company with branches in Bombay, Los Angeles, and San Francisco (magic names all) whose business was not specified but was quite patently successful.

Mehta had seen Barot's advertisement in the Marriages Offered section of the Delhi *Post* that was flown in to his office in San Francisco several days a week. He was looking for a bride for his younger brother, Laxman, acting as the family representative since their parents were both dead. Laxman was a boy of simple tastes, according to the letter, and both brothers preferred a traditional arranged marriage to the haphazard dangers of the American system. If the girl's family was willing to have their daughter emigrate to America, would they please send a photograph, details of the girl's life and accomplishments, and a signed letter from the village health worker to the effect that she was healthy and capable of bearing children.

The letter was couched in terms both more flowery and less direct than that, but all parties involved knew what was meant. She needed to be certified a virgin, she had to be shown to have the normal complement of eyes, ears, and teeth in a more or less pleasing arrangement, and they wanted something in writing that said who she was. Normally, a marriage broker or convenient uncle would take care of this, but the family seemed to have no relatives in the area, and they wanted assurance that their investment would reach them in an acceptable manner. Otherwise they would have to ship her home again, and the "no dowry" phrase had already established that Barot would be unable to reimburse them for the transportation costs.

Barot held the pristine white sheet of paper in his trembling, work-roughened fingers, examining the bold signature of the Chief Executive Officer as if it were the stamp of a god. Salvation was at hand; Pramilla was saved from the clutches of a freak or a wife-beater; he and his son would not starve. And America—unbelievable! The land of golden opportunity had opened up, reaching out to a dusty village in Rajasthan, for surely this would mean that when Pramilla's brother was grown to be a man, her husband, this godlike Laxman Mehta who was younger brother to an American Chief Executive Officer named Peter, would reach out again to bring the boy into the fold of his extended family.

It was only the cousin's wife who had doubts. Barot was from a good caste, granted, but the Mehtas were much higher. What did they want with a girl like Pramilla, when they could have someone both higher and with a degree? And San Francisco was so very far away, and Pramilla so young. Who knew this family of Mehtas? Was there no one here to speak for them?

But her protests, admittedly mild, went unheard, for Barot and his cousin and the entire village were filled with joy and excitement. Even Pramilla herself was speechless with the thrill of it (for she had known of the two other suitors hovering in the wings of her father's vision, and had shuddered at both of them).

The photographer was summoned from the next town, arriving with his heavy ancient camera and a choice of three grubby saris for the occasion. Pramilla yearned for the white sari heavy with silver thread, but the cousin's wife disapproved, saying it would make her look as if she could afford a dowry after all, and besides, the white would make her skin look much too dark even with rice powder. So she chose the sari with small sprigs of blue flowers on it, and dusted Pramilla's face and arms with the powder, and pronounced herself satisfied with the result.

Pramilla was fourteen and a half years old, and looked twelve in the picture that landed on Peter Mehta's desk two weeks later. He grunted, felt a brief regret that he was not himself in need of a luscious young bride, and passed it over to Laxman for approval—unnecessary, perhaps, but this was America after all, and there was no reason to be too medieval about this.

Laxman blushed and nodded, and the arrangements went ahead.

One thing the bride's father had asked (with fawning trepidation in his ornate phrases, and at the firm suggestion of the cousin's wife), and that was whether the wedding might not take place in India, preferably in Jaipur or, if that was not convenient, then Delhi—although the writer of the letter could fully understand if the Mehtas were to find this impossible, and it was only asked by the love Barot felt for this his last and most precious jewel of a daughter.

Actually, visa arrangements were vastly simpler if the wedding took place outside the United States and the bride could be introduced as a *fait accompli*. It would mean fiddling with the date on her birth certificate, but Peter knew a man in Pune who was good at that sort of thing. No, it would not be a problem, and would all in all be preferable to deal with the matter in India. He even sent three third-class rail tickets, so the bride's family could accompany her.

It was a full, no-expenses-spared Hindu wedding, with *shamiana* tents in the garden of the second-best hotel in Delhi, a white horse for the groom and rented jewelry for the bride, music until the early hours, and even some fireworks to light up the neighborhood and wake the restless beggars sleeping at the hotel gates. Barot was frankly terrified by Peter Mehta and had to fight down a sudden impulse to thrust Pramilla into the arms of the Chief Executive Officer who would soon be her brother-in-law and run away, but his first view of the younger brother, Laxman, brought with it a wave of relief mixed heavily with guilt.

Relief because the lad was more than presentable, he was beautiful, long-lashed as a cow, slim as a young Krishna, and he looked not much older than his bride.

He was older, Barot knew that, twice Pramilla's age, but he looked very like a young boy, white-faced and plucking at the front of his white silk *kurta* pajamas—more like a farm boy than a hard-driving company director, and infinitely more suited to Pramilla. And Barot knew guilt because he suspected that Pramilla was not really being given the man she deserved, but an immature boy who might never become anything else. All through that long day and night the farmer kept casting glances at the boy who would take his daughter, and in the end he decided that there was definitely something wrong with him. Not greatly so—he wasn't a drooling idiot by any means, just . . . slow.

His cousin's wife, who had come with him instead of Barot's young son, agreed with his assessment, and managed to take the young bride aside for a private conversation at which phrases such as "patience" and "a loving heart" and "you will need to be your husband's backbone" played a part. The earnest advice confused Pramilla somewhat, but lodged in her heart, and her "auntie" assured herself that the child would find them there and remember them when the time came. She patted the child's cold hand and told her to remember that even the great god Shiva was nothing without the energies of his wife, Shakti; as she put it: "Shiva is *shava* [corpse] without *shakti*" (*shakti* being, Kate remembered from Roz's television panel, both the word for energy and the name of the goddess). Pramilla nodded dutifully and went back to take her place beside her pale, silent boy-husband.

The marriage might never have been consummated had Pramilla waited for Laxman to make the first move. Indeed, it was not consummated in the five days they spent in Delhi, waiting for Peter to finish his business and for the authorities to come through with her travel papers. But once on the airplane, sitting in the roaring, rattling, utterly foreign compartment surrounded by poisonous smells, incomprehensible voices, and a husband who, though exceedingly beautiful, acted nothing like the *filmi* husbands she had seen on the flickering screen in her village, or even her neighbors' husbands, Pramilla Mehta watched in something close to terror as the sprawl of Delhi fell away beneath the wings of the plane, and the girl of not yet fifteen years began quietly to weep.

Had she plotted for days, she could not have come up with a better way of making the boy at her side cleave to her. He had spent the last week not far from tears himself, and twice had succumbed to them after the unsatisfactory nightly ritual of going to this pretty stranger's bedroom, sitting rigidly on the edge of her bed and making attempts at conversation in a language she could barely understand, and retreating again having done nothing but briefly touch the back of her hand, once.

But now she was the one in tears, this delicate, precious, daunting, sweet-faced young goddess, and without even pausing to consider his action, he reached out and took her hand. In response she sobbed aloud, and his heart simultaneously broke and swelled up in manly pride that at last he had found a role he could step into, even if it was only that of comforter.

Sleeping and awake, they held hands all the way to San Francisco.

It was not easy after that, and Pramilla was often in tears, but at least she had the vague comfort of knowing that her sorrows were those of all young wives, home in the village or here in this new country, and that she had only to endure and life would, in the end, sort itself out. Peter's wife, Rani, playing the part of mother in the family (and indeed, she was nearly old enough to be Laxman's mother), was hateful, even cruel, but that after all was what mothers-in-law were. She refused to speak Hindi with the newcomer, pretending that she did not understand the peasant girl's rural accents; she pinched Pramilla's arm when the girl put the spoons in the wrong place or failed to peel the vegetables to her satisfaction; worst of all from Pramilla's point of view,

Rani encouraged her own children (who were not actually all that far from Pramilla's age) to mock her and treat her as a rather stupid family pet. And Laxman . . . Her husband was not a simple person to be with, since he seemed to know that he had something missing and was short-tempered because of it. He lost patience with her at the slightest irritation and occasionally shouted and sometimes slapped her, and bed was never easy, since she did not seem able to be anything but dry and tight against him. Still, even that was a thing that her knowledge of village marriages had prepared her for, and she soon folded away her picture of *filmi* romance as an outgrown (if never actually worn) garment.

So Pramilla Mehta went her way in the New World, walking a tightrope between an inadequate and easily frustrated husband and an oppressive mother-in-law figure, with no friends or family or even familiar surroundings to bolster her. Tens of millions of women had done the same, and like them, Pramilla could have been happier, but at least she had the degree of contentment that comes when one's expectations are met.

The precarious balancing act held for precisely five months, until one evening when Rani, annoyed at some problem with a plumber and angry at Peter for working such long hours, pointed out with a voice that cut flesh that Laxman and 'Milla had been married for nearly half a year, why wasn't the girl pregnant?

All four Mehtas ended up in a shouting match, which broke apart only when Peter slammed out of the house, Rani turned her wrath on Pramilla, and Laxman retreated from the scene. Later that night he came to his wife's room expecting her to sniffle and cuddle and comfort him by her need for his manly comforting. Instead Pramilla, still smarting from Rani's cruel words and her own fresh, sharp fear of childlessness, turned on him and demanded furiously why he, her husband, had not been a real man and stood up for her against his brother and sister-in-law.

Laxman went berserk. He hit her and screamed at

her, forced himself on her, and then collapsed in a storm of teary self-recrimination, kissing her bruised face and saying over and over how she must never again make him do that.

She never did. In the seven months that remained to her, she was always careful, around him and around Rani (who conceived and miscarried what would have been her fifth child).

The only outlets to Pramilla's spirit were the daytime television programs, which taught her English with their simple plot lines and *filmi* dialogue, and brief, uncertain conversations with a woman who lived down the street and seemed to know everything that was going on in Pramilla's life with Laxman.

Her name was Amanda, and she was a being even more exotic to Pramilla than the people on the daytime television programs. She acted more like a man than any woman Pramilla had ever known, allowing her arms and legs to go bare—not like a prostitute, which was what many of these women looked like, but like the castes of women who carried stones and bricks to building projects, chattering loudly and ignoring their veils—or like the pictures of women athletes Pramilla had seen, strong and brazen. Pramilla couldn't understand why men weren't afraid of Amanda; she looked as if she would pull out a sword or a club at any moment, like Kali. She certainly frightened Pramilla, she was so overflowing with Western ease and power, and she fascinated Pramilla, because she was as strong and confident as Peter. Her independence was . . . god-like.

They met at the local market, where Pramilla was puzzling over a display of unfamiliar greenery. A bare, browned arm snaked past her to snatch up a head of curly purple leaves, and paused to shake it under Pramilla's nose.

"Great stuff," said the voice attached to the arm. "You ever try it?"

Pramilla glanced around to see if this stranger might not be speaking to someone else, then looked up into a face as sunburnt and roughened as that of a road-mender. She was as without manners as one of the road gangs, too, bluntly informal in that way that was both offensive and secretly appealing. Pramilla came up with a phrase her sister-in-law had used on a similar occasion. "I beg your pardon?" she said, but it did not come out the same way as Rani said it, and this Western woman took it as an invitation.

"Purple kale, it's called," she continued cheerfully. "Fry it for just a minute with butter and garlic, it's gorgeous and healthy, too."

Pramilla's English was sufficient to gather that the woman was telling her a recipe, although it sounded remarkably bland and nearly raw. Pretty, though, if the purple stayed in the leaves. Perhaps she could convince Rani to try it.

"Amanda Bonner," the woman said, and put the brown hand out at Pramilla. Very gingerly Pramilla extended her own fingers, allowing them to be clasped briefly and released.

"My name is Pramilla Mehta," she recited.

"Pramilla. What a beautiful name. You live down the block from my parents, I think. I've seen you on the street."

"Parents, yes."

"Sorry—I'm talking too fast, aren't I? Can you understand my English?"

"Understand, yes. I do not speak good. I hear the television, when they talk slow."

"How long have you lived here?"

"Seven, eight month."

"Is that all? Did you know any English when you came?" Amanda asked, sounding surprised.

"Some little. Hallo, goodbye, Tom Cruise, Superman." Pramilla shrugged her narrow shoulders gracefully.

"Well, I wouldn't have thought TV could have much to offer, but it obviously works for you. Do you watch the soaps?"

Pramilla knew that word from Peter's disparaging

remarks. "Yes, and cooking shows, news, cartoons. Game shows are too fast. They make me tired."

Amanda laughed, showing a lot of white teeth. "They make me tired, too, and I was born here. Your English is very good, though. You must practice."

Pramilla grimaced. "I have to. No one will speak anything else." Laxman knew little Hindi, Peter pretended he knew none, and Rani treated the language as something only an Untouchable would speak. It was English or go hungry.

"Immersion English, huh?" Amanda said and, seeing Pramilla's confusion, changed it to, "We have a saying: Sink or swim."

"I know," said Pramilla a touch grimly. "I know."

9

Help us to bring darkness into the light,
To lift out the pain, the anger,
Where it can be seen for what it is—
The balance-wheel for our vulnerable, aching love.

"You got all this from Amanda—what's her name?—Bonner?" Kate asked, since Roz seemed to have come to a pausing place.

"Most of it. Some of it I asked Pramilla herself."

"You met her, then?"

"I did. On Thursday night, in fact, the day after I mentioned her to you. Sweet little thing, looked about twelve years old, but quite bright and nobody's fool. Amanda thought she might listen to a woman who was also a priest."

"Listen to what?"

"Advice. Amanda thought the girl—I ought to call her 'young woman,' but it's hard to think of such a child that way. Amanda thought she was being abused by her husband and his family, and she wanted me to encourage Pramilla to get out before she found herself with a broken arm, or worse. When I heard the details of the story, I thought the 'or worse' all too likely. That file on bride burning is something I've been compiling for years, and when I saw the situation—a young bride far from her own support group, married over a year and not pregnant, with signs of escalating violence like the bruises on her arm where someone had grabbed her, hard—I became extremely concerned. I was right, but I wasn't concerned enough. I should have dragged her out of that house. Or gone there and made a stink to let them know someone was watching. I will never forgive myself that I did not."

"Roz, there's a mountain of guilt out there if you want to crawl under it. And you're not even sure it wasn't an accident, are you? Those damn garments they wear, I should think they're massively dangerous around open flame, all that loose silk waiting to catch on fire."

An odd expression took over Roz's features, memory wrestling with an unwillingness to relinquish the self-blame. "She didn't like cooking over electricity. She told us that. They had to buy her a little kerosene stove because it was closer to what she was used to. She could cook squatting on the floor."

Kate said nothing, merely meeting Roz's eyes and nodding. The door behind them opened briefly and shut again; she became aware that the temporary silence in the outer office had given way again to voices and movement. The church members had returned from their dinner and were awaiting the next commands of their beloved leader.

She closed her notebook and clipped the pen over the cover. "I'll make some calls, let whoever caught the case know that there's some question about it. And I'll try to have a look at the autopsy report myself."

Roz opened her mouth—to object, Kate knew, to the proposed noncommittal investigation—but was cut short by the door again, this time with a voice asking if Roz was nearly finished, because if so, that call that Roz had been waiting for . . .

Kate took advantage of the interruption to make her escape, but she was followed out the door by Roz's voice, calling, "Talk to Amanda, Kate. Hey, Jory? Give Kate Amanda Bonner's phone number, would you? I'll talk to you tomorrow, Kate—and thanks."

Roz obviously intended for Kate to leap right onto the case's back, may even have intended for Kate to phone Amanda Bonner from the office, but Kate was tired and hungry, so she went home.

Lee was in the kitchen making tantalizing smells to the sound of a classical guitar CD. Kate slipped up behind the cook's back and put her arms around Lee, just holding her, until Lee remembered that something on the stove was about to become inedible (if not burst into flames) and she unwrapped Kate's encircling arms, gently but firmly.

"Jon's out again?" Kate asked, going to the cupboard for a couple of wineglasses.

"In and out. Sione has the night off, so they're going to a movie."

"Sione being . . . ?"

"The dancer. From *Song*. Kate, you have been home this last week, you have heard about this."

"The dancer, right." The cause of Jon's falsetto renditions of "Why Do Fools Fall in Love?" and other gems of the fifties and sixties. "How much longer is *Song* running?" she asked. It seemed a safe question, and relevant as well, particularly if it was a traveling show and the current love of Jon's life was going off with it.

"Two and a half weeks, I think. Jon wants to know what night we want tickets for."

"You want to go?"

"Sure. It sounds wild."

"Okay. Well, the first part of the week should be safe, I'm not on call nights until Wednesday."

"Monday or Tuesday, then. Would you mind if we made a group of it and asked Roz and Maj? I mentioned it to Roz the other day and she said she could easily have someone take her group session at the shelter, if it needs to be Monday. Or do you think we've seen too much of them lately?"

"Never too much, they're good people," said Kate easily. She did, in truth, think that they'd been seeing an awful lot of them recently, between one thing and another, but if it made Lee happy she could put up with it. She put the full glasses next to Lee's spoon rest and stood behind her lover, wrapping her arms again around Lee's waist. "What about dinner before, or after? There's that good Chinese place not too far from there."

"Great. You want garlic bread?"

"With Chinese?"

"With this minestrone, you fool. Tonight."

"I'd rather have you."

Lee turned in Kate's arms and said, half purring, "You can have both, you know."

"Not at the same time. Too messy. Beans and stuff all over the place."

Lee drew back and pursed her lips in thought. "We could work on it."

"I don't want to work on anything, I'm taking the night off. When is Jon coming home?"

"Any minute," Lee murmured regretfully into Kate's hair.

"Then the garlic bread now," Kate said briskly, and disentangled herself to go and set the table.

Jon did indeed come in a few minutes later, humming a tune Kate remembered from the long-ago summer her periods began—positively modern by Jon's standards. At least he wasn't singing out loud.

Still, she braced herself for the other symptom of Jon's love life, which was an inability to talk about anything without dragging The One's name into it. A complaint about the garbage cans would trigger the observation that "Bryce was into recycling before curbside bins came"; a comment about kung pao chicken would bring forth the information that "Jacksen's allergic to chilis."

So when Lee said to Jon that they were going to try for *Song* on Monday or Tuesday, Kate braced herself for Sione's name in some form, but it didn't come. Jon merely nodded and said that would be great, he was sure they'd love the show.

She looked at him closely, but could see no sign that the affair had run its course already. He seemed pleased with the soup, happy to talk about anything or nothing—indeed, he seemed content, a word that had never before applied to Jon Sampson, who, though he was not clinically bipolar, tended to the extremes in his moods. Finally Kate couldn't stand it.

"So, Lee tells me you have a thing with one of the *Song* dancers."

He beamed at her, a simple, uncomplicated look of delight. "Sione Kalefu. He's so great. He's talented, intelligent, he even has a sense of humor. And he's flat-out, drop-dead gorgeous—like a young Polynesian Mick Jagger, if you can picture it." Kate tried, and failed. "In fact, when I told him that, he said that yeah, he'd often thought that when he retired he'd run a gay bar and call it Memphis."

Kate looked at him blankly, waiting for the explanation. Punch line, rather, judging by the expectant sparkle in his eyes.

"All right," she said. "I give. Why 'Memphis'?"

"What's the first line of 'Honky-Tonk Women'?"

Kate thought about it for a minute, and then felt her lips twitch. Jon threw back his head and laughed and Lee, who had heard this before, nonetheless snorted. "Oh, God, Jon, that's terrible," Kate protested, then began to laugh as well.

He cleared the dishes away, doing a bump-and-grind to the accompaniment of the nine-syllable phrase Jagger made out of "honky-tonk women," then he grabbed up his coat and took himself and his suggestive lyrics out the door to his Polynesian paramour.

"Well," pronounced Kate in the ensuing silence. "At least it's a change from 'Mrs. Brown you've got a loverly daughter' in bad Cockney."

"Or 'It's my party and I'll cry if I want to' à la Lesley Gore."

"Remember the time Bryce bought him those Timberland hiking shoes and we heard Nancy Sinatra for a week?"

"Oh, please don't remind me. They're all the sorts of songs that lodge in the back of your brain and circle around and around at three in the morning."

"Haw-aw-aw-aw-aw-nky-tonk women," Kate brayed.

They set the dishwasher going and went to bed early that night.

And were awakened when Jon came in at two in the morning, singing quietly to himself a half-familiar tune, the chorus of which came into Kate's mind as she was drifting off again: "Goodness gracious, great balls of fire." She fell asleep with a smile on her face.

In the dark of the night, while Kate had slept the sleep of the just and the overworked and Jon found joy in a pair of brown arms, the Ladies struck again. Kate sat and read all about it in the morning *Chronicle*. This time their attack involved the torching of the shiny, new, phallic-shaped car of a man who had been seen slapping his wife around in the park across the street. She had gone across to fetch their son from an after-noon soccer game, become involved in a conversation with the other mothers, and not been at her place in the kitchen when he arrived home from work. He went looking for her and literally dragged her home. The note the fire department found duct-taped to the fence near the burnt-out wreck read:

YOU TOUCH HER, WE TORCH YOU.
  —*the Ladies*

The reporter did not think much of the theory that the second verb was a typographical error. Kate folded the paper and threw it on the floor, thinking that it was time she just stopped reading anything that came before the comics.

"I went to see Roz yesterday," she told Lee, taking a bagel from the toaster and reaching for the jar of Maj's blackberry jam. "Just in case I wasn't busy enough, she called me and thought I'd like to look into another sus-picious death."

"The Indian girl?"

"You know about her?" Kate asked in surprise.

"Maj called to warn me that Roz was setting off on another Campaign. I figured she'd drag you into it."

"I don't know how draggable I am at the moment. These last two cases are going to eat up a lot of hours."

"Kate, if Roz wants you to do this, you know you're going to end up doing it. Easier to admit it now and get on with it."

"I thought the woman was supposed to be writing her doctoral thesis," Kate complained. "Why isn't she doing that, or painting the baby's room, or starting a bookmobile service for the homeless, or something?"

"She's probably doing all of them," Lee said, adding darkly, "I used to have that kind of energy."

"You never had that kind of energy. You just never slept."

"That's true. Not like now."

"God no, you do nothing but snooze. Must be up to, what—six hours a day? Lazy pig."

Lee stuck out a purple, crumb-covered tongue, a childish gesture that pleased Kate inordinately because there had been so few of them in the two years since Kate's job had cost Lee so dearly. The two women sat across the table from each other grinning like a pair of schoolgirls, and Kate's heart swelled in joy and pride and the precious nature of what they had and she picked up Lee's hand and kissed the palm.

"Sweetheart?"

"Yes, my Kate?"

"Back in . . ." No, not *Back in the bad time*, although that was how Kate thought of it. "Last year, you said you wanted to have a baby. I . . . over-reacted, because I didn't think you were ready. Physically. I mean, you were barely walking. And more than that, because I wasn't ready. I just want to say that if you still feel the same way, and if the doctors think you won't, I don't know, blow any fuses, then I'm willing to go into it with you."

Lee's head was drooped so far that Kate couldn't see her face, so she had no warning when Lee's shoulders began to heave silently. Kate's hand tightened on Lee's in distress.

"Lee, love, what is it? Don't cry, I only meant—"

Lee's head shot back and her free hand slapped down hard on the table, and Kate realized belatedly that her lover was laughing uncontrollably.

"What?" she demanded. *"What?"*

Lee shook her head and spluttered, " 'Blow any fuses'? Oh God, Kate, the technical language. The subtle grasp of medical terminology you've picked up—"

Both relieved and affronted, Kate retrieved her hand and her dignity.

"I can't seem to do anything right," she said plaintively, which made Lee laugh even harder. So Kate took herself back to the relatively simple business of tracking down killers.

10

It is time for the invocation, to atone
For what we fear most and have not dared to face:
Kali, the destroyer, cannot be overthrown;
We must stay, open-eyed, in the terrible place.

Before she buckled down to her own caseload, however, Kate dutifully dug up the detective in charge of investigating Pramilla Mehta's death. Tommy Boyle had caught the call, so Kate left a message to have him phone her, and went back to her report.

Or she tried to go back to her report. She became increasingly aware of a small, dark woman, little more than a child, standing quietly in the corner of her vision, waiting with the self-effacing patience that had characterized her whole short life, and may have led to her death. Try as Kate might, she could not ignore the girl, and when Boyle came into the Homicide room with a question on his face, she abandoned the paperwork with even more gratitude than such an interruption usually earned.

"Want a cup of coffee?" she offered, already on her feet.

"Sure," he said.

Kate had known Boyle for a couple of years, but not well, and they happened not to have actually worked a case together. He was a red-haired, green-eyed man with Hispanic features and brown skin, who had impressed Kate as a person interested mainly in getting on with his work; when in a group, he tended to be seen with his nose in a sheaf of case notes or a book on forensics. She liked him, but didn't know him well enough to know how to approach him on what could be taken as a touchy business, intruding on another's investigation. Kate spooned coffee grounds into the machine and tried to put together a question that wouldn't sound either nuts or pushy, and in the end gave it up.

"It's about that burn victim you caught Tuesday night. Pramilla Mehta."

"What about her?"

"You haven't written it off as an accident, have you?"

"Of course not. Haven't even got the path report back yet." He waited for her to tell him why she was interested.

"You know the name Rosalyn Hall?"

"Rosalyn—you mean Roz Hall, that minister? Oh jeez. Is she involved in this?"

"I'm afraid so. She thinks the husband did his wife."

"The husband's a true flake," he offered in agreement.

"Thing is, Roz is convinced that this is an American incident of bride burning, which they get a lot of in India."

"People in India burn their brides?" he asked dubiously. "I heard of widows throwing themselves on their husband's funeral pyre, but I always thought that was old women. And isn't it illegal there now? There was something about it in a novel I once read," he added, as if to explain away his knowledge.

"I think that's a different thing. This is young brides. They have this complicated system in India with the bride's family giving a dowry to the groom's family— not just money, but stuff like motorbikes and kitchen appliances—and if the groom's family is greedy and demands more, and doesn't get it, they sometimes get pissed and kill the bride. Especially if there are also no babies."

"That sounds insane."

"I know. And Roz may be off her rocker and be

seeing demons in the dark, but on the off chance she's on to something, I told her I'd make sure it's treated like a possible homicide, not just a domestic accident."

Boyle narrowed his incongruous emerald eyes at her. "It sounds like she's a friend of yours."

"Longtime acquaintance," she admitted, repressing a twinge of guilt at her disloyalty. "You probably know how she works. She's a politician, she goes to someone on the inside to get things done. So she came to me, and to get her off my back I told her I'd make sure it was being done right. One thing the department does not need is Roz Hall raising a stink about due process."

"God no. Sure, you go ahead and tell her we're handling things right. But you might also tell her that I don't appreciate anyone telling me how to do my job."

"I'll be sure to mention it. When I saw who had caught the case, I knew it'd be done by the book. What did the scene look like? If you don't mind my nosiness."

"Pictures should be ready this afternoon. It was messy—burnings always are. As to whether we're looking at a homicide or not, I couldn't right off tell whether she fell into the stove or the stove fell onto her, if you see what I mean. There was accelerant in either case—it was one of those portable kerosene cook stoves—and there wasn't a whole lot of her left to look at. The whole house nearly went up."

"Why didn't it?"

"The family was home. The sister-in-law was working in the main kitchen, and she saw—"

"They have two kitchens? Must be a mansion."

"Oh no, it's just that they had a separate cooking area in the garden, a shack really—no building permit, of course—where the girl, Pramilla, was working. Sort of what my grandmother would have called a summer kitchen, very sensible in a climate like Fresno, or I suppose India."

"I see. Um. Have you talked with the arson investigator?"

"Not yet. I left him there with Crime Scene, taking a million measurements. He said he'd get back to me. I've got to leave it to him; I'm supposed to be partnered with Sammy." Sammy Calvo, the department's most politically incorrect detective, who suffered (along with everyone around him) from chronic foot-in-mouth disease, was currently out with the shingles, one of those complaints that seemed like a joke to anyone who had never lived with it. She stifled the flip remark that it couldn't happen to a nicer guy; Boyle presumably was friends with his partner, to some extent at least.

"Would you like a hand with this one?"

"I could use it," he admitted. "But I wouldn't have thought that you need to go around drumming up business."

"I've got the two actives, a handful of cold ones, and I'd be happy to give you a couple of hours' follow-up on this one."

"Right, then. I have to be in court all day—do you want to give the ME and the arson investigator a call this afternoon, see what they have? You might even go see them, if you have the time." It being a recognized fact of life that the physical presence of an investigator was harder to ignore than a voice on the phone.

"I'll stop by if I can, pick up their reports. Anything to keep Reverend Hall off the chief's back," she told him. The machine on the counter had stopped gurgling, so Kate poured them each a cup of coffee and they went back to their desks.

One of those jobs came to her, saving her trekking across the city. Amanda Bonner phoned and said that Roz Hall (at the very mention of whose name Kate was beginning to develop a wince) had told her to call and tell Kate what she knew. Kate hesitated, decided that Boyle would be happy enough to hand the preliminary interview over to her, and told Bonner to come down. She was there within half an hour.

Kate could well imagine that a teenager out of village India would find Amanda Bonner an impressive figure. She herself found Bonner impressive. Six feet tall, a hundred sixty pounds of very solid bone and muscle, she made Kate feel short, pale, flabby, and ineffectual.

Her hand was dry and callused when she shook Kate's officeworker palm, and she shed her jacket in the warmth of the small interview room to reveal sculpted muscles beneath a tank top. Kate might have tagged her as a bodybuilder, but Bonner just dropped into a chair with no hint of arrangement or posing except that when she leaned forward to talk with Kate, the top of her shirt fell away from her chest, giving Kate a glimpse of unfettered breasts that were surprisingly generous, with a sprinkling of freckles and a tan that appeared to go all the way down. Kate averted her eyes and sat down firmly in her own chair, pulling up a businesslike notebook and pen to take the woman's statement.

As Roz had told Kate, Bonner had met Pramilla Mehta over a head of purple kale in the supermarket. She had seen the Indian girl numerous times before that, since Amanda's aging parents lived on the same block as the Mehtas and Amanda stopped in almost every day to shop and cook and generally check up on them.

"It's a pretty ritzy area, you know. The Mehtas are about the only ethnic people there—aside from the gardeners and cooks. A beautiful young girl wearing a *salwar kameez* and a dozen silver bracelets sticks out."

"What was your relationship with Pramilla Mehta?" Kate asked.

"Friendship, basically. Older sister stuff. If you're asking if I slept with her, the answer is no. Frankly, she wasn't my kind. For one thing, she was straight—or at least, she was too young and confused to think about being anything else. Personally, I prefer the strong, confident type. Don't you?"

Now Kate was certain that the gaping shirt had been no accident, though she kept her face as straight as Pramilla's orientation. It happened often enough, women flirting with her, since everyone in the city who read a paper or watched the news knew who and what Kate Martinelli was. All she could do was ignore it, as she had a dozen times before. No different, really, from a straight male cop with a female witness coming on to him. Amusing, but she mustn't show that; a smile would either offend or be taken as an encouragement.

"How did you communicate with the girl?" Kate asked. "I thought she didn't speak much English."

"I've traveled all over the world, and had a lot of experience in talking to people whose language I don't speak. It's mostly a matter of not being embarrassed about making a fool of yourself with sign language and asking for words. And besides, Pramilla understood a lot, and as soon as she realized that I wasn't going to make fun of her like her family did, she relaxed and could speak a lot better than when she was worried about getting it right."

"But I would expect that a lot of what you understood about her life was reading between the lines," Kate suggested.

"That's true. And I'm sure I read some of the more subtle things wrong. But then, that happens even between people who speak the same language, doesn't it?"

"Did she tell you that her husband hit her? In so many words?"

"One day she had a bad bruise on her cheek. I asked if Laxman had done it, and she nodded."

"Nodded, or shrugged?"

"That sort of Indian wag of the head. It means, 'Oh yes, but never mind.' "

It could mean any number of things, thought Kate to herself. "And the other abuses? You told Roz that Peter's wife, Rani, pinched her."

"And slapped her a couple of times. It's fairly traditional in families like that to find a younger relative imported as a servant—or an older one, which the Mehtas have as well. Slave is more like it, because they aren't usually paid wages, just given a bed and food. Pramilla at least had Laxman's allowance."

"Have you met Laxman?"

"Not directly. I've seen him a couple of times, once

with her in the market telling her what to buy, and once when they were getting off a bus. He was carrying this tiny parcel, a pie or something in a bakery box, and he got off first; she was behind him with this great arm-load of string bags of vegetables and two grocery bags, and she stumbled coming down the steps and nearly dropped the lot. He just shouted at her—in Hindi so I couldn't understand the words, but it was obvious that he was giving her hell. Then he walked away leaving her to carry the rest."

"What did you do?"

"What did I do? Nothing." Bitterness crept into Bonner's voice. "Pramilla had made it clear that it only made more problems for her when I tried to interfere. If I'd seen Laxman actually hit her, I would have stepped in, called the police, the whole nine yards. But since I didn't, I thought it would be better for her if she made the decision to leave him. She had my number, she knew I would come to her any time of the day or night. I even gave her a hot-line number, in case she wanted to talk to someone who understood better than I."

"Understood . . . ?"

"Her situation and her language. But as far as I know, she never called. Not then, anyway."

Kate lifted her eyebrows in a question. After a minute, Bonner reluctantly dredged up the rest of it. "I think she may have tried to call me, just before she was killed. I was out shopping for my parents, and when I got home there was a hang-up message on the answering machine. Nobody there, and when I tried to do that star sixty-nine thing to call back, it wouldn't go through. And then that afternoon when I went to take the groceries to my folks, there were all these police cars down the street. I can't help but wonder . . ."

"Yes," Kate said. "Well."

Had Pramilla Mehta been religious? Kate wondered as she walked Amanda Bonner to the elevator. Would she have said that fate—karma—kept her friend Amanda from being there when she needed her? And what about her death; would a fifteen-year-old girl agree that death was nothing, reincarnation all? Or was that a Buddhist conceit, not a Hindu one?

Assuming, of course, that the hang-up call was from Pramilla. The Mehta phone records would tell, although it would not be a kindness to confirm Amanda's fears. Maybe she'd just let it go.

Just after midday, Kate and Al drove up to talk with Matthew Banderas's boss, Janice Popper. The software company was in an uninspired strip of businesses just off the freeway, clean and tidily landscaped and working hard to appear both cutting-edge (a modern tangle of sculpture out front) and reassuringly stable (thick carpeting in the entrance foyer). They identified themselves to the receptionist, who picked up the phone and announced their arrival. Popper came out of the back and greeted them, ushering them back to her office with a declaration that Kate had heard dozens of times before in similar circumstances, although she freely admitted that very occasionally it was true.

"I don't think I can help you much," Popper told them. "I didn't really know the man."

"That's fine," Hawkin said, settling into his chair across the desk from her and presenting her with a genial smile. "We just need to be thorough. Let's see. You've only had this job a few months, is that right? Did you work for the company before that, or were you hired from outside?"

"Nine weeks now, and I was headhunted. Brought in from outside. That may have been one of the problems, with Matthew, that is. He applied for this position, although he wasn't really qualified. His experience was almost exclusively in sales, not general administration."

Janice Popper was a small, thin woman with a number of nervous habits involving her fingers, which made Kate wonder if she'd recently given up smoking and had to find something to do with her hands. Right now she was tugging irritably at the sleek dark brown hair that fell along her jawline, trying to tuck it behind her ear—without success, as it was about half an inch too short to stay tucked—and adjusting her titanium-framed designer glasses as if they were bothering the bridge of her nose.

"When did you find out about his criminal record?" Al asked her.

"My second week here. I never had a proper handover because the guy who did this job before me had a heart attack and wasn't up to briefing me, and personnel records were secondary to active contracts and ongoing negotiations. It took me a week or so to get my feet under me, begin to get a handle on the shape of the company. After that I started taking appointments with personnel, people with problems or urgent suggestions, wanting transfers or raises, that kind of thing. Most of them, of course, just wanting a chance to size up the new boss and make an impression. Banderas came in around the middle of that week, maybe Thursday. I always have my secretary give me a file on an appointment so I know something about them—single or five kids, war veteran or university graduate, anything like that. Nothing confidential you know, just background. So I open the file for my ten o'clock or whatever it was and see that Matthew Banderas was on record as a sex offender. I left the door wide open during that appointment, I can tell you."

"You said you had decided to fire him?" Hawkin asked.

"Not for that," she quickly said. "I'd have no right to fire him for a past offense, either legally or ethically, no matter how uncomfortable it made me feel. No, he was falling down on his job. The sales numbers just weren't coming in, and numbers are the bottom line. We work by salary plus commission, and we couldn't afford to pay somebody who wasn't bringing it in."

"But he'd been okay before you came?"

"Not really. He'd been slipping for some months." She paused, choosing her words. "I ran an analysis on his sales, trying to track it down, thinking I might help him out. I found that almost all of his successful sales contacts were men." She shook her head. "There's just too many women in charge of buying to write off that whole side of the market."

"He alienated women buyers, then?"

"Somehow, yes."

"Any way of finding out how?"

"I wouldn't want to ask them directly, if that's what you're saying. It's hardly a great sales technique, to remind buyers that you had a rep who was not only a prick but a rapist to boot, who on top of that managed to get himself murdered."

"On the other hand," Kate suggested, "it might clear the air if one of your female sales reps had a few woman-to-woman talks with people who turned Banderas down. Might get across the message that it wasn't going to happen again."

Popper sat still for a moment, staring at Kate and thinking. Her right hand came up to tuck the uncooperative lock behind her ear, and she nodded.

"You may be right. We'll run a trial, and tell you what—if I find anything out about Matthew, I'll pass it on to you."

"One other thing," Hawkin said, interrupting the forward shift in her body's position that presaged their dismissal. "Who else knew about Banderas's history?"

"I have no idea. No, really—I don't," she insisted. "I would guess that either everybody knew, or nobody. It's the sort of thing that tends to spread, but I haven't been here long enough to develop my own network within the company, and I've been too damn busy to ask around about him. Why don't you talk to my secretary—she's been here forever."

Both times Popper had said the phrase "my secretary," she had looked as if she were biting into something unpleasant, leading Kate to suspect that the secretary had been inherited with the job, and that Popper was none too pleased about it. She was probably temporarily dependent on the woman—and the woman's own "network" of knowledge and contacts—but somehow Kate thought that would not continue for long.

The woman in the outer office was pale, slow-moving, spoke with a trace of Texas in her voice, and was at least a decade older than her thin new boss with the nervous fingers.

"Oh, indeed," she told them. "Everybody knew. Everybody that mattered, that is. I made sure the new girls all heard, just so they wouldn't accept rides from Mr. Banderas, if you see what I mean. Not that he ever seemed to look close to home—as far as I know he never gave any of the girls here so much as a glance—but I thought it was good to be careful."

"Did you tell anyone outside of work?"

"I may have mentioned it to two or three friends," she replied stiffly, "but I wouldn't have told them his name."

"Has anyone ever contacted you, inquiring about Banderas?"

"No." And, her prim expression added, she would not have told them had they asked.

Hawkin thanked her in his warmest fashion, which made no impression at all on her disapproval. As he and Kate left, he glanced at his watch.

"Too late for lunch?" he asked, sounding hopeful.

"Didn't you eat?"

"I had a late breakfast. I don't really eat breakfast at home these days. Jani turns green if she's around anything but dry cereal and herb tea before noon. Morning sickness—though I don't know why they call it that, since it lasts most of the day."

"Let's go eat, then."

It was coffee that Al seemed to crave even more than food, since Jani's hormones had abruptly found the merest whiff of the stuff instantly nauseating. He seized the cup as soon as the waitress had filled it, drank half of it down, and sat back with a sigh of contentment.

"Is Jani okay other than morning sickness?"

"She's fine. She's even gaining a little weight, though I don't know how since she never seems to eat. She went in yesterday and heard the baby's heartbeat. Said it sounded like a bird's."

"I'm glad for you both. For all of you."

"Jules said to say hi, by the way. So," he said in an abrupt change of subject, "how do we tie these two bastards together?"

Two men who lived their lives miles apart, both literally and figuratively, brought together by the means of their deaths.

"Could it be a coincidence, that they both had a history of abusing women? A more or less random stalker?"

Al was shaking his head, not so much in disagreement as an expression of bafflement. "What're the odds? A blue-collar baggage handler in his fifties who beats his wife in South San Francisco and a young hotshot software salesman with a bachelor pad and a habit of raping strangers?"

"We need to take a closer look at Matty's victims. Maybe one of them has a brother who works at the airport."

"Be nice."

"Hey. Things happen sometimes."

"I'll hold my breath," Al said sourly.

"We're going to need to do all the airport interviews again, as well as follow-ups with all the people who worked with Banderas or lived near him," said Kate, making notes.

"The women, for sure."

"What about handing some of it over to what's-her-name—Wiley? She seemed good."

"If you think you can talk her into working with us instead of going it on her own, sure. She struck me as a one-man show. One-woman show."

"I'll talk to her."

"If she's available this afternoon, you could drop me back at the software place, I could get started on those."

"Might be better tomorrow," Kate said. "I need to be back in the City before five. I've set up a couple of interviews on another case and I'd like to clear them up."

"What case is that?"

"It's something I'm helping Boyle with, while Sammy's out." And as their lunch arrived and they both dug in, Kate told her partner the sad story of Pramilla Mehta, concluding, "It's probably just an accident, her silk skirt brushing against the kerosene stove. Like that woman in the camper van last winter." One of San Francisco's sizable population of transients, this one not strictly homeless although the roof over her head was attached to wheels, had been cooking up what investigators had originally suspected was a batch of drugs but had turned out to be supper, when either the stove malfunctioned or she had stumbled into it. The woman did not die, but she had spent many weeks in the burn unit wishing she had.

"And this is Boyle's case?"

"He caught the call. I had a word with him this morning, told him I'd make a few phone calls for him."

Hawkin knew his partner too well to be fooled by her casual tone. He fixed her with a stony eye. "How are those headaches of yours?"

"They're fine, Al. No problem."

He did not believe her. "See if you can get someone else to give Boyle a hand. You're going to be too busy to do it justice."

"I'm kind of committed, Al. And, I promised Roz Hall I'd look into it."

"Roz Hall? What's that woman got to do with the case?"

"That's just it: I'd rather she didn't have anything to do with it. She's convinced that Pramilla's death is a case of bride burning. I thought if I stepped in, it'd keep her from going on a crusade with the papers."

"Martinelli, you only have so many hours in the day."

"If things get too crazy, I'll ask you to explain that to Roz."

"Want me to write her an excuse slip, like I do for Jules?"

"Let's not go overboard on this fatherhood thing, okay, Al?"

11

She comes to purge the altars in her way,
And at her altar we shall have to pray.

"Homicide," the pathologist said to Kate, peering happily up at a set of X rays. "No doubt. See all that stuff just behind her right ear? Compression fracture. Made by something long and thick, like a piece of half-inch metal pipe or a fireplace poker, but not the sharp edge of the masonry hearth she was found next to. Nope, no way. Wrong angle, too. She'd have had to fall out of the sky onto it—with her arms at her sides—to get that angle of blow. She was hit, arranged, and set alight."

"Homicide," the arson expert declared, tapping lugubriously on the precise lines of his sketch. "The evidence is consistent with a scenario whereby the victim was rendered unconscious, the kerosene stove was raised and propelled across her supine form, then set alight. Note the path of the accelerant: Had she fallen directly into the stove, one would expect to see the deepest burns nearest the area onto which the kerosene spilled—the arm and upper torso had she hit the stove that way, along with a fan along the path of the spill. However, instead of that we see the body lying at approximately a right angle to the spill, and underneath it. In other words," he said, relenting, "she went down, then the stove went down but perpendicular to her fall. And before you ask, yes, she could conceivably have moved after the fire began, and repositioned herself, but considering the head injury I would say she was unconscious when the fire started."

"Murder," Kate said to Al, tossing the file temptingly onto the car seat next to him. "Somebody whacked her, laid her out to make it look like she'd hit her head on some bricks, and then kicked the stove over to burn the place down. Actual cause of death was smoke inhalation, but she'd have died of the burns or the head injury."

"Murder," repeated Hawkin, putting away the photographs they had picked up from the lab and taking up the file portrait of the victim, angling it to catch the fading light. "A pretty little thing. She doesn't look much older than Jules."

"She wasn't. That's the photo her father had taken back in India when Peter Mehta's inquiry letter first arrived. She was about fourteen."

"Mail-order brides, in this day and age. So who did it?"

"The husband sounds borderline retarded with a temper that's had the police out twice, the sister-in-law's a stone bitch, and Peter Mehta himself is a businessman who looks for results. And the girl wasn't pregnant a year after he'd bought her for his brother."

Hawkin shook his head, dropped the photo back into the file, and slipped his half-glasses into his breast pocket. "You still want to get involved with this?"

"I told Boyle I'd give him a few hours, like this business of getting the reports while he's in court, and I'll go along with him to the Mehta house this evening. I know we've got Larsen and Banderas, but that's it at the moment. That gangbanger case is solved, we're just waiting for him to show his face again, and there's not a hell of a lot more I can do on last month's drug dump. It's dead." This was closer to outright lie than exaggeration: a homicide detective was never without work. Still, the urgency of open cases varied considerably, and in recognition of this unhappy fact of life, Hawkin did not challenge her.

"Just don't let that Hall woman give you a hard time about it, okay?"

"She'd give me a harder time if I ducked out of it."

"Are you saying the girl was murdered, Inspector Boyle?" Peter Mehta asked in disbelief. It was an hour later, and he reached over and turned on the desk lamp as if to throw light on more than their faces. The window in his study fell instantly black.

Mehta was not what Kate had expected of a man who bought his brother an underaged wife from an Indian village. She wasn't quite sure what exactly she had expected, but it wasn't someone so very . . . American. His features were Indian, yes, and his clothes slightly more formal than she imagined the usual Californian executive wore at home. And the house itself was somehow ineffably foreign—the air scented with exotic spices instead of the usual stale coffee and air freshener, the furniture larger and ever-so-slightly more opulent, the colors more intense. Like the difference between a plain black dress on a skinny woman and a designer dress on a fashion model; hard to say where the difference came in, but it was clearly there.

Even Mehta's voice was faintly foreign as he addressed Tommy Boyle and, at his side as silent partner, Kate. Not so much an accent, she decided, as the feeling that his parents might have had accents. A rhythm, perhaps, that became more pronounced under stress. Such as now.

"Is that what you are telling me, Inspector? That the death of my brother's wife was a murder?"

"It looks that way, Mr. Mehta," Boyle told him.

"My God. And in my own home. Who would want to do something like that?"

"Did you have any visitors during the day, that you know of?"

"I am certain my wife would have told me. She is not in the habit of letting strangers into the house while I am away."

"But friends?"

"Women friends, sometimes, yes. But hers, not the girl's. She was allowed only to invite friends while I was home. We had a small problem once with Laxman becoming disturbed by one of her visitors, and so she saw her friends in the evenings and weekends, or out of the house."

"And you were not at home that day, Mr. Mehta?"

"It was this time of evening—no, a little earlier. We had not yet eaten dinner, but yes, I was home. Having a drink here in my study while my wife cooked."

"And your brother?"

"Upstairs in his room. At least, he came down from there when . . . I saw him come down the stairs when I came through the house to show the fire department where to go."

"And the children?"

"The younger ones were in their rooms, watching television. My son Rajiv was at the kitchen table doing his homework. He was the first to see the fire, and he shouted at my wife. She ran in here to get me, and I telephoned 911. But I told all this to a dozen people the other night."

"We're just confirming our notes, Mr. Mehta. Do you mind if we take a look at the place where Pramilla died?"

"Yes, certainly. You were here the other day, were you not?" he asked, looking from Boyle to Kate and back again. "Forgive me, there were so many people here, the police and the fire department . . ."

"I was here, yes. Inspector Martinelli was not."

"Of course. Please, come this way."

Mehta led them out of the office, which was just inside the front door, and back through the house, past a formal dining room and an adjoining closed door that gave off the fragrance of exotic spices and the mundane sounds of running water and dishes clattering. Mehta paused to switch on the lights, and a garden sprang into view. They stepped out of a sliding glass door onto a brick patio surrounded by a patch of lawn and some unimaginative shrubs. Patio and lawn were scattered with heavy cast-iron garden furniture, a child's tricycle, several dismembered dolls, and a soccer ball. A door with a curtained window in its upper half stood to their right, an entranceway to the breakfast area and the kitchen beyond.

In sharp contrast to the fragrant kitchen, the garden stank of smoke and wet ashes and a faint trace of burning flesh, a smell which no one who had worked with a charred corpse ever forgot. Yellow crime scene tape was festooned around the shrubs, everything in sight had a thick coating of gray ash, and one whole half of the garden looked as if it had been through a hurricane, the plants flattened, smaller flowers uprooted by the force of the fire hoses. Kate circled around a chaise longue with mildewing cushions and stepped down from the bricks onto a concrete driveway that ended abruptly at the source of all this devastation, the remnants of the burnt-out shed where the child-bride Pramilla Mehta had died.

It looked to have been a shoddy structure compared to the substantial bulk of the house, and it had burned fast and hot—judging by the heavy charring on the wooden fence ten feet away that had nearly gone up as well. A pan that looked like a shallow wok lay buried under the fallen roof, and a set of three metal kitchen canisters lay flattened, either by heat or under the boots of the firemen. Preservation of a crime scene was never high on the fire department's list of priorities.

"This was a sort of outdoor kitchen, as I understand it?" Kate asked Mehta.

"I had it built for her," he answered. "Two women in a kitchen is not always easy, and my wife, Rani, complained that the girl was becoming difficult. Always underfoot, wanting to use the stove to cook her own food—although she was not a good cook and it was not necessary, as the family eats together. In the interest of harmony, we needed a separate area for the girl."

"Why didn't you build a proper structure? Why a plywood shed with a kerosene cook stove?"

Mehta sighed and ran a hand over his face. "I must have been asked that question fifty times in the last few days, to the point that I now ask it of myself. The insurance people are the most insistent, and the building inspectors. I can only say that it seemed a logical idea at the time, to put up a strictly temporary structure—it was a kit, from a gardening supply shop—and furnish it the way the girl was used to. She came from a very poor background, the sort who cooks over a cow dung fire and dreams of the day when she could have a kerosene cook stove and a refrigerator proudly displayed in the living room with a doily across the top. I wasn't about to have an open fire out here, and I didn't want to run electricity into a shed, but I thought the stove a safe compromise. The entire project was my brother's suggestion, in fact, and it did serve to calm the waters. Until this."

"We'd like to speak with your brother, Mr. Mehta," Boyle told him.

The man sighed again, more deeply than before, and turned back to the house. "Are you finished out here, Inspectors? Because I need to talk to you about my brother before you see him."

Kate cast a last glance at the collapsed walls and the black, flattened shrubbery that surrounded them, rendered even more unearthly by the strange shadows cast by the garden spotlights. She and Boyle turned to follow Mehta back inside. The curtain on the kitchen door fell back, but not before she had caught a glimpse of a plump woman in a garish orange sari, watching them. Peter's wife, Rani, no doubt.

Back in the study Mehta sat again behind his broad mahogany desk, leaving them to choose between the two uncomfortable chairs on the other side, chairs whose seats were slightly lower than Mehta's. Boyle sat down, but Kate chose instead to stand, leaning up against the window frame with the light behind her and in a place that required Mehta to crane his neck around to see her. Two could play the one-upmanship game, and Kate had taken a dislike to Mehta, particularly the way he kept referring to Pramilla not by name, but as merely "the girl."

"What do you have to tell us, Mr. Mehta?" Tommy Boyle asked. He and Kate had talked over everything Roz and Amanda had told her, and she had in turn been given the details of his preliminary interview with Mehta the night of Pramilla's death. Now it was time to get down to details.

"My brother was too upset the other night to talk to you," Mehta began. "I made him take his sleeping pill early to calm him down, and he is still most disturbed. The doctor is *quite* concerned, in fact. I want to stress that interviewing him is not . . . how shall I say this? Not like interviewing other men."

"Are you telling me there's something wrong with your brother, Mr. Mehta?" Boyle asked bluntly. Roz had said there was, but it was best to hear it from the source.

"Yes," Mehta said with equal frankness. "There is something wrong with my brother. Laxman is more or less retarded. I have been told it was due to our mother's advanced age when she was pregnant with him, although it may have been a brief problem during the birth that affected him, but in either case he was starved of oxygen during a vital time, and it damaged his brain. He functions, he communicates, he can even read and write and do basic math, but he will never hold more than a low-scale job, and on his own he would never marry a woman with more wit than a ten-year-old.

"In India, caring for people like my brother would be easier. There may be fewer facilities, but more . . . flexibility, shall we say, and people willing to work for a pittance. But Laxman and I are both American citizens. We were born here, have lived here all our lives. Our mother was a pretty traditional Indian woman in some ways, and always dressed in a sari, but she made certain we spoke only English in the home, and she raised us, as well as she could, as Americans.

"She died six years ago, when Laxman was twenty-three. He missed her enormously—still does; he's never really gotten over her death. So Rani and I decided that the best solution was to bring him a kind of substitute mother, you might say: a wife. Their children . . . any children Laxman fathers will be normal, you understand; we were not being irresponsible. And from the wife's point of view, a village girl, even a bright one, wouldn't have the same expectations of a husband as someone who had grown up in a city. The girl we found was ideal. A little young by American standards, I realize, but not by Indian ones.

"And it seemed to work well at the beginning. Oh, the very beginning was a little rocky, but as soon as we got back here they settled in nicely. The girl was so quiet you hardly knew she was here, and Laxman seemed very fond of her. He found her soothing, began speaking a little more Hindi to her, dressing in *kurta* pajamas instead of jeans. I was very pleased, and God knows things went smoother, both here and at work, where Laxman had been trying to do jobs he couldn't possibly handle and creating untold difficulties for me. If only she'd gotten pregnant."

"That created a problem? They hadn't been married all that long."

"I didn't care one way or another. I have two sons and two daughters, so the family as a whole didn't need Laxman's sons. Frankly, I've had enough of babies and unsettled nights, and I knew that if they had children, the burden would end up on Rani's back, and mine.

"But my wife is more traditional, and thought it was unfortunate that the girl didn't catch.

"Understand, Inspector, that there was nothing wrong with my brother physically. His brain may not be too hot, but once he understood what the equipment between his legs was for, he went at it with an enthusiasm that other men would envy. I had to speak with him about the need to keep a closed door between them and others, especially the children."

Boyle's face gave away nothing, but Kate wondered why the apparently urbane Mehta felt the need to flaunt his brother's skills in such detail, verging on crudeness. Perhaps they were meant to think that he shared his brother's prowess? She had the urge to match his crudeness and ask whether Laxman and Pramilla had gone around fucking like rabbits, just to see how he reacted, but before she could say anything, Boyle mildly noted, "A man can be virile but sterile, Mr. Mehta. Although I'm sure you know that."

"Of course," he admitted, though not looking pleased. "I merely tell you because you need to understand what the girl was to Laxman. He was very fond of her, but she also changed. When she first came she was all sweetness and docility, giving her husband and his family the proper respect, but later, and especially recently, she became more difficult. She was learning English, and was very arrogant about it. She showed it off in front of Laxman and Rani—she would correct her husband and sister-in-law when they made a mistake, as if to point out how clever she was. She made inappropriate friendships with women in the neighborhood—"

"How were they inappropriate?"

"The women . . . they were not Hindu, to begin with, not even Indian, and one of them was divorced. Not the sort of friendships a proper young girl, a girl with family responsibilities, ought to cultivate. There was, for one thing, no supervision when men were present, which upset my brother greatly when he found out. I realize this is a part of the American custom, but it is unacceptable to a good Indian family."

"She was becoming American?" Boyle suggested.

"She was becoming irresponsible, neglecting her husband and her household duties to Rani. The outdoor kitchen was a way of encouraging her to be an independent woman, a wife and future mother, while at the same time strengthening her ties to her own past and her people."

It all sounded pretty sordid to Kate, a very small step from slavery, but again she tried to push her own feel-

ings down. Still, she could not suppress them completely, and they added an edge to her own question.

"You said it was your brother's idea to give Pramilla
a traditional Indian kitchen. Are you telling me now
that he was behind this fairly subtle . . . manipula-
tion, shall we say, of his wife?"

Mehta shifted in his chair to look at her. "Of course
not, not directly. But retarded though he might be, he is
not insensitive. I think what he actually said, following
a tiff between the two women, was, 'She misses the
smell of dung fire.' I talked with Rani, and between the
three of us we came up with the kitchen compromise. It
wasn't permanent, you understand. I could see that everyone would be much happier if Laxman and his wife
had their own establishment. It is the Indian way to
have all the family living together, but it is not always
the best. No, when the girl had been mature enough to
take care of a house and her husband, they would have
moved out. In fact, I had my eye on a place down the
street that was about to come on the market. It would
have been ideal, close enough that we could keep an eye
on them, but far enough away that they could stand on
their own. Without the girl, though . . ."

Kate suddenly found the man's resolute avoidance of
the name "Pramilla" unbearably irritating, on top of all
his other ideas and assumptions. She pushed herself
away from the window and said, "I think we should
talk to Laxman now, if you don't mind." She said it in
her cop voice, those tones of bored authority that made
gangbangers drift reluctantly away and drunks subside,
and it worked on the Chief Executive Officer of Mehta
Enterprises. He removed himself from the barrier of his
desk and led the two detectives back through the house,
this time passing through the dining room, down another hallway, and up some stairs to a door. He
knocked and opened it without waiting for an answer.

The suite of rooms Kate entered was a self-contained
apartment whose occupant had far stronger ties to the
Indian subcontinent than did the people downstairs.
The air smelled of sandalwood incense and curry, and

the walls were hung with garish prints: Krishna and his big-breasted milkmaids, the elephant-headed Ganesha, and Hanuman, the monkey god (which reminded Kate of Mina's antics on the school stage the week before). Gold thread shot through the heavy drapes and the sofa upholstery. The living room was blessed with at least six shiny brass lamps, and every horizontal surface—tables, shelves, the top of a huge television set, a pair of brightly colored ceramic stools from China, and the corners of the floor itself—was laden with objects, most of them shiny, and a few of them expensive, a couple of them beautiful, all of them looking newly acquired. One corner had a delicate triangular table set up with a sinuous statue of a maternal-looking figure, with the ash of incense and some wilted marigolds at its base. Pramilla's household shrine, most likely.

All in all, the apartment looked as if the contents of a large knickknack shop had been moved here in their entirety.

As they entered, Peter Mehta had glanced through an open doorway into what resembled a staff lunchroom, with a small table, two chairs, a half-sized refrigerator, and the basic necessities for producing hot drinks and warming leftovers. Finding it unoccupied, he led them into the knickknack shop of a living room before going to another door, which he opened, making a brief noise of impatience or irritation before stepping inside. Kate followed, and caught her first sight of Laxman Mehta.

Her first impression was of a small boy waiting in his bedroom for his parent to fetch him for some dutiful event such as a dinner at Grandma's. He sat fully dressed but for his shoes, perched at the end of a neatly made bed with his hands between his knees, looking at nothing. His brother bent over him and gave his shoulder a gentle shake.

"Laxman," he said. "Mani, come on, don't sit here all day. You've missed both tea and dinner, and Rani even made *samosas* for you. And look, there are two people here to talk to you, Inspector Boyle and Inspector Martinelli. They're with the police. Come on, Mani, it's time to move along."

The boy on the bed, whom Kate knew to be nearly her own age, roused himself and nodded. When he stood up it was with the slow deliberation of an old man, and Kate recognized the symptoms instantly: Laxman Mehta ached with grief.

His brother seemed oblivious, merely chattering his encouragement in a way that made Kate think that if she were not there, he would be considerably more brusque. Peter Mehta clearly found his brother a burden.

But a gorgeous burden, Kate saw. Even face-to-face, Laxman looked closer to twenty than thirty, his skin clear and unlined, the only sign of his recent tragedy the stance of his back and shoulders and a certain sunken distraction around his eyes. Although the distraction might be chronic, she reminded herself. Both Peter and Roz's informant had indicated that he was retarded.

As a decorative object, though, this male was extraordinarily beautiful. His long black eyelashes over those dark limpid eyes would make a poet croon, the creamy hairless skin on his face cried out to be touched, and unlike his stocky brother, Laxman was blessed with a slim, almost adolescent body that promised innocence and strength. If even a lesbian like herself felt the stir of his beauty, she could only assume that there were places in town where this man's presence would cause a riot. Half the men in the Castro would fling themselves at his feet while the other half were turning their backs in despair. He, however, would notice none of it—which was part of his attraction. He was quite oblivious of his own beauty. His family must have kept him under close wraps, and breathed a sigh of relief when he was safely married off.

Physically, at any rate, the farmer's daughter could have found herself with a less acceptable husband.

Kate stepped aside to allow the three men to return to the living room, but also so that she could take a closer look at the bedroom. The single bed was narrow, the walls stark and almost without decoration. It was austere compared with the collections in the main room, but there was a door beside the bed, and she took two quick steps over to it, and opened it into something out of a maharajah's harem. She had thought the living room was ornate, but this was a jewel box, packed to bursting with a thousand gaudy baubles, carved figures of lithe tigers and entwined couples, armfuls of silk flowers thrust into maroon and cobalt vases, two gilt-framed mirrors on the flocked wallpaper, a lace canopy over the bed and a heavily embroidered cover on it. The two silk lamp shades on either side of the bed had what appeared to be genuine pearls dangling from the lower rims. One of the lamps was on, but so low that the streetlight outside cast shadows through the delicate filigree of the magnificent carved screen that covered the window. Even dimly lit, however, the room's impression was quite clear. Kate backed off, closing the door quietly, discomfited by the sheer raw sensuality of the room. There was no doubt which bedroom the couple had slept in.

She found Boyle and the Mehta brothers in the diminutive kitchen. The room had no cooking facilities aside from a microwave oven and an electric kettle, which Peter was filling with water at a bar sink too narrow to hold a dinner plate. He put the kettle on the counter and switched it on, and Kate had it on the tip of her tongue to ask Mehta why he had not converted this room to a proper, if small, kitchen, when she glanced at Laxman's bereaved face and let the question subside for the moment.

Peter set four cups and a packet of tea bags on the sink and then turned to his brother.

"Laxman, these people would like to talk to you about, well—"

"Pramilla," said Laxman, and raised his lovely eyes to Kate. "You want to talk about my wife and the way she died, because you're policemen and that's what the police do when a person dies, they talk to the family."

"Laxman watches a lot of television," Peter offered

in explanation. Kate nodded and she and Boyle sat down in the chairs across the table from the boy-man. The tiny room was very full of people.

"All right, Mr. Mehta," Boyle began, "tell—"

"I'm Laxman. Mr. Mehta is my brother."

Both detectives found themselves smiling. "Okay, Laxman. Tell me, how do you think Pramilla died?"

"I killed her," Laxman said. Their smiles died a sudden death and Peter nearly dropped the teapot he was holding.

"Mani!" he exclaimed. "What are you saying? Oh, I knew this was not a good idea."

Boyle put out a hand to shut him up, and said to the beautiful young man across from him, keeping his voice even and gentle, "How do you mean, you killed her?"

"They all said I would if I hit her again, because I'm really very strong and she's so tiny. She was so tiny, I mean. So I didn't hit her and I didn't, even when she made me so angry with her teasing, but they said I would kill her and she's dead now, so I must have done it. I don't remember, but I must have."

"Did you hit her a lot, Laxman?"

"Three times. Three different times, I mean. I hit her one time when she made me mad by turning off the television. And the second time was when she . . . she was angry and she called me names. I hit her two or three times then, I don't remember exactly. And then the last time she was teasing me because she'd been talking with some other men and I didn't think that was right and I told her so and she laughed! She laughed at me and so I hit her and . . . and hit her. That time I made her bleed really bad and it scared me, and she cried and I told her I'd never do it again because if she did have a baby I didn't want her to lose it. So then I promised I would hit other things if I got mad, so I wouldn't hit her. And I did that twice. Once I punched a hole in the wall. I hurt my hand."

They looked at him, and he looked back at them. Finally Boyle cleared his throat. "On the afternoon Pramilla died, Laxman? What were you doing?"

Laxman gave Boyle a flat stare, not really seeing him, and Kate thought he had either not understood the question or was zoning out (was he on drugs, prescription or otherwise?), but after a minute his eyes focused again. "She was making me *panir pakharas*. They're my favorite. I was angry at her in the morning—not real mad but a little—and she went out and bought something." He stood up abruptly and walked out of the room, coming back with a small Chinese figure of a boy leading a water buffalo, which he put on the table in front of Kate. "She said she bought it because it was like me, and she was going to make me the *pakharas* so I would be happy. And I was, until I heard the sirens stop in front of the house and people shouting. And I haven't been happy since. I don't think I ever will be again."

Kate looked down at the crude little figurine, alone in the center of the table, and it occurred to her that Pramilla could easily have meant not that the boy in the statue reminded her of Laxman, but rather the lumbering beast who was being led. If the latter, then the girl had possessed a sharp sense of humor. Kate could well believe that this dull-witted man could have been driven to fury until the girl relented and made him his *pakharas*.

"She smelled bad," Laxman added suddenly.

"Who," Boyle asked. "Pramilla?"

"She was burned up and they wouldn't let me see her, but she smelled awful. Rani said that's how our people at home make funerals, by burning, but I don't like it. It's terrible."

"I agree, Laxman, it's not very pleasant. Tell me, Laxman, what did you do while Pramilla went out to cook the, er . . . ?"

Laxman regarded the detective blankly, as if he hadn't heard the question. It seemed to be a part of his thinking process, however, because after a minute he said, "She went to cook the *pakharas*. Cheese *pakharas*. I tried to watch my television programs, only I couldn't because I was still angry, and so I had a hot bath like she said to do when I got mad, it would make me feel better. And it did. So I went back to the TV. And then the sirens came."

"Laxman, did you happen—" Kate started to ask, but this time Laxman was not listening, and went on with his thought.

"She was good to me, and she was so pretty, and her hair smelled so sweet and her skin was soft. I miss her so much. If she came back I'd never be angry at her ever again. But she's dead and horrible and now I'll never be happy again." And with that he dropped his head onto his arms on the tabletop and began to sob as extravagantly as a child.

Embarrassed, Peter abandoned the tea he was trying to make and awkwardly comforted his howling brother. Kate glanced at Boyle, and could see in his face the agreement that they were not about to get a lot more out of either Mehta tonight. Boyle thanked Peter and Laxman in a loud voice, and they left.

They halted at the foot of the stairs.

"Do you want to try talking to Mrs. Mehta?" Boyle asked.

Kate shrugged. "We could try, and come back later with a translator if her English is too bad."

They found Rani Mehta in the kitchen with three of the children. A boy of about thirteen was sitting at the table with a stack of books: the eldest, Rajiv, no doubt. A girl of about six or seven occupied the chair across from him; in front of her was a row of naked dolls with frayed hair, some of them missing various limbs. She had two of them in her hands, carrying on a loud conversation for them concerning, Kate thought, swimming pools. The third child was of uncertain sex until it turned and they could see the gold loops in her ears. She was seated on the floor whining in a manner that indicated she had been there for quite a while, and that she had no real hope of being rescued anytime soon. Rani was crashing some pans into the sink, talking loudly in some jerky language that Kate thought might be Hindi. She did not seem to have an adult audience, but after a minute an elderly, stoop-shouldered woman came in from the next room with a couple of bowls. She stopped dead in the doorway and said something to the woman at the sink, who spun around as if she was being attacked. The two female children went silent in surprise, and even the oblivious Rajiv looked up from his books and blinked.

"I'm sorry to bother you, Mrs. Mehta," Kate said with a smile. "We've been talking with your husband and Laxman, and I wonder if we might have a word with you before we go. I'm Inspector Martinelli, this is Inspector Boyle."

Rani did not answer, but glanced across at the older woman as if in need of reassurance.

Boyle took a couple of steps over to where the boy was working. "Math?" he asked.

"Algebra," confirmed the boy.

"You must be Rajiv," Boyle said. "You're, what—thirteen?"

"Twelve," the boy corrected him shyly, looking pleased, and Kate recalled that Boyle had kids of his own.

"Does your mom speak English, Rajiv?"

"A little."

"She probably has trouble when she's surprised like this. Would you mind telling her what Inspector Martinelli said?"

Rajiv spoke to his mother, but even in translation their greeting did not seem to reassure her much.

"Rajiv, whenever there's a death like that of your aunt, we need to get a very clear idea of what was going on around the time she died. Could you ask your mother to tell us what—"

"You not bother the boy," Rani interrupted. "Rajiv, take your sisters upstairs."

"Just a minute, Rajiv," Boyle said as the boy obediently began to gather his books. "You were here, weren't you, that night?"

Rajiv nodded.

"Right here?"

Another nod.

"You were the first one to see the fire?"

Nod.

Kate walked over to glance out of the window beside the boy. From where he was seated, only the back half of the garden shed was visible—the fire would have been well and truly under way before he had seen it.

"Did you see anyone near your aunt's cook shed a little while before you saw the fire?"

"I was working," Rajiv told them. Having seen the boy's powers of concentration, Kate could well believe that a troop of mounted police could have ridden through the backyard without disturbing the scholar from his books.

"Go now, Rajiv," his mother said firmly, and waited while all three children left the room before she drew herself up to face the invading police.

Rani Mehta was a formidable woman, not tall but with rolls of brown flesh at the edges of her brilliant orange sari and its short flowered underblouse. She wore her hair in a heavy bun on the back of her head and had a dozen solid silver bracelets on her wrists like shackles. The red marriage mark on her forehead looked like a bleeding sore. Her features were heavy, her teeth strong and white, and she had a black mole on her face next to her nose. Not for the first time, Kate speculated about the attraction that the lithe young Pramilla might have had for her brother-in-law.

They discovered that the woman's understanding of their questions was pretty close to complete, and Kate recalled from someone's statement that Pramilla was accustomed to having the television on all day. Probably Rani did as well, which might also explain the paradox of her relatively clear understanding coupled with the difficulty she demonstrated in putting together an English sentence: A person does not generally carry on a two-way conversation with the TV.

"Mrs. Mehta," Boyle went on, "could you tell us please what you were doing that afternoon?"

"I cook," she said, looking down her slightly upturned nose at Kate as if understanding that this was a woman who neither cooked nor cared for children. "I made *mutter panir* and *dhal* and *kaju kari* and *brinjal* and two *chatnis*, and I was cooking the *parathas* when I heard Rajiv shout. I ran to get my husband in his room. He went to look, and then he call the fire."

"Do you know what Pramilla was doing in the cooking shed?"

The fat rolls shrugged. "Cooking. She take *panir*—cheese—to make *pakharas*. I say leave some for the *mutter panir*, she leave small piece. I think, oh well."

The colloquial expression sounded odd in the heavy accent, but neither detective smiled.

"What do you think happened, Mrs. Mehta?"

The woman pushed out her lower lip and gave a small eyebrow shrug. "I think she spill the hot oil into the fire. *Pakharas* is not for foolish girls to make."

"The, um, *pakharas* are cooked in hot oil?"

"Boiling oil," she said with relish. "Very boiling."

"I see. Well, thank you, Mrs. Mehta. We may want to speak with you again tomorrow, but we'll let you get on with your work."

Rani dried her hands on a towel and accompanied them to the front door—less, Kate thought, as a polite gesture than to ensure they did not poke into things on their way out. They thanked her again, and heard the lock turn behind them as they went down the front steps.

Boyle had driven, and would drop Kate home. As he put the car into forward, he said, "That woman is really something."

"She must have hated Pramilla the minute she set eyes on her. And to have the girl under the same roof as her husband. She might be a great cook and the mother of his children, but she was never a beauty."

"But Laxman loved the girl. Temper or no, he loved her."

Kate agreed; that bedroom shouted aloud the man's devotion, heaping beauteous objects on his wife. Yes, Laxman's extravagant grief had been real enough.

However, love went hand in hand with violence, as anyone who worked a domestic homicide could testify, and especially with the jealous knowledge of Pramilla's illicit conversations with other men riding in his mind. Grief in and of itself was no proof that Laxman's had not been the hand that knocked the girl down, any more than his disgust at her charred body could prove that he had not in rage or confusion or childish petulance splashed her with kerosene and set her alight.

No proof at all.

12

It is the time of burning, hate exposed.
We shall have to live with only Kali near.
She comes in her fury, early or late, disposed
To tantrums we have earned and must endure.

In the days that followed, Jimmy Larsen and Matty Banderas rode squarely in the center of Kate's sight, with Pramilla Mehta—who was, after all, Boyle's case—firmly pushed slightly off to one side, while on the periphery of her vision lurked all the other still-open cases, haunting the corners of her mind like so many cobwebbed gargoyles. A call from Janice Popper revealed that Matthew Banderas had made a pass at the manager of a software store, and when she had canceled their purchase contract, he had threatened to tell everyone that she was a lesbian. She just laughed and told him to go ahead, since it happened that she was. The woman also told Popper that she had been receiving an unusual number of wrong-number, dark-of-the-night phone calls and two whispered obscenities on her answering machine. None, incidentally, since Matthew Banderas had died.

One high point was a phone call from Martina Wiley, sounding like a cat at the cream. She practically purred as she told Kate that a rather firm interview with Melanie Gilbert had given them some prime hints not only about the Banderas sex life, which had been far kinkier than Gilbert had been willing to admit at first, but also led to a storage locker in Novato. It was currently being gone over with the finest-toothed combs in the Crime Scene repertoire, but it looked to be where Matty had stashed his rape souvenirs. His victims, and the police departments across the Bay Area, would begin to sleep more soundly.

On the Larsen homicide, a follow-up series of interviews at the airport turned up a fellow baggage handler who had run across Jimmy Larsen in a bar, and remembered Larsen mentioning sleep problems due to a strange woman calling in the middle of the night to hassle him. About what, he hadn't said, just that he was tired and fed up, but didn't want to leave the phone off the hook in case Emily phoned (his wife, he had hastened to tell his co-worker, was just off visiting her father, and would be home soon).

Kate worked long hours over the weekend, trekking south to the airport to question airport personnel, north of the bridge to talk to computer programmers, and closer to home to listen to the bereft and guilt-plagued Amanda Bonner.

On Monday, Kate had scheduled a few hours off to go with Lee, Roz, and Maj to see *Song*. They were to meet Jon there, and after the performance they would finally meet Sione, and have a late dinner together. However, the day's lack of any real progress meant a reluctance to call it quits, and at six o'clock Kate was still at her desk. When the phone rang, she knew who it would be before she picked it up, and indeed, Lee's voice came strongly over the line, demanding to know when Kate was planning to appear.

"I'm leaving in two minutes, honest," Kate pleaded, scribbling her signature on one report and reaching for the next.

"No, you're not. You are leaving right now."

"Yes, right now. As soon as I finish the—"

"Kate."

"Okay. I'm leaving. That's the sound of my desk drawer you hear. It's closing. I'm out the door."

"Now."

In three minutes Kate actually was heading out the

door when she was greeted by the startling sight of a slim woman being viciously assaulted by a burly man in the hallway right outside the homicide division, while a group of police officers, uniformed and plainclothes, looked on in nodding approval. Kate came to a sharp halt, then realized that the woman was actually a cop, and the man as well, and that the hard blows they were practicing were more noise than contact.

"What's this?" she asked a vice detective she had worked with on a couple of cases.

"Decoys. They're going to troll the parks tonight, see if we can get a bite from the LOPD when he starts slapping her around."

"Nice," she said. The woman of the antagonistic couple she now recognized as a patrol officer who had been twice commended for bravery, who had a black belt in some arcane form of martial art, spent her free time producing intricate oil paintings that sold for a small fortune, and loved life on the streets so much she refused to take the exams that she feared would move her up and behind a desk. At the moment, she looked remarkably like a suburban housewife.

"Makes for a change from playing a dealer or a hooker," the man from vice commented. Kate had to agree.

On the way home, however, she had time to reflect on the assumptions behind the scene she had witnessed. Without a doubt, fear was growing among the men of the city—ironic, that those normally most secure in the streets at night were those who were feeling an unaccustomed discomfort in the hours of darkness. The City's night life was suffering, its all-important tourist trade threatened, and if the quiet night streets made life easier for those responsible for patrolling them, the economic dip added to the fears felt by half the population meant that the pressure was on. At times like these, Kate was very glad she was not one of the brass.

Kate came through her front door at a trot, shedding equipment and clothing as she went, aware of Lee's disapproval floating up the stairs and following her into the shower. Kate's clothes were laid out for her, black silk pants and blouse with an elaborately embroidered vest to go on top. The shoes were as close to heels as she would wear, her hair was too short to worry about, and she even took thirty seconds to swipe some makeup across her eyelids. All terribly civilized, Kate thought, trotting down the stairs again and out to the street, where Lee waited in the passenger seat of Kate's car, pointedly studying her watch.

"You look delicious," Kate told her, kissed her, and turned the key in the ignition.

Mollified, either by the compliment or by the speed with which Kate had dressed, Lee's irritation subsided. They were going out for the evening, and Kate could feel Lee decide that she'd be damned if she would let even her own righteous indignation get in the way of pleasure.

Lee did look delicious in a shimmering gold blouse and loose white crepe pants. Jon wore velvet, Maj looked as majestic as a sailing ship, and Roz, though she swept in late, puffing and apologetic, was dressed in festive formality rather than a power suit and minister's collar.

The night before, Kate had braved Lee's study to refresh her memory of the Song of Songs, that Old Testament book attributed to Solomon (he of the many wives) that she remembered as being endearingly erotic, filled with odd descriptions of breasts like gazelles and cheeks like pomegranates. Lee had apparently had the same idea, because the Bible lay open on her desk. Kate sat down to read. Ten minutes later she closed the soft leather covers, vaguely disquieted. Erotic, yes, but some of the passages were also puzzling, others almost troubling. Perhaps, she thought, Roz was right, that more than the words had changed when the Bible was rendered into English. Certainly a reader was left with the distinct impression of various translators along the way tidying up and applying generous quantities of whitewash, and that underneath their quaint images lay a fairly explicit picture of ancient sex.

In *Song*, the whitewash had been pretty thoroughly scrubbed away.

When the women entered the small theater to take their seats beside Jon, the lights were dim, the buzz of anticipation damped down under the sensation that the performance was already beginning—as indeed it was, for on a platform raised up over the right side of the stage sat three figures dressed in white. They perched there motionless, their heads bent, but the audience was very aware of them and incomers took to their seats with hushed conversation and wary glances upward. Kate looked at the program and saw that the two main characters would be "Lover," played by someone called Kamsin Neale, and "Beloved," the part played by Sione Kalefu.

The set, as Maj had said the other night at dinner, was striking. Black dominated, punctuated by draped lengths of intensely colored net fabric, gold and ruby and lapis curtains against the dark. Some were supple, drifting and changing colors with the currents of air. Others were static, rigid as frozen flames leaping up from the stage to disappear into the hidden heights. The small overhead spots picked them out as clouds of sheer color, some of which sparkled as if they had been sprinkled with finely ground rubies and emeralds and sapphires. The set was both stark and sumptuous, empty and powerful.

The seats gradually filled, the anticipatory hush intensified, and the three figures crouched on the raised platform might have been statues. Finally came movement, as five black-clad men and women filed across the stage from the right, came down the short flight of steps on the left that led to the orchestra pit, and took up a peculiar variety of instruments: oboe, viola, drums and an assortment of bells and percussion objects, an electronic keyboard, and a sitar. They spent a few minutes tuning this unlikely chamber orchestra, the weird atonality of the notes mingling slowly until a sort of music came out, and then the instruments fell silent, and the audience slowly became aware that at some point the actors had entered the stage.

Song was a story, much more of a narrative than what Kate had read in Lee's black Bible. The two main characters, who in the original had been heterosexual lovers, were in this production both profoundly androgynous, to the extent that it took Kate a good twenty minutes to decide that Lover, the big muscular one dressed in reds and oranges, was played by the woman Kamsin, while the slim, dark, pursued character in blue—Beloved—was actually Jon's new friend Sione.

The viola began, to be joined a short time later by a throaty voice from the seated trio above, reciting the words of the Song of Solomon. "O that you would kiss me with the kisses of your mouth," the voice murmured, and the two dancers began to move slowly around each other, becoming acquainted, flirting, moving apart, glancing back at each other, until finally they came together in an exploratory embrace. Lee's fingers crept into Kate's in the dark, caressing palm and wrist, playing under the silken cuff of Kate's blouse. Kate shivered at the scrape of Lee's nail, and could feel Lee beside her smiling into the dark.

Other dancers swirled onstage and off: Beloved's disapproving brothers, Lover's friends, but each time the pair shook the others loose and returned to their increasingly passionate self-absorption. "Black am I, and beautiful," chanted the three narrators. "Sustain me with raisin cakes, strengthen me with apples, for I am faint with love." Beloved's brothers stormed in, angrily trying to separate them, but the two lovers slipped behind a cloud of glowing red voile, and were safely lost in each other again.

The dancing grew more intense, the music wilder. To a quickening beat, the pair on the stage caught up lengths of crimson and cobalt gauze that swirled about them, first concealing, then revealing (and going far to explain the production's X rating). The flurry of colors came to a climax in a rush of atonal music, and then breathlessly subsided. The spotlights dimmed on the entwined figures, the voices grew to drowsy murmurs. ("When the day breathes out and the shadows grow, turn to me, my love, like a buck, like a young stag on the mountains.")

The lights fell further, until the stage was dark and utterly silent. The silence held for a dozen or more heartbeats, broken only by a cough from the audience, and then a faint light flickered and grew off to the right, a beam that illuminated a section of wall and a single figure, lying alone in a heap: Beloved. Sione stirred, stretched languorously, and then rose, looking around with growing agitation for Lover. The distraught figure snatched up a small lamp, using it to search the room, and then burst through an opening in the prop wall and directly into the arms of a troop of uniformed guards. The voices identified them as "guards of the city, armed and trained against the terrors of night," but instead of protecting (and indeed, though clothed in khaki, one of them bore a startling resemblance to the burly cop Kate had seen at the Hall of Justice, preparing to "beat" his "wife" as bait for the night's avenging Ladies), the guards seized Beloved, began to laugh and pluck at the diaphanous blue garments. The voices for Beloved pleaded with the guards, asking them to say if they had seen Lover, but the guards merely laughed, and reached out, until Beloved twisted away from them and escaped.

Immediately, Lover appeared from offstage. Beloved flung "herself" at the strong figure, who wrapped strong arms around Beloved and snatched "her" away into a room. The two lovers embraced, but the note of the oboe, which had dominated the scene with the guards, remained, quiet and disquieting, in the background of the scenes that followed.

The reunited lovers, surrounding themselves with armed and uniformed soldiers of their own, retreated in safety and triumph to an enclosed garden, a womblike bower of shimmering green where they sang and danced and fed each other morsels of fruit until the night grew up to hide them, and silence fell.

For a second time, lamplight flared in the dark; again

the solitary figure reached for Lover, and again set out
to search; and this time, too, the five guards were waiting. But unlike the first harassment, Beloved did not slip
away. In utter, appalled silence the audience gaped as
the khaki-clad figures brutally tossed the slim blue one
back and forth between themselves, accompanied by
the oboe, the sitar, and the panicky heartbeat drum of
the tabla. The harsh whispers of the narrators and the
inarticulate cries of Sione punctuated the texture of
sound:

> The guards found me
>   They who patrol the city.

the narrators sang.

> They hit me.
> They hurt me.
> They stripped me.
>   The guards.

Over and over the last four lines were chanted, faster
and faster. The guards sprouted gray and black and
khaki veils, and Beloved sank down beneath a swirl of
obscuring darkness; one slim blue arm emerged in protest from the huddle, and was overcome. One by one
the guards detached themselves and stormed offstage,
boots beating on the floorboards, leaving behind them a
half-nude figure, heaped up beneath a drift of drab
cloth.

After a while, a stir came from the wings, and in
washed a flock of five giggling girls wearing the bright-
est of colors who emerged startlingly, almost painfully
from the dark. The abused figure pushed laboriously
upright, and made an effort to rearrange hair, pull together clothing, and pluck away the gray and khaki
shrouds. The girls came up, laughing and teasing, to
inquire where Lover had gone; Beloved asked them, in a
hoarse, faltering voice, if they would help look for
Lover. Completely oblivious of their friend's suffering,

the five colorful figures danced and primped and gossiped about Lover's charms, speculating teasingly about where Lover might have gone, and with whom. Desperately, Beloved reached up to seize an apricot-colored skirt, and cried out:

I beg you, girls of Jerusalem,
If you find my love,
  What will you tell him?
Tell him . . .

(Beloved's voice drifted off, and the five girls paused, paying attention at last and waiting for their companion to continue. Finally, the distraught figure in blue climbed slowly upright, swayed, straightened, and continued.)

Tell him . . . I am sick with love.

With that phrase, in swept Lover, as heedless of Beloved's distress as the girls had been, and flung strong arms around half-bare shoulders. Beloved cried out, in pain or in pleasure, but then to cover it up, began again to praise Lover, to flirt and act the coy and lighthearted one. All the while the oboe continued to sound its plaintive note, while the audience wondered when Lover would wake up to the realization that something was desperately wrong, would find out what had taken place and rise up in fury to take revenge on the guards.

Night fell again on the embracing couple, with no moment of revelation. The third lighting of lamps came, and a figure lying alone on the stage. This time, however, it was not the slim figure of Beloved who woke alone, but the strong one, Lover, waking alone in the warm and flickering light. But before Lover could do more than sit up and glance about, rubbing a sleepy eye in puzzlement, Beloved erupted back onto the stage, whirling like a dervish, like a small blue tornado, leaping and shouting over the quick beat of the music and holding up some object before her in triumph and adoration. Only when the dance brought Beloved to the very front of the stage, dropping down on both knees to face them, did the audience see clearly the object being held up: a dagger, gleaming silver and stained with blood. Beloved lifted it high, shouting in exultation, paused a moment with it in both hands, then drove the shining knife into the boards of the stage before whirling around again to face the still-seated Lover.

You are beautiful

said Lover, sounding a bit dubious.

You are as lovely as Jerusalem,
You are . . .
You are . . .
  You are terrible,

(Lover whispered, drawing back from Beloved, as the realization struck)

Terrible as an army with banners.
Turn your eyes away
  they disturb me.
But . . .
But your hair . . .
Your hair flows
  like a flock of goats
  spilling down the side of Mount Gilead.

Torn between these sudden, conflicting visions of Beloved, Lover shifted away while at the same time holding one hand outstretched.

Who is this that comes like the dawn
  Fair as the moon,
  Bright as the sun,
  Terrible as an army with banners?

Beloved rose and walked slowly over to Lover, leaving
the bloody knife quivering in the stage, and then solved
Lover's dilemma by dropping down, knee to knee, and
bringing their mouths together in a kiss.

"Love is stronger than death," chanted the voices as
the light dimmed over the embracing couple. "Passion
fiercer than hell, it starts flaming . . ."

The last thing to be seen on the stage as the light
dimmed was the dagger, silver and red in the narrow
spotlight.

"Whoa," said Kate uncertainly when the clapping had
eventually died and the curtain calls ended.

"My God," exclaimed Roz. "That was superb. Dramatically and theologically, to say nothing of psycho-
logically. And the virgin's dance with the dagger! I
wouldn't have thought—"

"*Virgin?*" Kate asked in disbelief. "You think that
girl was meant to be a virgin after all that?"

"Not *virgo intacta*," Roz said dismissively. "The
warrior-virgin, a goddess archetype. What an interpretation—straight out of Pope."

Kate was completely lost. She could not begin to
imagine what the pope could have to do with this particular version of the Song of Songs, but she could see
that Roz was not about to pause and explain. She
looked as exultant as the man/woman on stage had
been, her eyes dark with several kinds of arousal, the
enthusiasm coming off her in waves. Kate knew her
well enough to see that there would be no rational explanations until her passion had subsided—at which
time there would probably be more rational explanation than Kate actually wanted. Still, Roz was a pleasure to watch, and her excitement was contagious.

Then the pager in Kate's pocket began to throw itself
about furiously, if silently. Lee heard her exclamation
of disgust, turned to look at her, and diagnosed the
problem in an instant.

"You're being buzzed?"

In answer Kate fished the little thing out and shut it off. The number it displayed was that of Al and Jani, and she could only squeeze Lee's hand in apology, turn her over to Jon yet again, and (because she was not on call and Lee had pointedly refused to bring her own cell phone) go searching for a pay phone. She stood in the lobby with one finger pushed against her free ear and the receiver jammed up to the other, half shouting to be heard above the departing audience.

"Is that Jules? Oh, Jani—hi. Al paged me. What? I can't— He's where? Hold on just a second." She fished out a pen and a scrap of paper. "What was that address again? Okay. Right. But we're not on call, did he tell you why they called us? It's *who*? Oh, Christ. God damn it. Oh, I'm sorry, Jani. Thanks for the message, I'll probably get there before he does. Say hi to Jules for me."

Kate hung up and stood for a long moment with her hand still tight around the receiver, her eyes shut. Fury and confusion and dread all pushed at her, and useless self-criticism, but above all came sorrow, for the loss of such a thing of beauty.

Laxman Mehta had been found in an alley behind a bar in the Castro.

Dead.

Strangled.

And wearing handcuffs.

13

We have to listen to the harsh undertow
To reach the place where Kali can bestow.

The fading colors and images of the dance she had just seen jostled in her mind with the reality of what Kate was seeing. It was night here, too, the alley dark and filled up with flitting, shifting shadows, and there were the uniformed guards of the city's peace, moving about the alley as if it was a narrow stage depicting gritty, urban life. Her imaginary song of the city was as ominous as any of the oboe's notes, and the setting considerably uglier. All it needed was a bloody knife sticking out of the alleyway.

Kate shook her head to clear it of fantasy. No knife here, no theological speculation about virgin goddesses, no costumes and beautiful sets. Just brutal death, and a crowd of people. The ops center seemed to have pulled out all the stops on this one, and called in everyone from foot patrol to the lieutenant. Most of the personnel were standing around with nothing to do, since a scene had to be worked in sequence. Press photographers snapped away at the teams leaning against the wall and laughing, and she sent a uniform over to have the technicians take their waiting out of sight. Then Kate went forward to look at the body.

A person would never know that this had been a beautiful male creature. ("Black am I, and beautiful" echoed in Kate's ears in painful contrast to the swollen-tongued, dark-faced figure at her feet.) Between the distortion and suffusion of the strangulation and the postmortem trauma of being (apparently) dragged and kicked, the only thing Laxman Mehta looked like was dead.

She did not even bother to pull back the remains of his shirt to look for a taser burn. It was possible that an experienced pathologist in a brightly lit morgue would be able to pick out the difference between one slightly red area and another, but Kate couldn't, and certainly not in a dark alley.

The flash of cameras and a raised chorus of voices from the street made her look around to see Al Hawkin letting himself through the screens Kate had ordered put up. Nothing like a body behind a Castro district leather bar to pique the interest of readers over their morning coffee.

"You must've driven like a maniac," she greeted Al.

"Got lucky with traffic. Was the press here when you arrived?"

"Yeah, but the foot patrol had them under control. No scene contamination except for the guys who found him."

"Talked to them yet?"

"They're inside with the patrol. I told him to get them some coffee. Kitagawa caught this one. I guess he's the one who called you?"

With the possibility of a serial killer on their hands, word had been spread throughout the Bay Area that any dead male who had been strangled, showed taser marks, or had a history of abuse against women should be brought to their attention. She and Al had decided to keep the tenuous link of candy in the victims' pockets to themselves for the moment. Leaks were all too common, and it was good to sit on one mark of the killer—if mark it was.

"Yeah. I told him we'd assist. He said he'd get Crime Scene started here, then go tell the family and seal the guy's rooms until they can get over there." Al dropped his voice further. "You look at the pockets yet?"

"The ME did. Didn't find any candy exactly, but he found a little plastic bag of something that looked like seeds and stuff."

"Seeds? Like sensemilla, you mean?"

"More like caraway or something—and some little colored thingies mixed in with it. Like those sprinkles you put on top of kids' birthday cakes, you know?"

Al shrugged his shoulders. "Doesn't sound much like caramel chews and chocolate bars to me, but we'll see what the lab says. Are they about finished here?"

"I think so." Kate signaled that the body could be bagged and taken away, and walked with Al toward the kitchen entrance of the bar. "Al, one thing. You didn't meet him, but that was one gorgeous young man when he was alive."

"Why, Martinelli, I didn't know you cared."

"I'm not interested, Al, but I'm not blind. I remember thinking at the time that he'd cause a riot in a place like this."

A stranger might be excused from thinking there was already a riot going on inside. It occurred to Kate that the insulation in the walls and windows must have cost a pretty sum; from the outside all she had heard was the muffled hum of a beehive with an underlying thudding sound of a beating heart. Inside, Al had to shout in her ear to be heard.

"Is Kitagawa still here?"

"He's gone to notify the family," she shouted in return. "He said he'd bring back a photo."

The bar was just what the Christian Right had in mind when it referred to the hellfire sins of San Francisco, Sodom-by-the-Bay. Had one of their straight-ace photographers made it inside the door, he could have shot a random roll that would have scared the socks off Middle America and made them join in fervent prayer for an earthquake along the San Andreas Fault.

Kate, though, had no problems with the place. Were it not for the stink of sweaty males with booze and controlled substances oozing from their pores, she might even have enjoyed it, if for nothing more than the display (using the word in more than one sense) of black leather fashions and the impressive creativity of the human male when it came to threading sharp metal objects through parts of his anatomy. Put one of those gigantic car-lifting magnets in the ceiling and switch it on, she reflected, and half the men here would slap up against it, spread-eagled like flies on a windshield.

"What are you grinning at, Martinelli?" Al yelled in her ear. She just shook her head and pushed forward toward the bar.

There were two men working, expertly banging down full glasses and change with one hand and scooping up empties and money with the other, bantering at the top of their lungs with the customers and singing occasional snatches of music with the recorded cacophony belting out of the speakers. Kate, the only woman in the place as far as she could see, leaned against the corner of the polished wood and waited for the nearer bartender to approach. When he did, she flipped open her badge holder to identify herself and in one smooth movement the man's hamlike hand shot out and folded the ID shut and back into her palm before anyone noticed it.

He leaned across the bar at her. "You want to shut the place, Martinelli, or you want to talk to me?"

Kate drew back to study his face and realized that she knew him—or at least, she'd met him. She thought.

"Dimitri?" The man who had passed through her kitchen some months before, working on some project with Lee and Jon, had left her with the impression of a retired wrestler in a tweed jacket, not this slab of muscle glued into a garment that was more than half missing. He had also been lighter by about six ounces of surgical steel, some of which Kate had to deduce by the shapes of the hoops and bumps under the sleek leather. He grinned at her with perfect white teeth and pulled up the top of the bar to let himself out. Nodding amiably at Hawkin behind Kate's shoulder, the bartender paused to swat a willowy figure on one half-protruding and nicely shaped buttock and, when his victim whirled around, Dimitri jerked his thumb in the direction of the huge mirror in back of the bar. The shapely man extricated himself from his companions and made for the service side of the bar, leaving Dimitri to push his way through the crowded room with Kate and Al Hawkin on his heels.

The office was also heavily insulated, and a relief. He waved them to a tight circle of half a dozen chairs and continued on through a narrow door, leaving it ajar so he could talk.

"You're here about that boy in the alley?" he called to them.

"You know anything about it, Dimitri?"

"Only that two of my customers stepped out for a breath of air and had the shock of their lives. Your nice patrolman took them home, by the way—one of them couldn't stop crying and began to need his asthma inhaler. I have their address for you."

The sound of running water stopped, followed by a soft pop followed by a slick rubbing noise. Dimitri came out, drying his face in a towel and smelling of deodorant. Kate made the introductions, she and Al both shook the man's nice clean hand, and then he dropped into a chair, swiveling it around to open a tiny refrigerator at his knee. He pulled out a bottle of mineral water, offered them a drink (which both refused), and unscrewed the cap to empty half the bottle down his throat in a series of muscular gulps.

"Sorry," he said when he came up again for air. "Gets hot in there. What can I do for you?"

"Do you know the man who was found in the alley?"

"I didn't go look at him, just saw him for a second from the kitchen door before I was shoved back inside, but he didn't look familiar. Do you know who it was?"

"His name was Laxman Mehta."

"Indian? No, I think I would've noticed an Indian.

We don't get too many in here—they tend to be a little . . . conservative."

"You'd certainly have noticed this one. Five six, slim, soft brown skin, long eyelashes, high cheekbones. Like a doe on two legs. Looked about sixteen, was actually in his late twenties."

Dimitri raised his eyebrows. "I couldn't have missed the effect he would have had on the place."

"You don't think he was in here, then?"

"Was he into the leather scene?"

"I shouldn't think so. I don't even think he was gay."

"A waste," Dimitri commented.

"Are you the owner here, Mr. . . . ?" Hawkin spoke up, trying for the Russian's surname, but defeated before he began. A massive arm waved away the attempt.

"Nobody can say my last name. That's why I chose it—I was born Travers. Call me Dimitri. And yes, I'm the owner—or, me and the bank anyway."

"Are you here most of the time?"

"Six days a week, opening to closing. We're shut Sundays. Remember the Sabbath, to keep it holy."

Hawkin peered at the man to see if he was serious, and decided he was joking, but Kate vaguely remembered that Dimitri had been a devout member of the Russian Orthodox Church. Hawkin continued. "And you didn't hear anything in the alleyway? Sounds of a fight, say, or a car engine?"

"I was out there earlier, dumping the garbage, and after that things got busy. And before you ask, no, he wasn't there when I went out."

"When would that have been?"

"Let's see. Definitely after six 'cause the news I watch was over, but before six-fifteen. Can't get closer than that."

Kate checked her notes: The first call to 911 had come in at 8:42. She'd been buzzed about forty-five minutes later, and it was now nearly tomorrow.

"Do you get many women in here?" Kate asked without much hope. Whether they were LOPD Ladies or simply women, a female would stand out in Dimitri's.

"Did you see many? Oh, we get a few, mostly they drop in on a dare, sometimes they come in with friends. They don't stay. And I don't remember any tonight."

"Can you give us a list of your customers' names, Dimitri? Anyone who would have been here between six and eight-thirty?"

"God, you don't ask for much, do you? You know, the best thing would be to come back tomorrow night and ask them yourselves. Weekdays like this, my guys tend to be regulars, especially that early in the evening. Then I could give you some names, they could give you others, you'd get a more complete list."

"You don't mind having your . . . patrons questioned?" Al asked him.

"I stopped your partner flashing her badge because this time of night's an entirely different crowd, and they won't have heard about the killing yet. By tomorrow they'll all know, and even if your man wasn't gay, he sounds pretty enough that a passing gay-basher would have assumed he was. You'll find my customers'll be willing to help, especially the early crowd. They're more, I suppose you could call it family-oriented."

" 'Family-oriented,' " Al repeated.

"Do you have a problem with my place of business?" demanded the big man, his eyebrows coming together. "Because if so, maybe it'd be better if Martinelli came back alone."

"Problem? No, I don't have any problems with your bar or its clientele. It just seems so . . ." Al paused to consider his word, while Dimitri's shoulders bulged menacingly and Kate prepared to duck. "So old-fashioned."

Dimitri's muscles deflated comically. "So *what*?"

"Quaint, I suppose. I mean, you almost expect to be issued a towel at the door."

He blinked blandly at Dimitri, who finally decided that his leg was being pulled, and gave a great bellow of laughter. He slapped Al affectionately on the shoulder, nearly shooting him off the chair.

" 'Old-fashioned,' " he said, chuckling. "I like that. But yeah, you know, a place like this really is about as close to the old bathhouse energy as you're going to get in this day and age. You could say I'm helping my people find their roots." He laughed again, hugely amused, and Kate and Al left him to a contemplation of his quaint and old-fashioned leather-bound and metal-studded customers.

The two detectives paused on the bar's back step to look over the taped-off alley, waiting for the light of day to search for its forensic secrets. After a minute Kate snorted.

"God, Al, I thought you were going to insult that guy and I'd have to peel you off the wall. 'Quaint,' yet."

"Well, sure. Places like this are so nineteenth-century, they're positively archaic. Wealthy male aristocrats with a taste for being spanked go to private clubs where they can dress up in uncomfortable clothing and masks for a bit of anonymous fun and then go home to their regular lives. Hell, the Victorians even invented the nipple ring."

Looking at the side of his face in the half-light spilling into the alleyway, Kate could not tell if he was making a joke or if he meant it.

In either case, it was an interpretation of leather bars that had never before occurred to Kate, and she made a mental note to try it out on Lee. And Jon.

14

But she must have her dreadful empire first
Until the prisons of the mind are broken free
And every suffering center at its worst
Can be appealed to her dark mystery.

Dimitri's two customers had seen nothing and no one when they set off on their shortcut through the alley, except for Laxman's body, which they nearly stepped on. The men were a longtime couple, a month past their tenth anniversary, and the younger one, the one gripping the asthma inhaler as a talisman, had never seen anything like it before. His older partner seemed more resigned, certainly less shocked, which made sense when he told them that he had spent two years as a medic in Vietnam.

They had not noticed anyone out of the ordinary in the hour or so they had been in Dimitri's, and certainly no women. The older man thought he had seen a car drive out of the end of the alley, something boxy and light in color, but he couldn't swear to it because just then his partner had stumbled and screamed at what lay at his feet. When asked, they worked out a list of who had been there at the same time. Many of the names were less than helpful, since they consisted of nicknames like Studly and Dragon (for metalwork and a tattoo, respectively), but Dimitri would no doubt be able to translate them, and the task cheered the asthmatic up considerably.

Kitagawa called them to say that Peter Mehta was

too upset to talk to them that night and that his wife had already taken her sleeping pill and gone to bed. Kitagawa had reluctantly agreed to return the next day, and wondered if Kate and Al considered a watch on the house necessary. They decided it was not. In the meantime, Kitagawa would take the photograph of Laxman he had gotten from Peter and leave it to be copied overnight, to help their neighborhood canvass.

When they got back to Dimitri's they found that even the media had packed up their cameras and returned to their beds, leaving the Castro to its family-oriented residents and the few late-night denizens whose voices echoed down the thinly populated streets as they walked off beneath the street lamps, leaving behind that remnant of a free-and-easy, pre-AIDS past called Dimitri's.

"You want a bed?" Kate asked her partner, who was looking at a forty-minute drive home. Plus, with the Laxman killing, it was time to upgrade the task force: an early-morning meeting had been called, a long-overdue gathering of all the disparate law enforcement individuals concentrating on the series of killings, including the feds. Al would want to be alert for that, and had taken her up on such offers a number of times before, since marrying Jani and giving up his apartment in San Francisco. He even kept a clean shirt and a razor in the guest room.

"I don't know. Jani worries."

"Send her an e-mail, or fax." This too had been done before, to let Jani know where he was without waking her.

"Yeah, I guess I could. Thanks."

He followed her across town to the silent house on Russian Hill, joined her in a sandwich and some unfocused and low-voiced conversation in the kitchen, and then they both fell into their beds for the luxury of five unbroken hours of sleep.

The two detectives dressed with care in the morning, checking shirt-fronts for old stains and hair for stray tufts. They walked into a room which held one lieutenant, one captain, one secretary, Detectives Boyle and Kitagawa from Homicide and Deaver from the LOPD task force, a large pot of fresh coffee, a plate of doughnuts, and an unknown figure whose reputation preceded him, the local FBI agent Benjamin Marcowitz. He was known as Marc to his very few friends, Benny to his numerous enemies, and the Man in Black to most of the people who worked with and for him, both for his habitual choice of dark suit and for his resemblance to a slimmer, younger Tommy Lee Jones in the movie of that name.

Kate had never seen an FBI agent who more precisely resembled the caricature straight-faced, straitlaced, clean-cut male in the suit. All he needed was a coil of wire emerging from his ear to complete the picture. Marcowitz's handshake was the least expressive touch of flesh she had ever experienced: It might have been a leather glove filled with sand.

Despite first impressions, however, he was not as bad as he might have been. At this point, he made clear, he was prepared to run a more or less parallel operation, concentrating on the national search for similar killings and on providing manpower, backup, and coordination for the SFPD. He was, in a word, altogether too reasonable, and the locals eyed him warily.

To Kate's astonishment, a brief smile appeared on his face, then vanished. "In the past," he told the room, "the Bureau has generated a lot of ill will by its tendency to take over cases that might be better handled by the local police departments. We're actually better used in assistance, on regional cases. I don't want to get grabby, and I'll do my best to give you anything we come up with. I hope that works the other way, as well."

Eyebrows were raised at this innovation of an FBI running interference instead of carrying the ball, but it was a nice thought.

In a short time, decisions were made and responsibilities divided up. Having three teams of detectives related to this one case meant tying up practically the entire SFPD homicide detail, and once the tasers brought in the Ladies task force as well, it was clearly time to sort things out. Kitagawa had taken the Laxman Mehta call, but Pramilla's death—which was Boyle's case—was clearly a consideration, and over them all was the possible link with Al and Kate's serial. At the end of the meeting it had been agreed that, in order to streamline matters, Al and Kate would be the primaries on this one, with Kitagawa and Boyle feeding them information so as not to do everything twice and with Marcowitz kept up-to-date so that, if the time came for the feds to take what he called "a more active role," there would be no delay. The FBI, in the meantime, would turn its mighty mind to the problem of the Ladies, although whether it would give them what it found was anyone's guess. Kitagawa, on the other hand, was the very essence of cooperation, having printed off multiple copies of his notes from the night before (typically enough, typed neatly and thoroughly legible), including the brief preliminary interview with Peter Mehta. Laxman's rooms on the upper floor had been sealed off for them, and for the crime scene team, if necessary.

The morning was fairly thoroughly gone by the time Kate and Al drove off through a light rain to interview Peter Mehta. Speaking over the rhythm of the windshield wipers and the blowing defogger, Al said, "You've met Mehta; how do you want to handle him?"

"He's definitely a man's man. You'd better start on the questions, I'll jump in when it's time to make him uncomfortable."

"Thought of anything else I should know?" They had spent a couple of hours, not only that morning but the night before, reviewing what Kate knew of the case and its chronology. She thought about what she had already told him, and what she had not.

"Did I mention the thought that there could have been something between Peter and Pramilla? Not that I have anything concrete, just my naturally suspicious mind. She was very pretty and he's very full of himself. At the very least, he found her attractive."

"Jealous of Laxman, you think?"

"Who in turn may have picked up on it, and bashed his wife. Just something to keep in mind. Of course, there's also the fact that Laxman resented his wife's talking to men on one of her outings. It was the cause of one of his beatings. It could have led to him doing her in."

"Which would make it very likely that Laxman was one of our Ladies' serials. Was there anyone in particular that she was 'talking to'?"

"It's on my list of things to find out. I thought I'd give Amanda Bonner a call later today."

"What about Mehta's wife, Rani? Did you get the sense that she suspected something between her husband and her sister-in-law?"

"She's a puzzle. Far too much of a wife-and-mother for me to get much out of her, and her English isn't good enough to get much subtlety out of it. If there was something—*if*—she'd be aware of it. How could she not be, all under the same roof? But I will say that according to Roz's material on bride burning, it's usually the mother-in-law—which in this case would be Rani—who is most involved in dowry harassment."

"Really?"

"Ironic, isn't it? So much for the solidarity of the oppressed."

When they arrived at the Mehta house, they discovered that it would have been redundant to park a uniformed at the curb: The place was awash with media. They had to push their way through to the two uniforms who were trying to keep the reporters out of the rosebushes. Three women in rain parkas carrying hand-lettered signs reading CHILDREN ARE NOT FOR MARRYING walked back and forth in front of the next-door neighbor's house, which was as close as they could get to their target. Al mounted the front steps and, before pushing the doorbell, asked the uniformed how it was going.

"Oh, fine sir. It was a little crazy about an hour ago when he came out to talk to the reporters, but some of 'em left after that. Wish it would rain harder."

"You mean Mehta? He made a statement?"

"Yes sir. Right here on the steps. I had some job keeping them from following him inside afterward."

"What did he say?"

"That he and his family were being 'hounded,' that was his word, by a bunch of women who had no understanding of Hindu customs or sensitivities. That was more or less what he said."

Hawkin glanced at Kate grimly. "Did he name names?"

"Not directly. Although he had a quiet word with one or two of the reporters, I didn't hear what he told them."

"I guess there's nothing we can do about it now. Anything you need out here?"

"We're going to be going off in a while, they'll send replacements."

"Okay. Well, thanks." He rang the bell and, after the peephole darkened momentarily and the locks were slid noisily back, they stepped into the besieged Mehta house and followed Peter Mehta into his study.

Kate introduced Al Hawkin, and then as they had agreed, she sat down and faded into the background. "Mr. Mehta," Al began. "Could you please tell us what happened last night?"

"What do you mean, 'what happened'? My brother was killed, is what happened. Foully murdered and his body left in a—a corrupt and disgusting place, and his murderer walks the streets of San Francisco with impunity."

Kate suppressed a tug of amusement at Mehta's flowery language. She was well aware that many of the city's ethnic minorities tended more toward histrionics when confronted with tragedy than did the Anglo-Saxons (she herself, after all, came from an Italian family), although she was mildly surprised at the dramatic response of Peter Mehta, who previously had seemed as

American as they came. Apparently his American skin was thin in places. He was on his feet now, pacing the carpeted floor of his study, his hands playing restlessly over his lapels, buttons, the backs of furniture, and each other.

"Sir," Al was saying patiently, "we need to question everyone who came in contact with your brother last night."

Mehta came to a halt and turned to Hawkin, affronted. "You would question *me*?" His lilting accent was stronger now, such was his perturbation.

"We are questioning everyone, sir. Now—"

"My wife? You would question her?"

"Yes, when we're fin—"

"And the children, perhaps? Will you question my son Indrapal who is not yet two years old concerning the foul murder of his uncle? Why are you not out there searching for these female animals who are killing the men of our city? Why do you come and torment the suffering family? This is intolerable!"

"Sir," Hawkin said sharply. "Each death must be treated individually. Even if your brother's murder is related to someone else's, it is distinct. You're a sensible man, Mr. Mehta. Surely you can see that we have to begin at the beginning, to trace your brother's last movements, and to do that we have to question the people who were closest to him. Do you have any objections to that?"

Abruptly, Mehta subsided. "No," he said, and retreated to his chair behind the desk. "No, of course I don't. I'm just . . . It is all most upsetting. I was fond of my little brother. He was not an easy person, but I did my best to love him and care for him. And now this. *Achcha,*" he said, and then drew himself together. "You wish to know where we were last night. I worked in this study until eleven o'clock. My wife worked in the kitchen with the servant, Lali, and then Lali left and Rani put the children to bed at nine o'clock. She was asleep by the time I went up, and I was asleep myself twenty minutes later. I did not see Laxman all evening, although his lights were on. They usually are."

"Do you know why your brother was in the Castro district last night? Was he meeting a friend, perhaps?"

"My brother had no friends. He had his family, and until a week ago he had his wife."

"I understand that he and his wife were very close."

"He worshiped her," Mehta declared fiercely, although Kate thought that was not exactly the same thing.

"Do you think your brother killed his wife?" Al asked bluntly. Too bluntly, because Mehta turned his swivel chair around to look out the window at the slowing rain.

"I don't want to think that, no," he said after a while.

"But you think it possible?"

Mehta did not answer. Hawkin left it for the moment.

"When did you last see your brother?"

"In the afternoon, I went up to his rooms to see if I could persuade him to come down and eat dinner with the family. He had not done so since the girl died."

"You mean he stayed up in his rooms all the time?"

"During the day."

"But at night . . . ?"

Mehta gave a deep sigh. "I do not know, but I think he went out at night. My wife thought she heard him come in early one morning, and two days ago I found the front door unlatched when I went out for the newspaper."

"Where would he go?"

"My God, who would know? He had no friends, he didn't drive. Where is there to walk to here?"

Kate could have listed half a dozen late-night hot spots less than half an hour from the house by foot, including Dimitri's leather bar, but neither she nor Al chose to enlighten the man. Instead, Hawkin asked him, "Did your brother have his own phone line?"

"No, just an extension of the family line."

"Would you have heard an incoming phone call during the night?"

"Of course."

"In that case, I'll need to see a printout of the calls made on your number since your sister-in-law died." It would save another round of search warrant forms if Mehta were willing to provide the records—but he was already nodding in agreement.

"I'll ask the phone company for one."

"What about phone calls this last week, Mr. Mehta? Any threatening calls, hang-ups, wrong numbers at strange hours?"

Mehta nodded vigorously. "Two. We had two after Pramilla died." He was using her name now, Kate noted. "Women, both of them. I hung up on them. And told my wife and children not to answer the phone, to let the answering machine take it. There have been a lot of hang-ups on the recorder."

The two detectives were silent for a minute, wondering if they ought to have known, if they should have put a tracer on the line as soon as they had a man fitting their profile of victim. Could they have foreseen the threat to Laxman Mehta, and prevented his death? Or would they have had to be psychic to guess?

"Your brother's income, Mr. Mehta," Al asked. "Did he have his own bank account, charge cards, ATM card, that sort of thing?"

"As I told your colleague, Laxman was mildly retarded. He could handle simple cash transactions—he was actually pretty good with numbers—but the *concept* of money was beyond him. I handled all money matters for him, gave him a cash allowance to spend at the market. He enjoyed shopping for clothes, and for knickknacks at the tourist shops. Anything bigger, I went with him to purchase."

Something in the phrase "handled all money matters" snagged at Kate's attention, and she thought she ought to clarify this. "Do you mean that Laxman had money of his own? Or was he dependent on you?"

"Of course he was dependent on me," Mehta said impatiently. "You met him, you saw the problem."

"Financially, I mean, Mr. Mehta. Did your brother have any money of his own?"

"In a manner of speaking, yes. Our father wished to be fair, so he left a small portion of his estate in trust for Laxman."

"How does that work, to have money in trust?" she asked innocently, to see how he would respond.

Mehta picked up a gold pen from his desk and fiddled with it, put it down and picked up a small bronze figurine. "The money is there, in an account and stocks, and the income goes into another account that is jointly in my name with that of Laxman. Theoretically, he could have drawn from it, although he could not have touched the capital."

"And you were the, what do they call it, executor?" Al stepped in to resume the questions. Kate had no doubt that her partner knew perfectly well what the word was.

"I was. Am, since I am also the executor for Laxman's estate."

"And now that he is dead, who inherits?"

"Inspector, I really don't know why—"

"Just answer the question please, Mr. Mehta."

"My brother was killed by . . . by terrorists, and you sit here questioning me about my financial affairs?" Mehta spluttered indignantly.

"We can find out easily enough, Mr. Mehta."

"My children," he told them furiously. "My four children will inherit their uncle's estate. Mani's nephews and nieces."

"Although it will, I assume, be in trust for them until they reach the age of twenty-one? Isn't that how such things usually work?"

"It is." The terse response showed that Mehta well understood the implications a suspicious detective might place on the transfer of money, but there was no hesitation in his answers. "At the time my eldest reaches twenty-one it will be legally presumed that my wife and I are having no more children, and Mani's estate will then be divided equally between however many there are."

"Until then, you are in charge of your brother's estate?"

"Yes."

"And how much money is actually involved?"

Mehta's eyes came up to meet Hawkin's. "In the vicinity of a million dollars. Depending on the state of the stock market, you understand."

Hawkin nodded sympathetically, as if the recent downswing in stock values had inconvenienced him as well. "Mr. Mehta, are you sure there was no such provision in your father's will, that Laxman should inherit the money at the age of twenty-one?"

A muscle in the line of Mehta's jaw jumped, once, and he picked up the pen again as if thinking deeply.

"He did inherit, didn't he?" Al prompted.

"No! For heaven's sake, Inspector, Laxman was already twenty-two when our father died. There was no question of his inheriting. Unless," Mehta continued in a slow and reluctant voice, "circumstances changed."

"Those circumstances being . . . ?"

"Our father was trying to be fair, especially to any children Laxman may have had. The doctors told him that any children Laxman might have would be normal, that his mental condition would not be passed on."

"So Laxman would have inherited if Pramilla had children?"

"Not Laxman. Our father knew he couldn't manage more than a few dollars on his own."

"Mr. Mehta," Al said, his voice showing impatience for the first time, "if you are refusing to tell us what financial arrangements your father made concerning your brother, then say so. Don't assume I won't find out the details on my own. With a homicide like this one, I can easily get a warrant, and your lawyer will be required to tell me. Everything."

That final threat got to Mehta. He exhaled, and put down the pen. "My brother had inherited the money the day he married. I was still a signator on the account, and I had planned on using some of it as a down payment on the house down the street for him and his wife. I did not tell Laxman at the time, because it would have confused him."

"And Pramilla?" Kate asked coldly.

"What about her?"

"Did she know that her husband was in himself a wealthy man, not just a person living off his brother? Or did you not want to confuse her, either?"

"You make all this sound so sinister," Mehta complained. "The girl was a peasant. She could barely read, couldn't speak a word of English when she came here. I wanted to give her a chance to grow up, to learn about her position and her responsibility. Tell me what you would have done, Inspector. Would you have told a fifteen-year-old, virtually illiterate village girl that by writing her name on a piece of paper, she could have anything she wanted? Any clothing in the shops, any flashy car, a house she couldn't begin to care for? Would you?"

Al and Kate just looked at Mehta, and Al asked if they might speak with his wife.

Today Rani Mehta was squeezed into a hot pink sari with a blue and pink underblouse, and she stood quivering with barely suppressed outrage at the invasion of her home. Her husband stood at her shoulder while she was being interviewed, asserting that her English was not good enough to have her interviewed on her own. Even without the language problem she was not a helpful witness. She resented their presence in her house almost as much as she had resented the presence of her childish brother-in-law and his increasingly difficult (and undeniably pretty) young wife, and her answers through her husband's translation were brusque and unhelpful. Eventually they let her go and told Mehta that they were ready to see Laxman's apartment.

The ornate rooms, in the absence of the people who had created them, looked merely tawdry. The boy-and-buffalo figurine stood on the mantelpiece over an electric fireplace, in poignant juxtaposition with an ornately framed photograph of Pramilla and Laxman in their wedding finery, both of them looking very young and rigid with terror. Kate contemplated the arrangement for a long time, and found herself wondering what on earth the village girl had made of this glowing electric imitation fire, the thick off-white carpet, the man to whom she had given over her future.

They found nothing in the apartment. Aside from a sunken patch of wallboard behind a hanging, which Mehta told them was where Laxman had driven his fist in a tantrum, there was no sign that any act of violence had taken place in the rooms, no bloodstains, no sign of dragging on the carpets, not even any disarray. They could find no indication of why Laxman had left the house that night, no telephone numbers scribbled on pads by the phone or balled-up messages in the wastebaskets. The redial button on the only telephone in the rooms connected with an answering machine and a woman's voice announcing, "Hi, this is Amanda's machine," which Kate recognized as that of Amanda Bonner. As Bonner had suspected, she had been Pramilla Mehta's last call. Kate broke the connection before the tone could sound.

They finished the search, thanked Peter Mehta, and went back out into the rain. Outside the house, the press had thinned out somewhat, and the three placard-wielding women had moved their demonstration over in front of the Mehta house. The two detectives nodded to the uniformed police on guard, told the reporters that they had no comment, and strode briskly down the block to where they had left the car.

"That's a fair amount of money involved," Kate noted as she pulled away from the curb.

"Even with those troublesome market swings. You think it was only a million?"

"Not for a minute." Any interrogator recognized instantly the look of open candor that accompanied an outright lie.

Kate made a mental note to dig out the truth of the

Mehta finances. It was never good to assume that, with the family of a victim, the first interview was anything more than reconnaissance. They would return after Laxman's autopsy results and preliminary lab work were in.

"We also need to know if Laxman might have got ahold of some money on his own. Sold a statue, pawned a wristwatch, something of that sort. He understood money enough to know that you can buy or sell things, and if he watched a lot of TV it's the kind of thing he might've seen and copied. Even if he was thick as two bricks."

"We also need those phone records."

"Ask Peter and his wife separately if Laxman had any mail. Postman might remember, too." Al was thinking out loud. "Even the kids in the house. But the big question here is, if this is the work of the serial, how'd the killer find out that Laxman hit his wife sometimes, that he may have been responsible for her death?"

Kate took a deep breath. "Roz Hall knew. Amanda Bonner told her, and if Roz knew, anyone in the city could have known."

"That doesn't narrow things down much."

"God," she said, "if you'd planned it, you couldn't have come up with three more different victims."

"James Larsen, Matthew Banderas, and Laxman Mehta. Affirmative action murders," Al said with heavy irony. "The United Nations of victims."

"Taking political correctness to an extreme," she agreed.

"You'd think there would be a few chronic husband-beaters available as well, hiding in the woodwork. Balance things out a little."

Black humor was one thing; this was becoming bleak. Kate asked, dropping the joke, "You'd say this is definitely a woman thing, then? Standing up for her—or their—downtrodden sisters, revenging their mistreatment and, in Pramilla's case, death?"

"Taking back the night in a big way," Al commented

dryly. "I can't see any other link, can you? Nothing but the history of the victims and their violence toward women. I think we've got a vigilante. Or a group of them."

"The Ladies?"

"I just don't know. Might be them, but it feels different—someone inspired by them, a sort of copycat. What do you think?"

"I agree—it doesn't have at all the same flavor. But then it's pretty hard to inject duct-tape humor into a murder."

In a different voice, Al said, "The press is going to have a field day with this." He was, Kate knew, repeating his offer to let her step quietly out of the way.

"Well," she said, having none of it, "we'll just have to keep one step ahead of them, won't we?"

15

What we have pushed aside and tried to bury
Lives with a staggering thrust we cannot parry.

It was Jon, oddly enough and in a roundabout way, who gave them the break they needed.

After the morning drizzle, the sky cleared and the weather took one of those odd warm turns that spring sometimes comes up with in San Francisco, to fool the gray city's inhabitants into thinking they live in sunny California. Late Wednesday afternoon, after a day spent in a stuffy building with pathology reports and the interviews of a couple dozen of Dimitri's clientele, in endless phone calls and meetings with a dozen stripes of law enforcement, the migraine that had been lurking in the back of Kate's skull all week finally found an opening, flowering in the long, irregular hours and the stress of the entangled cases. She spent a solid half hour on the telephone with Amanda Bonner, who could think of no possible male object of Pramilla's affections, or even fantasies, although she spun out the potential candidates, all the men Pramilla had met in Amanda's presence, until Kate felt like telling the woman that a simple no would have done it and slamming the phone down. Instead, she was polite, and thanked her, and hung up softly. Unfortunately, Hawkin came in just as Kate was tipping the tablets out into her palm.

"You told me the headaches were okay," he accused.

"They were. Are. This is just a normal one, not like before."

"Sure. Go home, Martinelli."

"I'm fine, Al."

"Martinelli, we can't afford to have you on your back for a couple of days. You go home now and do nothing related to the case, or I'll call Lee and the department doctor, in that order."

Either one would be a problem, involving hours of explanation and concealment. Better to capitulate.

"Okay. I'll go. See you in the morning."

"I'm going to check with Lee tonight to make sure you're not working," he warned her.

"Christ, Al, don't be an old woman."

"Now I know you're sick. You'd never use an insult like 'old woman' if you were in your right mind."

Kate laughed in spite of herself. "All right. I promise not to do any work until tomorrow morning, if you promise not to call Lee to check up on me."

"Deal," Al said, and Kate switched off her computer.

Two years ago—even six months ago—Kate would have tackled all the cases on her desk head-on, throwing herself into seventeen-hour days fueled by fast-food meals washed down with gallons of coffee, seeing everyone, doing everything, refusing help and rest as signs of weakness.

However, there was nothing like nearly losing your lover—first her life and then her presence—and then getting your brains scrambled by a kid with a length of galvanized pipe to give you a sense of perspective. The headaches that had pounded through her skull much of the winter had indeed faded, but today was proof that they were not gone, just lurking in the synapses, a menace waiting for stress and overwork to open the door again. Al was right: If she made herself eat properly, sleep adequately, and take a few hours off now and then, she would have a better chance of lasting to the end. As Lee had said, some cops operated under the conviction that they were a victim's only hope, but those cops tended not to make it to retirement in one piece. Kate had proved herself, more than once; now it was time to settle in for the long run.

So she went home.

First thing in the door, Kate did something she'd been intending for what seemed like weeks: She phoned Jules. Conversation with that precocious young woman did nothing for Kate's headache, but it distracted her from business and made her feel as if she'd accomplished something with the day. After half an hour of chat about Jules's social life (i.e., boys) and a project she was doing on human psychology, they made a vague date for an outing. When she had hung up, Kate continued through the house and opened the French doors into what Lee optimistically referred to as a garden, with the thought of pulling weeds, or scrubbing mildew, or just sitting mindlessly in a folding chair, basking in the warmth of the late-afternoon sun.

It was an unexpected hour of respite, what Roz might call a gift of grace, and Kate stood in the overgrown backyard, drawing in deep breaths of the mild, oxygen-rich April breeze and wondering why no painter ever managed to capture the colors in the skies of approaching dusk, when she decided that what she really wanted to do was pollute that sweet evening air with the smoke of charcoal briquettes. Lee made a phone call and sent Jon off to the market while Kate dug out the little barbecue grill, scraped off the accumulated gunk from the previous summer, and fired it up, first to sterilize the metal surface, and then to lay on it the marinated skirt steaks and the slabs of ahi tuna. Soon she stood with a beer in one hand and a two-footlong turner in the other, enjoying both the fantasy of suburbia and the brief holiday from the cases. After all, everyone had to eat sometime, even homicide detectives, and ahi took less time to cook than sitting in a restaurant waiting for food. And, she realized, at some point in the last hour, her headache had shriveled up and crept away.

Jon came out of the house onto the small brick patio,

carrying two salads and some plates. He was followed by Sione, lithe and graceful even when burdened by a tray piled high with bread, drinks, and silverware, a checkered tablecloth draped over his left forearm, and a folding chair clamped under his right armpit.

Lee retrieved the chair from under his grasping elbow and quickly draped the cloth over a small tiled table that really should have been scrubbed first. Sione politely ignored the table's gray scurf of city dirt and dried mildew and set about transferring the contents of his tray onto the cheerful cloth.

He and Jon were talking about their afternoon, laughing easily and brushing against each other from time to time. Kate found herself smiling, and raised her gaze to the darkening bay, her thoughts going to another young couple. Laxman and Pramilla Mehta had been two individuals every bit as beautiful as Sione Kalefu, caught up in an arranged relationship that had twisted into something dark and deadly. Jon asked her something, and she blinked.

"Sorry?"

"I wanted to know if you thought I would swagger like that if I wore a carpenter's apron."

"Swagger like what?"

"Kate, hello? Where are you? I took Sione downtown to whistle at the construction workers, and he noticed how the guys with the carpenter's belts walk. I said it's just the weight of the things; he says it's attitude."

"Could be either. Patrol cops walk the same way."

"Ah," Jon sighed. "Men in uniform."

They giggled together like teenaged girls. Spring is in the air, thought Kate with a sudden sour twinge in her gut. Like pollen, and love, and babies.

Meat and fish cooked, salads and bread distributed, the quartet bent over their food in the soft evening light. Roz and Maj were coming over shortly, bringing Mina and one of Maj's luscious desserts—if Roz didn't get called away, if Kate's beeper didn't go off, if the earth didn't move beneath their feet.

In the meantime, they would behave as if they were normal people who lived in a world where such interruptions never occurred. Kate forced herself to eat slowly, to push away the very possibility of the telephone from her mind, to make jokes as if she had all the time in the world, to listen to Lee's easy conversation with Sione about how a Polynesian boy from Tahiti came to be dancing with a New York based troupe in San Francisco.

As they listened to his story, told in a melodious half-French accent that even without the rest of the package would have explained Jon's infatuation, it struck Kate how different the young man was from Jon's usual lovers, who tended to be white-collar professionals with gym memberships and identity problems. Sione was as colorful and exotic as a tropical bird, and as comfortable with himself. Jon's attitude, too, was a different thing this time, affectionate rather than admiring, relaxed where he was usually so concerned with making an impression. He and Sione had only known each other a couple of weeks, but they seemed old friends. All in all, thought Kate, a very hopeful state of affairs.

"Who wrote *Song*?" Lee was now asking. "That business you do with the knife, for example—that's not in the Bible. Is it?"

"Oh, no." Sione smiled, an expression as slow and sure as his movements or his low voice. "*Song* began several years ago, when I first came to New York. One of the dancers in our studio, Dina Moreli, was attacked by a man she thought she knew well. A friend, he had been. Dina trusted him, and he raped her.

"She was unable to dance afterward, not just because of the injuries, but because she could not bring herself to go on stage. To trust her audience, you see? She couldn't work for a long time, two years or more. She came to the studio twice a week, but other than that she stayed inside her apartment and became a hermit. She did dance on her own, and she tried to write a journal of what had happened to her. She also spent a lot of time reading books she had always meant to read.

I suppose she thought that her time away from work should not be a complete loss.

"One of the books she took up was the Bible. But the more she read, the angrier it made her, what she called 'man's inhumanity to woman.' The story of the man entertaining important visitors who gives his concubine to a drunken mob to abuse and kill, so as to save his guests. Or Tamar, the young widow who dresses up as a prostitute and seduces her own father-in-law to force her husband's family to undertake their responsibilities toward her. Jephthah's daughter, nameless even as a sacrifice. And the *Song of Solomon*, where a young girl out looking for her lover falls into the hands of a group of soldiers, is raped, and then, when she finds her lover again, is forced by her own needs and by his assumptions to act as if nothing had happened.

"That is not exactly how the Bible describes it, but as you probably know, interpretation depends on the eye of the reader, and the experience of being raped changed Dina's way of looking at the world. It explains why she wrote the dance the way she did, exaggerating the abuse of the guards but also giving Beloved the power to strike back, not only against her attackers, but against the need to hide her rape from Lover."

The doorbell punctuated his last sentence and Jon started to rise, but Kate waved him back to his seat. She took a tray of dirty plates to the kitchen, pausing to switch on the already-filled coffeemaker, then went to let in Roz, Maj, and Mina. The two adults were carrying containers, and Mina's arms were wrapped around a bunch of bananas the size of her chest. Shutting the door, Kate asked, "Will we need bowls or plates?"

"Bowls," said Maj. "Big ones."

"Everyone's outside on the patio, I think it's still warm enough. I'll bring some bowls and utensils."

Maj had brought the makings for very high-class banana splits: homemade ice cream yellow with egg yolk and speckled with vanilla bean, bitter chocolate sauce, crumbled pralines, and creme anglaise, with maraschino cherries for the top and delicate, brittle rolled cookies for the side. This was what Jon referred to as *cuisine amusante*, or gourmet junk food, and it succeeded completely in defeating the nice, healthy dinner they had eaten. In no time at all, the only things left were a few cherries and some cookie crumbs. The evening sky had shifted from blue through rose to dusky lavender and finally to no color at all, and they sat in easy companionship and admired the quarter moon riding low against the city. Eventually, it was getting too cool to sit outside, and they moved in for coffee. Mina asked for the globe puzzle again, and Lee obediently fetched it for her to dismantle.

Roz wanted to talk about *Song*, and Sione repeated for her benefit the history of the production.

Roz was thrilled. She sat forward on the edge of her seat as if she could pull theological and psychological truths out of the dancer by force.

"Beloved submitting to her lover's expectations and his lack of sympathy," she declared, "is just like all the women who fail to report rape, even now. And in a patriarchal society, when the woman's purity reflects directly on her menfolk, she wouldn't dare tell him— look at those poor women in Muslim countries who get murdered by their brothers for daring to shame the family by getting themselves raped."

Maj offered another interpretation. "You don't think Beloved is simply afraid that if she tells Lover she was attacked, he would go after the guards and be beaten up himself, or killed? That she's protecting him?"

Roz waved away her partner's suggestion impatiently. "'Tell him I am sick with love,' Beloved says. She's hiding her injuries because she knows that if she doesn't, he'll be so put off by her lack of purity that he'll leave her."

"Interesting, isn't it," Lee commented mildly, "that we call Beloved 'she' and Lover 'he' even though the players were reversed?"

Sione, dressed in khakis, loafers, and a fleece pullover and showing not the least sign of transvestism or gender bending off the stage, smiled. "As it is written, the parts could be played by either sex, but the director had the two of us at hand, and thought it was more interesting this way. 'A piquant touch,' one of the reviewers said."

"But why Beloved's rage?" Roz demanded. "Why did Moreli decide to have Beloved come in with the bloody knife and then settle back into business as usual with Lover? Is that her idea of happily ever after?"

Maj spoke up. "I'm sure it's your old friend the warrior-virgin, Roz love. Even if Dina Moreli didn't have that figure consciously in mind when she wrote the interpretation—after all, that's what an archetype is, a powerful upwelling from the unconscious. Women's *shakti,* like those women on the panel called it."

"Oh," Lee broke in, "I meant to tell you how much I enjoyed that program. I taped it and watched it the other night."

Roz glanced involuntarily at Kate, looking uncomfortable, and Kate wondered in amusement which of the statements Roz had made during the discussion was embarrassing her in hindsight. Roz turned back to Sione.

"But where did that interpretation come from? Did she just pull it out of thin air?"

Sione shrugged apologetically. "I do not really know why Dina wrote it that way. I am only the dancer, not the person who created it. But," he added, seeing Roz's impatience, "are Beloved's actions not, after all, what people do? When driven to uncharacteristic acts, do not most people then fade back into the obscurity of their daily lives?"

Roz opened her mouth to argue, caught Maj's eye, and then threw out her hands with a smile. "I'm sorry, I realize it isn't your dance. It's just that it's so precisely what I've been working on for my dissertation, the juxtaposition of love and rage. And I find it exciting to come across an intelligent and sympathetic interpretation of a biblical text. So many people pretty things up and make them so sweet you want to vomit. Or they go the other direction and dismiss the whole thing as the tool of an oppressive patriarchy."

"You would see it somewhere in between?" Sione asked dutifully. Maj made a noise and rolled her eyes, but Roz ignored her partner.

"Religion *is* passion," the minister of God declared passionately. "The Bible is our document as well as theirs, and it holds all the human experience of fear and love and despair and terror and revenge, of power and the rights of the powerless. It is a paradigm of human behavior. Its theology is one of liberation, and not just in the hands of Latin American Marxism."

Sione was starting to look bewildered, Jon bored, and Lee stirred and objected mildly, "There is a lot of ugly stuff in the Bible, Roz; you have to admit that."

"Precisely. Because there's a lot of ugly stuff in daily life, and pretending there isn't doesn't make it so. Life isn't a fairy tale; the good guys sometimes lose. Hell, even fairy tales aren't pretty except in twentieth-century America. The original Grimm tales—have you ever read them? Grim's the word. Little Red Riding Hood doesn't rescue her granny, she finds her chopped up, bottled, and hanging in the smokehouse."

"Roz!" Maj protested, looking over to where Mina was kneeling, concentrating on the thick plastic shapes that Lee was fitting together for her. Roz started to bristle, but Sione got in first with a distraction.

"I have always thought that Christianity and left-wing politics were poor bedfellows, which has been a sorrow to me, because the church of my childhood was such a place of joy, full of big women in white hats singing full-throated to the heavens."

Roz was nodding her head before he finished his sentence. "It is a terrible pity that the right wing has laid exclusive claim to the Bible, so inextricably that it seems impossible to reject the one without the other. But to do so only gives them a victory. It's not their Bible, and the fact that I claim the same Holy Book makes the Right angrier than anything else I can do. If I rejected their religion entirely I would simply be another poor lost heathen in need of their prayers. By declaring myself a Christian, by knowing the Bible better than most of them do, I became a maddening enigma. And I mean literally maddening: Twice I've had men try to rip off my collar."

"And she regularly gets threatening letters," Maj told them.

"You never said anything about threats," Kate said sharply. "What kind—"

"Kate," Roz interrupted her, shooting a stern glance sideways at her partner. "Don't worry about it."

"Why the hell not? You have to take threats seriously these days. There are a lot of nuts out there."

"You think I don't know that? Of course I take them seriously, but I don't want you to get involved. One of your colleagues knows all about the problem."

"But—"

"Kate, please. Unless one of them actually carries out his threat, it's not going to be your job."

"For Christ sake, Roz, that's not at all funny."

Lee spoke up as well. "Roz, please don't joke about this. It isn't fair to the people who care about you."

"Sorry, sorry. Anonymous letters come with the territory, and although I assure you that I take the nuts seriously, I have to say that I find the whole subject tedious, and can we please talk about something else?"

"The threats to your immortal soul are much more worrying," Maj commented, sounding considerably more amused than worried. She explained, "Roz seems to be a regular sermon topic at that grotesque church that tries to quote 'heal' gays and dykes."

Roz laughed aloud. "The last one was in retaliation for an article I'd written and they had obviously not bothered to read, about Hitler claiming to have been a Christian."

"Did he?" Jon asked, interested.

"I have no doubt that he thought of himself as a good Christian leader."

"Like those maniacs who bomb abortion clinics, killing to save lives," Jon agreed. "They're mostly right-wing Christians. The guy who runs that Web site giving the names and addresses of abortionists that's little more than a hit list—he calls himself a man of God."

"We humans have a deep need to justify our behavior, especially the more extreme acts," Lee commented, pausing in fitting the boot of Italy into the Mediterranean. "We drag God in to stand at our side, even if we have to bend reality to do it."

"Poor old God," Jon said. "Must be frustrating having everyone claim your support. Like Albert Einstein being dragged in to advertise everything from Coke to computers."

"God definitely needs a press agent," Lee said. Sione was looking ever more puzzled.

"Issuing statements to clarify policy," Roz agreed.

"Headline: God says, 'I do not support Pat Robertson,'" Lee joked.

"God announces: 'Only gay feminists of color admitted to heaven,'" Maj suggested.

"God unveils heavenly affirmative action plan: One percent Christian Right to be admitted, qualified or not," Roz contributed.

The jokes escalated, the intellectual content plummeted, and a couple of minutes later Lee, seeing Sione looking worried and Mina positively alarmed at this incomprehensible adult descent into hilarity, leaned over and spoke to Kate.

"How about some more coffee, hon? Kate?" Lee reached out and put her hand on Kate's knee, bringing her back to the present from some far-off place.

"Huh?" Kate said, blinking.

"Could you put on another pot of coffee?"

"Sure," she said, and went off to do it.

Her mind was not on the chore, however. In fact, she had heard nothing of the discussion and joking, nothing after Jon's mention of the abortion clinic murders, an offhand remark that had sent a small tingle rising up in the back of Kate's mind, the kind of sensation that carries the phrase, "Listen to me."

Hit list. Web site. Maniac. *Listen.*

Kate listened, and speculated in a state of distraction while the coffee was made and drunk, and the dishes were cleaned, and Jon and Sione left to feed Sione's recently adopted Siamese kitten. She helped gather up Maj's empty containers and walked with them out to Roz's car. The night sky was still clear, a rarity in the city of fog, and mild enough that none of them wore a jacket. Maj opened the Jeep's rear door and took the bowls from Kate, who leaned against the passenger door and addressed herself to Roz's backside, emerging from the back of the car while she buckled Mina into the car seat.

"There were three women with picket signs in front of Peter Mehta's house yesterday morning. You know anything about that?"

"I know that they've moved on to his place of business. Much more visible. Can you scoot back a bit, honey?" Roz asked, which Kate assumed was addressed to the child in the car seat.

"It's an interesting question, isn't it, how much we allow immigrants to keep the customs of their birth country," Kate noted. "When we have laws to the contrary. Like the conservative groups who refuse to send their kids to public schools."

"Customs or not, marrying off children is wrong."

"So is allowing half the kids in the country to go without medical care. So is spending a million dollars for a missile to drop on civilians."

Roz pulled her head out of the car and grinned at Kate. "Martinelli, we're going to make a flaming liberal of you yet."

"Roz, who did you tell about Pramilla Mehta's death?"

Roz shut Mina's door and stepped back so Maj could approach the passenger door. Kate too stepped away from the car.

"Why do you ask this, Kate?" Maj's voice asked, but it was Roz's gaze Kate held as she answered.

"Someone may have known that Laxman was being investigated for his wife's death, and decided not to wait for the police. If we can narrow down the people who had that information, it might help us find his murderer. Roz knew of Laxman's violence against his wife. Roz and Amanda Bonner."

Maj answered before her partner could. "Roz knew. I knew. About eighty other people knew. And then whoever those people may have told."

"Eighty people?" Even for Roz, that seemed like a lot of phone calls.

"I preached on it, Sunday morning," Roz explained.

Kate winced. "Mentioning names?"

"Yes."

And on Monday night, Laxman Mehta had been killed.

Maj reached for the passenger door, breaking the staring contest. Roz walked around the car to the driver's side.

"It was good to see you," Maj told Kate. "I hope you're taking care of yourself."

"Lee makes me." To say nothing of her other partner, Al.

"She is looking so well."

"She's doing great." Kate opened her mouth again to say something further about Roz's threatening letters, and then closed it firmly. They were big girls, and neither of them naive.

"Shall we go, my Maj?" Roz asked. *Mymy*, her favorite pun on Maj's name.

Maj leaned forward and gave Kate an affectionate kiss on the cheek. Both women got in and closed their doors, Maj with some difficulty, which indicated that the Jeep's argument with the Yosemite rock face had damaged more than paint. The engine ground into life (something wrong under the hood as well—Roz's pet mechanic must have left the congregation) and the red car slid off down the hill.

Kate stood for another minute with her face upturned to the faint impression of stars, then she went back inside, poured the dregs of the coffee into a cup, and took it upstairs, where she turned on the computer and then walked away from it, ending up on the small balcony off the guest room. Half an hour later Lee found her there, sitting and watching an overhead airplane rise up into the heavens.

"What are you doing?" Lee asked.

"Sitting."

"You okay?"

"I am perfect," Kate told her.

Lee came up behind her chair and leaned down to kiss her on the same cheek Maj had used earlier. She smelled of soap and toothpaste. "You turned the computer on. Are you working tonight?"

"You detective, you. Al thought I needed a night off, so I promised him I wouldn't work until tomorrow morning."

"So you're waiting until midnight," Lee diagnosed. She laughed.

"Tell me something," Kate asked her. "Roz did something in India that gave you the creeps. What was it?"

Lee stood still for a moment, and then with a sigh she put her hands back through the cuffs of the crutches and shifted over to sit down on the narrow bench.

"I don't really want to go into detail, but basically what happened was Roz disappeared from the hotel and went off to live with a group of *dacoits* for a few days. What we would call, I don't know, a band of outlaws, I guess. Nasty people. Personally, I've always thought that she was given some powerful drug, a hallucinogen I'd say. She swore she wasn't, but it was all pretty ugly, and it took a major effort to get her out of there, and out of the country without being thrown in jail."

"I . . ." Kate shook her head. "I can't picture it."

"Completely uncharacteristic," Lee agreed. "Which is why I decided she'd been given something. I've never known Roz to do drugs, other than that time. And at the end of it we were both more than a little uncomfortable around each other."

"You've never talked about it?"

"Never. She may not even remember it, not in detail."

"Thanks for telling me." Though, Kate reflected, it was hard to know what, if anything, to make of this long-ago episode of youthful indiscretion. Except . . .

"I don't suppose that there was one of the, what do you call them, *dacoots*, in particular?"

"*Dacoits*," Lee corrected, the wicked smile on her face clear even in the dark. "And how did you guess?" She stood up, kissed Kate's other cheek, and merely said, "I'm going to bed."

"Okay, sweetheart," Kate said absently. "I'll be there in a bit."

"Don't work too late."

Kate did work late—or rather, early, when a faint light in the east was bringing definition to the Bay and the northern shore beyond. Through the night, while the traffic fell silent and the streetlights dominated the darkness, while the sea haze coalesced into clouds and set the house's downspouts to their musical tapping, Kate searched the tangled threads of the Web for three lonely names, and eventually, working backward from Roz's Web site, using search engine and Web links, she found them.

"Womyn of the EVEning," they called themselves, and their Web site began with a soliloquy on the night.

Eve was the first, a creature of the darkness, who with her apple freed her children from the tyranny of the Ruler of paradise. Eve, whose thirst for knowledge was so great, it changed humynkind. Eve, whose act was called shameful by males, who stands in pride and strength as the Mother of us all.

We, too, are creatures of the night. Night is a Goddess who wraps Her dark cloak around us, allowing us to become invisible as we work Her will. For too long, womyn has been invisible in the daylight, a being with no voice, no face, whose labors in the home are only seen if they are not done, whose birthing and raising of children is only noticed when she fails.

Males call us weak, males attack us with their stronger muscles, males try to convince us that the Night is a place of danger, that we must stay inside, lock our doors against the lurking, unseen threats of the dark.

Why do we believe this? In truth, for too many of us, it is the well-lighted home that places us in danger, the locked and bolted door that traps us and makes us vulnerable.

In truth it is the dark, all-concealing Night outside that will make us safe, Night's dark cloak that shields us with invisibility. Our weakness and our fear shall become our strength and our weapon, until it is the male who hides in the light, cowering from womyn's dark vengeance.

The night is ours, to do with as we please.

The dark is ours, to punish the evildoer.

Here are some of the males who would deny us our dark safety.

And then came the names.

Gritty-eyed and unwashed, Kate stumbled off and collapsed between the sheets for three hours, when she was dragged out of unconsciousness by a steaming mug and Lee's voice.

"Your hair," Lee purred into her lover's ear, sinking her fingers into the matted brown tangle on the pillow. " 'Your hair flows like a flock of goats, spilling down the side of Mount Gilead.' "

Kate opened one eye to glare at the face of her partner, who was convulsed with hilarity at her own wit. "You woke me up to tell me that?"

"I woke you up to remind you that you have an appointment in Marin at eight o'clock."

Kate looked at the clock, and then nearly knocked the mug out of Lee's grasp as her own hand shot out for the telephone. She punched in the number, as familiar as her own, and then grimaced at the woman's voice that answered.

" 'Morning, Jani," she said carefully. "This is Kate. Have I missed Al?"

"He's in the shower, Kate. Can I have him call you back?"

"Okay. I'm at home. It's kind of urgent, Jani."

"Isn't it always?" Jani commented, and the phone went dead. Kate put her own phone down, wondering if she should read anything into Jani's brusque dismissal, and if so, how much. She had seemed okay on the phone the other night, so maybe it didn't mean anything.

"What's wrong?" Lee asked, again holding out the mug. Kate took it gratefully, slurped off the top inch, and arranged a couple of pillows behind her head.

"Jani didn't sound very happy to hear me," Kate told her. "I'd thought it was calming down with her, but maybe not." Jani still held Kate to blame for the kidnapping of her daughter, Jules, while under Kate's supervision just before Christmas. Since in Kate's opinion Jani was right, she could hardly complain at the woman's treatment of her. Still, it added a degree of tension to her partnership with Al that was sometimes awkward.

Lee, however, had an alternative explanation for the exchange

"It's probably her morning sickness. Didn't you tell me she was about ten weeks along? She was probably just trying not to vomit into the receiver."

"You think so?"

"I think it's possible. You might check with Al before you get het up about nothing."

"Is 'het up' a medical term, Doctor?"

"Definitely. New Age terminology meets the Victorian era." Lee drew a deep breath, looking down at her hands, and Kate went instantly wary. "Sweetheart," Lee began, "I've been thinking about what you said the other night."

Kate made no pretense at not knowing what Lee was talking about. There was only one subject at the moment that called for low voice and lowered gaze.

"About a baby?"

"Indirectly. Or rather, on the way to a baby. I've never really apologized properly for what I put you through last summer."

"That's not—"

"Let me say it. I treated you like shit. I made you crawl and then shoved you away, just to prove I could. And when I finally heard that you'd been hurt, nearly killed, it was like—oh, I don't know. Like having a bucket of ice water dumped into my brain. All I could think of was, if you'd died, you would have gone thinking that I wasn't coming back. It was a shock, that idea, it made me feel . . . I can't begin to describe how I felt," admitted the articulate psychotherapist. "I think about it every day. And I am sorry. Mostly—" she held out a hand to stop Kate's protest. "Mostly I'm sorry for what my actions did to us. You've been insecure about us ever since, which I can understand. But let me say, here and now, that I am not going anywhere. I love you, and I am staying here with you. If you can just think of the other as a sort of temporary insanity, I would be very grateful."

Kate was not exactly proud of the memory of her own response to Lee's abrupt exit, which had gone from drunken self-pity to reckless rage for weeks. She had not told Lee, would not tell her now, but merely took her lover into her arms and held her.

After a minute, Lee stirred. "Now we can talk about the baby thing. I've found an OB/GYN over in Berkeley who is willing to work with a disabled lesbian. I made an appointment for early next month. I'd like you to come with me."

Kate smoothed Lee's own unruly curls. "You're very sure about this?"

Lee sat up again to meet her eyes, taking Kate's hand. "I think I'm sure, if that makes sense. What I mean is, I want very badly to try, but if at any point along the way the difficulties become too major—if the doctor says absolutely not, if the insemination doesn't take, if problems crop up—I will back off. You may need to remind me of that promise, by the way," she said, her smile a bit lopsided. "If I'm becoming fixated, let me know. Loudly."

"That's a deal."

"One more thing."

"Only one?"

"At the moment. We haven't talked about money."

"We'll manage."

"A baby's an expensive addition. And if we commit ourselves to in vitro, it gets really expensive. Plus, I can't see myself working full-time, either before or after." Her attitude was not simply one of warning Kate, but of leading up to something.

"So you want me to rob a bank?" Kate asked lightly. "Or are you and Jon cooking up a little computer fraud and you want a couple of tips?"

"Uh, no. I think I'll avoid anything that would land one of us in jail. I hear they're bad places to raise children. No, I was thinking that we might have to sell this house, move someplace cheaper."

It was not entirely unexpected; in fact, it was a suggestion Kate had made any number of times over the years since Lee had inherited the property following the death of her authoritative and strongly disapproving mother, but it still sent a sharp pang of regret through her. Objectively speaking, it was worth a small fortune, but Kate had put herself into this house, her sweat and her commitment, and she loved it as she never thought she would love a mere building. She also knew without question that they were both well and truly spoiled for any lesser house they might find to replace it.

She kissed Lee and smiled at her. "I'll miss the view of the Bay," she said, and left it at that.

Al's return call found her about to step into her own shower. She turned off the water and sat down on the toilet in front of the glowing bars of the ancient wall heater.

"Jani said you needed to talk."

"Look, Al, is Jani okay with me?" she asked bluntly. "She sounded pissed off."

"Jani?" Al's surprise was all the answer she needed. "No, she's not pissed off with you. With life in general, maybe, and with hormones and a dry cracker diet in particular, but she's good with you."

"I'm glad."

"We're both waiting for the second trimester to get under way. It usually settles down then."

Hawkin the expectant father, Kate thought in amusement, and wondered idly if she and he would share hints and complaints when and if Lee was in Jani's condition. The thought brought the entire possibility of Lee and a baby into abrupt focus, and for a long moment Kate sat naked on the toilet seat, bemused by the whole situation. Al's growl jerked her to attention.

"Martinelli, is that all you phoned to ask?"

"No, Al, sorry. Didn't get much sleep last night. Do you have a minute?"

"Go ahead."

"Okay. Last night we had Roz and Maj over, and got to talking about religion and the conservative Right with their anti-gay programs and the bombing of abortion clinics. And then Jon mentioned that Web site that everyone was talking about when the doctor back East was shot, the Web site that lists doctors and clinic directors, their families and home addresses, all kinds of things nobody would want a nut to get ahold of."

"The hit list."

"Exactly."

"Do I see where this is going?" Al asked slowly, and Kate knew him well enough to hear the excitement in his voice. She hugged herself to keep warm.

"You do. It took me forever, but I found one that is a kind of mirror image. It's called Womyn of the EVEning—that's w-o-m-y-n, and the e-v-e in evening is capitalized. It's only been online since January, which may be why nobody's heard about it. It isn't one of those governmental lists, notifying residents they might have a sex offender as a neighbor. This one's a list of suspects who are known to beat their wives, abuse kids physically or sexually, or rape women. Each guy is given a case history, his arrest and conviction record, and a list of the things he's suspected of that he didn't get taken down for because the courts weren't able to prove anything further. You know the routine—tainted evidence, a withdrawn statement by a victim or witness, circumstantial evidence without direct corroboration, that sort of thing. There were a couple of plea bargains for lesser offenses. God knows where all their information came from, though it looks to me like somebody's getting into things they shouldn't."

"Hackers?"

"Or an inside source."

"How many on the list?"

"Two hundred fourteen names."

"*What*? In four months? Christ, Martinelli."

"Makes you think, doesn't it? It's compiled by a woman who seems to be somewhere in Nebraska. People send her names, and if they match her criteria— that's what she calls it—she adds them to the list, with their phone numbers and addresses. I've sent her an imaginary case, to see what she does with it, what kind of checks she runs."

"Are any of our—" Al started, but Kate was already there.

"They're all on it. All three."

Al was silent, then said what was on both their minds.

"That takes it out of our hands for sure. Have you called Marcowitz yet?"

"My next call, after I talked to you."

"The feds'll be embarrassed that you found it first," he said, pleased at the idea.

"I thought I might point that out, if they try to cut us out of the loop completely."

"Blackmail, Martinelli? Not nice."

"Just doing my job, Al."

"Sure you are. Find anything else interesting on the list?"

"Don't know about interesting, but there's going to be a hell of a lot of work there. But Al? There are a bunch of connecting sites, things like legal information for victims, do-it-yourself PI work, how to go underground, that kind of thing. I haven't been through all of them yet, but I had two interesting hits. One of them was a self-defense site that talked about, among other things, buying and using various kinds of taser." Hawkin grunted in reaction. "The other—frankly, I don't know what to think. Roz Hall's church has a Web site two links away."

16

Every creation is born out of the dark.
Every birth is bloody. Something gets torn.
Kali is there to do her sovereign work
Or else the living child will be still-born.

Kate had not been inside Roz and Maj's house since the previous Thanksgiving. It looked as if she was not about to enter it today, either, since there was no response to either doorbell or knuckles. She had thought she was early enough to catch them, and Roz's red Jeep stood in the driveway, but the house was empty. Try again later.

She had her car door open when Maj's boxy white BMW rounded the corner, lights on and wipers going against the morning drizzle. It signaled its turn to an empty street and pulled sedately into the drive. While Kate waited for the doors to open, she reflected that either cars were no indication of personality, or else a certain degree of incompatibility was no bad thing in a relationship: Whereas Roz drove a big, battered, once-flashy but still new vehicle that already had a dozen political stickers superimposed in layers on the back bumper, Maj stuck to the car she had bought new twelve years before, a car as immaculate and scrupulously maintained as its owner, which usually wore a single bumper sticker, scraped off and changed two or three times a year at Maj's whim, its message either puzzling or humorous, if not both. Her most recent one, Kate noticed, declared that REAL WOMEN DRIVE STICK. The BMW, needless to say, had a manual transmission.

The car doors opened and the two women got out, followed by a large black dog, which shook itself damply, spotted Kate, and launched itself down the sidewalk toward her as if she was either a long-lost soul mate or a mortal enemy. Before Kate could decide between pulling her gun or a swift retreat into her car, Roz spoke sharply and the dog skidded to a halt, casting Kate a longing glance before it returned to Roz's side.

"You're up and around early," Roz declared. "Were you looking for us?"

"I thought I missed you. I should've called first."

"Maj just dropped Mina off at school and circled around to pick me up from my run. I don't think you've met the newest addition—this is Mouton, also known as Mutton, or Mutt to his friends."

"Mutt?"

"What can I say? It's what he answers to."

"Because he's a mutt?"

"No," said Roz, bending down to take the dog's damp head between her hands and rub it vigorously back and forth. "It's because he's just an overgrown lamb," she crooned at him, to his ecstasy.

Mutt was mostly black Lab with the addition of something from the fluffier end of the gene pool, and he did look a bit like a sheep. A wet, smelly, wriggling sheep who, when his mistress had released him, wanted nothing but to bound up into Kate's arms but settled for washing the back of her outstretched hand with an enthusiastic tongue. Perhaps a black sheep, Kate thought, noticing Maj's disapproving glance at the animal's damp and sandy feet. How did one train a dog to wipe his feet at the door?

"He's very nice," she said obediently, though she'd never been much for dogs. "How long have you had him?"

"Couple of months. He belongs to a friend who moved back to England. She couldn't stand the thought of locking him up for their six-month quarantine, so we sort of inherited him, unless she decides to come back. Mina adores him, and Maj approves of the way he forces me to get some exercise. Want a cup of coffee?"

"Love one."

"Are you in a hurry?" Roz asked over her shoulder, her key in the lock. "If you're not, I'll jump in and out of the shower first so we don't have to leave all the windows open. Mutt doesn't mind my delicate fragrance, but human noses tend to twitch."

"Shower ahead, there's no rush."

Mutt did have the manners to shake himself before entering the house, and he pounded up the stairs on Roz's heels. Maj shook her head affectionately and led Kate back into the large, spotless, very Scandinavian-looking kitchen to put on a pot of coffee for Roz and Kate and a cup of herbal tea for herself and the baby. She moved more heavily these days, balancing against the weight in front, and Kate reflected that on the way over this morning she had seen four other pregnant women, at various places along the streets. Either half the city was pregnant, or she had babies on the brain.

"The smell of coffee doesn't bother you?" Kate asked. Giving up coffee for nine months if Lee got pregnant was not an appealing thought.

"No," Maj replied. "Should it?"

"My partner Al's wife is pregnant and says that coffee makes her sick. I just wondered if it's a common reaction."

"Coffee doesn't affect me. It's odd things like chicken and celery that get to me." She shrugged. "Who knows?"

"How's my step-goddaughter? Over her monkey phase yet?"

"I wish. She found a book on Jane Goodall last week. Now she wants to go to Africa and live with the chimpanzees."

"And you? Getting any work done?" A person tended to forget that Maj Freiling had a life out from the shadow of Roz Hall and the family structure, but that was partly due to the general uncertainty about what Maj's job was. It was neither psychology nor brain surgery, but existed somewhere between the two, and seemed to consist of conversations with researchers on how people thought. She was, Kate knew, working on and off writing a book, which Lee had explained as having to do with sex-linked characteristics and gender role expectations, but that too was made up of apparently unrelated fragments rather than a unifying thesis. Today's conversation was typical.

"Oh, yes," Maj answered. "I came across an interesting man at San Francisco State who is looking at the complexity of our perception of a person's voice, how we can judge sex and age, education and authority just by a few words over the telephone. He is working from an evolutionary viewpoint, the question of why a person's voice perception is so capable of reading subtle clues, almost as much as visual perception. I am more interested in the consequences, but I am thinking of adding a chapter, or at any rate a few pages, on the subject. It is most distracting," she added with a laugh, seeing that Kate was not following any of it. Her accent, almost nonexistent in everyday conversation, became more precisely European when she spoke about her work, Kate noticed, and wondered what message this voice perception carried.

They drank their hot drinks and talked about this and that, and then Roz came back in, her hair wet and Mutt's nearly dry, to pour herself some coffee and a bowl of cereal.

"Want anything to eat?" she asked Kate, who declined the offer. "Well, let me fill up your cup again and we'll get out from under Maj's feet."

Roz's office was as untidy as the kitchen was neat, bookshelves sagging, a door-on-sawhorses set up at a right angle to a sturdy oak desk, both entirely buried in books and files and computer printouts. Roz walked around to the niche surrounded by desks and shelves and balanced her bowl and cup on top of a stack of folders. She waved Kate to the chair across from her and began to spoon up her breakfast.

"What have you found about Pramilla Mehta?" she asked around a mouthful of granola. "Can you prove yet that her husband killed her?"

"The investigation is, as they say, ongoing."

Roz peered at her over the laden desk. "You can't talk about it."

Kate pulled a face. "It's difficult. He was clearly mentally deficient, and possibly mentally disturbed. We're having a profile put together, to see if he had a potential for violent outbursts followed by careful planning. I mean, we know he could be violent, but the cover-up is the question. I personally don't think he did, but then I only met him once, and he wasn't in very good shape at the time." If Roz was either surprised or suspicious at Kate's willingness to share information, she did not show it, but Kate knew that there would be no forthcoming information from Roz if Kate did not at least give the appearance of openness. And she had actually not given Roz anything that wasn't in the papers.

Roz chewed for a minute and washed it down with a swallow of coffee. "I've had a word with the mayor and your chief of police last night, suggesting that the murder of Pramilla Mehta may need closer examination. It's going to be a touchy subject—the Indian community is not going to be thrilled to be accused of the barbaric act of burning young brides—but at the same time we can't ignore it. This'll be a political hot potato."

Kate gaped at her, unwilling to believe what she had just heard, but unable to put any other interpretation on it. "Roz, what the hell did you do that for? How do you expect us to carry out an investigation with a bunch of politicians sitting on our shoulders?"

"Are you angry?" Roz sounded puzzled, and Kate for a moment thought it might be an honest reaction. But no—it had to be an act; no one as well versed in the workings of the city as Roz Hall could fail to grasp consequences so innocently.

"Of course I'm angry. You shove the case into my hands and then, when two days go by without an arrest, you snatch it away and say that nothing's being done. For Christ sake, Roz, I've got the FBI and a hundred reporters to deal with and now—you might have warned me you were about to drop City Hall on me as well."

"I thought you could use the additional manpower," Roz protested. "I told them you were doing the best you—"

"Christ, Roz, you know full well what this'll involve. A string of meetings holding hands and explaining how we have to do it, hours and hours eaten up that could be better spent—" Kate realized that Roz was not paying any attention to her words, but was looking past her at the door. Kate turned in her chair and saw Maj's apologetic face looking in.

"It's Jory on the phone," she said to Roz. "There's a problem with the information packets for the meeting this afternoon. Something about copyright questions and the copy shop?"

Roz rubbed at her face in irritation and stood up. "I'm sorry Kate, I have to deal with this. I'll be back in a minute." She followed Maj out of the room, although there was a telephone on the desk, and closed the door. Kate too got to her feet and paced up and down the crowded room. She paused at Roz's desk to glance at the books Roz was reading now, and found her usual wild assortment of titles: *Evoking the Goddess; Awakening Female Power; When the Drummers Were Women*. Kate reflected that the first time she'd met Roz, the minister had been holding an armful of odd titles. She smiled at the memory, and at a framed picture of Mina and Maj at the zoo, in front of the orangutan enclosure.

Roz was probably only trying to help, in her own heavy-handed way, Kate told herself. It was a pain, but not a disaster; hell, it might even mean she and Hawkin got some help with the scut work and typing.

Kate realized that the object on the desk in front of

her was a bound copy of Roz's thesis, firmly described on the front page as a "first draft." It was titled "Women's Rage and Men's Dishonor: Manifestations of the Violent Goddess in the Hebrew Bible." She opened it curiously to glance over what Roz was doing.

The brief introduction was relatively intelligible, as academic writing went. Roz seemed to be looking at ways in which the warrior-goddesses of the ancient Near East (Ishtar and Asherah Kate had heard of, though not Anat or Hathor), their stories, songs, and characteristics, welled up in the tales and ideas of the Old Testament. After a general introduction, however, the writing seemed to become more technical and heavily footnoted, sprinkled with Roman numeral references, foreign phrases, capitalized abbreviations, and words like Masoretic and Septuagintal. Lee might make sense of it, Kate thought, but for someone who hadn't done any scholarly reading in too many years to count, it did not look like easy bedtime reading.

Thumbing through the thick document, Kate spotted a few pages that were not text. Some were reproductions of archaeological reports, alternating with pen-and-ink sketches and photocopies of photographs. One picture showed a sculpture of a female head and torso with glaring eyes, her sharp teeth pulled back from a grotesquely long protruding tongue, with a variety of objects in her four hands. The caption said "Durga," and Kate figured she was an Indian goddess like Kali because of the multiple arms. Not a warm and friendly goddess, though. Even Mutton would hesitate to give those hands an affectionate tongue-bath.

The door opened and Roz came back in. Kate let the thesis fall shut and moved away so Roz could resume her place and her breakfast.

"Sorry, Kate, but Jory is not the most competent secretary I've ever had, and I have to have a report together by this afternoon. Look, I'm really sorry about going over your head. I just didn't think."

"Don't worry about it," Kate heard herself saying.

"I'm sure it'll work out. Finish your breakfast, your granola will get soggy."

"Granola never gets soggy," Roz pointed out, taking up her spoon. "It's like wood fiber, needs to go rotten before it gives up its cellulose. Did you come to see me about Pramilla Mehta? And what can I do—to help rather than hinder?"

"Just back off, and I'll call if you can help. No, it's not specifically about her, though it may have to do with her husband's death. I wanted to ask, what do you know about a Web site called 'Womyn of the EVEning'?"

Kate, watching Roz carefully, saw the wariness descend.

"I've heard of it," Roz told her, which Kate decided meant that she knew the site but hesitated to admit it until she could see where this was heading.

"Your church's site and that one are linked through a third site that gives information on self-defense for women. Dirty self-defense—eye-gouging, breaking eardrums, biting off various body parts." She was being deliberately abrasive, but Roz did not react, merely responded.

"It's a nasty world."

"And attackers deserve to lose ears and penises, and habitual abusers deserve to be killed."

"Is that what their Web site's line is?" Roz said evenly. "If that's true, I may have to ask them to sever the link with our church."

"Roz, you can't expect me to believe that there's a Web site with a provocative name two steps away from yours that you haven't visited."

For a moment Kate thought that was precisely what Roz would assert, which meant that unless Kate could get a warrant to find what sites Roz's computer had visited, and she could prove that only Roz used the computer, she might as well walk away now.

But Roz relented. "Yes," she said. "I have glanced at the Web site."

"I have three murders on my hands whose names were on that site. I'm not going to ask you why nobody happened to bring this to my attention, not at the moment anyway, but I'm troubled by the fact that the only link we've been able to find between two of the men is that Web site. A Web site that your church is closely tied to."

Roz finally flared up. "Neither the church nor my own parish has anything to do with that list. You can hardly hold us responsible for the killing of three men just because we share a link on the Internet."

"I don't hold you responsible," said Kate evenly. "But I think you should brace yourselves for when the media finds out about it."

Roz half rose in her chair, putting both palms on the littered desk as if about to come over the top of it at Kate. "You wouldn't. If you dare to leak any of this—"

"I won't have to leak anything, Roz, you know that. It's surprising that no enterprising reporter has come up with it already."

"Kate, if I find that you—"

Kate's composure abruptly snapped. "Don't, Roz. Do not threaten me."

They glared at each other over Roz's life's work, and in the end the minister gave ground before the cop. Her gaze wavered and Kate could see her decide that this was not the best way to handle the situation. Her hackles went down, her palms came off the desk and went back to her lap as she settled down in the chair. She even tried for a crooked smile.

"No. Sorry, I know you wouldn't do that to me. God—you of all people wouldn't turn a friend over to the media sharks. I apologize."

"Actually, Roz, they may be the least of your problems. Because of the Internet aspect, the FBI is now going to take over a large part of this investigation. Al and I are still involved," she added with satisfaction— Roz Hall was not the only skilled manipulator in the room—"but it's out of our hands now. I'll do as much as I can to run interference with them, but they'll want answers, and if I can't get the answers for them, they'll come to you direct. One of the things they'll ask you is,

Do you know who submitted the names of James Larsen, Matthew Banderas, and Laxman Mehta to the Web site?"

"No," Roz answered—too quickly, Kate thought.

"Would you tell me if you did?" Kate demanded.

"Probably not."

"But you do know who has been responsible for the actions of the group known as the LOPD." Kate made it a statement, and Roz did not try to deny it outright.

"I may have heard some rumors, but they are not connected with these deaths, Kate. I swear I do not think they are."

"Give me their names, I'll ask them. Myself, not just handing the names over to the feds," Kate offered, but Roz was shaking her head before the sentence was finished.

"I can't do that, Kate, I'm sorry."

"You're willing to play God, condemn to death men even the courts can't? To be an accomplice?"

"I told you, I don't know who put their names on the list, I don't know who killed them." This time Kate let the silence stretch out, until Roz gave way and broke it. "As for playing God, it works the other way, too. Even if I knew, it would be playing God to turn the killers in. If what you're saying is true, they've chosen to become judges in a society that refuses to take that responsibility. I'd have to think long and hard before I could decide they were wrong."

"Judge and executioner," Kate pointed out.

"Judge and executioner," Roz accepted. "The ultimate in responsibility."

"I thought God wanted us to practice forgiveness."

"There are times when God would have us practice justice instead."

"Or revenge?"

"There are times to turn the other cheek, and times to get out the whip and overturn the tables of the corrupt in the Temple. This may be one of the second."

"And you wouldn't tell me who's doing it."

"If I knew, I would regard it as privileged information."

"The FBI is going to turn you inside out."

"They can try."

"There are better causes to choose if you want martyrdom, Roz."

"Not very many. Kate, my church does not have ritualized, formal confession like the Roman Catholics do, but if someone were to tell me of their involvement in this, as an ordained priest I would regard it as inviolable. To you or to the FBI.

"All of which," she hastened to say, "is theoretical. Since I don't actually know anything."

"Tell me about your Ph.D. thesis."

"My what?" Roz asked, thrown off balance by the abrupt change in direction.

"Your thesis. About women's rage."

Roz flushed, an interesting reaction. "In the Old Testament," she said with force. "It's largely about how the pre-Israelite goddesses influenced the developing cult of Yahweh. It's a Ph.D. thesis, for Christ sake. You should know they never have anything to do with real life."

Kate nodded as if Roz had actually told her something, and then abruptly stood up, thanked Roz, and left. She was not certain just what she had accomplished—other than severely disconcerting the woman behind the desk. Still, it was not easy to throw Roz Hall, and surely having done so counted for something.

17

Out of destruction she comes to wrest
The juice from the cactus, its harsh spine,
And until she, the destroyer, has been blest,
There will be no child, no flower, and no wine.

Over the course of that damp morning, the FBI's information came dutifully in, as trickles or in undigested lumps. Five additional men on the Web site list that Kate had uncovered had died in the last few months, and several others were simply missing. Late in the afternoon came news of a cluster of three men, from Georgia up through the Carolinas, that gave Kate a nasty feeling, since all of them just disappeared from their daily lives into thin air. In one case a badly decomposed body had been found out in the woods by the first hikers of spring. It was suspected to be the missing man from South Carolina; DNA testing was under way.

Of the five known dead, three had clearly been murdered, two of those gunned down in New York a month apart by the same gun, and no suspects identified. There was one accident on the list (and reading the faxed report of the man's blood alcohol level and the absence of skid marks or mechanical failure, Kate had to agree that he had simply passed out at the wheel and gone off the road and into a bridge support at high speed) and another man had committed suicide, but if the suicide was not actually assisted, his family swore he had been more or less driven to death's door and handed a gun. For weeks before he had put a bullet in his head, the convicted child abuser had been the object of a barrage of letters, photos, and phone calls, threatening, taunting, and merciless. At home and at work, his colleagues and his neighbors included, the pressure had been unrelenting and around the clock. Until he killed himself. In the three weeks since his death, his family had received nothing further.

The fifth death, the third confirmed murder victim, was close to home, both physically and in regards to their investigation. His name was Larry Goff, and he had died in Sacramento, less than three hours from downtown San Francisco, with strapping tape on his wrists.

Goff's wife, Tamara, according to the Web site and the Sacramento detective Kate talked to, had been to the hospital emergency room five times in two years for treatment of chronic "accidents," and had separated from her husband, with a restraining order in place. In early November, Goff was accused of kidnapping their two children—picking them up from school on a Friday afternoon and taking them for the weekend without telling his wife. He brought them back to her on the Sunday, and when arrested he claimed that she had given him permission, but the kidnap charges stood. He was granted bail, and the subsequent investigation had been wending its slow way through the court system when Tamara was found in her bedroom one morning in December, dead of an overdose of prescription pain pills. At the time of death, she had a fresh plaster cast on one arm and two broken teeth in the left side of her jaw. There was no indication of suicide, and nothing to show that she had been force-fed the pills. She was simply in pain, and she made a mistake.

Tamara's sister claimed the children, and with the pending kidnap charge hanging over their father, the courts granted her temporary custody. Then two weeks later, a few days before New Year's, Goff was found in a hotel frequented by prostitutes, bound, gagged, and strangled to death. His wallet and watch had been missing, though not his gold wedding band. Police investi-

gators determined that he had been lured to the room
by a woman the manager had not seen before, although
he surmised her profession by her clothing. Once in the
room, she and possibly an accomplice had overpowered
Goff, killed, and robbed him.

"Do you have a copy of the autopsy report in front
of you?" Kate asked the Sacramento detective over the
phone.

"Sure. You want me to fax it to you?"

"That would be helpful. I'm looking for any red
mark on the torso. A taser burn."

A minute of silence broken only by distant voices
and the sound of pages turning was ended with a
"Nope. Don't see anything like that here. There were
some marks—you can see them in the photographs—
but they looked more like immediately premortem
bruising."

"Okay. You haven't seen anything else with that
MO?"

"No, and we've been watching, since it's such an
oddity. I mean, how many hookers use strapping tape
for bondage games? Hairy guy like Goff, he'd have little
bald patches all over him. Imagine explaining that to
your girlfriend back home."

Kate had to laugh at the image.

"You'll see when you get the photos that his beard's
kinda mangy looking. That's from cutting away the
tape. In fact, I heard about your duct-tape guys the
other day, and I was going to call you—different stuff, I
know, but close. Then something came up and I forgot
about it."

"That happens," Kate said. Not to her, damn it, but
she tried to keep the irritation from her voice; there was
no point in alienating a colleague, particularly one who
had a file she wanted to see. "Did you develop any
suspects?"

"Nada. We thought at first it might be revenge, you
know, since the wife died, but as far as anyone knew,
Tamara had no contact with prostitutes, was never ar-

rested, our informants had never seen her on the streets, so it wasn't some friends doing a little payback. This was Tamara's second marriage, so we looked at her first husband, just in case, but he's out of the picture, happily remarried and living in Miami, no indication that he was away at the time of the murder. No brother or father around that we could find, not even a mother, though a friend of Tamara's said there is one somewhere. The two kids are with Tamara's sister now, she's looking to adopt if she can talk the ex-husband in Florida into it. His wife doesn't want them, and only one of them is his, the other's Goff's."

Kate thanked the detective, and when the fax came through a while later she studied the face with the small blue eyes, trimmed beard, and dark mole on the left side of the nose, but neither the picture nor the report told her much. No sign of candy on the body, not in the report at any rate. She filed it away, and went back to her phone calls.

Of the 200 or so living (presumably living) members of the abuser's hit list, by the end of the day, the team had succeeded in making contact with just over half. The others had either moved or had their phones disconnected, and the investigators were forced to wait for the local departments and regional agents to report back. Two of the deaths came to light in this way, but for most of the remaining names it would be days before the locals got a chance to check the individuals out and get back to them.

In the meantime, of the 127 men the team had found, men scattered from Key Biscayne to Seattle, nearly all said that they had received some form of threatening communication, and three-quarters of them had gotten a dozen or more letters, faxes, three A.M. phone calls, or anonymous e-mail messages. Due to their own legal entanglements, the men on the list were less likely than the general population to complain to the police, but a number of them had, although neither police nor telephone companies had been able to iden-

tify the anonymous senders. Even the e-mail had come
from public computers in libraries and Internet cafés.

The Web site did prove to be operated by a woman
in Nebraska, which struck Kate as incongruous, for
some reason. Still, remote or not, Stella DeVries knew
her rights and her high-powered lawyer refused to let
her say anything aside from a public declaration that
she had not advocated any act of harassment or violence, and that freedom of speech included listing the
names of accused offenders with the disclaimer that
they were innocent until found guilty in a court of
law—which disclaimer was indeed prominently displayed on the Web site, albeit at the very end.

The entire Internet side of the investigation was now
the property of the federal authorities, and Kate had no
choice but to let other law enforcement agencies deal
with Ms. DeVries and her well-prepared law team. Kate
and Al could only walk around the edges and try to see
how their cases tied in.

Finally, late that evening, Al laid his hand on Kate's
collar and dragged her away from her computer terminal to a late-night diner much beloved of the cops who
worked out of the Hall of Justice. Kate's back felt permanently hunched, her fingers crabbed into the typing
position. She couldn't remember when she had last
eaten, or what.

They had been living on coffee for all that long day
and craving a strong drink for the last half of it, so they
both compromised and had a beer with their hamburg-
ers. Kate swallowed deeply and closed her eyes in appreciation; following that brief vacation she sat forward
and returned to work.

"I can't believe how long it takes sometimes for
things like this Web site to come to light," she groaned.

"It's only been up for, what was it, twelve weeks?"

"Closer to fourteen."

"And there's obviously a lot of personal support for
the list, off-Web contacts that can't be traced. All the
Web site says is, Here's the guy's name and where he

lives; here's what he's accused of; let him know how you feel. Nothing about murdering him or hounding him to suicide. I personally can't see that there's anything illegal about it. What's the precedent, anyway? Can you get a restraining order against a Web site?" Hawkin wondered.

"Unless there's a really clear link between a violent act and a Web site's ranting, it's hard to shut it down," Kate reminded him. Al no doubt knew this, but he tended to push the electronic world as far away from his life as he could.

Their food arrived, hot and beautifully greasy, and they turned their attention to it. In a short time Kate was contemplating a few limp and lonely french fries and thinking that the hamburger really hadn't been as large as it looked. The waitress, standing by the table as if summoned, asked if they wanted something else.

"Actually," Kate told her, "I'd like the same again."

"For me, too," said Al. "And another couple of beers."

The two partners sat without speaking, suspended between the points of work and companionship, hunger and satiation. When the second half of their meal came they ate and drank with an almost ritual slowness, and both sighed at the end.

"I didn't realize I was so hungry," Al said, sounding amused.

"What's that phrase? My sides were clapping together like an empty portmanteau." Kate belched demurely and pushed away the plate, leaving the trimmings of lettuce and orange slice. "Whatever a portmanteau is. So, Al. What do we do? Are these about to become the feds' completely, or still ours, or what?"

"They're still ours until they kick us off. The hit list is their business—we just uncovered it. You did. Though I wouldn't wait for any more thanks than you've got."

"I won't. So it's back to our very own trio of abusers."

"And possibly what's-his-name, Goff, in Sacramento."

"Be nice to find out if anyone in the city has regular contact with Ms. DeVries and her list. You suppose the FBI will tell us?"

"I don't think we should wait for that either."

It was frustrating not knowing what information would come from the federal investigation—and frustrating to know that the feds might well solve all three murders in one day, by working them from the opposite direction.

"We go on as before?" Kate asked.

"Who knows? We might even get there first."

"I suppose," Kate said thoughtfully, "it doesn't really matter where the killer—or killers—found out about their victims. I mean, they could have gotten the names out of newspapers and court reports, inside contacts in the hospitals and shelters, even just word of mouth. Man beats wife, the neighbors know. That seems to be the way the Ladies find their victims. Barry Doyle and the rest of the LOPD victims aren't on the Web site."

"But, who would respond to a stranger's troubles by killing the stranger's abuser, or rapist? A lot of people might want to, but wanting is a long way from doing. Strangling an unconscious stranger isn't a thing just anybody can do. Assuming, as we have been, that they are strangers."

"I agree," she said. "It takes someone with a major load of resentment and anger. Cold rage." The word brought to Kate's mind the troubling title she'd seen on Roz's desk. "You know, Roz Hall's Ph.D. thesis is on 'women's rage' and something about violent goddesses. Maybe I should take a closer look at it."

Hawkin cocked his head at the tone of her voice. "And at her?"

Kate rubbed her face tiredly. "I've been turning that over in my mind a lot, and I just can't say what I think. She's an obvious candidate, because she's so involved in the movement here, but you know, I can't see it, can't see her working herself up to that kind of hatred. Still, God knows she's a woman with a lot of sides to her. I think it may be time to ask some hard questions about her alibis for the nights involved."

"Probably better if I do it. I'm not a friend."

"Let me start, see what I come up with. I'll hand it over to you if there's not a conclusive negative."

"Who else, other than her?"

Kate gazed off into the night street outside the diner, assembling her thoughts. "We tend to think of anger as a sudden thing, an eruption into violence that fades and is over, either permanently or until the next time." Most of the homicides they dealt with were this way, either in the home fueled by alcohol and stress or on the street corner fueled by drugs, territoriality, and young male hormones. Hawkin nodded, and Kate went on. "Serial killers are something else, of course. They work either on voices in their heads or sexual impulses. Anger feeds into it, but it's secondary." Again Hawkin nodded, and Kate sat forward, laying her forearms out on the worn Formica table.

"Then there are the terrorists, mass or serial killers who tie their anger in with their intellect." God, she thought uneasily; could I describe Roz Hall any more clearly? "For them, rage is channeled through political action; their personal resentments and injuries, all their personal histories are given meaning by what they do. Revenge is taken not on the individual soldier who beat you up or the guy from the other side who blew up your little sister with a pipe bomb, but on all of 'them,' the whole group that soldier or the bomb-thrower represent."

"Sounds like you've talked this over with Lee," Al commented.

"No." He looked up at the tight, brief negative, and she had to explain. "I can't go into this without making Roz a part of it, and Lee and Roz are close. They were lovers, a long time ago, and Roz has done an enormous amount in bringing Lee back to life. We owe her a lot. I owe her. They're family."

"I see."

"I don't know that Roz has anything to do with these murders—like I said, I can't believe she does. But I think she has either knowledge or at least her suspicions. She talked about the inviolability of confession in a way that sounded . . . potential. As if nobody had come to her yet to confess, but she thought they might. And the subject matter of her thesis shows she's been thinking about the idea of women's anger for a while."

"Terrorism, like Peter Mehta said. Against abusers." Hawkin sounded more thoughtful than dubious.

"Selective terrorism. Although if they could come up with a way to eliminate large numbers of abusers at one throw, I doubt that they'd hesitate." Kate thought of the flyer advocating poison pills for male babies, triggered at the first sign that the boy was becoming abusive.

"Terrorists generally go for publicity," Al objected. "Why haven't they sent in a manifesto to Channel Five or the *New York Times*?"

"Maybe they thought they'd see how many they could get away with before it came out and the abusers started to watch their backs."

Hawkin took a thoughtful bite of his elderly orange slice. "So, not one vigilante, but 'they.' How many do you see here?"

"I suppose it could be one person."

"Male or female?"

Kate started to answer, then closed her mouth and thought for a minute. "You know, we've been thinking of this as a woman's thing, but there's no reason it couldn't be a man. Someone who lost a sister, maybe, or whose daughter was raped. God," she said with a laugh, "wouldn't that be ironic? Woman's revenge carried out by a man."

"Sensitive New Age guy goes overboard."

Kate rolled her eyes. "Now you're writing newspaper headlines?"

"I may need a second job to support the new kid. But you were saying it could be one, or—?"

"If it's a single individual, a woman, she's got to be strong enough physically to handle a man the size of James Larsen, and with an immensely strong personality that could plan and carry out a series of methodical murders without falling apart."

"Either that or she's nuts."

"Either that or she's nuts," Kate agreed. "But even that is a form of strength. If it's a group, on the other hand, I'd say it has to be a small one, probably no more than two or three. Like you said, finding a person who could help you commit murder in cold blood wouldn't be that easy. Anything but a very tight group, you'd have someone who talked or bragged or fell to pieces with remorse."

"I agree. But finding them through the Web site is no longer our business. Unless, of course, we happen across the bigger picture in our own investigation." Hawkin scratched his bristly jaw and shoved back his chair. "Time to go home, Martinelli. Get your beauty sleep, give Lee a back rub, sing Gilbert and Sullivan karaoke with Jon."

Kate too got to her feet. "You make it sound so attractive, Hawkin."

They sorted out dollar bills for the waitress, and went their separate ways.

When Kate got home she found the lights turned down and the house's other residents asleep. She also found a package waiting for her on the table in the hall, an oversized mailing envelope containing something the shape and weight of a box of typing paper. Clipped to the end of the envelope was a note in Lee's writing that said:

Roz came by with this tonight, said she had the impression that you wanted to see it so she printed you a copy.

Hope you're not going to try to read it in bed.

—L.

It was a box of typing paper, or 487 sheets of it, anyway, unbound. On the first page was the title.

WOMEN'S RAGE AND MEN'S DISHONOR: MANIFESTATIONS OF THE VIOLENT GODDESS IN THE HEBREW BIBLE

18

How then to set her free or come to terms
With the volcano itself, the fierce power
Erupting injuries, shrieking alarms?
Kali among her skulls must have her hour.

Kate had no intention of settling in to read 487 pages of turgid doctoral prose, not after the day—the string of days—she'd had. She made herself a cup of decaf coffee that was mostly hot milk and sat at the kitchen table with the massive piece of work to glance through it, more so she could tell Roz she'd done so than from any great interest.

Two and a half hours later she suddenly realized that if she didn't go to bed soon, she would not be going to bed at all. Once she had decided to skip over the lengthy footnotes with their detailed discussions of opposing points of view and debates of the subtle meanings of words and objects, the text moved right along. Indeed, instead of the usual dry technical language employed by every thesis Kate had ever seen, Roz wrote in straightforward, even lyrical English prose that drew the reader on, and in, as if this was a popular work designed to inspire a general audience. Why was she surprised, Kate asked herself; everything that damn woman set her hand to was compelling, why not her doctoral thesis?

Like most nominal Christians, and most enthusiastic believers as well, Kate had never given much thought to what came Before Christ. Oh sure, the Old Testament had been around before the New, which explained its complexity and seeming lack of unifying theme, but before the Old Testament there were what? Patriarchs and Canaanites and goatherds and things, wandering dimly through the desert.

In Roz's hands the Bible came alive, revealing itself as a document of the human spirit with roots reaching far back into the history of humankind, before the stories were written down, back to an age when high-tech weaponry was made out of bronze, and even stone.

The name Baal appeared on page three, abruptly calling to mind Kate's long-ago Sunday School classes taught by the tightly girdled Miss Steinlaker. The priests of Baal, it had been (and for an instant Kate was back in that drafty church classroom with Miss Steinlaker looming over her, smelling of chalk, perfume, menthol cigarettes, and the musk of unwashed clothing). The priests of Baal had lit something on fire, hadn't they? Or perhaps had failed to do so. Kate blinked, and the classroom vanished, and Roz was explaining that Baal was a Canaanite storm god, a young warrior deity about whom hymns were written down on clay tablets, describing Baal as the Rider on the Clouds. Then a thousand years later the Israelites came out from Egypt and settled in the land, and soon they, too, were speaking of their God as a young warrior heaving thunderbolts across the sky, calling Him "Rider on the Clouds."

It was not stealing, Roz explained firmly, and it should not be thought that the people of Israel were trying to change their God's nature or attach other gods to His coattails in a sort of religious corporate takeover bid. It had to do with framing a language of theology, using the images and descriptions of others to more richly describe the wonder of the one true God's majesty and complexity.

If this was so, Roz then asked rhetorically, what of the images and language that described the unique actions and characteristics of the goddess figures so common in the ancient Near East, Anat and Asherah, Ishtar and Inanna? Were they simply condemned as idolatry, as the Prophets would have us believe? Or did their poetry and songs, their epithets and personalities, resonate so strongly in the minds of the people that, despite the goddesses' inextricable connection with the forbidden fertility cults and their obvious antithesis to the masculine figure of Yahweh, God of Israel, some of their nature survived in Him, some of the goddesses' stories became adopted and adapted by the people of Israel?

This question came a bare twenty pages into the document, and amounted to Roz's introduction, laying the groundwork for the thesis itself.

The thesis being that Yahweh did indeed come to incorporate certain characteristics of a group of Near Eastern goddess figures whom Roz classified as Warrior Virgins—virginity, as Roz had mentioned the night of *Song* but had been too distracted to explain, being for divine beings not indicative of physical innocence but rather a state of proud independence from males, of not being defined by their male consort.

As role models for women set on taking back the night, these goddesses were a fearsome bunch. Take the verses illustrating the goddess Anat:

> *Heads roll about like balls,*
> * hands fly up like locusts,*
> * like a swarm of grasshoppers, the warriors' hands.*
> *Anat ties the heads as a necklace,*
> * she fastens the hands around her waist. . . .*
> *Her soul swells up with laughter,*
> * her heart bursts with joy.*
> *Anat's soul is joyous*
> * as she wades to her knees in the blood of soldiers,*
> * to her thighs in the gore of warriors.*

No, thought Kate, Miss Steinlaker had never told her Sunday School class about this.

There was the goddess Inanna, who aside from being a goddess of fertility was also a fearsome warrior:

In the mountain stronghold that holds back homage,
  the very vegetation is cursed,
The city's great gates,
  O Inanna,
  you have burnt to ash.
Its rivers run with blood,
  the people cannot drink.

Then came the Indian goddess Kali, a close cousin to the virgin warriors of the Middle East, who lived in the cremation grounds, ate pieces of the bodies, and wore a necklace of human heads and a belt decorated with severed hands. She was followed by a description of the bloodthirsty Egyptian Hathor, appeased only by a great flood of red beer poured across the land like the blood she takes it to be. The Mesopotamian Ishtar called down a raging storm on humanity until they floated like dead fish on the sea, and the Greek Demeter condemned the earth to bare sterility to revenge the abduction and rape of her daughter.

Why do people think of goddesses as wide-hipped, large-breasted, loving bringers of fertility? Kate wondered uncomfortably. These women were terrifying.

Kate went to pour herself a glass of wine, looked at the rich red liquid in the glass, and dumped it down the sink, taking instead a shot of nice safe amber brandy from the cooking supplies. She continued reading, about revenge and wrath and the sheer joy of killing, and she winced when she came to Roz's description of Kali:

She is young and beautiful, old and haggard, dark-skinned as a blow in the face of the pale, high-ranking Aryan castes, savage and loving and utterly enamored with bloodshed. Kali is created by the great goddess Durga for the express purpose of conquering a monster able to kill any man who comes up against him—but not, it turns out, any woman. Kali glories in death, decorates herself with pieces of her victims, and allows no man supremacy, not her enemies, not even her consort, who lies beneath her in intercourse. She is the advocate and protector of India's poor, India's acknowledgment that inside every woman lurks a force of immense power that, when loosed, exults in the destruction of men, that longs to trample even the most beloved of males underfoot, to wade in his blood and eat his carcass.

Sweet Jesus, Kate reflected, taking a large gulp of the brandy, what must Roz's thesis supervisor be making of this? And did Roz need to be quite so graphic, even loving, in these descriptions of gore and destruction?

Perhaps that was the point: that even an ordained minister with a pet dog named Mutt, a weekly salary, and a mortgage could feel that urge, primal and terrible.

With a convulsive shudder Kate shoved the entire thesis together and back in its box. She felt trapped by a visualization of what this group of vigilantes—selective terrorists—could do if they took this stuff seriously. Would they begin gutting men next, instead of a nice tidy strangulation? Hacking off body parts for Kali to wear? or—Christ!—eat?

She drained her glass, considered and rejected a refill, and, knowing she'd never get to sleep with those images crowding into her mind, went in to the television. An old movie, she decided—if she could find one without gore, abuse of women, or a woman taking revenge. Which left out Jon's collection of Bette Davis films, and half the suspense movies. She was faced with Jon's musicals or Lee's science fiction, and whereas the latter often involved wholesale slaughter, the former induced in Kate the very desire to commit it that she was trying to avoid. Even *Men in Black* had a downtrodden woman whose husband gets his due. To say nothing of reminding her of Agent Marcowitz.

In the end she fed an old Peter Sellers *Pink Panther* movie into the player, and fell asleep on the sofa before it was through.

By the clear light of a far too early morning, it was difficult to justify the night's heebie-jeebies as anything but overwork and an overactive imagination. After all, none of the corpses had been mutilated and there was no sign of escalation into mass slaughter. The Ph.D. thesis Roz was writing might have some link with the hit list victims, but it was, as Roz herself had said and Kate had to admit, an academic investigation, not a vigilante manifesto.

Still, Kate could not shake the image of the warrior-goddess wading in a pool of men's blood, that "immense power that exults in the destruction of men" loosed on the world. (How did *Song* put it? "Lovely as Jerusalem, terrible as an army with banners.") Kate did not want to read the rest of the pages, but she knew she would, and that night, after a day spent in painstaking and excruciatingly slow telephonic investigation, she picked up the typescript again, warily.

It appeared, however, that the worst of Roz's flight of fancy (if that was what it was) had been confined to the beginning, and the author now set about demonstrating just how the worship of goddess figures might have been transferred over to the cult of Yahweh. Roz took a passage in the Gilgamesh epic where the goddess Ishtar "cries out like a woman in travail" bemoaning her destruction of her people, for "are they not my own people, whom I brought forth?" and compared it with Yahweh's cry "like a woman in travail" in the Book of Isaiah. She then set about building on the common theme throughout the Old Testament (which Roz consistently called the Hebrew Bible) of God's wrath overflowing, the furious arm of a vengeful God turned against his faithless people, only to be drawn back before complete destruction could descend.

And this is the point, Roz asserted, at which God and goddess are one, that God's love—often using a word based on the Hebrew for womb—is love "as of a mother for the child of her body." God could no more destroy his—or her—people than a mother could cease to love a child she had given birth to.

All very heavy stuff, and although Kate didn't exactly feel a headache coming on, she found herself hoping that she would, so she would have an excuse to stop reading. It soon became obvious, however, that the bulk of the tome's latter half was made up of the highly technical material of pure thesis, heavily footnoted, concerned with alternate translations, parallel meanings, the problems of something called a *hapax legomenon* (whatever that was), and the minutiae of dating texts and text fragments. Kate leafed through page after page of typescript studded with what looked like three different alphabets, one of which was Hebrew. Some of the footnotes in this section took two or three pages to work themselves out, and Kate made no attempt at following any of it, relieved that it was nearly over.

Then, at the very end, after the bibliography in fact, an additional and still-rough chapter had been appended. After a moment Kate realized that it was the result of the *Song* performance they had all seen the other night, the interpretation of the Song of Songs that had so excited Roz. "Pope," it seemed, was not the Roman pontiff but one Marvin Pope, who had developed the idea of a link between the Indian Kali and the Canaanite Anat, both of whom took vast joy in spilling blood, both wearing belts of hands and necklaces of skulls, both being absolutely essential, in spite of their murderous tendencies, to the continuation of the universe. Or rather, precisely because of their tendency to give vent to murderous bouts of rage, for without Anat's fury, Baal the storm god could not bring the life-giving rains and the land would go sterile; without Kali, Shiva's dance that heralded both the end and the beginning of time would fail.

Kate felt as if her head was about to explode. She scratched her scalp hard with her short fingernails, wondering why she was wasting so many hours on this airy-fairy nonsense that she hadn't a chance of fully understanding. It was pointless—after all, wasn't *point-*

less one synonym for the word *academic*?—but she could not shake the feeling of a connection here. She could smell it coming off the paper in front of her, faint and evocative but there.

But how? And where?

One more possible victim had been added to their list during the day. A resident of King City, a few hours' drive into the Central Valley south of San Francisco, had disappeared five weeks ago and been found last week in a brushy area frequented by coyotes and half a dozen other kinds of scavengers. About all the pathologist could tell was that the man had been strangled. Whether he'd been zapped by a taser or once had a candy bar in his pocket was anybody's guess. He was, however, a wife-beater, and his name was on the hit list, along with his address and phone number.

Quite a number of other men on the list had admitted to receiving harassing calls and letters. The majority assumed at first that the team's call was yet another one, so the people wielding the phones had learned to speak fast, firmly, and with blatant if not entirely genuine expressions of sympathy in order to avoid hang-ups.

Two men thought they were currently being stalked, one in Huntsville, Texas, the other in Reno. Seven had been attacked already, either personally or by something being thrown at, splashed against, or painted onto their houses. One man had seized on the suggestion of a taser-wielding attacker that one of the less experienced members of the team had let slip, but further interviews made it fairly clear that he was more than a little unbalanced and would have taken up the mention of alien abduction with equal enthusiasm.

Five men had disappeared completely, seven had moved but been in communication with family or friends, and three names were either mistakes or jokes or complete fabrications—one of them Kate's suggested addition to the list, a hardened but exceedingly wily child-abuser by the name of Al Martini. That had appeared during the afternoon, causing a few minutes of near-hysterical levity on the part of the frustrated and overworked team, bent over their terminals.

Kate decided enough was enough, said good night to Al and the others, and took herself home. Lee was still awake, and called down the stairs as Kate was unloading her burden on the hallway table.

"That you, Kate?"

"What's left of me."

"Would you give Roz a call? I told her that if you were in before eleven, you would."

"What does she want?"

"She didn't say."

Kate seriously considered ignoring the request, but in the end she did phone Roz's number, bracing herself for another demand from Roz: an illicit look at someone's file, perhaps, or a request to be on a panel in Washington, D.C. But to her surprise, Roz did not seem to want anything, only to know if Kate had had a chance to glance at the manuscript, and if she had any questions. Kate rubbed her forehead wearily, grateful that telephones did not have viewers, and told her that no, she did not.

Kate then climbed the stairs to bed, and to Lee, and then to sleep.

To jerk awake at 3:09 the next morning with the phone shouting at her, and Al's voice on the other end of the line.

Telling her there had been another one.

Only this one was still alive.

19

Anguish is always there, lurking at night,
Wakes us like a scourge, the creeping sweat
As rage is remembered, self-inflicted blight.
What is it in us we have not mastered yet?

"Detective's name is Hillman," Hawkin told her in the car on the empty freeway headed south down the peninsula. "Ever meet him?"

"No. He must be after my time in San Jose."

"Sounded competent, but a little irritated that the feds are all over him."

"I can understand that. Are they taking it over?"

"No. Just getting in his way at the moment."

"What'd he say about the MO?"

"Two attackers, a taser for sure, regulation handcuffs, they had a scarf around his throat before they were interrupted. Didn't wait around to finish him off, just ran. Cops didn't see them go, they went out the other side of the building."

"What about the candy?"

"Ah. Marcowitz hadn't gotten around to mentioning that to him. I asked Hillman to look, and to keep it under his hat, both that I'd asked and if he found any. He called me back just before you picked me up, to say they'd found a handful clear at the other entrance. One print—they're running it now."

"A print? That's great," said Kate, meaning it profoundly. Any small thing to break the back of this increasingly scary case was fine with her. "Who's the vic?"

"Guy named Traynor, Lennie Traynor. A true creep. Makes Larsen and Banderas look like Citizen of the Month, gives Mehta a run for the stupid prize."

"What does he do, murder grannies?"

"Plays with kids," Hawkin said succinctly. They drove in silence through the night.

Lennie Traynor, both in history and in the flesh, was the sort of creature guaranteed to make a cop bristle. Knowing he'd probably been abused as a child himself didn't help; both of them—particularly Hawkin, with an adolescent stepdaughter at home and a baby on the way—saw him sitting in the hospital bed and felt a quick urge to grind him underfoot and finish the assailants' job. Traynor felt their instantly suppressed contempt, and cringed further. That too did not help.

Traynor had one felony conviction behind him, for raping a thirteen-year-old girl with Down's syndrome, and a string of other charges, two of which had been plea-bargained down to misdemeanors. He had been driven out of two communities unwilling to harbor a sex offender before he landed in an industrial area of San Jose with few families, and found an employer who was happy enough to hire the unhirable, on the cheap and no questions asked. Traynor worked as a janitor in a small assembly plant for low-tech computer parts, and was given a dank room in exchange for doubling as night watchman.

His nocturnal lifestyle undoubtedly contributed to his crawled-out-from-under-a-rock appearance, but all in all, the police faced with his problem wished that he had stayed under his rock, or died there quietly.

Instead, unlikely as it seemed, Traynor had been lucky. Bashed, taser-zapped, and half strangled he might be, but he was alive, and as he told his story for what must have been the dozenth time, it became obvious that only luck had saved him.

Traynor's job was literally half his life. His commitment ran from six at night to six in the morning, day in and day out. He was free to take days (or rather, nights) off with prior arrangement, but he had only done so a handful of times in the three years he'd worked there, and his two-week annual holiday was more often than not cut short by boredom.

His sole forms of entertainment, it seemed, were the walks he took every morning when his shift had ended and the cyber-crawls he indulged in on his top-of-the-line computer system. His declarations of healthy exercise and intellectual curiosity were dismissed by Kate and Al, as they had been by every investigator who had stood in the room before them, but whether or not he logged on to child pornography sites was not currently their concern. It was the walks they were interested in, the long wanders in the surrounding housing developments during the hours when children were walking to school or waiting for buses.

He'd been seen, and recognized, three and a half months before, and for the third time a group of concerned parents began to organize a neighborhood against him. Mothers pointedly shepherded their children to the school gates, petitions were drawn up, the kids began to watch for him. So he retreated, and for six weeks had stayed in his cave.

Things quieted down, and Traynor lay low, and interest waned. He bought an elderly dog from the pound to keep him company, a quiet dog that slept most of the day and was content with walks around the weed-lined parking lot. After a while, though, when Traynor judged that interest had moved on, he snapped the dog's leash on, piled him into the car, and drove him a few miles away for a daily walk—at the hour when the neighborhood was waking and its bright and freshly scrubbed children were going off to school.

Had the dog been more lively or appealing, Traynor might have gone his way in peace for a good long time. The dog, though, was as scruffy and unkempt as its owner, and a few weeks later one mother who jogged in the mornings was talking to another mother at a parents' meeting, and his identity came out.

There was nothing against him but distaste and profound apprehension, no evidence whatsoever of wrongdoing, but a sex offender was required to register with the police in a new area, and although he was not proposing to move into the neighborhood, he was frequenting its sidewalks.

It might well have died down, given time. After all, Traynor had a car, a twelve-hour day, and all the residential neighborhoods of the Bay Area at his command. However, in the midst of it a young girl disappeared from her home two miles from Traynor's factory, and even though he had a firm alibi for the time (three of the factory workers had seen him walking the dog in the parking lot) and even though the police quickly determined that the girl was a runaway (the diary entry she left might have been ambiguous, but the story she told her best friend was not), Traynor had already been put in the spotlight. Two days later his name was on the Web site hit list. Letters began to arrive, notices went up on phone poles throughout the area, and pickets set up outside the gates. Phone calls came, so that when the task force team had reached him the day before, he thought it another one and cut them off hastily. His increasingly nervous boss gave him two weeks' notice, one of the factory workers who had four children put a brick through Traynor's windshield, and shrill voices were raised in the City Council meeting.

Then the night before, a few minutes short of eleven-thirty, a pair of black-clad figures wearing hoods and gloves broke into the factory with a pair of bolt cutters. They ambushed Traynor on his rounds, stunned him with a taser, slapped handcuffs on his nerveless wrists, and prepared to throttle him with a length of red silk. Unfortunately for them, but to the dubious benefit of Traynor's life, they assumed that the night watchman was the sum total of security at the factory, and on their way in the door tripped an old but still efficient silent alarm. One of Traynor's assailants heard the sound of an approaching vehicle, looked out the window, and saw the patrol car responding to the alarm. The two intruders fled with their job half complete, although the blow one of them dealt Traynor's head, either with a boot or the abandoned bolt cutters found nearby, added to the bad gash he had sustained in his original fall, nearly did him in.

So here he lay in his hospital bed in the small hours of the morning, a victim no one had the least scrap of sympathy or indignation for, his lank and thinning hair half shaved off to mend the two scalp wounds, black of eye, hoarse of voice, and trying hard to maintain the moral superiority of the assault victim under the cold, knowing stares of hospital staff, police, and the dread FBI. Even his fingers were repellent, thin white tentacles plucking nervously at the sheets, and Kate found herself wondering what had happened to the only true victim here, the poor dog.

She realized that Traynor had come to the end of his well-practiced narrative and was waiting for questions with resigned apprehension. Hawkin had his back to the room, looking out of the third-floor window, apparently leaving it up to her.

"Do you have any idea who they were, Mr. Traynor?" she asked, but he was shaking his head before the question was over.

"They could have been anyone. Just that they were women."

"How do you know that, Mr. Traynor?"

"How do I . . . ? You mean, how did I know they were women?"

"Yes," she said with exaggerated patience. "Their voices, their bodies, did they smell of feminine hygiene spray, what?"

The pasty face went pink with embarrassment. "I . . . well, the way they moved, I guess. And their clothing was not so heavy I couldn't tell, er—"

"That they had breasts and hips?"

His blush deepened at her blatant reference to a woman's body; he nodded, studying his hands.

"What about their voices?"

"The only thing they said—the only thing I heard them say—was when I was already half unconscious. I heard the word 'cops,' and then the pressure went off my throat and after that I passed out. I suppose when they hit my head."

"Just the one word?"

"Nothing else. Their silence was . . . scary. Unearthly. Just some grunts while I was . . . I was screaming, I'm afraid, as soon as I had my voice back, asking them why they were doing this. Begging them to stop. They never said a thing."

For the first time Kate was aware of a faint brush of compassion for Lennie Traynor, but it did not last long. Instead, she pressed him for details about the two figures.

One, it seemed, had been taller and stronger than the other, and it had been this taller person who was in charge. She (if she it had been) had come at him with the taser in hand and had handled him like a rag doll, flipping his stunned body over and wrenching his arms back for the bite of the handcuffs. It had been her black hood looming over him when he found himself faceup again, she who whipped a silken billow of dark red out of a pocket and wrapped it around his throat, she who tightened and twisted and began to fade from view as the oxygen ceased to reach his brain.

"What was the hood like?" Kate asked.

"Black. One of those knitted ski things."

"So it had eyeholes?"

"I saw her eyes, yes."

"What color were they?"

"Brownish, I guess."

"Mr. Traynor, you were looking into her eyes while she was trying to kill you. Surely you remember what color they were."

"Light brown. Lighter than yours. Maybe hazel?"

"And the skin color around them?"

"She was white, not black. Maybe a light Hispanic. Not Asian, anyway."

"Makeup?"

"No," he said, not sounding at all certain.

"Perfume?"

"Unh-uh. She smelled like sweat."

"Bad? Like she hadn't washed in a while?"

"No. Sweat like she'd been exercising. Fresh. Not stale or strong."

Not a nervous sweat, then, the smell of fear that Traynor had been giving off since they entered his room.

"About how tall was she?"

"I went over all this with the others," he protested feebly, his hand coming up to touch his bruised throat.

"Nearly finished. How tall?"

"Taller than me—but then, dressed all in black and standing over me, she seemed bigger than she was, I think. I was only facing her for a second or two, but she still seemed a little taller than me. Maybe a couple of inches. I'm five seven."

Brown-eyed Roz Hall stood five feet ten, Kate's traitorous mind got in before she ruthlessly turned it to other things.

"Mr. Traynor, were you aware of people hanging around the factory at night, telephone calls, that kind of thing?"

He looked at her as if she were raving. "It's been nuts around here the last few weeks. I told you about the picketers and the—"

"I mean single people, not groups of protesters. A car parked across from the entrance, say, or the dog barking at the darkness."

"Maybe. I don't know, I've been kind of jumpy."

"What did you think you saw?"

"Well, Popeye—he's my dog, or he was until I took him back to the pound over the weekend. Anyway, he was showing the strain about, oh, maybe a week ago. I'd be sweeping up or doing my rounds and he'd be whining at the door to get out or getting under my feet. Drove me crazy."

"What night was this?"

"There were a coupla nights. Monday maybe? And then not the next night, he slept like usual, but again on Wednesday."

"What time would it have been?"

"Late on Monday—yeah, I'm sure it was Monday, first day of the week—or really Tuesday morning, I guess. After *Late Night* was over anyway. But Wednesday night was earlier, I was mopping the rest rooms and he kept trying to track across where I'd just mopped. Maybe nine, ten? Close to nine, I guess."

"But you yourself didn't hear or see anything?"

"Nah. Just the dog. Jeez, maybe he was trying to warn me, you think? Maybe I should get him back from the pound. Problem is, I don't know where I'm going to be. I don't suppose you know . . . ?"

Kate shook her head and snapped shut the notebook she'd been writing in. "We're from San Francisco," she told him. "You're not our—our responsibility." She had nearly said problem, which would have been the simple truth. Nobody liked protecting a piece of slime like Traynor, though obviously they had to. It was complicated by the question of his own potential as a suspect of purveying kiddie porn, and how the authorities might take the evidence that had fallen into their laps completely by accident and in the course of a different case, and render that evidence both useful and untainted by questionable means. One tangle, thank God, that she and Al could walk away from.

Which they did. They said a thanks to the room in general, which could be taken as being aimed at Traynor but which they all knew was meant for the cop at his side, and left the battered pedophile to his ambiguous future.

20

She cannot be cast out (she is here for good)
Nor battled to the end. Who wins that war?
She cannot be forgotten, jailed, or killed.
Heaven must still be balanced against her.

Al was silent as they passed through the sterile corridors of the hospital, as he had been during the entire interview with Traynor. "So, what do you think?" she asked him as she got in behind the wheel of the car.

"I think that if I saw him walking that dog of his next to Jules's school, I'd castrate the bastard myself with a dull knife."

The sentiment and the mild obscenity were so unlike Hawkin that Kate stared at his profile. He was not kidding. She opened her mouth to make a joke about the effects of pregnancy hormones on the human male, but then she noticed the hard clench of his jaw and decided that maybe she'd let it pass. In her experience, limited though it was, she'd found that pregnant women seemed to develop areas of humorlessness. It appeared to be contagious to the partner.

She put the car into gear and began to thread her way out of the hospital parking lot. "No security cams in the factory building," she said after a minute. "That's too bad."

"Have any of the victims on the hit list been black?" Hawkin asked in an abrupt non sequitur.

Kate thought about it. "I think some of the guys are. Yeah, I'm sure there were half a dozen black guys—I remember at least two of the photos. As for actual victims, the auto mechanic in New York was black, I'm pretty sure."

"But none in the Bay Area."

"Larsen and the guy in Sacramento, Goff, were both Anglo, and now Traynor. Banderas was Hispanic, but I thought he looked more Mediterranean, Italian or Greek. Mehta was Indian, but again, pretty light-skinned."

"Does that say anything to you?" he asked.

"Not really. Could be they're white women, like Traynor thought, and they're either afraid of messing with black men or else they figure it's not their business. Maybe they just haven't gotten around to that community yet. On the other hand, they could be black women out to eliminate their traditional tormentors. I don't think we can make any assumptions, Al."

"What about methodology?"

"For our guys, or the list as a whole?"

"Both."

"I'd say that, countrywide, we're looking at two or three different groups of killers: one here, one centered somewhere between Georgia and South Carolina, and one farther up the East Coast. The New York bunch are into quick, clean, distance kills with a handgun. Unadorned executions. The Southerners may be more hands-on, maybe use a taser like ours, or a gun to force their target into a car before driving him into the woods to dump him. It's hard to know exactly how long the groups have been working, since people vanish every day, but if I had to guess I'd say it started about when the Web site hit list came online in January."

None of this was new, and the FBI was probably miles ahead of them, but their investigations worked best when they reviewed and explored, over and over again, watching for unnoticed bumps and oddities in the terrain. Most of the ideas they tossed around were not original, but sometimes the patterns the ideas formed when they landed were.

"And our own ladies, or womyn-with-a-y. What about them?"

"Up close and personal, wouldn't you say?" she asked.

"Can't get much more intimate than strangulation, that's for sure. The very definition of hands-on."

"But they leave the bodies to be found, so there's no reason for the notes, other than the statement."

"The others are more, what would you call it—strictly functional? Do 'em and leave 'em like the garbage they are, whereas ours are a little bit angrier about their victims, and want the world to know. Yes?"

"I agree. But what's the candy got to do with it?"

"Don't take it from strangers? Maybe one of the women was raped and her attacker called her 'sweet' or 'sugar'? I'd say it's a pathological twist that we won't know about until we find the perp. Or perps."

"Something obvious to her, or them, but personal?"

"Of course, if we find someone whose sister named Candy got killed by a rapist, we might take a look," Kate suggested facetiously.

"Or whose abusive husband owned a candy shop."

"I can see the search base getting dangerously cumbersome. And you're the one in charge of computer searches," Al said, beginning to sound a little happier about things.

"Actually, this sounds to me ideal for one of your million-scraps-of-paper-tacked-to-the-wall approaches, Al. Much more intuitive."

They were on the freeway now, the easiest way to get from the hospital to the industrial area where Traynor had been attacked, driving past shopping malls and residential sprawl through the increasing traffic of a city before dawn. Near the airport, with an approaching jet screaming overhead, the phone sounded in Al's pocket. Al's end of the conversation consisted of a few grunts, a yes, "San Jose airport" to identify their location, and then he was reaching for his pen and notebook and scribbling an address.

"What was that?" she asked when he'd tucked the phone away again.

"The lab ID'd a fingerprint on the candy they found on the stairway. Belongs to a woman with a conviction for drunk and disorderly, lives in East Palo Alto. Hillman's looking into it, thought we might like to tag along. Get off here and circle back to 101 north," he suggested, but she was already moving into the exit lane.

The woman's name was Miriam Mkele, changed from Maryanne Martin when she had gotten out of jail three years before, and if she was either surprised or frightened when she opened the door to five plainclothes detectives and two uniformed patrol, she did not show it. She just stood in her doorway, six feet of proud African-American woman, and raised her eyebrow at them. The local detective did the identification, and after he had run through his own name and rank and those of the two San Jose cops (Hillman and his partner, Gonsalves) and the two San Francisco detectives (Kate and Al), he was running out of steam and Mkele was looking, if anything, amused.

"And these two good boys, who they be?" she asked, raising her chin briefly at the two uniformed officers. The East Palo Alto man dutifully extended his introduction to include the uniforms, who were acting as bodyguards more than anything in this rough area just across the freeway from the intellectual elite of Stanford University. East Palo Alto had one of the highest murder rates in the United States; Miriam Mkele looked as if she had known many of the victims, and held the hands of a fair number of the survivors.

"Do you people want to come in?" she asked.

"We'd appreciate it, ma'am," Al spoke up. "It's not getting any warmer out here."

Mkele looked him over, and looked up at the sky as if to judge the attractive possibility of it beginning to rain on their heads, but the clouds were light and high and the breeze cold enough to suck the heat from her house, so she stepped back and the five detectives filed in, leaving the two patrolmen to retreat to their car.

The small house was warm, in temperature and in emotional impact, and scrubbed spotless beneath the signs of wear and tear. African woodcarvings clustered along one wall, tribal masks hung on another, the curtains were brightly colored block prints and the sofa scattered with kente cloth pillows. Mkele closed the door, walked between them to take up a position on the other side of the room, and, still standing, crossed her arms.

"What you want?" she asked.

"These people have some questions about an attempted murder that took place last night in San Jose, Ms. Mkele," the local man explained.

"Do I need a lawyer?"

Hawkin pushed forward. "You're welcome to have one if you'd feel more comfortable of course, but at this point we're just trying to clear up a couple of questions. You are under no suspicion of a crime." No more than any physically powerful female would have been, Kate added silently.

Mkele nodded, a sign that he should continue.

"Your fingerprint was found on an object left at the scene, possibly by the attackers. Just for the record, can you tell us where you were last night?"

"What time?"

"Between nine P.M. and midnight."

"Worked until nine, came home and cooked a late dinner for some friends, and went to bed 'bout eleven-thirty."

Like a cop on the stand, Mkele did not volunteer any information beyond the bare question.

"Where do you work?"

"The Safeway on El Camino, just off the freeway."

"What do you do there?"

"I work the registers. Cashier. Smile and say thank you," she said. Kate could not picture Mkele with a smile on her face.

"Responsible job," Hillman commented.

"For an ex-con, you mean, dee-tective? I finished with the life that drove me to alcohol. I worked three years cleanin' the floors and stockin' the shelves to prove I was dependable, and they trust me with money now, yes."

"Do you know—" Hillman was starting to say, but Kate had been struck by a sudden thought and spoke over his voice.

"Ms. Mkele, do you still stock the shelves sometimes?"

The dark eyes studied her pensively, as if looking for the trick in the question. "No," she said.

Ah well, thought Kate, it was an idea, but Mkele spoke again.

"I do not gen'rally stock shelves at my own store. There's a, what you call, hierarchy, you understand? And I'm gonna be a manager one day, so it's not good for my image to stock shelves. But sometimes I help out at other stores, and then I do what is needed. In South San Francisco I even cleaned the toilets once. Haven't done that since I got out."

"In the last few months," Kate asked, her voice taut despite her effort to control it, "have you ever stocked one of those self-service candy bins?"

Mkele put her head to one side, not so much searching her memory as considering.

"Was it on one of those pieces of candy that you found my fingerprint?" she asked after a minute. Kate did not have to answer; her silence gave her away. Shockingly, then, Mkele threw back her head and laughed, long and richly, at the discomfiture on the faces before her. "Oh, you poor people," she said at last. "If I tell you yes, I may be lying so's to explain that fingerprint, but if I tell you no, you are left with one great puzzle. Well, I'm gonna tell you yes, as far as I can remember, I stocked those bins twice in the last half year or so, once in Fremont, where I worked in October, and the other in my own store just before Christmas when three men were out sick and the shelves were bare in the evening. I'd have to look up the precise dates."

That she did not expect them to believe her was clear in her stance and the tip of her head. Kate figured the woman's alibi must be ironclad, for her to so patently not care if they believed her or not—although very possibly she would still show them an amused defiance if she had no more to vouch for her than her own empty bed. Kate found herself liking the woman, rare enough when it came to a witness and a potential suspect, for her straight spine and her simple ambitions and her willingness to take a stand here in this community of little hope.

"Any chance you might have handled any of that candy any other time?" she asked. "Maybe helping someone scoop some out, or a bag spilling at the register, something like that?"

Mkele thought about it, and then shrugged her strong shoulders. "I don't remember that happening, but it's not impossible that it did. Things get busy, you know, 'specially if you're talking about as far back as Christmas. By the end of the day you wouldn't remember if you fed a whole cow over the scanner."

Kate nodded, took a card from the pocket in her notebook, flipped the book shut, and dropped it in her pocket. She stepped forward with the card in her left hand and her right hand outstretched.

"Thank you, Ms. Mkele," she said. "Let us know when you figure out those dates, or if there was any other time you might have handled wrapped candies. We'll give you a call if anything needs clarifying." Mkele looked at Kate, and at her hand; then she reached out and took both card and hand.

The local man and Hawkin moved with Kate toward the door. The two San Jose detectives hesitated but followed in the end, leaving Miriam Mkele in command of her diminutive but colorful field of battle.

21

Put the wild hunger where it belongs,
Within the act of creation,
Crude power that forges a balance
Between hate and love.

Dismissing the two patrolmen to resume their centurion duties, the detectives moved off to safer ground, a twenty-four-hour coffee shop next to the freeway. Its garish color scheme, Kate had read somewhere, was specifically designed to discourage customers from lingering over their coffee.

It worked on five plainclothes cops as well as it did on the sales reps and the families heading for Portland or Los Angeles. They discussed briefly the odds that Mkele had been lying to them and that she was somehow involved, decided that they had no evidence either way, divided up the tasks of checking up on her story, and in twenty minutes they were out the door.

In the parking lot Hillman, the older of the two San Jose detectives, took Kate aside in that helpful and avuncular manner that always made her jaw clench.

"Look, Martinelli," he began, "we weren't actually finished with Mkele."

"No? We had her answers, and she said she'd call us back with the other information."

"She's an ex-con. You have to push them. Always."

"Thanks for the tip, Hillman, but let's see if she comes across before we go back and push her around."

"It's just that you really can't be friendly with a witness, especially a shady one. Like that business with the handshake—what if she'd refused to shake? You'd have looked like an idiot."

"Well, Hillman, I guess I don't mind looking like an idiot. Better than actually being one. I'll let you know when she calls." Kate stood her ground and waited for Hillman and the others to get into their cars and drive away. Al leaned against their car with his face turned away, so none of them but Kate knew that he was grinning at the exchange.

When the others had left, Al went back inside to phone Marcowitz from a ground line, for the added security. When he came out of the restaurant, Kate watched him closely, trying to guess what the Man in Black had said, but Al just walked along, head down either in thought or in well-concealed anger.

"Well?" she asked when he was sitting beside her.

"They're doing the interviews."

"Ah. Well, we knew they'd take over eventually. What does he want us to do? Type up their field notes?"

"Not quite that bad. I told him I wanted to take another look at the Traynor crime scene, he said fine."

Kate suspected that it had not been quite such a simple exchange, but she would not argue. She started the car and, without discussing the matter, took the entrance for the freeway north and drove for three miles. She then exited, circled under the freeway, and resumed the trip heading south, back toward San Jose. After a mile, the sign for the Safeway market where Mkele worked came up on the right, readily visible from all lanes in both directions, instantly accessible from an exit two hundred yards from the front doors. Kate kept her foot on the accelerator, saying only, "I assume we don't need to see the inside of the store."

"We could stop off and pick up some milk on our way home," Hawkin answered. "If curiosity gets the better of us." From the sound of his voice, that was not likely.

The factory where Lennie Traynor worked, lived, and had nearly died was a seedy three-story cement-block cube dropped into a parking lot. It was half a mile from the flight path of the low-flying jets, whose exhaust had deposited black shadows on every upper surface. All the grimy windows on the lower floor had bars on them, and a scattering of boarded-over windows on the upper floors testified to the accurate aim of the local throwing arms. Traynor's room was on the southwest corner of the top floor. The metal fire escapes on two sides did not appear to have been extended down or even greased in decades, which meant that entrance by Traynor's attackers had to have been through the doors.

A new chain hung on the metal gate that a San Jose officer opened for them. The original chain, with its cut link and the lock still attached, was in the San Jose lab for comparison with the bolt cutters. Kate drove through the gate and around the cube to pull in near the five unmarked and two patrol cars that were parked at the side entrance. She flipped her badge at the uniformed who popped out of the door; the woman nodded and stepped back inside.

Traynor's two black-clad attackers had jumped him as soon as he came out the side door on his rounds, firing the taser into their victim's back and then, as soon as he dropped, cuffing him and hauling him back through the door. He had fallen onto the edge of the step, giving him the scalp wound that left drops and smears up the steps and through the doorway, each drop now flagged and numbered for the police photographs. In two places, feet had stepped into drops of blood, and the lab was working on identifying the shoe by the scraps of track left on the worn linoleum.

Traynor's keys had been found on the floor near where he lay, dropped there after his attackers let themselves in. Their mistake had been in assuming that Traynor had not set the alarm as he came out through the door: The alarm set itself automatically every time the door was closed, and sounded in the local precinct house if it was not coded off within ninety seconds. The relatively sophisticated system had been installed eight years earlier at the insistence of the insurance company when intruders had snuck in twice while the night watchman was off in the grounds. It had been a pain in the neck of the local patrol under previous night watchmen, but Traynor never once forgot to code it off, and the police had not responded to the factory alarm since he had taken over.

Al paused on the doorstep and looked across the parking lot at the chain link, razor-wire-topped fence and the street beyond.

"They must've been watching him, to get his rounds down," he said. "Just not close enough to see him punch in the code. From a car down the street it'd just look like he was slow in putting the key in the lock every time."

Kate looked up at the inadequate bulb in the fixture overhead, and agreed: At night, the subtle shift in the arm movements of a man, particularly one wearing a heavy jacket and seen from the back, would not be easy to catch.

They walked through the open door and into a familiar world of crime scene investigation, flags and chalk marks and swags of yellow tape. Fingerprint powder added its grime to all the likely nearby surfaces, but it didn't look as if the intruders had left behind any prints except that of Miriam Mkele on the cellophane wrapper of a piece of butterscotch. Traynor's keys had given up only his own prints, smudged in places by their rubber gloves.

Traynor had been dragged inside less than ten feet, just far enough to get the door closed, leaving him well away from the window. Blood from his scalp had formed a pool the size of a man's hand in the place where he had lain until the paramedics arrived. Although two shoe-prints outside held out some hope as belonging to the invaders, the inside evidence had been tracked and smeared into uselessness during the urgent process of saving Traynor's life. Crime Scene personnel had done their best with sketches and photographs and evidence bags, but truth to tell, a nice cold, obviously dead corpse that everybody stayed well away from was much easier to work with; here, the most they could hope for was that somewhere down the line they would find traces of Traynor's blood on a suspect's shoes.

Kate stood and read from the rough report she'd been given, comparing the statements of Hillman and the reporting officers with the scene before her. Everybody seemed to agree that Traynor had been dragged into the office, turned onto his back, had a length of red silk, light but strong and measuring fifteen by forty-nine inches, twisted around his throat. The state of his fingernails and the marks his boot heels had left on the floor showed that he had been conscious enough to struggle, but there was no doubt he would have succumbed had not the local patrol car happened to be bare minutes away when the alarm call came, and had one of the attackers not happened to see the marked car approaching. The attackers had fled, pausing only to kick Traynor or bash him with the bolt cutters (in petulance, or rage, or a last attempt at quick murder?) before escaping down the hallway toward the main doors. No breach of the fence had been found, so it was assumed the black-clad would-be killers had slipped back out through the ill-lit parking lot and the wide-open gate while the patrol officers were busy discovering Traynor. One of the patrol officers noted that he had glimpsed a very clean, light-colored, late-model four-door compact parked on the street a couple of blocks away, noticeable because it was an incongruity in the area, and that when he had driven past the spot after processing the Traynor crime, the car was no longer there.

Kate and Al walked away from the relative bustle of the office where the attack had taken place, through the echoing factory building. The owner had closed the place for a couple of days to reassure the workers that he cared, not so much for Traynor but for the safety of his fellow employees. The two San Francisco detectives traced the route of the two attackers where they had raced through the lower floor, taking a couple of wrong turns that resulted in knocked-over equipment and piles of paperwork and indicating that they did not know the building from within. The intruders had finally reached the double glass doors that faced the street. There one of them had paused to fling a handful of nine mixed, cellophane-wrapped candies back into the entrance hall and across the receptionist's desk. Now a scattering of flags showed where they had landed: mostly on and under the desk, where they might well have been over-looked as something the receptionist had dropped had Hawkin not specifically asked Hillman about them.

The attackers had left no prints; they had made a careful surveillance of their victim's habits; and they knew that there was a backup escape route, if not its exact path.

"They're careful," Al said, voicing Kate's thought.

"What about that car?"

"San Jose's out canvassing the neighborhood, to see if anyone in the area saw it. And they'll stick up a no-tice board if they don't get anything, see if some pas-serby remembers it."

"Pretty anonymous vehicle," Kate remarked.

"You think deliberately?"

"If I were knocking off a guy, I sure wouldn't leave my own car around the corner."

"Rental, then? Clean, white, four-door?"

"Worth a try, don't you think?"

"The feds probably thought the same," Hawkin said repressively.

"Well, I guess we'll find out as soon as we start ask-ing, if there's been someone ahead of us."

"You want to begin with the airport? Biggest car rental around, I'd have thought. Of course, we'd more or less have to tell Hillman what we were doing, it being his patch. And Marcowitz, of course."

"Of course. But maybe we shouldn't waste his time until we've finished."

"That's what I like about working with you, Marti-nelli," her partner said with satisfaction. "It's the meet-ing of true minds."

With FBI involvement, any line of inquiry on the part of the local forces ought to be directed by the feds. If, however, the local cops didn't get around to mentioning some ongoing piece of their investigation while it was actually being pursued, well, that was understandable—sometimes you had to go back and dot the i's and cross the t's later. And if they happened to find something that contributed to the case, and managed to run it down before returning to their desks and dutifully reporting in, any official reprimand would be more than balanced by their own satisfaction—and that of their departmental colleagues. Especially if that contribution was large enough. Solving the crime and getting killers off the street was obviously the main goal, and they would not do anything deliberately to compromise that, but it was always nice when the overworked and under-equipped locals pulled off something the big guys couldn't.

So their slow and circuitous route back to the Hall of Justice took them into virtually every car rental place on the peninsula. Most of the agencies said, with greater or lesser degrees of enthusiasm, that they would draw up a list of cars matching their description and which had been out the night before, and who had rented them, and get the list to them in a day or so. The two biggest agencies at San Francisco International, though, were both highly automated and eager to help, and both offered to provide a printout. And no, there had been no one else around asking for that information in the last day.

They drove out to the airport and picked up both lists, added them to the growing stack, then retreated to a nearby restaurant to replenish their energies with a drippy hamburger for Al and a blackened chicken salad for Kate. They spread their papers out to look them over as they ate.

It was a daunting pile, even for detectives well used to paper chases. There were hundreds, thousands of white four-doors for hire in the peninsula, and most of them were in circulation. Some of the lists were handwritten and half legible; others gave every car in the agency regardless of make and color and left it up to them to decipher the identifying code. Some of the lists went back weeks; one was dated for April, but of the previous year.

Kate sighed, turning over the cold remnants of her fries with her forefinger, and decided to phone home. She got up to use the toilet, tried the public phone, found the line busy, and came back to find Hawkin digging into a huge construction that seemed to be equal parts chocolate and whipping cream. She ordered a double espresso for herself and thumbed disconsolately through the stack of papers.

"This is hopeless," she began to say, when simultaneously her beeper went off and her eye snagged on a name. The name had to be a coincidence, if an odd one, and the number on the pager display was her own. Still, she tugged the piece of paper out to mark the place before she went back to the pay phone.

Annoyingly, the number was again busy. She hung up, waited half a minute, and tried again. This time Lee had it on the first ring.

"Hello?"

"Hi babe, it's me. I got your page—I tried to reach you myself ten minutes ago. What's up?"

"When are you coming home?" Lee's voice sounded either tired or stressed, and Kate's fingers whitened on the receiver.

"Why? What's wrong?"

"Just—" Lee bit off a sharp demand, and went on with deliberate calm: her reasonable therapist's voice. "I just need to know when you'll be back."

"I could be there in forty minutes, less if Al lets me stick the flasher on. What do you need?"

"It's not that urgent, I'm just trying to organize something and it was stupid to make arrangements for a ride if you were about to walk through the door, is all. You sound like you're occupied."

"I am, but it's nothing urgent. I'll drop Al at the—"

"Kate, stop. It's fine. It's just that Jon is out with

Sione and I hate to beep him, but Maj called up all in a dither about something Roz is doing, so I told her I'd go over and hold her hand. It's nearly Mina's bedtime, or she'd come here. I could get the Saab out, but I know that—"

"Lee, no, that's a really terrible idea. I'll be home in half an hour, surely it can wait that long?"

"No, no, I don't want you to break off, I only wanted to know if you happened to be about to drive up any minute. I'll call a cab."

"Promise me you won't try to drive?" Lee hadn't driven a car since she had been shot, and although her legs were stronger, their reaction time was undependable. On city streets, in city traffic, it would be criminally foolhardy.

"I promise."

Maj in a dither didn't sound like anything worth breaking speed limits for; indeed, considering the frequency of Roz's passionate causes, it didn't even sound like something worth missing her coffee for.

"But Maj is okay?" she asked Lee, just to make sure.

"Oh yeah, I'm sure she is. Just upset." Lee herself sounded calmer, and Kate's grip on the phone relaxed.

"In a dither, huh?"

"Completely ditherized. What does that word mean, anyway? How's your day going?"

"I'm playing tag with some evidence the FBI might think I should have turned over to them, hoping it gives me some meaning. Doesn't look like it, though."

"Another productive day."

"That's how it goes. But I met a woman who could be a poster girl for the black and beautiful campaign, whose goal in life is to manage a Safeway store."

Lee, after a silent moment, asked, "Have you been drinking?"

"Iced tea, I swear."

"Is Hawkin with you?"

"Yes, Mother."

At that Lee finally laughed. "Yeah, right—why I should trust him to keep you in line I can't imagine."

"You're sure a cab is okay, hon?"

"Cost a fortune, but I'll let Maj pay half."

"How long do you think you'll be with her?"

"Couple of hours. Less if Roz shows up—I won't stick around for that stage of the conversation, thank you."

"Okay. Well, if I'm back in town before—what does that make it, eleven?—I'll call there, give you a ride home."

"If it's convenient, that'd be great. Don't work too hard."

"Never."

"Sure. Why don't I tell Roz to just chill out, while I'm at it?" But she chuckled as she said it, and they talked about nothing in particular for another minute or two before they hung up and went their separate ways.

Back at the table Kate finished her tepid espresso in one quick swallow, then reached out and pulled the puzzling sheet from its neighbors. She turned it around and laid it in front of Hawkin, tapping the name that had caught her eye.

"Don't you think that's odd?" she asked him.

He looked down at the name and his eyebrows went up. He nodded his head slowly.

A white car had been rented the previous morning to a woman named Jane Larsen.

22

She keeps us from being what we long to be;
Tenderness withers under her iron laws.
We may hold her like a lunatic, but it is she
Held down, who bloodies with her claws.

"Did James Larsen have a sister?" Kate asked her partner.

"We've never come across one."

"I don't know which I like less, the idea of coincidence or the thought of some seventy-five-year-old avenging mother on the scene. Talk about Disgruntled Ladies."

"Do you have Emily Larsen's phone number with you?"

Kate didn't, but she got it from information, and Emily answered, the noise of canned television laughter in the background. Kate identified herself, asked how she was doing, and then asked her question.

"No," Emily said, sounding confused. "Jimmy never had a sister. He has a brother who lives back East, Philadelphia I think, but we haven't heard from him in years."

"Is the brother married?"

"Not that I knew of. Jimmy always said Danny was too mean to get married."

"Do you have his last address, Ms. Larsen?"

"I have an address, sure, but like I said it's really old. We haven't even gotten a Christmas card from him in maybe five years."

"It'll have to do." The telephone went down and Kate was treated to several minutes of laugh track and manic gabbling before it was picked up again. Emily gave her an address and phone number, and Daniel Larsen's full name, and then asked Kate the inevitable question.

"What do you want to know this for?"

"Oh, a woman with the same last name has popped up in a related matter. Probably nothing. Thanks for your help, Ms. Larsen."

"Any time. Say, while I have you on the line, can I ask you something?"

"What's that?"

"Do you need to report when a credit card's missing?"

The question dropped into Kate's mind with the slow electric tingle of discovered evidence. "Is this one of your credit cards we're talking about?"

"It was Jimmy's. I mean, I could sign on it, but he didn't want me to have my own in case I used it. I forgot all about it until the other day when the monthly bill came and I realized the card wasn't with his other stuff that I got back, and when I went looking for it I couldn't find it."

"Did he usually carry it with him?"

"I guess."

"Is anything else missing?"

"Oh heavens," she said with a little laugh, "I'm losing all kinds of things. The therapist I'm seeing says it's a common sign of stress, to lose things."

"What have you lost?" Kate's voice remained light, but it was an effort.

"All kinds of things," Emily repeated, beginning to sound embarrassed. "I brushed my hair in the guest bathroom and forgot, so I couldn't find my brush for two days. I left my housekeys in the market, talk about stupid, I had to go back for them. Now it's my whole wallet. I can't think where I could have left that. Isn't that silly? Hello? Inspector, are you there?"

"Yes. Sorry, Ms. Larsen, I was thinking. I'm sure it'll

turn up. You probably just left it somewhere, maybe last night?"

"I wonder . . . You know, I was at the shelter on Friday night, they invited me up for dinner. I wonder if . . . I'll call and ask them."

"Actually, Emily, I'm going over to the shelter first thing in the morning. Rather than bother them tonight, considering how busy they always are in the evenings, why don't I just ask for you when I'm there, maybe take a look around to see if your wallet fell into the back of the sofa or something?" If the missing wallet was of any importance, the last thing Kate wanted was for its thief to be forewarned that she was coming.

"Would you? That's very nice of you. It's green, looks just like leather, with a gold clasp along the top. Jimmy gave it to me for my birthday three years ago."

"I'm glad you're keeping in touch with the shelter," Kate said with elaborate casualness. "I saw Roz the other day myself, she was saying that she wished she could spend more time there."

"Roz was there Friday, but she had to run. She asked Phoebe—you know, Carla's secretary?—to give me a ride home, though, and she did, which was nice of her, it's really out of her way. The insurance company is still dragging their feet over replacing Jimmy's car."

Kate made sympathetic noises, and then nudged Emily a little further down the evidence trail. "That explains why I couldn't reach you—I didn't want to call too late."

"Yes, it was after eleven when we got home. I hated to have Phoebe come all the way down here, considering how busy she is, but the buses don't run as much that late."

"I see," Kate said, afraid that she was beginning to.

"What did you want?" Emily interrupted Kate's thoughts to ask.

"Sorry? Oh, you mean the other night. It was nothing, just clarification of a detail. We worked it out." She wished the woman luck with getting the insurance company to replace the trashed car, and hung up before Emily could ask again about canceling the credit card.

Hawkin had paid and was standing near the door, so she waited until they were in the car to tell him what Emily Larsen had said.

"His credit card and her ID, both gone missing," Hawkin mused. "What you might call thought-provoking."

"Not much we can do about it tonight, though," Kate said hopefully.

After a minute, to her relief, Hawkin nodded his head in agreement. They had been on the road for eighteen hours, since the San Jose people had made the connection between their hospitalized pedophile and the SFPD's dead bodies, and Kate for one knew that her day was not over yet.

"That car was rented out to Jane Larsen at around ten A.M.," Al noted. "We might find the same staff on duty that time tomorrow."

"How 'bout if I take you home, pick you up in the morning?"

"More driving for you—you could just drop me at the Hall, I'd use an unmarked."

"It's only twenty minutes to your place, Al, and not much farther in the morning."

"Then I accept. Might even see Jani today, awake."

The apartment Al shared with Jani, a professor of medieval history, and her teenaged daughter, Jules, was north of Jani's work and south of his. Kate and he talked mostly about Jules on the short drive there, about her brilliance and her resilience in recovering from the traumatic experiences she had been through over the winter.

"I finally managed to call her the other day," Kate told him. "It was good to talk to her. I told her we'd go bowling in a week or two."

"She'd like that. She misses you. You know, the other day she told me she was thinking of writing to that bastard in prison. She didn't say anything to you about it, did she?"

"God, no, she didn't. She isn't serious, is she?"

" 'Fraid so. She thought it might, and I quote, 'aid the healing process.' I don't know if she's insane or incredibly well balanced."

"Lee would tell you that at a certain point, the two are the same."

"Thanks a ton. Meanwhile, what do I tell Jules?"

"Oh no, I'm not going to touch that one. You're the dad here." And then, for the first time and tentatively, she told him about Lee's decision. "Lee wants to try for a child. She has an appointment at the clinic in a couple of weeks."

"Hey," Hawkin said warmly. "That's great. Really great news."

"Not news yet, just an intention, and if you'd keep it to yourself." You'd think she'd get used to the invasions of the world into her private life, Kate thought to herself, but sometimes it felt like living in a house with glass walls, and all the world outside with rocks in hand.

"Sure. Can I tell Jani?"

"Of course—but let's have Jules out of the loop for a while, okay? We can tell her when there's something to tell."

"I hope it all goes smoothly. Give Lee my best, would you?"

"God—I nearly forgot. Would you dial a number for me?"

Lee was still at Roz and Maj's house, and sounded relieved to hear from her. Whatever the crisis was, Lee was already tired of it and glad of an excuse to leave. Kate told her she'd be there within forty minutes.

"I think Roz is off on one of her campaigns," Kate told Al in explanation. "She gets involved in some cause or another and everything gets thrown up into the air until she loses interest. It's kind of hard on Maj."

"What is it this time? Handicapped parking permits for the meals-on-wheels delivery folk? City investments in anti-gay corporations?"

"I don't know. Yet."

"Well, I hope you get some sleep. See you at nine? We can get some coffee on our way to the car place."

"Jani still can't stand the smell, huh?"

"You notice I didn't have any tonight—I don't like sleeping on the couch."

Kate hoped this was not a sign of things to come.

She dropped Al off, made a U-turn in the quiet night street, and headed back north. When she pulled up in front of Roz and Maj's house, the red Jeep was not on the street, and when Maj opened the door it was obvious that she'd been crying earlier in the evening. She seemed calm now, and so Kate ruthlessly extracted Lee from the troubled house; in truth, Maj seemed nearly as relieved at her departure as Lee was herself.

Kate settled Lee in the passenger seat, tossed the cuffed crutches over the back, and drove briskly away before Roz could arrive and precipitate them all back into the crisis. Lee drew a deep breath, blew it out with feeling, and let her head drop back against the headrest.

"Might be easier if you could charge them by the hour," Kate offered by way of sympathetic opener.

"I love Roz," Lee said tiredly, "but the woman can be a fucking maniac."

First Al, now Lee—two people who never cursed letting fly with easy obscenity, and both in the same day. A third one and San Francisco might well slip into the sea.

"What's Roz got in her teeth now?"

"It's that Indian girl again, Pramilla Mehta," Lee said. "Roz has decided to link up in solidarity with a group in India that's working to expose dowry deaths for what they are."

Kate dragged her thoughts away from San Jose and back to the larger picture. "But I thought she was convinced that Laxman Mehta killed her? What can she do about him? He's dead—our problem now, not hers."

"She thinks the family encouraged him, maybe even drove him to it."

"Christ. So what is she going to do?"

"Big picket lines in front of his company, and the

city is looking into the contracts it has with him, think-ing of canceling."

"Well, that certainly sounds like Roz."

"They're also putting together a public memorial service for Pramilla."

"Who is they?"

"I swear, Roz has half the organizations in Northern California involved. This is going to be big. Huge. And, I'm afraid, divisive. There's a large Indian community in the Bay Area, and they're all going to feel targeted, even those who have nothing to do with dowries. You know how it goes with ethnic groups, they all get jum-bled together in the popular mind. Anyone wearing a turban is a follower of the Ayatollah; anyone with an Arab name sides with Saddam."

"I know. But I'm sorry, babe, this all sounds like business as usual for Roz. Why is Maj so upset about it this time?"

"A combination of things. Maj's not feeling very well, and the pregnancy is interfering with her own work. And the timing is bad, coming just when her work is going through a demanding phase, and Roz had promised to be more available for Mina. Plus that, Roz's church is making noises about cutting back her funding—they say they're paying her to be a parish priest, not a political organizer, and the congregation is being neglected. So there's that worry as well. But I think what has Maj so concerned is the degree of Roz's involvement. For some reason this girl's killing has pulled all of Roz's levers at once, and it's making her a little crazy. That's not a diagnosis, by the way," Lee added, in a welcome breath of humor. "She's out to make Pramilla Mehta a saint and a martyr, or at least a household name, and you know how good she is at playing the media game."

Kate agreed: Roz was an artist at manipulating the media.

"But it takes a massive jolt of energy to get the PR wheels going, so she's pulled out all the stops. State-ments issued, photo ops, interviews on national television, in and out of the mayor's office and the supervisors', phone calls to the governor and any senators she can get through to. The president has heard of her, and Oprah is interested."

"So she's running on empty, no food or sleep, and Maj is waiting for the crash."

"You know, it really is an addiction, this kind of righteous campaign. When it ends, as it has to, the drop-off is a steep one."

They had seen it before, but Maj had to live with it, and would be picking up the pieces at a time when she would be ill equipped to do so.

"Is there anything you can do?" Kate asked.

"Not really. You know Roz. If you try to shake some sense into her, it just makes you the enemy."

"Hard on Maj."

"Yes. And Mina is confused, too. But enough—it won't help anyone if you and I get sucked in. What happened with your day?"

"We're closing in," Kate told her. She rarely went into detail with Lee on an active case, both from professional scruples and as a way of separating home from job, but this case in particular had developed so many prickly areas—from Roz's presence in its periphery to the ambiguous righteousness of the feminist vigilante— that she did not know where to pick up the thread even if she wanted to. Better to let the tangled story sort itself out without Lee's involvement, especially considering the hour. So it was merely, "We're closing in," and a few minor details before she threw down the distraction of Jules writing to her jailed abductor, which kept Lee happily chewing on that question until they were pulling up to their curb.

23

It is time for the invocation:
Kali, be with us.
Violence, destruction, receive our homage.

"I was busy," protested the young woman at the airport car rental agency. It was nine-twenty on Monday morning, and Britany Pihalik was still busy, fending off telephones, customers, and pushy cops all at the same time. Kate kept any mote of sympathy off her face, knowing that to appear implacable was in the end the quickest for everyone, and eventually the young woman gave in, turned her name card around on the counter, and led the two detectives into an empty break room. She offered them coffee, which they declined, took a can of diet Coke from the refrigerator for herself, and settled them at a table.

Kate handed her the printout with the name Jane Larsen circled on it. "What can you tell us about this woman?"

"I'd have to look it up—no, wait a minute. I remember her. It was the lady with the mangled card." She gave them a perky look as if happy to have satisfied their curiosity and ready to get back to work now, and seemed mildly surprised that they had more questions.

"Could you tell us about her, please?" Hawkin asked.

"Nice lady, truly ugly hair, kind of stupid—her, I mean, not her hair. Though her hair was pretty stupid, too. Anyway, she hands me this credit card that looks like she fed it to a pit bull, said it'd fallen out of her purse and her husband ran over it with the car. But the computer took it, I didn't even have to enter the numbers like we do sometimes when the magnetic strip is wrecked, so it was okay."

"Did you take a close look at it?"

"No," she said flatly, clearly thinking the question, to use her favorite word, stupid.

"Did she have any other form of ID?" Kate asked.

"Of course." Ms. Pihalik obviously was getting no very high opinion of the police department. "We can't let them rent a car without a valid driver's license. She had one, I rented her a car, she left."

"Was the name on the license Jane Larsen?"

"Yes. No. No, it was her middle name. Elizabeth, something like that. Maybe not Elizabeth, because it was something as, you know, dreary as Jane, and I remember thinking it was too bad she didn't have at least one interesting name to choose from. But then she was pretty dreary herself."

"Was the name Janet? Mary?" Headshakes, continuing through the suggestions of "Patricia? Cathy? Susan?" until Kate got to "Emily?" A headshake began, cut off by consideration.

"Emily might've been it. Yeah, that sounds right, I think it was Emily."

Kate did not kiss her, although it was tempting. "You don't have security cameras here, do you?" she asked. Unless they were hidden, Kate hadn't seen any.

"Not inside. There's some in the lot."

"What did the woman look like?"

"Like I said, dreary. Dull. That ugly black hair—a really crappy dye job, might've even been a wig—and with these heavy glasses that were all wrong for her. Baggy clothes, like she didn't want anyone to see her body, though it didn't really look that bad to me. Little bit fat, maybe." Coming from a broomstick like Britany Pihalik, Kate guessed that "fat" described anything more than three percent body fat.

"Height?" Kate asked. "Eye color?"

"Taller than me, three or four inches—and I had heels on, so she was maybe five, um, nine? ten? Big, like I said. Not really fat, I guess, just kinda, what? Chunky? Muscular, like. I don't remember her eyes. They might have been blue, or brown."

Helpful, Kate thought; at least they knew not to look at anyone with pink or purple eyes.

"Your machine didn't make an actual impression of the card, did it?" Hawkin asked.

"Like one of those old back-and-forth machines with the what-you-call-it, carbons? No, it reads off the strip unless that's been scrambled by the person keeping it in an eelskin wallet or putting it down next to a strong magnet. Then we have to key in the numbers by hand. But like I said, hers was okay."

"Ms. Pihalik, the list you gave us yesterday was reservations and a few walk-ins. I'd like to see the actual final list of names taken from the credit cards themselves."

"I'd have to ask about that. I don't know if I'm allowed to give it to you."

"Maybe we should check with your supervisor?" Hawkin gently suggested.

She look relieved. "Sure, just a minute," she said, and went to the door to call in a taciturn young man not much older than she was, who wore a lapel pin declaring him to be Jim Tolliver. He heard their request, scratched for a moment at a flare of acne on one cheek, and then shrugged.

"I don't know why not. But it'd be faster if you could just look at the screen instead of printing out everything."

So Ms. Pihalik went back to her customers and Mr. Tolliver went to a free terminal, and while the detectives looked over his shoulder he scrolled through the previous day's rentals until he came to LARSEN. But it was not JANE; it was JAMES. The card's user might have hammered the S and the second half of the M into invisibility, but the computer was not fooled, and had Britany Pihalik not been so distracted, she might have noticed.

Mr. Tolliver seemed to think she should have, distraction of line-out-the-door customers or no distraction. He bristled in righteous anger, leaving Kate and Al to study the record. There was, however, little to see except that the signature had been close enough to pass at a glance.

As evidence, the faked car rental could have been more specifically damning, but there was no doubt that it constituted a solid piece of work. They had sat on it for too long, however, and could not justify the additional hours of going through the videotapes of the external security cameras in hopes of glimpsing a face. It was time to report in.

"Reporting in" quickly evolved into "being called on the carpet." The official disapproval of their independent tactics—from lieutenant, captain, and deputy chief, everyone, it seemed, but the chief of police and the mayor himself—was indeed balanced against the quality of the evidence they had dug up (in the minds and faces of their own people—Marcowitz was not so easily mollified), and by hanging their heads in meek (if mock) submissiveness while they continued to thrust out in front of them the tangible results of their borderline insubordination, they defused the wrath of officialdom to a tongue-lashing none of them took very seriously. When it was over, the higher ranks left, satisfied that the lieutenant could handle it from here.

However, Agent Marcowitz remained, sitting in a chair slightly removed from the police department personnel and saying nothing. The Man in Black (actually a dark charcoal, Kate noticed, and very nicely cut) dominated the meeting precisely by doing nothing, not even shifting in his seat, until the official reprimand had run its course. Then he uncrossed his legs, and the three remaining members of the SFPD turned to him as if for judgment.

"We agreed that you would keep me in the loop at all times," he said.

"We phoned you as soon as we had something firm." Kate's protest sounded feeble even to her own ears; far better to have stayed silent.

"What do you propose to do now? If I may be allowed to ask."

"The videotapes of the rental lot need to be gone over, the car found and checked for prints."

"I've already sent agents to get that under way."

"Traynor's own history needs to be looked into, in case this is the work of one of his victims, parents at the school, that kind of—"

"We are assisting Detective Hillman with that line of inquiry."

"Which leaves the interviews of our own pool of suspects here."

"Suspects."

"Possible suspects, should I say? Nothing on any of them except opportunity."

"And an agreement with the philosophy of the group calling itself the Ladies."

"What philosophy? That some men are lowlifes and need to be stepped on? I don't know too many people who would disagree, cops included."

"Alibis," Marcowitz merely said, a cool word to let the air out of her heated digression.

"We were told that your people were taking over there. That's why Al and I took the time to go hunting down the car."

"The preliminary interviews are under way. I understand you yourself give Rosalyn Hall an alibi."

"That's right. I talked with her on the phone at about ten-forty Saturday night."

"Did she phone you?"

"I phoned her, returning her call. On her home number, not her cell phone," she added before Marcowitz could ask.

"Any reason to think she was actually at home when she took it?"

With an effort, Kate reined in her patience. "I heard the dog—all right, I heard *a* dog," she corrected herself before he did. "But no noises to indicate she wasn't at home. I suppose it's conceivable that she had the call forwarded to her cell number, but the delay in ringing is usually noticeable. Does she have call forwarding on her home phone?"

Marcowitz did not bother to answer. "What had she called you about?"

"Nothing, really. Just to ask if I'd gotten a manuscript she'd left at the house, and to talk about how things were going. Just conversation."

"At twenty minutes to eleven?"

"Roz is a night owl."

"So she arranged for you, a friend and investigating officer, to give her an alibi on the night a man was attacked, wanting only to talk about her Ph.D. thesis."

Put that way, the call sounded far too convenient for words, but Kate could only shrug and say, "It's awfully elaborate. And shaky. How could she know when I would call?"

"It wouldn't matter when you called, would it? If she was home at ten-forty, and she left immediately after you hung up, granted she would have to move fast, but she could conceivably have been present at the Traynor assault. The silent alarm was triggered at eleven twenty-seven."

"Barely. And she didn't know I was going to call, she wouldn't have had any reason to wait around at home." Unlikely did not make an alibi, and they all knew that, but Kate had done what she could. "Have you talked with Roz, or Maj?"

"I had another agent take their preliminary statements. Maj Freiling was not cooperative, and Reverend Hall seemed more interested in making a speech. My colleague decided to suspend the interviews for the time being, thinking that if a second attempt has similar results, we can bring them in for questioning."

"I'd be very careful about that," Kate warned him. "Roz Hall is a woman of considerable influence—I wouldn't try to mess with her unless you've got a warrant in your hand. Which I don't think you're going to get, at this point. And dragging in Maj, who is seven months' pregnant, could be even worse. You could find yourself knee-deep in lawsuits."

Marcowitz might not have heard her, for all the reaction he showed. "There is one thing I had hoped you might help us with, Inspector, until you went incommunicado on us. Statements must be taken from the residents of the women's shelter run by Diana Lomax, and she strongly requested that you be the one to take them, having been there before."

"I'd be happy to."

"I will accompany you."

"That's not necessary."

"Yes," he said. "It is."

"The women in there are very uncomfortable when men invade their private space," she objected. "It really would be best if—"

"I will go with you."

"Don't you at least have a woman agent you can send instead?" she suggested, trying not to plead.

"They are busy, I am not, and you need backup. Either I go with you, or Inspector Hawkin and I will do it ourselves."

"Two men, yeah, that'd be great. Okay, but you have to let me do the talking, and if Diana Lomax refuses, then we wait for one of your women agents. When do you want to go?"

"Now."

"Right now? I—" Kate stopped, and shrugged. "Okay. Just let me make a couple of calls first. Five minutes?"

Only one call proved necessary, since Lee was home so Kate didn't have to hunt down Jon.

"Hi, babe," she said. "I thought you guys'd be out shopping," that having been the plan when Kate left the house that morning.

"Finished early, we got some gorgeous little artichokes that I'm fixing right now."

"Hell. Will they be okay cold?"

"You're going to be late," Lee said in resignation. "Well, if you get a chance, give me a call later, let me know when you'll be getting in."

"I'll try, but don't wait up for me. Things may drag on."

"You astonish me," Lee said sarcastically.

"I try. Enjoy the artichokes. Love you."

"Me too you."

They hung up together and Kate looked up to see Marcowitz standing iron-spined ten feet away, having heard every word.

"Shall we go?" he said.

Kate responded by taking her holstered gun from her desk drawer, putting on gun and jacket, and following him to the elevator and the parking lot. He was driving.

Marcowitz did not ask for directions, and did not need them. He drove with watchful confidence, although as far as Kate knew he had only been in San Francisco a couple of months. She considered asking the Man in Black a question about his background, then decided against it, and sat in silence.

He pulled up near the shelter, put on the parking brake, and then said something that had Kate open-mouthed in astonishment.

"Before we go in," he told her, "I just wanted you to know that my mother was beaten to death by her boyfriend when I was twelve. Just in case you don't think I'm sympathetic to the women who come to a shelter."

Without waiting for a response, he got out of the car and started walking toward the group home. Kate scrambled to follow.

"I'm sorry," she said inadequately when she had caught up with him.

"I didn't tell you that as a play for sympathy," he said stiffly. "Merely so you know where I'm coming from on this." And he turned and pressed his finger on the doorbell, then stepped back so that her face would be first at the door.

The shelter was bustling; that was apparent even on

the wrong side of the sturdy door, with the children inside working off a day shut up in classrooms, their voices raised and bodies racing. One of them answered the bell, and Kate leaned forward to speak to the small face, only to have the door slammed on her nose. The sounds of an altercation arose from inside, which after a minute Kate decided was an older child giving the younger door-opener hell for a lack of caution.

She and the FBI agent waited as the shouts moved off and relative silence fell, and Marcowitz was putting out his hand to ring the bell again when a single adult set of footsteps approached. The locks clattered and Diana Lomax stood before them, thunderclouds of disapproval on her brow.

"Hello, Ms. Lomax," Kate said. "This is agent Marcowitz of the FBI. Sorry, but we need to ask the residents some questions."

"This is not a good time."

"It won't take long." I hope, Kate added under her breath.

"All right, if you absolutely have to. But the agent can wait outside."

"I'm afraid that won't do," Marcowitz said, firmly but without the body language of the affronted male, remaining behind Kate instead of pushing forward and crowding his targeted foe with raised shoulders. Kate couldn't help giving him points for his reasonableness, and even Diana Lomax seemed to think again.

"Okay," she said finally. "But you'll have to stay in my office. I won't have you intruding on the privacy of the residents."

"Fine," he said, and she then let them in, locking the front door behind them before leading them down the hall to the office. Before Kate went through the door, she glanced ahead into the kitchen, source of a rich fragrance of Italian herbs, and spotted Crystal Navarro standing before a huge bowl of lettuce and tomatoes, looking in alarm at their passing. Kate raised her hand as a greeting, and followed Lomax and agent Marcowitz through the door marked OFFICE.

"May I ask what this is about?" Lomax demanded as soon as the door was shut. Marcowitz took his time in perching on the arm of the sofa, where he crossed his arms in a display of authority that Kate knew from experience left his right hand just inches from the butt of his gun, and met Lomax's angry gaze.

"Three nights ago while she was here for dinner, Emily Larsen's wallet disappeared from her purse." He paused for reaction, of which there was none. "Yesterday the identification taken from that wallet was used in the commission of a crime."

Lomax waited, then asked, "Is that all?"

"It's enough to tie this shelter to three murders and one attempted murder."

Lomax stood without moving for a long moment, then reached for the phone on the desk (Marcowitz's hand twitched, but he did not draw his gun). She dialed seven digits, and said to whoever answered, "Inspector Martinelli is in my office with evidence that links the shelter to a series of murders. I think Carla should be here." She waited for the response, said "Thanks," and then hung up.

She did not seem very upset, concerned rather than worried. She left her hand on the telephone for a minute as she stared unseeing into space, then gave herself a shake and walked around the desk to sit in her chair. Had she pulled open a drawer and reached inside, Kate knew that the agent would have drawn on her, but she merely played with a pen that lay on top of the desk and chewed at her lip. Kate shifted on her feet near the door, and Lomax's eyes immediately came up.

"I don't know if I need a lawyer or not while I'm talking to you, but Carla will want to be here, just in case. Do you two want a cup of coffee or something while we're waiting?"

Before Marcowitz could refuse, Kate said, "That'd be nice."

"Crystal's in the kitchen, she'll show you where the cups are. I have to ask you not to question her, however."

"Nothing more urgent than where to find the milk," Kate agreed with a smile. No reason not to keep this friendly. Marcowitz might doubt, but Kate knew, as surely that the sun was going down outside the house, that Diana Lomax would not produce a gun—or cause others to produce theirs—in a house filled with her women and children. Marcowitz was safe on his own, and in the few minutes they had before Carla Lomax arrived with her legal objections, Kate might nose something out. Ignoring her temporary partner's glare and keeping her voice and stance as casual as she could, she said, "Marcowitz, you want anything?"

"No."

"Okay." Kate paused at the door to ask Diana, again with great care to be offhand, "You mind if I take a look around? I didn't really get a chance to see it the other day."

To her surprise, Lomax nodded. "Sure, look around. Not in the residents' rooms, though. Not without a warrant."

If they'd had enough evidence to back up a warrant, the FBI man wouldn't be sitting on the arm of the sofa. A missing wallet would only make a judge laugh. But being given permission to roam opened the place up— not to a full search, perhaps, but to a close scrutiny. She ducked out of the room and did actually go into the kitchen for coffee, keeping one eye on the hallway the whole time so she could see if the office door opened, but it did not, and Kate nonchalantly thanked Crystal before going back up the hall to look into the other three rooms that opened off it.

Leaving the kitchen, the office was the first room on her left. She turned to the door directly across the hall from it, marked TRAINING, and found behind it a tiny windowless room with two long folding tables, two computers (one so old she wondered if it was compatible to anything at all), and an electric typewriter. If this was the shelter's sole job training, she decided, it was a miracle that any of the residents found employment.

The next room, behind the sign MEETING ROOM, was

much larger. Although it, too, had no outside windows, since the building was attached to neighbors on both sides, it did have a piece of stained glass set into the end wall that separated it from the entrance foyer. The pseudo-window, combined with several airy watercolor prints on the pale green walls, added to the impression of space, and the room's random assortment of love seats, armchairs, backless hassocks, and a couple of wooden rocking chairs were arranged against the walls in a wide circle around an oval braided rug that reminded Kate of her grandmother. Kate didn't need the disproportionate number of tissue boxes to tell her this was the room used for group therapy. It was functional but comforting, the color and prints on the wall so similar to those in Roz's church offices that they might have been chosen at the same time.

Kate went back out into the hallway, checked the office door to be sure it was still closed and silent, glanced into the entrance vestibule with its hodgepodge of outdoor clothing, children's equipment, message board, and stairs leading up to the bedrooms, then reached for the fourth doorknob, the room adjoining the office. She turned the knob, and stepped into the shelter's chapel.

This was no ordinary chapel, however, with an altar at one end and pews all in a row. This one looked more like a teenager's bedroom, had the teenager been tidy and interested in religion and spirituality instead of handsome actors and rock bands.

The wall to Kate's right represented more or less the Roman Catholic faith. Its central figure was the Virgin Mother rather than a bleeding Christ, but the steadily burning candles in tall amber glasses were those of Kate's childhood, and the inspirational pictures pinned up all around the Virgin were those she remembered from Sunday school and from the edges of her mother's dresser mirror. Sayings, scraps of prayer, and biblical quotations fluttered gently in the air rising off the candles, and on the floor at the Virgin's feet stood a large pottery bowl spilling over with small pieces of paper, folded or crumpled into thumbnail-sized wads. Feeling far more guilty than any police investigator should, she glanced at the empty doorway before reaching for one of the scraps. *Thank you Mother for Rebecca's math grade*, she read, and on another, *Please help me get the job in your Son's name we pray*. She put them back and stood up to study more closely the offerings and exhortations around the Virgin. The simple name *Mary*, written on a three-inch-square yellow Post-it and heavily decorated with an elaborate green vine with purple and lavender flowers, had been stuck to the wall over the Virgin's halo like a miniature illuminated manuscript. Other Post-its, torn-off squares of typing paper, and wide-lined sheets from children's schoolbooks had quotes ranging from reassurance that *God notes the sparrow's fall* to the command (which reminded Kate of her recent discussions with Roz, and which seemed remarkably inappropriate in a shelter for battered women) *If anyone strikes you on the right cheek, turn to him the other also.* Around the bowl of prayer-wads, offerings had been laid, many of them floral and either wilted or artificial. They were interspersed with coins, a cross-stitched bookmark, and a string of lumpish beads made of the bright oven-baked plasticine that Kate recognized from Jon's experiment with Christmas ornaments. It was all sweet and rather pathetic, and Kate turned away to see what else the room contained.

Four backless benches of polished oak had been arranged in an open square in the center of the room, facing the four walls. The Virgin Mary's shrine wall was to the right of the door; the wall with the door in it bore only a plain wooden cross with a tall candle in front, dignified and simple to the point of starkness. The left-hand wall, across the room from the Virgin, was mounted with a deep wooden shelf about six feet wide, roughly three feet off the floor. On the shelf was propped a painting done on cheap canvas-board, a crudely done landscape of hills, trees, and river, with an angel flying in the clouds over it. The angel did not appear aerodynamic nor the landscape very probable,

but there were half a dozen other pictures leaning
against the wall to choose from, and Kate put her
empty cup down on one of the benches and went to flip
through them. They included an intricate mandala, a
Star of David, the enlarged photograph of a tropical
island, and three framed prints: a Berthe Morisot
mother and child, an old-fashioned painting of children
splashing in a river, and a famous Eva Vaughn study of
three children, the original of which Kate had actually
seen in the artist's studio. She greeted it like a friend
and thought about putting it up in place of the nonaer-
odynamic angel, but resisted the temptation.

This left the fourth wall, which was completely concealed by a heavy, dark red velvet curtain that stretched
from wall to wall and ceiling to floor. She pulled the left
edge away from the wall, saw that there did indeed
seem to be something other than blank wall behind it,
and found a curtain pull. She tugged at the cords, the
drapes obediently parted, and then Kate was stumbling
back, badly startled.

For a brief but intense moment, she thought that she
was being attacked by a wild woman with blood on her
teeth. She could almost smell the blood, splashed
around the woman in a pool, and then the hallucination
faded, leaving her to gaze in mingled amazement and
horror at the image before her.

The painting on the wall was enough to give a man
nightmares. It showed a woman of sorts, but this was a
woman who would have caused a playboy to shrivel,
would have given pause to the most ardent feminist,
would have had a Freudian rapidly retracting that
plaintive, worn, masculine query concerning what
women wanted.

For what this lady wanted was blood.

And had it, as Kate could well see. The deep blue,
larger-than-life female was wading through a lake of
the stuff, splashing it around, looking drunk with it.
Kate recognized her instantly as the subject of Roz's
thesis, Kali with the necklace of skulls and the belt of
human hands, laughing her terrible pleasure at the de-

capitated head she held up in one of her four arms, a
bearded face with blue eyes and a mole next to his nose,
which seemed oddly familiar to Kate. Gentle Jesus meek
and mild would be eaten alive by the goddess, and Kate
could understand why the curtain normally hid her
from view.

There were not as many prayers and thanks offerings
in the two bowls attached to her wall, either, clear indication that Kali was a bit strong for most of the women
who came here to free themselves from a battering relationship. It would take most women some time to get in
touch with this degree of anger.

But if that was so, then whose slips of paper were
these? They read only *Thank you Kali Ma* and *Be with
us*, and were for the most part printed anonymously.
Marigolds lay in Kali's thanks bowl, mixed with a few
still-fragrant narcissus, a child-sized glass bracelet, a
gold wedding band, and a Polaroid snapshot of the
Golden Gate Bridge.

And right at the bottom, uprooted by Kate's curious
forefinger, a lump of cellophane-wrapped butterscotch.

24

Help us to be the always hopeful
Gardeners of the spirit
Who know that without darkness
Nothing comes to birth
As without light
Nothing flowers.

Kate snatched her hand out of the bowl as if she'd been burned, but she scarcely had time to contemplate the awful implications of contaminated evidence before a noise came from behind her back. She whirled around, her hand plunging of its own accord toward the butt of her gun, but she froze when she saw the cluster of women in the doorway.

Diana Lomax stood just inside the room, taken aback at Kate's sudden reaction. Behind her stood Crystal Navarro and a couple of the other residents, with two young children. Crystal and the children had quite obviously never seen the painting of Kali, because all three were gaping at it, bug-eyed.

"Blessed Jesus!" Crystal blurted out. "I didn't know them curtains had anything—"

"Who did this?" Kate demanded of the shelter director.

"Did what?" Diana asked in confusion.

"That . . . thing on the wall. Who painted it?"

"That? It is a bit strong, isn't it? One of our volunteers asked if we—"

"Who. Painted. It." Kate leaned forward, and Diana took a step back.

"Phoebe Weatherman. Carla's secretary?"

"We've met," Kate told her, not entirely accurately. "When did she paint it?"

"Not very long ago. January, maybe? Yes, it must have been just after the first of the year, because her daughter-in-law Tamara was killed by her second husband just before Christmas. Phoebe loved Tamara like a daughter, far more than she loved her own son."

"Tamara." A woman of that name had appeared somewhere in the history of this convoluted case. Who . . . ?

"Yes. Tamara Pickford. A lovely, lovely person. She was one of our first residents, nearly seven years ago. That's when Phoebe began to get involved," she added.

"Phoebe," Kate repeated, and revelation opened in her mind like a flower. Phoebe Weatherman, a physically strong woman with a figurine of Kali the Destroyer on her desk, who four months ago had been handed a whole world of pain, cause enough to hate the entire male sex. Phoebe Weatherman, always in the background—how did the Womyn Web site put it?—cloaked in invisibility? Who was more invisible than a dowdy secretary? What better disguise for a vengeful goddess to assume?

And that bearded head . . . "What was Tamara's husband's name?" Kate asked sharply. She became aware of Agent Marcowitz looking over the heads of the women, alert but not knowing yet what had happened.

Diana thought for a minute before shaking her head. "It was her second husband and I don't remember . . ." Then she turned to crane her head at the hallway, looking past the women at a figure who stood just out of Kate's line of vision, near the front vestibule. "Carla?" she called. "What was the name of Tamara's second husband?"

An instant of silence fell over the gathering, and then came a voice, clear and pregnant with meaning.

"His name was Lawrence Goff," Carla Lomax said, and took a step forward so she could meet Kate's eyes. That was why the face on Kali's decapitated head looked familiar: Larry Goff, the December victim, killed in a Sacramento hotel by a woman dressed as a prostitute.

"Marcowitz," Kate began to shout, Stop her, Marcowitz, but she got no further than his name before the knot at the door flew apart in several directions at once. Crystal Navarro had abruptly realized that the two young children were staring in fascination at the naked, brutal, blood-soaked painting on the wall, and over their loud protests she seized their shoulders to force them out of the room. A split second later, Carla Lomax grabbed a couple of the women, shoved them hard at Marcowitz, and ordered, "Keep him here."

And then the lawyer turned and fled.

The women rose up in fierce obedience against the agent, protecting their advocate against this unknown male oppressor in the suit, just as Crystal's two small charges came smack between them, and the hallway burst instantly into a welter of struggling, shouting man, women, and children. Kate lunged for Carla, came face-to-face with her cousin instead, and spent five critical seconds wrestling with Diana before need overcame caution and she flipped the director hard into the pile of shrieking, outraged women (Marcowitz ending up on the floor beneath them all) and waded through legs and over backs and out of the chapel doorway. The front door had opened and slammed shut again before Kate had made it into clear hallway; Carla's back was disappearing around the corner by the time Kate worked the automatic door latches and flung herself into the shelter's front yard.

Kate scrambled after the lawyer, who had kicked off her heeled shoes to sprint along the pavement in her stocking feet. It quickly became apparent that Lomax had spent more hours running the hills of the city than Kate, and many more than Marcowitz, somewhere in the rear. Kate wasted no breath in shouting; she merely ran, chin down and arms pumping, gaining slowly and painfully, risking cars' bumpers at crowded street corners, dodging kids with basketballs and homeless

women with shopping carts, pounding along the sidewalks to the shouts of protest and anger and the encouragement of a pair of enthusiastic prostitutes on
their way to work who whooped and shouted, "You
go, girl!" as the two women flew past.

Where the hell was a cop when you needed one? she
cursed silently. Or the goddamn FBI? And why would
good citizens ring 911 when the neighbors had a loud
party but not when a plainclothes cop was trying her
damnedest to run down a suspect?

The end came in a flash, more than half a mile from
where it began. Carla chose a street thick with
commute-hour crowds, where she lost ground breaking
through the pedestrians as surely as if she had been
breaking trail through deep snow. She felt Kate closing
behind her, shot a glance behind and saw her pursuer
too close, and shot to the right to risk a desperate leap
in front of a moving bus that would have cut Kate off
had Carla made it.

She did not. The bus was traveling slowly, but the
inexorable force of it hurled the lawyer into the air to
smash against the side of a parked car. She lay draped
across the hood for a moment, then melted down onto
the ground and lay still.

Twenty minutes later, Kate's breath had almost returned to normal, Marcowitz had summoned uniformed cops from all over the city, the paramedics had
forced their way into the center of the chaos, and Carla
Lomax was still alive. Unconscious, and so she remained. Kate stayed with her until the lawyer was
taken through the doors of the operating room, and
then she paced up and down in the sterile corridor
while the surgeons worked.

The corridor was where Hawkin finally caught up
with her. They'd spoken a number of times in the four
hours since Kate had found herself standing over Carla
Lomax's still form, and she was quite aware of the case
going on in her absence, but the dull meaty thud of the

bus hitting Carla's body, the inarticulate cry and the uncoordinated flail of limbs had dominated every intervening moment.

"How is she?" were Hawkin's first words.

"Broken bones, her spine is okay, but there's cranial swelling. They're trying to relieve it—she's been in there a couple of hours. No idea what damage there might be, probably won't know for a day or two." She ran a hand through her short hair, feeling suddenly as if taking a step, even speaking, would be more effort than she could face. Hawkin saw it and pushed her into a nearby plastic chair. She shook her head in despair. "If I'd just up and shot her she might be in better shape."

"If you up and shot her, she might be dead," he pointed out. "How's your blood sugar?"

"What?"

"Food. Lee told me to tell you that lunch was a long time ago."

She tipped her head back against the wall and closed her eyes. "I want to crawl onto that gurney and go to sleep. Have somebody put a sign on me so they don't roll me into the OR and cut something off, would you?"

Instead, he bullied her to the hospital cafeteria, a place that dispensed calories and caffeine around the clock. When she was looking less gray, he reached into his pocket and pulled out a sheaf of at least fifteen message slips. She groaned.

"I've been through them," Hawkin hastened to say. "I made some of the calls while I was waiting to see the Man in Black. Most of them are routine, though you might like to know that Miriam Mkele phoned, to tell you that she might've handled a bag of spilled candies at the register the first week of February, a Wednesday or Thursday. What that tells us I don't know. The only thing I couldn't deal with were the ten calls from Peter Mehta. I phoned him back but he didn't want to talk to me, so I said you'd get to him when you could. He said any time no matter how late, but since that was a couple of hours ago he's probably left half a dozen more messages by now."

"You get what it was about?"

"Roz Hall."

"Shit."

"She's called a news conference tomorrow morning, told Mehta that she intends to tell the world that he and his whole community burn brides."

Kate put her aching head in her hands, feeling the dry sandwich she'd just eaten turning to stone in her stomach, and feeling the world begin to whirl slowly around. While she'd been busy stamping out one flare-up, behind her back a volcano had begun to swell. "Shit," she said again. "Lee must be going nuts. Do you want me to call Mehta? What time is it, anyway? Midnight?"

"Not quite. It's eleven-fifteen."

"I was sure my watch had stopped. I want to stay around until she comes out of surgery."

"Do you need to wait here? Or we could go see Mehta, then come back and check on her? He said he'd be up late."

"Oh hell, there's nothing I can do here. Let's go. But look, what did Crime Scene find at the shelter?"

"No prints on the candy, sorry to say, except the edge of your finger. But the Kali painting was definitely done by Carla's assistant, Phoebe Weatherman. And Weatherman's house is full of the same kind of pictures."

Kate's brain began sluggishly to move. "She was also active in the shelter—she was there for a while the night James Larsen was killed. And she fits the description of Traynor's bigger attacker. And even the woman who rented the car—with a black wig and glasses . . ."

"Anyway, she's skipped—I've just come from her place, Crime Scene's taking it apart now. There's a warrant out for her. Her daughter-in-law, name of Tamara Pickford, wasn't actually killed by her ex-husband. She died of—"

"An accidental overdose of pain pills, after her husband violated a restraining order and left her with a broken arm and a smashed jaw. I remember from the report on Goff. Damn it all, anyway. Phoebe Weatherman," Kate said. "Set off by her daughter-in-law's death. Why the hell didn't her name come up in the Goff investigation reports?"

"A very convoluted set of name changes—Weatherman is the woman's third name since she gave birth to the child who was first husband of Tamara Goff-formerly-Pickford-formerly-Lopes."

"It wasn't Roz, then, after all." She did not know how she felt about that, probably wouldn't know for some time, but even then she was aware that the relief she felt was heavily colored with shame, and that she would not be able to look at Roz Hall for a long time without being aware of it.

"Certainly she wasn't directly involved in Traynor's attack," Al confirmed. "She's been far too visible the last few days."

"Thank God for small favors."

"That doesn't mean she isn't in there somewhere," he warned.

"Oh, she's involved somewhere, even if it's only planting the idea of a vengeful goddess into Phoebe's mind. Or Carla's. And she knows it, or suspects it. I wonder if that's why she's gone after the Mehtas with such a passion. Denial and guilt and the feeling that if she wasn't involved, she should have been? God knows. I'll have to ask Lee," she said, completely unaware of her identification of Lee with the Almighty.

"You stay here," Hawkin told her. "I'll round up a uniform to baby-sit Lomax if she comes out of surgery before we get back."

"Expecting a confession, Al?" Her voice was bitter; he glanced at her sharply, but said nothing.

Considering Carla Lomax's condition, the uniformed guard was probably a waste of the taxpayers' money, but she was there as much to keep camera lenses out as to keep Lomax from escaping, and Kate suspected she would earn her pay. They gave her their

various numbers, she promised to pass the information
on to any replacement guard, and Kate and Al left her
to it. Halfway to the elevators, the two detectives came
to a dead halt. Diana Lomax was emerging from the
steel doors, deep in conversation with several support-
ers, among them Maj Freiling. Kate could see the coming confrontation, and she quailed.

"I can't face them, Al," Kate told him in something
close to despair.

"So don't," he said simply, and took her arm to steer
her back down the other way, up and down a lot of
stairs, and eventually through the still-crowded emergency room (more dormitory for the area's homeless at
this hour than it was hospital) to the parking lot.

"Where the hell did I leave my car, anyway?" Kate
asked Al. "Oh yeah, Marcowitz drove to the shelter, so
it's still at the lot. You'll have to drive me by so I can
fetch it. Ah, hell; what am I thinking about? The hospital doesn't need me to watch over Carla Lomax. Let's
go and pat Mehta's hand, and then you can take me
home and I'll see if I can get Lee to talk Roz out of her
news conference, and then we'll all get twelve hours'
sleep and live happily ever after."

"If that was an offer of your guest bed," Al said,
"thanks, but I think that tonight I need to be in my
own. I can drop you by your house, or the lot."

"The lot, thanks. Is there any reason to go by the
shelter, or the two women's houses?"

"Marcowitz has his teeth into those."

A vivid and surreal image floated through Kate's
tired mind, of the strong, shiny teeth of the Man in
Black sunk deep into the front corner of a trim little
cottage. She shook her head to clear it.

"Did he say anything to you about what happened at
the shelter?"

"Not much, just enough so it was obvious he feels he
screwed up."

"He did. We both did." And Carla Lomax was paying the price.

Kate half hoped they would find the Mehta house

dark and silent, allowing them to pass by to their waiting beds, but such was not to be. All the outside lights were glaring and the downstairs windows were lit up, including Mehta's front study. The two detectives sighed simultaneously, and got out of the car.

The moment they set foot on the walkway, the front door flew open, revealing an unshaven, uncombed Peter Mehta, dressed in a dark jogging suit and carrying a heavy stick in his right hand. They froze.

Hawkin cleared his throat. "Mr. Mehta, would you please put down your club?"

The man in the doorway looked at the object in his hand and reached down to prop it in the corner. The two detectives resumed their journey up the walk and into the house. Mehta began speaking rapidly before the door was shut.

"That madwoman! You must do something about her. This is America—she has no right to torment my family. I will buy a gun to protect my wife and children! You have to make her stop."

Kate put a hand on his arm, which surprised him into sudden silence. Wondering vaguely if she'd violated some cultural taboo, she removed her hand and used it to gesture toward the man's study. "Shall we talk, Mr. Mehta?" she asked in a calm voice, and when they were all settled, she took out her notebook, although she doubted she would be writing anything in it—or if she did, that she would be able to decipher it in the morning.

"Now, Mr. Mehta, can you tell us what this is about?"

"She threatened me, my family."

"Who threatened you?"

"That Hall woman who calls herself a minister and her minion, the—what is the word?—dyke who led little Pramilla astray. Amanda something, and some other woman, and my God, the press! But mostly the Hall woman. She said she would burn us as little Pramilla was burned." It was "little Pramilla" now, Kate noted, not "the girl." The belated affection soured her stomach even further.

"That's a very serious charge, Mr. Mehta," Al said.

"It was in the newspaper. They did not name her, but it was what the voice told me on the telephone, that she would do to us what happened to Pramilla. Look," he demanded, "I have lost my sister-in-law, and then my own brother. Killed by those—those harridans, I have no doubt. Do I need to arm myself—or even take my whole family back to India, to escape their wrath? You must protect us."

It was difficult to separate Mehta's honest distress from his dramatic excesses and the unfortunate humor his increasingly singsong accent brought along; still, they had no choice but to take him at face value, at least for the moment. Kate asked if she could borrow his telephone to make the necessary arrangements.

"We'll have the house watched tonight and during the day tomorrow. Ms. Hall is due to speak with the press in the morning, but I'll see if we can reach her before then, ask her to tone down her remarks until we've had a chance to look into her accusations. Now," Kate said firmly, holding her hand up to stem his protest, "we can't stop her from speaking to reporters, any more than we tried to stop you. If I try to force her, it will only make matters worse." Mehta subsided, grumbling to himself at the innate unfairness of the American system, protecting the criminals and leaving a man to protect his family alone.

Kate felt suddenly flattened by exhaustion, and she snapped, "Mr. Mehta, we've just spent a very long day cleaning up after a bunch of vigilantes who thought the same thing. If we hear you've gone out and bought a gun, I for one am going to be really unhappy."

"No, no, I did not mean that. I do not want a gun— what do I know of guns but that children find them and shoot each other? I will let your officer do his work, and hope only that you will talk some sense into the madwoman."

Kate winced at the description of a woman she still

thought of as a friend, but she didn't argue with it. She
didn't want to argue with anyone else, wanted only to
tumble over onto Mehta's sofa and pass out, but she
had to stay rational until they could turn him over to
the uniformed officer.

While Al and Mehta walked around the house and
checked the doors and windows, Kate used Mehta's
phone a second time to call the hospital. Carla was out
of surgery, her condition critical but stable, whatever
that meant. She hung up and wandered around the office, suspecting that if she sat down she'd fall asleep.
The books on Mehta's shelves looked unread, there because a man's study needed a lot of hardcover spines.
Many of them were in some squiggly alphabet, and
some of them were on India and Indian art. That reminded Kate of a question she'd carried around for
days now, so when Mehta came back she asked him.

"Does your family . . ." How did one ask this?
Kate wondered. "Do you worship the goddess Kali,
Mr. Mehta?"

"Of course not," he said, sounding affronted. "Only
the . . . lower castes worship Kali. And tribals."

The outcasts and the marginalized. The invisible
ones again.

"Well, do you know anything about her worship?"

"Only in general. I have never been to one of her
temples, if that's what you mean, never witnessed a sacrifice."

"Sacrifice? What, like animals?"

"Goats most usually, smaller animals and birds for
the poorer people."

"Do you by any chance know if they're strangled?"

"What, the animals?" Mehta said, his voice rising in
protest at the question.

"Yes, the goats and such."

He took a deep breath, and said primly, "I believe
their throats are cut."

"But I thought Hindus were vegetarians?"

"They don't *eat* the animals." Mehta was now
frankly appalled, even more offended than he had been

at the idea of his family worshiping this dark goddess. Kate just looked at him, wondering if his answers would have made sense if she weren't so damned groggy, and then doggedly backtracked to where she had begun.

"I just asked about her worship because I was wondering if candy was a usual offering to Kali."

"Candy?"

She was beginning to regret that she'd asked. "Yes, pieces of candy. Chocolate, hard sweets, that kind of thing."

"I have never heard of that, although I suppose one could offer anything to a god, and foodstuffs are commonly used. *Ghee*—melted butter—is often used to anoint . . . objects of spiritual energy. But I have never heard of pieces of candy." Kate started to tell him thanks and it was not important, but he was not through. "Now if you'd asked me about *Candi*," he said, giving it a different pronunciation, "that I could help you with. Candi is another name for the goddess Kali, what you might call another manifestation of the primary goddess Durga. Hindu mythology is a little complicated," he said, sounding apologetic.

"Yes," murmured Kate. "So I understand."

"Do Indians eat candy, Mr. Mehta?" Al asked.

Mehta looked puzzled at this bizarre conversation, but he answered readily enough. "Yes, we eat candy—at least, the children do, when their mother lets them. In India there is little chocolate, because of the heat, you know, but we have many sweetmeats made from milk and nuts, and using fruits and vegetables. Very rich, but actually not bad for you. Would you like to try some? My wife buys it in Berkeley."

Kate would have demurred, but Hawkin said yes, he would be interested, and there seemed to be nothing else to do while they waited for the patrol officer, so Mehta, polite if uncomprehending, led them back to the kitchen and took out several clear plastic deli boxes filled with soft squares, white, orange, and a bilious pink color.

"Burfi," he said, offering them a square of mealy and cloyingly sweet white stuff that tasted like perfume. "Carrot *halwa*, and almond *burfi*. And there are also *gulab jaman* and *jelabis*, which my wife makes sometimes, but I would call those desserts or pastries, not candy."

Kate was having trouble with the substance in her mouth, but Hawkin swallowed hard and said thickly, "What about those little assorted seeds and stuff?"

"Seeds? You mean *saumf*? Not candy, no. You might call it a snack, I suppose, though I'd say it's more a breath freshener." He rummaged through another shelf and came out with a packet of loose seed mix with colored specks, apparently identical to the little bag of seeds Laxman had carried in his pocket. "Americans don't tend to chew things, other than gum, but we chew *betal*, which makes one spit, or *saumf*, which doesn't. Chewing or not chewing is a cultural difference."

"But it's not candy?"

"Not by any stretch of the imagination, Inspector."

Their strange questions had woken his curiosity, but they did not choose to enlighten him. The patrolman arrived a minute later, and they left, reassuring Mehta, hit by a sudden return of anxiety, that they would do their best to deflect Roz Hall. They turned the house over to the uniform and settled into their car, with Hawkin behind the wheel.

Kate, oddly, felt less tired than she had. That *burfi* or whatever it was had been sweet enough to raise the blood sugar of a corpse; maybe the department should lay in a supply for those long night shifts.

"So the candy is a pun," she mused, "an offering of Kali to Kali. And that was very interesting about the seedy stuff not being candy, to his mind anyway."

"But would Carla and Phoebe have known it wasn't an Indian kind of candy?"

"They know about Kali."

"That doesn't mean they know Indian culture."

"True," she agreed, and sat motionless in the moving car. Outside the windows, the city's night song came to

Kate's ears, muted and atonal, unpleasant and as jangled as her nerves. After a few blocks, she said, "I'll ask Lee to call Roz first thing in the morning, see if she can persuade her to lay off Mehta. If there's anyone she'll listen to, it's Lee."

"It'd be nice to be able to stop her without having to put a gun to her head," Hawkin said. Kate was not sure he was actually joking.

At the parking lot beneath the perpetually laden freeway, Kate's car started immediately, to her relief, and it seemed to drive itself up the silent streets to the old house on Russian Hill. The house was still and quiescent when she let herself in, the entrance and hallway lights the only bulbs left burning. She phoned the hospital again, which gave her no changes, and then, hating the world, the city, and her job in that order, Kate set the alarm for six A.M., less than four hours away, stripped her clothes off into a heap on the floor, and crept into the blessed shelter of the bed.

Lee woke up and turned over, nuzzling into Kate with a questioning noise in the back of her throat and then an actual question.

"Is everything okay?"

Kate, realizing that she could trade a few minutes now for a longer sleep in the morning, shifted around to put an arm around Lee.

"I need you to do something for me, sweetheart. Did you know Roz has called a press conference in the morning about the Mehta family?"

"God, do I ever. Maj was on the phone most of the evening."

"Well, there may not be anything that any of us can do, but Roz might just possibly listen to you." Lee started to protest, but Kate pushed on. "Carla Lomax and her secretary were the ones behind those murders. We haven't actually arrested either of them, because Carla ran in front of a bus while I was chasing her and is still in recovery and Phoebe's disappeared, but they will be charged with Larsen and Banderas for sure, as well as a man in Sacramento and probably in a few days Laxman Mehta, although the investigation's still going on. Oh yes, and the attempted murder of a guy named Traynor in San Jose."

Lee was fully awake now. "God, Kate, that's—what, five assaults? Why? And what does Roz have to do with it?"

"They began with straightforward revenge, it looks like, and from there decided to become vigilantes. And I believe that the reason Roz is so hot to get Mehta is that she knew, on some level, that the two women were involved in something. I think we'll find that she introduced them to the idea of the goddess Kali as a feminist avenger, and they ran with it. Sweetheart, blackmail her, for my sake. Play on her guilt, her responsibility for twisting those two women. Even if it's not true, it'll make her slow down and think. Yes, love," she said over Lee's protests, "I know it's unscrupulous and unfair and everything else, but Roz is about to set loose a tornado on the city that'll make it nearly impossible to investigate the Mehta case with any hope of conviction, and might well drive the Mehtas back to India and out of our jurisdiction. And you can tell her that, too, if she'll shut up about it; tell her anything, just so she gives me time."

Kate felt as if her voice was at the end of a dim corridor, echoing and growing fainter, but she waited until Lee had agreed to try, agreed to reach Roz early in the morning, before she let herself go. The last thing Kate said before sleep claimed her was, "Could you change the alarm clock to eight?"

25

Bear the roots in mind,
You, the dark one, Kali,
Awesome power.

It was not eight, she saw, it was twenty past seven, and it was not the alarm, but the telephone.

"Martinelli," she croaked into the receiver.

"It's me, love," Lee's voice said into her ear, "I thought you should know that I just got to Roz's house and she isn't home. We're heading over to the church; I'll ring you back as soon as we find her."

"You blessed among women," Kate said, already on her feet. "I love you."

"I know you do. Now go have a shower."

Kate's shower lasted perhaps ninety seconds and then she was pulling on clothes over her still-damp skin and running a comb through her wet hair. She trotted downstairs and had just poured herself a cup of very stale coffee when the phone rang again.

"Roz's secretary said that Roz phoned Peter Mehta at about quarter to seven this morning. They had a short talk and then she just drove off, about five minutes ago."

"Okay. She may have gone over there for a private talk, a little last-minute conflict resolution." It would be like Roz, but it made Kate uncomfortable to think of Roz facing the furious Peter Mehta by herself. "Look, I think I'll run by there, see if I can get her to leave him alone. You stay put, I'll phone you when I find her."

"There's coffee in the—"

"Got it. 'Bye."

She took one large swallow of the hot greenish substance and abandoned the cup.

The Mehta house was about ten minutes away on a good day. Kate made it in eight, charging up the hills and squealing around the corners, and even managed to punch in Hawkin's pager number at an unavoidable red light to leave a message.

Still, Roz had gotten there first. Her Jeep was in the driveway but there was no sign of her, or of Mehta. Kate eyed the drawn drapes, and decided that she did not really want to be in there alone with an angry man who met police officers at the door with a club in his hand—the memory of the last time she had ventured into an unknown situation with minimal backup was all too clear in her mind and on her scalp. Feeling a little abashed, she put in a call for assistance, but did not wait for the patrol car to arrive.

The doorbell brought no immediate response, nor did a heavy fist on the door. If the family heard her, they probably thought she was just an early reporter. She eyed the sturdy wood briefly before deciding that, even if she could think of an excuse, her shoulder would shatter before the door budged, so she headed around the house toward the remembered kitchen door, where she might well find the family at breakfast, Roz with a cup of coffee in her hand, beaming at them all in her inimitable friendly manner, creating reason and compromise out of angry divisiveness as she had so often done.

The gate in the high wooden fence was latched. Kate cursed under her breath, made sure her gun was secure in its underarm holster, and scrabbled up to pull herself over. She paused to peer over before committing her heel to the fence top, lest Mehta be standing there with his club—or a shotgun—but the empty driveway stretched out along the wall of the house to end at the burnt-out patch that had been Pramilla's kitchen, and her pyre. Kate continued pulling herself up, and over, and landed on the other side only slightly bruised and winded.

Kate was not aware of sliding her gun out of its holster, but somehow it was in her hand as she moved briskly down the concrete drive and rounded the corner of the house, and then the world blew up in her face.

Twin shrieks of pain and terror soared above the breathy *whump* of exploding gasoline. Without thought Kate hit the hard ground rolling, and felt more than saw the expanding cloud flash over her head and puff out, leaving at its source a dancing pond of flames from which two figures trailed streams of fire. Mehta's arm was alight to his elbow, but he was already pulling off his dressing gown and beating at the flames with it. At his feet, wavering in the heat, lay a compact black shape that a part of Kate's mind registered as a taser.

Mehta was up and out of danger, but not Roz. She was lying with her legs deep in the very hottest part of the flames, writhing feebly and trying with a clear lack of coordination to pull herself away. Her trousers were burning and her cries of terror and pain seemed to fill the air. Kate's gun went into its holster as she ran to grab Roz under the arms to drag her back from the worst of the flames, but the fire followed them, loath to let its prey go, and Roz still burned. Casting around desperately for something to smother the flames, Kate spotted the mildewy cushions of the lawn furniture; she snatched them up and threw them over Roz; the stubborn flames hesitated, then billowed up again around the thick pads. It was a nightmare, this heaving tangle of flowered cushions and squirting blue fire and flailing limbs, and as Kate jerked off her jacket to beat at the fire, an exquisite pain wrapped around her left arm, and she beat on until at last the fire on Roz flared and died out.

Roz's high-pitched mewls of agony were audible even over the dying roar of the flames, but then Mehta's voice came shouting, taut with pain and what might have been rage but Kate knew was in truth fear.

"What are you doing? That madwoman attacked me, she tried to burn down my sleeping house, let her burn, she ought to—"

His voice strangled at the sight of Kate's drawn gun. "What are you doing?" he said again, openly afraid now.

"You brought her here to kill her, you bastard. Set her on fire like you did Pramilla, knocked her helpless first like you did with Laxman. You thought we'd count your brother's murder as just one more of the series. Was it a million dollars your father left him, or was it maybe a little more? Peter Mehta, you are under arrest for the murder—"

That was as far as Kate got before the back door of the house crashed open on its hinges and Rani Mehta charged out, as vengeful as Kali and every bit as bent on destruction. She ran full tilt across the brick patio at them, oblivious of the gun, heedless of any official warnings, intent only on the rescue of her husband. She threw herself at Kate, shrieking and clawing, and Kate, in an agony of conflict, simply could not bring herself to shoot the woman at point-blank range. Instead, she curled over to protect her face from those fearsome nails, switched the gun into her left hand, and then rose up and drove her right fist directly up into the woman's plump chin with all the strength in her arm.

Rani sagged, and in that instant Kate yanked her handcuffs out and slapped one end around Rani's waving wrist, and then she felt Mehta beginning to move toward her and she let go of Rani to turn the gun on the husband. Unlike his wife, Mehta was very aware of the threat in Kate's hand, but it was Rani whom Kate had to neutralize, a recovering Rani about to launch a second attack. Kate shouted at her, "I'll shoot your husband."

Rani caught herself, and looked down at the gun, seeing it for the first time. She followed its aim, and in that moment of hesitation, Kate reached out with foot and hand to trip the big woman onto the hard knobs of the heavy cast-iron chaise longue; Rani's sharp cry of pain overrode the click of the cuffs over the metal frame. Gulping to catch her breath, aware of her own complete dishevelment and three of the Mehta children with the old servant Lali staring at her aghast from the doorway of the house, Kate panted her way through the arrest procedures. Even if she had carried a second set of cuffs, she could not have brought herself to clamp a handcuff over the raw and blackened skin of Mehta's right arm, but she did pat him down and kept an eye on him, as well as on the house behind him, until the sirens drew near, cutting off on the residential street, and the doors of several cars slammed in the street. She made Mehta go with her to the gate and unlatch it, and there she turned him over to a pair of uniforms to await the paramedics. She would meet up with him later, when a doctor had cleared him for interrogation.

She ignored Rani and the rest of the family, going to kneel at last by Roz's side. Roz was wearing her clerical collar; her face was as white as the plastic strip. She was conscious but shivering, crying and tight-faced with shock. When the paramedics arrived, Kate insisted that they take Roz first, leaving Mehta for the next ambulance.

On their way to the burn center, Kate sat holding Roz's unscathed hand with her own. Roz's pain came in waves, indicated by a clenching of her grip. At the height of one spasm, she turned her head and gasped, "Talk to me."

"About what, Roz?"

"Anything. Take my mind off this."

Kate seriously doubted that words alone would make much progress in pain management, but if words Roz wanted, then words she would have. And, Kate figured, the stronger the better.

"We caught Carla Lomax," she told her, and waited for Roz to ask what Carla had been caught for. Roz did not ask, which confirmed a number of Kate's suspicions. "And Phoebe Weatherman is on the run. Did you actually know, Roz? Or just suspect?"

The searing agony from Roz's legs was clearly battering at the woman, on the edge of overwhelming her. It was, Kate tried to reassure herself, a far better sign than lack of feeling—the fire had not gone deeply enough into Roz's skin to destroy the nerves. Roz held herself rigid and spoke in short gasps, but her words and thoughts were clear, as if willpower and grammatical precision were enough to keep the pain at bay.

"I told you. I did not know. I suppose. I did not want to. If I had. I would. Have told you. I said I wouldn't. That was a lie. I do not condone. Murder. As a way of solving problems."

Oddly enough, Kate believed her.

"Phoebe's gone. Underground. You won't . . . catch her." The last phrase coincided with a sudden buildup of pain, and Roz panted and groaned in the back of her throat until the wave had passed. When her eyes came open again, they were commanding Kate to continue, and Kate realized that words were indeed an effective analgesic; they'd certainly taken her mind off her own pain for a moment or two. And from a more selfish point of view, taking into account Roz's temporary dependence on rigid order, questions put to her were likely to be answered before Roz stopped to consider what she was doing. Reluctantly, then, Kate continued.

"You don't have any idea where Phoebe has gone?"

Roz shook her head.

"Roz, she's killed three people."

"Kate. I do not. Know."

Kate decided that was all she was going to get at the moment, and she sat looking at Roz and thinking about going underground, and about choosing invisibility as a way of life, as a form of self-defense. At the thought, and at her growing awareness of the community of invisible women out there, waiting to enfold Phoebe Weatherman, she had to smile in spite of the pain shooting up her arm. With a glance at the paramedic, she leaned over to speak quietly in Roz's ear.

"And what about the LOPD? That's Maj, isn't it?"

In Roz's pinched features, alarm mingled with the pain, and Kate hastened to explain herself.

"I figured it out when I realized that the reason we didn't focus on Phoebe Weatherman was because she was just a secretary. Of course, she wasn't 'just' anything, but she was invisible—like the Web site said. And like Maj always seems to be. Roz, I promise you, anything you say to me in the current circumstances will be completely inadmissible. There's not a judge in the country would allow it as testimony. So you're safe to tell me: I know Maj has had nothing to do with the murders, but she is behind the actions of the Ladies, isn't she? She's written all over it, her kind of humor."

"I can't . . ."

"Roz, I swear to you, on anything I hold precious. On Lee's head, if you like: Even if I could, I will not do anything with what you tell me."

The injured woman said nothing, but eventually, her eyes holding Kate's, she nodded, and the faint twist of a smile, affectionate and admiring, came across her mouth. Yes, it was Maj.

"Roz, I love the two of you. I owe you both one hell of a lot. So I'm not even going to ask for the names of the women who did the actual assaults—which I assume that Maj had nothing to do with, considering the shape she's in at the moment." The image of Maj Freiling, seven months' pregnant and dressed as a ninja assault warrior armed with a roll of duct tape, danced through Kate's mind, nowhere near as impossible as she would have wished. She pushed the image away, but she knew it would return at unlikely moments. "I want you to tell Maj that if she stops now, if she closes down the Ladies and doesn't attack any more men, I won't go any further with it. But she's got to stop. Now."

Roz held her eyes, and nodded again. Kate sat back, palm still clasped to palm, satisfied.

Roz's eyes drooped and then shut, which Kate hoped

meant that she had drifted off, but after a minute Roz said, "Still, it was a great Campaign while it lasted, wasn't it?"

Kate struggled to keep her face straight, and failed. "I hope—" she began, and then snorted loudly, startling the ambulance attendant. "I hope you guys bought stock in duct tape before you started." The alarmed paramedic stared at the two injured women with the tears starting down their faces, and fumbled hastily for his bag.

At the hospital, Roz was whisked away, and Kate put off treatment of her own burns to phone Lee. She told her to bring Maj to the hospital, reassured Lee that her own burns were minor, put down the receiver, and looked up to see Al Hawkin furiously shouldering his way through uniforms and nurses alike. He stopped when he saw her standing there—half her hair burnt to a frazzle, her shirtsleeves scorched and covered with ash, stinking to high heaven, her left forearm wrapped in the paramedic's gauze—and most of the storm clouds left his face.

"God damn it, Martinelli, don't do that to me. Lee would wrap those crutches of hers around my neck if I let anything else happen to you."

She tried to stir up some resentment at his protectiveness, but failed. She did manage a stir of feeble humor, however.

"Oh, you know me, Al. I like my cases to end with a bang."

And on the other side of town, in a pool of blood on the wall of the shelter for battered women, dark Kali smiled.

ABOUT THE AUTHOR

LAURIE R. KING lives with her family in the hills above Monterey Bay in northern California. Her background includes such diverse interests as Old Testament theology and construction work, and she has been writing crime fiction since 1987. The winner of both the Edgar and the John Creasey Awards for Best First Novel for *A Grave Talent*, the debut of the Kate Martinelli series, she is also the author of five mysteries in the Mary Russell series, including *The Beekeeper's Apprentice*, and most recently, *O Jerusalem*, as well as a thriller, *A Darker Place*. She is at work on her eleventh novel, *Folly*.

"Rousing . . . Riveting . . . Suspenseful."
—*The Chicago Tribune* on *The Beekeeper's Apprentice*

"A lively adventure in the very best
of intellectual company."
—*The New York Times Book Review* on *A Letter of Mary*

"A literary thriller to end all
literary thrillers."
—*Booknews* from The Poisoned Pen on *A Darker Place*

Enter the spellbinding world of

LAURIE R. KING

The thrill of the chase . . . literate, harrowing suspense . . . There's nothing elementary about the mysteries of Laurie R. King!

Since 1993, Laurie R. King has been tantalizing readers with her award-winning, internationally-acclaimed novels of mystery and suspense. Turn the page for a special look at Laurie King's books, along with excerpts from the more recent novels. Each is available now wherever Bantam Books are sold.

THE BEEKEEPER'S APPRENTICE
A Mary Russell and Sherlock Holmes Mystery

In 1915, long since retired from his observations of criminal humanity, Sherlock Holmes is engaged in a reclusive study of honeybee behavior on the Sussex Downs. Never did he think to meet an intellect to match his own—until his acquaintance with Miss Mary Russell, a very modern fifteen-year-old whose mental acuity is equaled only by her audacity, tenacity, and penchant for trousers and cloth caps, unthinkable in any young lady of Holmes's own generation. . . .

I was fifteen when I first met Sherlock Holmes, fifteen years old with my nose in a book as I walked the Sussex Downs, and nearly stepped on him. In my defence I must say it was an engrossing book, and it was very rare to come across another person in that particular part of the world in that war year of 1915. In my seven weeks of peripatetic reading amongst the sheep (which tended to move out of my way) and the gorse bushes (to which I had painfully developed an instinctive awareness) I had never before stepped on a person.

It was a cool, sunny day in early April, and the book was by Virgil. I had set out at dawn from the silent farmhouse, chosen a different direction from my usual, and spent the intervening hours wrestling with Latin verbs, climbing unconsciously over stone walls, and unthinkingly circling hedgerows, and would probably not have noticed the sea until I stepped off one of the chalk cliffs into it.

As it was, my first awareness that there was another soul in the universe was when a male throat cleared itself loudly not four feet from me. The Latin text flew into the air, followed closely by an Anglo-Saxon oath. Heart pounding, I hastily pulled together what dignity I could and glared down through my spectacles at this figure hunched up at my feet: a gaunt, greying man in his fifties wearing a cloth cap, ancient tweed greatcoat, and decent shoes, with a threadbare Army rucksack on the ground beside him. A tramp perhaps, who had left the rest of his possessions stashed beneath a bush. Or an Eccentric. Certainly no shepherd. . . .

"**The Beekeeper's Apprentice has power to charm the most grizzled Baker Street Irregular.**"—*Daily News*, New York.

TO PLAY THE FOOL
A Kate Martinelli Mystery

When a band of homeless people cremate a beloved dog in San Francisco's Golden Gate Park, the authorities are willing to overlook a few broken regulations. But three weeks later, when the dog's owner gets the same fiery send-off, the SFPD has a real headache on its hands. The autopsy suggests homicide, but Inspector Kate Martinelli and her partner have little else to go on. They have a homeless victim without a positive ID, a group of witnesses who have little love for the cops, and a possible suspect, known only as Brother Erasmus, whose history leads Kate along a twisting road to a disbanded cult, long-buried secrets, the thirst for spirituality, and the hunger for bloody vengeance.

His breath huffing in clouds and the news announcer still jabbering against his unemployed ears, the currently unemployed former Bank of America vice presidential assistant was slogging his disconsolate way alongside Kennedy Drive in the park when, to his instant and unreasoning fury, he was attacked for a second time by a branch-wielding bearded man from the shrubbery. Three weeks of ego deflation blew up like a rage-powered air bag. He instantly took four rapid steps forward and clobbered the unkempt head with the only thing he carried, which happened to be a Walkman stereo. Fortunately for both men, the case collapsed the moment it made contact with the wool cap, but the maddened former bank assistant stood over the terrified and hungover former real estate broker and pummeled away with his crumbling handful of plastic shards and electronic components. A passing commuter saw them, snatched up her car telephone, and dialed 911.

Three minutes later, the eyes of the two responding police officers were greeted by the sight of a pair of men seated side by side on the frost-rimed grass: One was shocked, bleeding into his shaggy beard, and even at twenty feet stank of cheap wine and old sweat; the other was clean-shaven, clean-clothed, and wore a pair of two-hundred-dollar running shoes on his feet.

The two officers never were absolutely certain about what happened, but they filled out their forms and saw the two partners in adversity safely tucked into the ambulance. Just before the door closed, the female officer thought to ask why the homeless man had been dragging branches out of the woods in the first place.

By the time the two officers pounded up the pathway into the baseball clearing, the second funeral pyre had caught and flames were roaring up to the gray sky in great billows of sparks and burning leaves. It was a much larger pile of wood than had been under the small dog Theophilus three weeks earlier, but then, it had to be.

On the top of this pyre lay the body of a man.

A MONSTROUS REGIMENT OF WOMEN
A Mary Russell and Sherlock Holmes Mystery

The dawn of 1921 finds Mary Russell, Sherlock Holmes's brilliant young apprentice, about to come into a considerable inheritance. Nevertheless, she still enjoys her nighttime prowls in disguise through London's grimy streets, where one night she encounters an old friend, now a charity worker among the poor.

Veronica Beaconsfield introduces Russell to the New Temple of God, a curious amalgam of church and feminist movement, led by the enigmatic, electrifying Margery Childe. Part suffragette, part mystic, she lives quite well for a woman of God from supposedly humble origins. Despite herself, Russell is drawn ever deeper into Childe's circle . . . far closer to heaven than Mary Russell would like. . . .

The door closed behind Veronica, and I was half-aware of her voice calling out to Marie and then fading down the corridor as I sat and allowed myself to be scrutinised, slowly, thoroughly, impassively. When the blonde woman finally turned away and kicked her shoes off under a low table, I let out the breath I hadn't realised I was holding and offered up thanks to Holmes's tutoring, badgering, and endless criticism that had brought me to the place where I might endure such scrutiny without flinching—at least not outwardly.

She padded silently across the thick carpet to the disorder of bottles and chose a glass, some ice, a large dollop from a gin bottle, and a generous splash of tonic. She half-turned to me with a question in her eyebrow, accepted my negative shake without comment, went to a drawer, took out a cigarette case and a matching enamelled matchbox, gathered up an ashtray, and came back to her chair, moving all the while with an unconscious feline grace—that of a small domestic tabby rather than anything more exotic or angular. She tucked her feet under her in the chair precisely like the cat in Mrs Hudson's kitchen, lit her cigarette, dropped the spent match into the ashtray balanced on the arm of the chair, and filled her lungs deeply before letting the smoke drift slowly from nose and mouth. The first swallow from the glass was equally savoured, and she shut her eyes for a long moment.

When she opened them, the magic had gone out of her, and she was just a small, tired, dishevelled woman in an expensive dress, with a much-needed drink and cigarette to hand. I revised my estimate of her age upward a few years, to nearly forty, and wondered if I ought to leave.

"Why are you here, Mary Russell?"

"King has a gift for the rich, decisive detail and the narrative crispness that distinguished Conan Doyle's writing."—*The Washington Post Book World*

WITH CHILD
A Kate Martinelli Mystery

Adrift in mist-shrouded San Francisco mornings and alcohol-fogged nights, homicide detective Kate Martinelli can't escape the void left by her departed lover, who has gone off to rethink their relationship. But when twelve-year-old Jules Cameron comes to Kate for a professional consultation, Kate's not sure she's that desperate for distraction. Jules is worried about her friend Dio, a homeless boy she met in a park. Dio has disappeared without a word of farewell, and Jules wants Kate to find him. Reluctant as she is, Kate can't say no—and soon finds herself forming a friendship with the bright, quirky girl. But the search for Dio will prove to be much more than either bargained for. . . .

And still, all that fall, she looked for Dio. Once a week, she made the rounds of the homeless, asking about him. Always she asked among her network of informants, the dealers and hookers and petty thieves, and invariably received a shake of the head. Twice she heard rumors of him, once at a house for runaway teenagers, where one of the current residents had a friend who had met a boy of his description; and a second time, when one of her informants told her there was a boy-toy of that name in a house used by pederasts over near the marina. She phoned a couple of old friends in the Berkeley and Oakland departments to ask them to keep an ear out, and she arranged to be in on the raid of the marina house, but neither came up with anything more substantial than the ghost she already had. She doubted he was in the Bay Area, and told Jules that, but she also kept looking.

That autumn, in one of those flukes that even the statistician will admit happens occasionally, it seemed for a while that every case the Homicide Department handled involved kids. A two-year-old with old scars on his back and broken bones in various states of mending died in an emergency room from having been shaken violently by his eighteen-year-old mother. Three boys aged sixteen to twenty died from gunshot wounds. Four bright seventeen-year-old students in a private school did a research project on explosives, using the public library, and sent a very effective pipe bomb to a hated teacher. It failed, but only because the man was as paranoid as he was infuriating. A seven-year-old in a pirate costume was separated from his friends on Halloween; he was found the next morning, raped and bludgeoned to death. Kate saw two of her colleagues in tears within ten days, one of them a tough, experienced beat cop who had seen everything but still couldn't bring himself to look again at the baby in the cot. The detectives on the fourth floor of the Department of Justice made morbid jokes about it being the Year of the Child, and they either answered the phone gingerly or with a snarl, according to their personalities. . . .

"Like a slow-burning fire, the story makes you hurt deeply for King's characters before you realize what's happening to you."—*Kirkus Reviews* (starred)

A LETTER OF MARY
A Mary Russell and Sherlock Holmes Mystery

Late in the summer of 1923, Mary Russell Holmes and her husband, the illustrious Sherlock Holmes, are en-

sconced in their home on the Sussex Downs, giving themselves over to their studies: Russell to her theology, and Holmes to his malodorous chemical experiments. Interrupting the idyllic scene, amateur archaeologist Miss Dorothy Ruskin visits with a startling puzzle. Working in the Holy Land, she has unearthed a tattered roll of papyrus with a message from Mary Magdalene. Miss Ruskin wants Russell to safeguard the letter. But when Miss Ruskin is killed in a traffic accident, Russell and Holmes find themselves on the trail of a fiendishly clever murderer.

The next day, *The Times* arrived at one o'clock in the afternoon. It still lay folded when I turned off the lights and went upstairs, and it had not moved when I came back through the house on Friday for an early cup of tea. Two hours later, Holmes came down for breakfast and picked it up absently as he passed. So it was that nearly forty hours had elapsed between the time I saw Miss Ruskin off on the train and the time Holmes gave a cry of surprise and sat up straight over the paper, his cup of tea forgotten in one hand.

"What is it? Holmes?" I stood up and went to see what had caught his attention so dramatically. It was a police notice, a small leaded box, inserted awkwardly into a middle page, no doubt just as the paper was going to press.

IDENTITY SOUGHT OF LONDON
ACCIDENT VICTIM

Police are asking for the assistance of any person who might identify a woman killed in a traffic accident late yesterday evening. . . .

I sat down heavily next to Holmes.

"No. Oh surely not. Dear God. What night would that have been? Wednesday? She had a dinner engagement at nine o'clock."

In answer, Holmes put his cup absently into his toast and went to the telephone. After much waiting and shouting over the bad connexion, he established that the woman had not yet been identified. The voice at the other end squawked at him as he hung up the earpiece. I took my eyes from Miss Ruskin's wooden box, which inexplicably seeemed to have followed me downstairs, and got to my feet, feeling very cold. My voice seemed to come from elsewhere.

"**A wonderful book, simultaneously inventive, charming, witty, and suspenseful. I loved it.**"—Elizabeth George

---

THE MOOR
A Mary Russell and Sherlock Holmes Mystery

Though theirs is a marriage of true equals, when Sherlock Holmes summons his wife and partner Mary Russell to the eerie scene of his most celebrated case, she abandons her Oxford studies to aid his investigation. But this time, on Dartmoor, there is more to the matter than a phantom hound. Sightings of a spectral coach carrying a long-dead noblewoman over the moonlit moor have heralded a mysterious death, the corpse surrounded by oversize paw prints. . . .

The telegram in my hand read:

> RUSSELL NEED YOU IN DEVONSHIRE. IF
> FREE TAKE EARLIEST TRAIN CORYTON. IF
> NOT FREE COME ANYWAY. BRING COMPASS.
> > HOLMES

To say I was irritated would be an understatement. We had only just pulled ourselves from the mire of a difficult and emotionally draining case and now, less than a month later, with my mind firmly turned to the work awaiting me in this, my spiritual home, Oxford, my husband and longtime partner Sherlock Holmes proposed with this peremptory telegram to haul me away into his world once more. With an effort, I gave my landlady's housemaid a smile, told her there was no reply (Holmes had neglected to send the address for a response—no accident on his part), and shut the door. I refused to speculate on why he wanted me, what purpose a compass would serve, or indeed what he was doing in Devon at all, since when last I had heard he was setting off to look into an interesting little case of burglary from an impregnable vault in Berlin. I squelched all impulse to curiosity, and returned to my desk.

Two hours later the girl interrupted my reading again, with another flimsy envelope. This one read:

> ALSO SIX INCH MAPS EXETER TAVISTOCK
> OKEHAMPTON, CLOSE YOUR BOOKS. LEAVE
> NOW.
>
> HOLMES

Damn the man, he knew me far too well.

"The great marvel of King's series is that she's managed to preserve the integrity of Holmes's character and yet somehow conjure up a woman astute, edgy, and compelling enough to be the partner of his mind as well as his heart."—*The Washington Post Book World*

A DARKER PLACE

Called "one of the most original talents to emerge in the 90's" by *Kirkus Reviews*, award-winning author Laurie R. King delivers a terrifying drama of good and evil, unlike any she has written before. . . .

A respected university professor, Anne Waverly has a past known to few: Years ago, her own unwitting act cost Anne her husband and her daughter. Fewer still know that this history and her academic speciality— alternative religious movements—have made her a brilliant FBI operative. Four times she has infiltrated suspect communities, escaping her own memories of loss and carnage to find a measure of atonement. Now, as she begins to savor life once more, she has no intention of taking another assignment. Until she learns of more than one hundred children living in the Change movement's Arizona compound. . . .

Y ou don't think that hauling a middle-aged professor of religion out of her ivory tower and into the field to investigate a cult is a little unusual?"

"I wouldn't use the word 'cult' in her hearing if I were you," Glen McCarthy suggested. "Not unless you're interested in a twenty-minute lecture on the difference between cult, sect, and new religious movement."

Gillian Farmer was not to be diverted. "It still sounds like something out of an Indiana Jones movie, not at all like a setup the FBI would come within a mile of."

"The bureau has changed since the days of J. Edgar. Now we do whatever works."

"And you think this will work?"

"It has three times before."

"And, as I understand it, once it didn't. People died."

"We were too late there—the final stages were already in motion before Anne could work her way in. I don't think even she can still feel much guilt about that one."

"Why on earth does she do it?" Gillian demanded. "Undercover work has got to be the most nerve-racking job in the world, and she's not even a cop."

But the man from the FBI was not ready to answer that question.

"A nail-biter thriller."—*The New York Times Book Review*

O JERUSALEM
A Mary Russell and Sherlock Holmes Mystery

In 1918, Russell and Holmes enter British-occupied Palestine under the auspices of Holmes's enigmatic brother, Mycroft, and find themselves at the service of two travel-grimed Arab figures who receive them in the orange groves fringing the Holy Land. A rash of murders seems unrelated to the growing tensions between Jew, Moslem, and Christian, yet Holmes is adamant that he must reconstruct the most recent one in the gully where it occurred. His findings will lead him and Russell into mortal danger.

The skiff was black, its gunwales scant inches above the waves. Like my two companions, I was dressed in dark clothing, my face smeared with lamp-black. The rowlocks were wrapped and muffled; the loudest sounds in all the night were the light slap of water on wood and the rhythmic rustle of Steven's clothing as he pulled at the oars.

Holmes stiffened first, then Steven's oars went still, and finally I too heard it; a distant deep thrum of engines off the starboard side. It was not the boat we had come on, but it was approaching fast, much too fast to outrun. Steven shipped the oars without a sound, and the three of us folded up into the bottom of the skiff.

The engines grew, and grew, until they filled the night and seemed to be right upon us, and still they grew, until I began to doubt the wisdom of this enterprise before it had even begun. Holmes and I kept our faces pressed against the boards and stared up at the outline that was Steven, his head raised slightly above the boat. He turned to us, and I could see the faint gleam of his teeth as he spoke.

"They're coming this way, might not see us if they don't put their searchlights on. If they're going to hit us, I'll give you ten seconds' warning. Fill your lungs, dive off to the stern as far as you can, and swim like the living hell. Best take your shoes off now."

Holmes and I wrestled with each other's laces and tugged, then lay again waiting. The heavy churn seemed just feet away, but Steven said nothing. We remained frozen. The thud of the ship's engines became my heart-beat, and then terrifyingly a huge wall loomed above us and dim lights flew past our heads. Without warning the skiff dropped and then leapt into the air, spinning about in time to hit the next wave broadside, drenching us and coming within a hair's-breadth of overturning before we were slapped back into place by the following one. Down and up and down and around we were tossed until eventually, wet through and dizzy as a child's top, we bobbled on the sea like the piece of flotsam we were and listened to the engines fade.

"Welcome to Palestine," Steven whispered, grinning ferociously.

"O Jerusalem is a standout!"—*The Washington Post Book World*

If you enjoyed Laurie R. King's *Night Work*, you won't want to miss her stand-alone thriller,

FOLLY

coming soon in hardcover from
Bantam Books.

Celebrated woodworker Rae Newborn sets foot on the uninhabited Pacific Northwest island known as Folly, about to embark on the most important project of her life. She intends to restore a long-abandoned ruin—the house built 70 years ago by her great-uncle Desmond Newborn—and thus rebuild her own life, shattered by tragedy and shadowed by devastating depression.

The gray-haired woman stood with her boots planted on the rocky promontory, and watched what was left of her family pull away. The *Orca Queen*'s engines deepened as the boat cleared the cove entrance, and its nose swung around, a magnet oriented toward civilization.

Go, she told them silently. *Don't slow down, don't even look back, just leave.*

But then Petra's jacketed arm shot out from the boat's cabin, drab and shapeless and waving a wild adolescent farewell. Rae's own hand came up in an involuntary response, to wave her own goodbye—except that in the air, her wave changed, the hand reaching forward, stretched out in protest and cry for help, as if her outstretched fingers could pull them back to her, as if she was about to take off down the beach, scrambling desperately over rocks and water to call and scream and—. She caught the gesture before any of the three people on the boat could see it, snapped the offending arm down to her side and stood at rigid attention. The boat dwindled, rounded the end of the island, and was gone.

Thank God they didn't see that, Rae thought. *The*

last thing I want is for Tamara to think I doubt what I'm doing.

So why do I feel like some ancient grandmother in one of those harsh nomadic tribes, left behind on the icy steppes for the good of the group? I chose this. I wanted this.

The engine's growl softened with the distance, grew faint, then merged into the island hush. No low mutter of far-away traffic, no neighbor's dogs and children, not even the pound of surf in this protected sea. A small airplane off to the north; the rusty-wheel squeak of a bird; the patter of tiny waves; and silence.

Alone, at last. For better or for worse.

MANDIE
AND THE
MYSTERIOUS
BELLS

Lois Gladys Leppard

BETHANY HOUSE PUBLISHERS
MINNEAPOLIS, MINNESOTA 55438
A Division of Bethany Fellowship, Inc.

Mandie and the Mysterious Bells

Lois Gladys Leppard

Library of Congress Catalog Card Number 87–72792

ISBN 1–55661–000–9

Published by Bethany House Publishers
A Division of Bethany Fellowship, Inc.
6820 Auto Club Road, Minneapolis, Minnesota 55438

Printed in the United States of America

With love
to my other granddaughter,
Jordan Leigh Leppard,
that adorable, brown-eyed dear,
who knows Mandie's story
but can't read it herself yet.

"Blessed are the merciful; for they shall obtain mercy."

St. Matthew 5:7

About the Author

LOIS GLADYS LEPPARD has been a Federal Civil Service employee in various countries around the world. She makes her home in Greenville, South Carolina.

The stories of her own mother's childhood are the basis for many of the incidents incorporated in this series. This is her tenth book.

Table of Contents

Chapter 1 Grandmother's Mystery 9
Chapter 2 Strangers in the Church 25
Chapter 3 April's Threat 38
Chapter 4 Concern for Hilda 51
Chapter 5 Trapped! 60
Chapter 6 No Way to Escape? 71
Chapter 7 Back to School 85
Chapter 8 More Trouble 95
Chapter 9 Discovery in the Belfry 107
Chapter 10 Phineas Prattworthy 118
Chapter 11 The Robber 131
Chapter 12 An Angry Mob 143

Chapter 1 / Grandmother's Mystery

As Mandie stepped off the train with Jason Bond in Asheville, North Carolina, she found her good friend Celia waiting on the depot platform.

"Celia!" she exclaimed. "How did you get here?"

"Your grandmother sent me," Celia replied. The two girls embraced each other. "You see, she asked my mother to let me come back a day early for school on account of the mystery that she wrote you about."

Mandie pulled her coat around her more tightly to keep out the cold wind. "Has she told you what it's all about yet?" she asked eagerly.

"No, she's waiting for you," Celia answered. She turned to greet Mandie's companion. "How are you, Mr. Bond?"

"Fine, little lady," Mr. Bond replied, smiling down at the girl. "Mr. and Mrs. Shaw were busy, so they sent me with Miss Amanda."

"Come on," Celia urged. "Ben is waiting with the rig over there." She led the way down the platform. "Here he comes now. Have you got all your baggage?"

"I'll get the trunk, Missy," Mr. Bond offered, hurrying to where all the luggage had been unloaded from the train.

Ben drove the rig over to pick up the baggage, and

the two men loaded the trunk and the bag Mandie was carrying.

Ben smiled at Mandie. "Welcome home, Missy. We'se glad to have you back."

Mandie laughed. "Thanks, Ben, but my grandmother's house is not home," she reminded him. "My mother and stepfather, Uncle John, back in Franklin would have a fit if they heard you call this home."

"But you lives at dat Miz Heathwoods' school back up yonder on de hill . . ." Ben looked puzzled.

"Only while school is going on," Mandie explained as they climbed into the horse-drawn vehicle.

"Den you lives different places, don't you now?" Ben shook the reins and the horses started on their way.

"Yes, I suppose so—ever since I met up with Mr. Jason here at my Uncle John's house in Franklin," Mandie said, reaching over to squeeze Mr. Bond's hand. "He's my uncle's caretaker, you know. And he helps us solve our mysteries sometimes."

"Now, Miss Amanda . . ." Jason Bond laughed. "All I really do when you're at home is try to keep up with whatever you're into next."

Ben looked at Mr. Bond and winked. "Dat's impossible, Mistuh Bond," he said. "Impossible to keep up wid dese two girls."

Jason Bond smiled.

"Well, Ben, we have a brand new mystery," Mandie announced. "And as soon as my grandmother tells us about it, we'll get right to work on it." Her blue eyes sparkled as she talked. "Grandmother sent me a message to come back to school a day early so I could spend the night with her. She said something mysterious is going on here in Asheville."

Ben grinned. "Good luck!"

"I'm thankful I have to go back home tomorrow," Mr. Bond joked.

Mandie and Celia laughed.

Ben pulled the rig up in front of Mrs. Taft's huge mansion. The girls jumped down and ran to the door.

They found Mrs. Taft sitting in the parlor by the big open fireplace, where logs blazed and crackled their own welcome. As Mandie's grandmother rose to greet them, she smoothed her faded blonde hair. She was a tall woman, and very dignified except when she was helping her granddaughter solve mysteries.

Mandie gave her a big hug. "Tell us about the mystery, Grandmother!" she cried excitedly.

"Not until you get your coats off," Mrs. Taft replied. She turned to greet Mr. Bond, who had followed the girls into the room. "Thanks for bringing Amanda," she said.

"I was glad to do it, ma'am," Jason Bond said. "It sure feels good in here. It's gettin' purty cold out there now."

The two girls hastily removed their coats and hats and handed them to the maid who stood waiting. Mr. Bond gave the maid his coat, and she hung everything on the hall tree just outside the parlor doorway.

"I imagine it is cold out there," Mrs. Taft said. "Come on over by the fire." She turned to the maid. "Ella, we'll be ready for some hot coffee and cocoa when you finish there."

"Yes, ma'am," Ella answered from the doorway. "I'll git it right heah." She hurried on down the hallway.

"Do sit down, Mr. Bond," Mrs. Taft told the man, indicating the armchair opposite hers by the fireplace. "We'll have something to warm us up in a few minutes. Then in a little while the cook will have dinner ready."

Mr. Bond took the chair opposite Mrs. Taft as Mandie and Celia sat on footstools by the hearth.

"Where is Hilda?" Mandie asked.

"She's staying with the Smiths next door until y'all go back to school," Mrs. Taft replied. "I didn't want her involved in this adventure. You know how she is. She runs away every chance she gets, and I'm afraid one day we might not find her."

"You're a mighty good lady to give her a home," Mr. Bond remarked.

"Well, I had to," Mrs. Taft insisted. "I couldn't let her be put in some mental institution, especially since it was Mandie and Celia who found her hiding in the school attic."

"But she's getting better," Mandie reminded them. "Dr. Woodard said she is."

"Yes, she is," Mrs. Taft agreed.

"She's bound to improve now that her parents can't keep her shut up in a room like they did," Mr. Bond smiled.

"I think so too. But now, Grandmother, please tell us about the mystery—please!" Mandie begged, clasping her small white hands around her knees.

"Well, it's like this," her grandmother began. "There's something very mysterious going on here in Asheville. The bells on our church downtown have been ringing thirteen times at the stroke of midnight."

"Do they ring thirteen times at noon, too?" Mandie asked.

"No, just at midnight," her grandmother replied. "And no one can figure out what's wrong. The bells are activated by the clock on the hour and half past the hour. Several people have examined the bells and the clock mechanism, but they haven't found a thing wrong," she explained.

"Sounds spooky," Celia whispered.

"Some folks say it's a bad omen, and the whole town is upset because no one can solve the mystery." Mrs. Taft paused for a moment. "I know you girls are good at things like this, so I thought maybe you'd like to look into it."

"Sure, Grandmother," Mandie quickly agreed. "I think we could find out what's wrong. Don't you, Celia?"

"Well, we could try," Celia replied.

"We have almost all day today, and we don't have to check into school until tomorrow afternoon," Mandie said. "Grandmother, could we all just go down to the church and look around?"

"It's too cold out there for me, but if Mr. Bond would agree to escort you two girls, you may go after we eat," Mrs. Taft promised. "You'll have to bundle up, though. There's no heat in the church except when there's a service, you know."

"Mr. Jason, will you take us, please?" Mandie begged.

"I reckon I can go with you girls, long as you don't stay too long," he replied. "Like your grandmother said, it's cold out there for these old bones."

"Thanks," Mandie said, reaching over to squeeze his hand.

"How do we get inside?" Celia asked. "Who has the key?"

"It never is locked, dear," Mrs. Taft answered, "until the sexton makes his rounds about bedtime. Then he locks the doors. But he opens them again early every morning."

As Mrs. Taft finished speaking, the church bells rang in the distance. They all listened and counted.

Mandie pointed to the china clock on the mantelpiece. "That clock says it's eleven o'clock," she said, "but the bells rang twelve times. I counted."

"I did, too," Celia agreed.

"You're right," Mrs. Taft said. "So now the bells are not correct in the daytime either. Did you count the rings, Mr. Bond? Was it twelve?"

The old man nodded. "Yes, you're right. It was twelve. Maybe the clock mechanism needs repair."

"Several workmen have examined everything, but they found nothing wrong," Mrs. Taft repeated. "Of course, they didn't tear the clock apart, from what I un-

derstand, but they did inspect all the connections between the clock and the bells. There just doesn't seem
to be anything wrong."

Ella the maid entered the room carrying a large silver
tray with a steaming silver coffeepot and a silver teapot
of hot cocoa. She set the tray on the low table by Mrs.
Taft.

"I'll pour it, Ella. Thank you," Mrs. Taft said. "Would
you let us know just as soon as dinner is ready?"

"Yes, ma'am," Ella replied, leaving the room.

"I know you girls like hot cocoa," Mrs. Taft said as she
leaned forward to pour for them, "but what about you,
Mr. Bond? Would you care for coffee or cocoa?"

"Coffee—black, please, ma'am," he answered. "Once
I got old enough to drink coffee, I've never stopped. Guess
you'd call me an old coffee sot," he laughed.

Mrs. Taft passed him a cup of steaming coffee, and
then poured some for herself. "I suppose I am, too," she
said, sipping the hot coffee. "However, once in a great
while I get a taste for hot cocoa."

Mandie warmed her hands on her hot mug of cocoa
and took a drink. "Grandmother, Joe said he would be
here this weekend with his father," she said. "He promised to bring Snowball with them since they'll be coming
in the buggy. I didn't want to bother with Snowball on the
train."

"I knew they were coming," Grandmother acknowl-
edged. "Dr. Woodard told me when I was at your house
for Thanksgiving last week. And I knew they would bring
that cat of yours." She smiled and took another sip of
her coffee. "Now as soon as you girls finish your cocoa,
run upstairs to your rooms and freshen up for dinner."

"Rooms?" Mandie questioned. "We only need one
room, Grandmother."

"Well, I had Annie make up two rooms next to each
other," Grandmother Taft explained, "but if you want to

share one, that's all right. Just don't stay awake talking all night."

"We won't. Thanks," Mandie said. She and Celia quickly put their empty cups on the silver tray and jumped up. "We'll be back in a few minutes."

Grabbing their coats and bonnets from the hall tree, they headed upstairs.

The girls' baggage had been put in separate rooms, but the door between was standing open.

"I think I'll change into something more comfortable," Mandie called to Celia in the other room. She hung her coat and bonnet in the huge wardrobe.

"And warmer," Celia called back from the other room.

"I think I'll wear this." Mandie took an indigo woolen dress from the trunk and held it up for Celia to see through the doorway. "And I'll wear my wool cape with the hood so I don't have to wear a bonnet."

"Me, too," Celia said, holding up a dark green woolen dress. "And I'll wear this."

Mandie changed her clothes quickly. "Don't forget your boots," she reminded her friend.

Celia laughed. "You'd think we were going to the North Pole!"

"Well, it does seem awfully cold—a lot colder than it was at home," Mandie said. "Was it cold in Richmond?"

"I suppose so. I didn't really notice because I wasn't outdoors much, what little time I was there," Celia answered. "By the time I left your house after Thanksgiving and got home to Richmond, your grandmother had sent my mother a message asking if I could come back to school a day early and spend the night with her."

Celia finished dressing first and joined Mandie in her room. Sitting on the footstool by the warm fireplace, she straightened her stockings above the top of her shiny black boots.

"Just think," Mandie said as she shook down her long

skirt which partially covered her boots, "the year 1900 will soon be gone. Thanksgiving has passed and Christmas is coming up." She turned to the tall mirror standing nearby and smoothed the long blonde braid which hung down her back.

"Time sure does fly," Celia agreed. "We're almost halfway through our first year at the Heathwoods' school, but it seems like we just started a few weeks ago."

"Maybe that's because we seem to get so many holidays," Mandie laughed. "Pretty soon we'll be getting out for Christmas."

Celia grew quiet. "It'll be the first Christmas for both of us without our fathers, won't it?" she said softly.

Mandie nodded. "I remember Christmas morning last year back there in Swain County," she said. "My father had brought in a small Christmas tree and we had decorated it. I got up so early I caught him wrapping presents by the tree, but he just laughed and said it wasn't time to get up yet. I stayed up, though, and helped him finish." She blinked back tears in her blue eyes.

"Our whole family was at our house for Christmas last year," Celia recalled. "All my aunts, uncles, and cousins—everybody. They stayed for days and days." Her eyes brightened. "My father gave me my pony for Christmas." She smiled.

"I know y'all raise horses," Mandie said, approaching a touchy subject carefully, "and you said your father was killed when he was thrown from a horse. Was it a new horse, or had y'all had it a long time?"

"He had just bought it the day before." Celia's voice quivered. "Mother sold it after it threw my father."

"I guess I was lucky that my father didn't die so suddenly," Mandie conceded. "He got a bad cold that turned into pneumonia." She drew a long breath. "He died in April, right when the weather was turning warm and the wildflowers were beginning to bloom."

A light tap on the door made the girls look up. Mandie opened the door to find Annie, the upstairs maid, standing there.

"Miz Taft, she say fo' you girls to git downstairs. Dinnuh be on de table," Annie announced.

"Thanks, Annie," Mandie smiled. "We're coming right down." As the maid left, Mandie turned to Celia. "Guess we'd better get going."

"Yes, let's hurry so we can get through dinner and go down to the church," Celia agreed.

The girls rushed through the meal as fast as they could. Mrs. Taft and Mr. Bond seemed to be in no hurry. They sat talking and sipping coffee while Mandie and Celia squirmed in their seats.

When Ella came in to refill the coffee cups, Mrs. Taft smiled at the girls. "Ella," she said, "ask Ben to bring the rig around to the front door, please. These girls seem anxious to leave."

"Let us walk, please, Grandmother," Mandie begged. "It's not far."

Ella waited.

"No, it's too cold out there today," Mrs. Taft replied. "Besides, you forget that Mr. Bond's legs are not as young as yours." She looked up at the maid. "Go ahead, Ella, and tell Ben."

As the maid left the room, Mandie smiled at Jason Bond. "Sorry, Mr. Jason," she said. "I keep forgetting that you are older than we are."

Everyone laughed.

"A good bit older, young lady," Mr. Bond teased. "I know you're used to your old Indian friend, Uncle Ned, chasing around on adventures with you, but I'm just too old for that—or maybe I should say too old and too lazy."

Mandie smiled across the table at him. "We love you anyhow, Mr. Jason."

"You girls may be excused." Mrs. Taft looked amused.

"Wrap up good now," she called as they hurried from the room.

Taking the steps two at a time, they stopped in their rooms only long enough to snatch up their cloaks and gloves. Mr. Bond buttoned up his warm coat and waited in the front hallway.

When they were all in the rig, Ben shook the reins and sent the horses flying. The girls squealed with delight and held on tightly. Jason Bond looked from them to Ben but didn't say a word.

Ben grinned broadly. "I loves to go fast," he explained, "but Miz Taft, she don't like it, so I'se glad to have some fun and git y'all to the church quick."

Mandie and Celia laughed, but Jason Bond just held on and looked straight ahead.

After a few minutes Ben pulled the horses up sharply in front of the big brick church and everyone lurched. Ben grinned again.

"Thanks, Ben," Mandie said, scrambling down from the rig with Celia and Mr. Bond close behind. "I guess you did get us to the church quick. That was fun!"

"Yeh, Missy," the Negro man replied. "Now, is I s'posed to wait heah or come back latuh to git y'all?"

Mr. Bond spoke up. "You'd better wait here, Ben," he said. "We won't be inside very long. You can come inside with us if you think it's too cold to sit out here."

"I be all right out heah," Ben replied, settling back in his seat.

The girls and Mr. Bond stopped to stare up at the tall steeple where the huge clock was mounted. They could faintly see the bells inside the belfry.

"Looks normal," Mr. Bond remarked.

"But it's—" The bells interrupted Mandie to ring once for one o'clock. "Well, it rang right this time," she said.

"Must be something wrong inside," Celia suggested

as they started up the wide steps to the double front doors on the porch of the church.

Mr. Bond stepped ahead of the girls to open the door for them and ushered them inside.

Mandie looked around the familiar sanctuary. "This is where we go to church while we're at the Heathwoods' school, Mr. Bond," she said. "Grandmother Taft is a member here."

"Sure is a big church," the old man commented as he walked around.

"Let's go up in the gallery," Mandie suggested.

"I'll stay down here," Mr. Bond said, sitting down in a nearby pew. "Just don't get into anything up there now."

"Come on, Celia!" Mandie led the way to a door at the back of the church. Opening the door, she started up the steps to the gallery, and Celia followed.

At the top of the stairs, Mandie surveyed the rows and rows of benches. "I've never been up here before," she said.

"I don't see any bells. How do we get to them?" Celia asked.

As the girls looked around, they spotted another door at the end of the gallery. They hurried over to open it. There, high above their heads, hung the huge bells in the belfry. Heavy ropes dangled down in various places.

"How can we get up there?" Mandie asked. "There aren't any steps going up to the bells."

"It looks awfully high from down here," Celia noted.

Mandie touched the ropes carefully for fear she would cause the bells to ring. Then she saw that some of the rope was actually a rope ladder extending up into the belfry. "Here!" she exclaimed, shaking the rope. "We have to go up this ladder."

Celia looked at the rope in fright. "Go up a rope ladder? We can't do that, Mandie."

"Yes, we can," Mandie assured her. "It won't be any

worse than walking over a swinging bridge, and I've done that lots of times without falling."

"But I've never been on a swinging bridge," Celia protested. "That thing will swing around and we could fall off."

"We won't if we're careful to hold on real tight," Mandie said. Quickly removing her cape and gloves, she threw them on a nearby bench and grasped the first rung of the rope ladder. "Come on."

Celia slowly removed her cape as she stood watching. "I'll get all dizzy and fall," she argued.

"No you won't," Mandie assured her. "Just don't look down. Keep looking up. Come on." She swung onto the next rung of the ladder and began to make her way up.

Celia nervously watched the ladder swing with Mandie's weight. She didn't move.

Reaching the top, Mandie stepped into the belfry and looked around at the huge bells. "Come on, Celia. You can see the whole town from up here," she called down to her friend. "You won't fall if you hold on with all your might. Come on."

"Well, all right. I'll try," Celia finally agreed. As she reached up and grasped the first rung of the ladder, it swung around and she stopped. Her heart beat wildly and her hands grew clammy.

Mandie knelt down on the floor of the belfry at the top of the ladder. "Reach up for the next rung, Celia," she called. "Keep looking up. Don't look down."

Celia took a deep breath and did what her friend said. Slowly, carefully, she made her way up the ropes. After several minutes she grasped the top rung and started to reach for Mandie's extended hand, but then she looked down. "Oh!" she gasped, shaking with fright. "Look how far it is down to the floor!"

Mandie grabbed Celia's hand and gave her such a hard pull that Celia sprawled onto the floor of the belfry beside her.

Celia closed her eyes. "I just know I'll never make it back down," she moaned.

"Come on. Get up," Mandie said, helping her to her feet. "Look outside. You can see everywhere from up here."

There were rafters running every which way. The only floor to walk on was a small piece supporting the bells, and a narrow walkway around the outer edge of the belfry. Celia held onto Mandie's hand as they carefully made their way around the narrow walkway to peer outside at the town.

"I thought you were the one who got dizzy-headed from heights," Celia reminded Mandie. "Remember telling me about the widow's walk at Tommy's house in Charleston?"

"But that was completely outside where if you slipped, you could fall all the way down to the ground," Mandie explained. "Up here we have these walls to protect us." She pointed down to the road. "Look, there's Ben in the rig down there."

Celia quickly turned back to look at the huge bells. "Let's get this exploration over with," she begged. "Just what are we looking for anyway?"

"Anything we can find," Mandie replied. As she stepped back over to the bells, Celia followed slowly and carefully.

Mandie's eyes searched the walls of the belfry. "Where are the connections to the clock?" she wondered aloud. "Where is the clock located from here?"

"Do you think the clock on the outside is as far up as the bells are?" Celia asked. "The clock is on the front side, remember?"

Mandie turned back to the front of the belfry. "No, I believe the clock is lower than the bells."

Celia found some wires and ropes coming out of the front wall. "Here it is!" she exclaimed. "The clock is on the outside of these wires and things. See? They go on over to the bells."

"You're right," Mandie agreed, carefully moving over to examine what Celia had found.

"But how does the clock make the bells ring, Mandie?" Celia asked.

"Well, I guess it's sort of like that big grandfather clock that my grandmother has. The pendulum trips something inside the clock and makes it chime," Mandie explained, tracing the wires.

"But how does the clock know how many times to strike?" Celia was baffled.

"Oh, Celia, I don't know everything," Mandie fussed as she traced the wires. "It just does somehow. The insides are made with one notch, two notches, or whatever, I suppose, to allow the clock to strike as it rotates—or something. Anyhow, these wires do go to the bells. See?"

Celia watched as Mandie followed the length of the wires to the bells. "I don't see anything wrong with them, do you?" she asked.

"No, they're all connected," Mandie replied.

Suddenly the girls felt the floor beneath their feet tremble slightly. Then there was a hard thud from somewhere below. They grabbed each other's hand.

"What was that?" Celia gasped.

"The whole place shook!" Mandie exclaimed.

"I think we'd better go back down," Celia decided.

"Yes, I suppose we'd better for now," Mandie agreed. "But we'll have to come back later. You go down the ladder first."

Celia sat down on the floor to grasp the rope ladder swinging below. After a few tries she finally got into a position to slide down onto the first rung. She held her breath and looked up at Mandie.

"Now don't look down," Mandie cautioned her from above.

At that moment one of Celia's hands missed a rung, and she grasped wildly into the air. Her hand found a rope hanging down from above. She grabbed it and hung on with all her might. Suddenly the bells started ringing. She was so frightened she slid down the rope and landed in a heap on the floor below. When she let go, the bells stopped ringing.

"Oh, Celia, are you all right?" Mandie called to her as she quickly came down to her. "I guess that rope is there to ring the bells by hand."

"At least it gave me some way to get down," Celia answered, trying to get her breath.

Just then they heard Mr. Bond's voice. "What are you girls doing up there?" he called from below. "I think you'd better get down here fast."

"We're coming," Mandie called back.

They grabbed their cloaks and gloves, and scurried around the gallery to the steps leading down into the sanctuary.

"We still don't know what was shaking everything or what that noise was," Celia reminded her friend as they reached the bottom of the stairs.

"I know, but we'll come back and find out," Mandie promised. "Anyway, we know what everything looks like up there now. Maybe Joe can help us when he gets here this weekend."

Mr. Bond was waiting for them at the bottom of the steps. "You know you'll have the whole town here in a minute, ringing those bells that way," he scolded. "What on earth were you doing up there?"

"I'm sorry, Mr. Bond," Celia apologized. "It was my fault. I slipped on the ladder and caught hold of the extra rope. I didn't know it would ring the bells."

"What ladder?" Mr. Bond wanted to know.

Celia glanced at Mandie. "The ladder to the belfry," she answered slowly.

"Now don't you girls go climbing any more ladders while you're in my care," the old man said. "Let's go outside and get going."

"Thanks for coming with us, Mr. Jason," Mandie said as they stepped into the rig where Ben was waiting.

Ben shook the reins, and the horses started off. "Did y'all find out whut makin' dem bells ring de wrong number at de wrong time?" he asked.

"No, but we will," Mandie promised.

"You hope," Celia whispered to her friend.

As they sped around the corner in the rig, the bells on the church rang three times. Everyone looked at each other.

"They rang three times, but it is really two o'clock," Celia said.

"I have an idea someone went up there as soon as we left," Mandie whispered.

"Thank goodness they didn't come up there *while* we were there," Celia replied.

"But we might have caught them if they had," Mandie reminded her.

Chapter 2 / Strangers in the Church

Mandie and Celia were awake before daylight the next morning, excited because Mrs. Taft had promised them they could go back to the church. They lay there in the warm bed discussing the mystery of the bells. The wind was blowing cold and hard outside and rattling the shutters. Annie had not yet come to start the fire in the fireplace in the room. "What are we going to do this time when we go to the church?" Celia asked.

"I thought we could just stay there a while and watch to see if anyone comes into the church, especially when the clock strikes twelve noon," Mandie replied, pushing up her pillow so she could sit up in bed.

Celia did likewise and the two tugged at the heavy quilts to cover their shoulders.

"But if somebody comes into the church, what will we do?" Celia asked.

"We won't let them see us," Mandie replied. "We'll just hide somewhere where *they* can't see us but *we* can see them."

"That'll be hard to do in that big church," Celia noted. "It's so wide open."

"There are draperies on each side of the place where the choir sits, and there's a low short curtain that runs across the platform behind where the preacher stands.

The pews are so tall we might be able to hide between some of them, too," Mandie suggested.

"Well, what do we do if someone does come in?"

"We'll wait to see what they do, and then we'll just come out and ask them who they are, I suppose," Mandie answered.

"I sure hope no criminals come into the church while we're there." The way the bed was placed in the room the girls were facing the door directly. Celia was looking that way when the door softly and slowly came open. She moved closer to Mandie and gasped. As Annie appeared through the doorway, Mandie laughed and said, "It's Annie."

"Mornin', Missies," Annie greeted them as she went over to the fireplace. "Y'all awake nice and early. I'll jes' git dis heah fire goin' now, and it'll be warm in heah in no time, it will."

"Thanks, Annie," Mandie said. "It is cold in here."

The maid quickly cleaned out the ashes and put them in the bucket on the hearth. Then, after laying kindling for a new fire, she took a match from the pocket of her long white apron and lit the wood. The fire spread quickly and the logs crackled.

"I heard my grandmother tell my mother that she was going to have that steam heat put in, Annie," Mandie said. "You know, the kind of heat that you just turn a knob on this thing standing in the room and the heat comes right out. Then you won't have to build fires in the fireplaces anymore."

"Steam heat? Whut kinda heat be dat, Missy?" Annie stooped and fanned the fire with her apron to make it burn better.

"Like they have in Edwards' Dry Goods Store downtown," Mandie replied. "You know how warm it always is in there."

"Oh, you mean dem big hot metal things whut stand

up on de floor?" Annie rose from the hearth. "Well, dey ain't 'zackly magic. Dey gotta have a fire goin' somewheres to make 'em git hot."

"I know," Mandie agreed, sliding out of bed and reaching for her slippers. "But I think it's just one big fire that makes them hot, probably in the basement, so you'd have only one fire to tend to." She hurried to stand in front of the warm fireplace as she quickly put on her robe.

Celia followed. "That's the kind of heat we have at home," she said, wrapping her robe around her. "Just about everybody in Richmond has that kind of heat now, but I don't know for sure how it works."

"Well, right now we ain't got it," Annie said, turning to leave the room, "so I'se got to go build more fires."

"Don't forget, Annie. Grandmother said you could go with us to the church this morning," Mandie reminded her.

"Lawsy mercy, Missy," Annie sighed. "I don't be knowin' why y'all wants to go traipsin' down to dat spooky church. Dem spooks down there is liable to git us."

"Oh, Annie, there's no such things as spooks," Mandie replied, smiling. "You wait and see. All that trouble with the bells is being caused by some good, solid human being—not something you can't catch hold of."

"Well, I sho' hopes dem bad human bein's don't git ahold of us," Annie mumbled as she went out the door.

"I do believe Annie is afraid to go with us," Mandie said, laughing as she and Celia sat on the rug by the fire.

"But, Mandie, it could be something—or someone— we *should* be afraid of," Celia reminded her.

At that moment the girls heard the church bells ringing in the distance. Silently, they counted to seven, and looked at the clock on the mantel.

"Right that time," Mandie said.

"Maybe they'll quit acting crazy and ring right all the time," Celia said.

"But then we wouldn't have a mystery to solve," Mandie argued. "I'm getting hungry. Let's get dressed and go find some breakfast."

After a delicious, hot breakfast, the girls were allowed to go to the church. Ben brought the rig around to the front door, and they were soon on their way.

The wind was still blowing hard and cold. The few people they saw walking on the streets were bundled up in heavy winter clothes. Winter had arrived.

Ben coaxed the horses to a fast speed, and Annie held onto her seat in fright.

"Now, you listen heah, you, Ben," she said sternly. "Don't you go runnin' wild like dat. You liable to git us all killed."

"But de Missies, dey like ridin' fast, don't you now?" he called back to the girls.

"Not too fast, please, Ben," Celia replied.

"We don't want to scare Annie, so would you please slow down a little, Ben?" Mandie asked.

"All righty, Missy. We sho' don't wanta skeer dis old woman up heah beside me, does we now?" Ben replied, laughing as he slowed the horses.

Annie twisted around and gave Ben a mean look. "Whut old woman?" she demanded. "Ain't me. I ain't old as you are. Won't be eighteen 'til next summer."

"Well, if you ain't old, den quit actin' like you wuz," Ben replied. As he pulled the rig up in front of the church, he turned to grin at the girls. "Heah we be's," he announced.

The girls jumped down from the rig and waited for Annie. She looked back at Ben. "Ain't you comin' wid us?"

"I stays right heah," Ben replied, settling back comfortably in the driver's seat.

"He can't go in with us, Annie," Mandie told the maid.

"That would be too many people to hide. There are three of us already. Come on."

As they entered the church, they looked around. There was no one in the vestibule or the sanctuary.

"Annie, we have to hide you somewhere," Mandie said, walking toward the altar. "How about standing behind those draperies up there where the choir sits?"

"Lawsy mercy, Missy. Why I got to hide?" Annie asked nervously.

"We came here to watch to see if anyone goes up there and rings the bells. We all have to hide," Mandie explained. "Come on. You can get behind those draperies. It'll be more comfortable than sitting down on the floor behind that low curtain across the platform like we're going to do."

Annie reluctantly followed Mandie and Celia to the draperies. The girls showed her how to keep herself hidden. There was even a small stool back there where she could just barely have room to sit.

The girls stepped back to look at the dark red plush draperies as they fell into folds and concealed Annie.

"Just right," Celia remarked.

"Annie, please don't make any noise or come out unless we come back there to get you," Mandie warned.

"I sho' won't, Missy. Jes' you don't fo'git and leave me heah all day," Annie answered from behind the draperies.

"We won't. We're only going to stay until the bells ring at twelve noon. Then we have to go back and get ready to check into school," Mandie explained.

The girls hurried over to the low curtain across the platform behind the pulpit. They stepped behind it and sat down on the floor.

Celia looked at the curtain in front of her, which was only a little higher than her head. "It just barely hides us," she said.

"We can peek through the holes where the curtain

rings are, though. See?" Mandie said, bending forward to fit her eye to the opening for the rod. "Mandie! I just thought of something!" Celia said suddenly. "We forgot to look up in the gallery and the belfry to see if anyone was already up there."

Mandie sprang to her feet. "You're right," she said. "We need to be sure there's no one there. Let's go see."

They dropped their capes and gloves behind the curtain where they had been hiding, and started for the stairs.

"Where you two gwine now?" Annie called from behind the draperies.

"We're just going to look upstairs, Annie. We'll be right back." Mandie answered. "Please stay where you are."

"I ain't stayin' heah long by myself," Annie called back.

"We'll be back in a minute," Mandie promised.

The girls hurried to the door and raced up the stairs to the gallery. No one was there. They opened the door to look up into the belfry. No one was there, either.

"We can't see inside the whole belfry from down here," Mandie said, moving around to look upward. She grabbed the end of the rope ladder. "You stay right here. I'm going up there to look around."

"Be careful," Celia whispered, as Mandie quickly climbed up the rope ladder.

At the top Mandie walked around. "Nobody up here, either," she called. She quickly came back down the swinging rope ladder. As she let go of the last rung, she sat down hard on the floor.

"Are you all right?" Celia bent down to make sure her friend wasn't hurt.

"I'm all right," Mandie assured her. "I came down too fast, and it made the ladder swing too much. I just let go to keep from swinging around." She stood up and brushed off her skirt.

The girls again took up their watch behind the low curtains. They sat still and talked only in whispers in case someone suddenly came into the church. During a long silence, the girls were startled when Annie sneezed loudly.

"Bless you," Celia called to the maid.

"I hope you're not getting a cold, Annie," Mandie said in a loud whisper.

"I ain't got no cold yet, but I will have if I has to stay in dis cold place much longer," Annie complained. Suddenly the draperies moved, there was a loud crash, and the Negro girl fell through the opening in the draperies.

Mandie and Celia jumped up and ran to her rescue.

"I be all right." Annie got up from the floor. "Dis dadblasted stool jes' turned over. Dat's all." She set the stool upright again. "Y'all go on back and git dis over wid so's we kin go home." She returned to her hiding place.

Mandie and Celia resumed their watch from behind the low curtains.

"It won't be long till twelve o'clock, Annie," Mandie called.

She and Celia put their capes around themselves and huddled together. It was cold in the church.

Before long the huge double doors of the church made a loud squeaking noise.

"Sh-h!" Mandie whispered.

As she and Celia peered through the holes in the curtain, an expensively dressed woman appeared inside the sanctuary. A tall, neatly attired man followed her from the vestibule down the center aisle.

Mandie's heart did flipflops as she watched and waited. Celia grabbed Mandie's hand tightly.

The couple talked in low voices as they walked down the aisle, pausing to look into each pew on both sides, making their way toward the front.

Mandie strained her ears but couldn't make out what the strangers were saying. She just hoped Annie would stay out of sight.

As the strangers neared the altar, Mandie could hear

a little of what they were saying.

"I know it's got to be here," the woman said. "I was . . ."

Mandie couldn't hear the end of the sentence because the woman had leaned down between the pews.

"Well, we have to find it," the man said firmly. "If someone else finds it, that wouldn't be too good."

"Oh, dear," the woman sighed. She seemed almost in tears.

"We've got to find it," the man repeated. "You go up that aisle over there, and I'll take this one over here." He indicated the two aisles at the sides of the church.

The woman started looking in the pews on the left as the man went to the right. "If only you'd stop blaming me," she moaned.

"I know it wasn't intentional, but it was your fault," the man told the woman. "If you hadn't decided to come into this church to keep from being seen you wouldn't have lost it."

"You told me to hide and I didn't know what else to do," the woman protested.

"Well, if you had stayed in one place instead of walking around looking at all those stained glass windows we'd know what area to search," he said. "It could be almost anywhere in here."

"I was afraid someone would come in and see me if I just sat still," the woman said. As the strangers got farther away up the aisles, Mandie couldn't make out what they were saying, but by the time they reached the back of the church, they were obviously arguing.

The man took the woman's arm and pointed to the last pew. She pulled her arm away and slid into the pew. But when the man sat down next to her, she moved away from him. Then taking a handkerchief from her purse, she dabbed at her eyes.

Mandie and Celia looked at each other. They dared

not even whisper for fear of being heard. The man seemed so angry, and the woman seemed to be afraid of him. The man was doing most of the talking. Oh, how the girls wished they could hear their conversation!

Finally, the strangers got up and started back down the outside aisles. This time they moved slower, carefully bending to look at the seat of each pew and then stooping to look beneath each one. They finally met in front.

"Nothing," the woman sobbed.

"Nothing over there, either. Let's go up this center aisle once more," the man said. "And please be sure you look very carefully."

As they walked along together, the woman took the left side and the man, the right. Once in a while the man would watch the woman when she wasn't looking as though he wanted to be sure of what she was doing.

Mandie realized her foot had gone to sleep from being cramped up behind the curtain, but she dared not change positions.

Celia shivered again and wrapped her arms about herself.

The strangers finally met at the back of the church, but just as the man opened his mouth to speak, the bells started ringing in the belfry. The man grabbed the woman by the arm and pushed her ahead of him as they rushed out the doors of the church.

Mandie and Celia sat stunned for a moment, looking at each other and mouthing the numbers as the bells rang—one, two, three ... Finally Mandie jumped up, stomping the foot that had gone to sleep, and hurriedly limped toward the stairs to the gallery. "Let's see who's in the belfry," she said.

Celia didn't seem in a hurry to run into someone up there, but she followed anyway.

As they ran up the stairs, they kept counting—out loud now. Across the gallery, they jerked open the door to the belfry.

"I'll go first," Mandie offered, grabbing the rope.

"You're not really going up there, are you?" Celia's voice quivered.

"Of course," Mandie called back.

The bells stopped after twelve rings and then sounded a weak, shaky thirteenth ring.

Mandie hurried up the ladder as Celia stood below and watched. She put her head through the opening at the top, and looked around before she got off the ladder. "There's nobody up here," she called, climbing onto the belfry floor. "I don't see a thing."

"Come on back down then," Celia hollered.

Then suddenly Mandie heard her name, "M-M-Mandie!" She looked down to see Celia frozen on the spot and white as a sheet.

A hand reached out and touched Celia on the shoulder. Celia screamed.

"Look behind you, Celia," Mandie yelled. "It's only Annie."

Trembling all over, Celia turned slightly.

Annie came around her and apologized. "I'se sorry, Missy," she said. "I didn't mean to skeer you. Y'all went and left me alone down there, and I jes' got skeered."

"Th-that's all right, Annie," Celia managed to say.

Annie looked up into the belfry just as Mandie hurried down the rope ladder. The hem of Mandie's long skirt was tucked into her waistband to keep it out of her way.

As Mandie swung onto the floor and straightened her skirt, Annie gasped. "Lawsy mercy, Missy. Miz Taft have a heart 'tack if she know you go climbin' round dat way."

"You worry too much, Annie," Mandie said. She turned to Celia. "Are you all right?"

Celia took a deep breath. "I am now," she said, her voice still trembling. "But I was sure whoever has been messing with the bells had caught me."

"I'm sorry, Celia," Mandie said. "I guess we'd better

go now. We have to get to school, you know."

"Thank goodness!" Celia exclaimed.

The three made their way through the gallery to the stairs.

"I didn't see anything going on up there, but there's got to be something wrong somewhere," Mandie said.

At the bottom of the stairs, Celia stopped. "And those people who were here a while ago," she said, "I wonder who they were and what they were looking for."

"I do, too," Mandie said as they went on through the vestibule. "Have you ever seen them before, Annie?"

"Now, Missy, jes' 'cause I lives in Asheville ain't no sign I knows ev'rybody in town," Annie said, opening the front door. " 'Sides, dis be white folks' church. I goes to my own church. I don't mix wid no white folks."

Mandie and Celia looked at each other and smiled as they went on down the front steps. Ben was waiting in the rig. He saw them coming and stepped down to the road by the rig.

"Not only dat," Annie continued, "dat lady didn't look like she come from dis heah town."

"What makes you say that?" Mandie asked.

"She jes' look too high uppity," Annie replied. "You know, too fancy dressed."

"Aren't there any fancy, uppity people in this town?" Mandie teased.

"No, not de likes of huh," Annie shook her head. "I don't think she live in dis heah town."

Mandie turned to Celia. "Why don't we look around outside while we're here?"

"We should go back to your grandmother's, shouldn't we?" Celia reminded her friend.

"Ben can walk with us if you're afraid we might find somebody," Mandie suggested. Without waiting for Celia's reply, she called the Negro man, "Ben, would you walk around the church with us?"

Ben walked over to them with a puzzled look on his face. "Why, 'course, Missy."

"Dat man couldn't catch nobody fo' you," Annie said with a teasing glance at the driver. "He too slow, dat Ben is."

Ben scowled at her. "Fust you says I'm too fast, and now you says I'm too slow," he grumbled. "Woman, make yo' mind up, or ain't you got one?"

Annie ignored him and walked on around the side of the church. The girls grinned at Ben and followed the Negro girl around the building.

Thick shrubbery grew against the church, but since it was wintertime, there weren't any leaves, and they could see right through the bushes. Annie stayed ahead of the other two girls, and Ben lagged behind as they all carefully looked over the outside of the building and the yard.

When they turned the back corner and faced the rear of the church, the girls stopped in amazement then ran up to the wall. There, all over the brick, was a lot of huge, illegible handwriting, evidently written with whitewash.

"What does it say?" Celia gasped.

"I cain't read dat," Annie fussed.

Ben stared at the writing with the others. "You cain't read nohow," he mumbled.

"I don't think it says anything," Mandie decided. She brushed her hand over the mess. "It's dry now, but it either dripped and ran together, or whoever wrote it didn't know how to write."

"Who in the world could have done such a thing? Imagine messing up a church building with all that!" Celia said.

"It's probably connected with the mystery of the bells," Mandie replied.

"Missy, I think we better git goin'," Annie spoke up.

"Let's just walk the rest of the way around the building," Mandie urged. "We can hurry."

She led the way. They returned to the front of the church without finding anything else unusual.

The girls were puzzled. What was that mess supposed to be? A message? A warning? And when did it get there? No one had mentioned that strange writing before.

The mystery was deepening.

Chapter 3 / April's Threat

Later that day Ben loaded the luggage and drove the girls to school. As they rode up the half-circle graveled driveway, the huge, white clapboard house at the top of the hill came into view. Gray curls of smoke rose out of the tall chimneys. The giant magnolia trees surrounding the school were now bare.

The rig came to a halt in front of the long, two-story porch supported by six huge, white pillars. A small sign to the left of the heavy double doors read *The Misses Heathwood's School for Girls*. Tall narrow windows trimmed with stained glass flanked each side of the doors. Above the doors, matching stained glass edged a fan-shaped transom of glass panes.

The white rocking chairs, with their bare cane bottoms, were still sitting along the veranda behind the banisters. The green flowered cushions had been removed and taken inside for the winter. The wooden swing hung bleakly on its chains attached to the ceiling. Uncle Cal, the old Negro man who worked for the school, came out to help unload the baggage.

"Hello, Uncle Cal," Mandie greeted him as she and Celia stepped down from the rig. "Did you and Aunt Phoebe have a nice Thanksgiving?"

"Sho' did, Missy 'Manda, but we'se glad to see you

38

back," the old man replied. "You, too, Missy," he told Celia.

"Thanks, Uncle Cal," Celia replied, tossing back her long auburn hair. "Guess what! We have another mystery to solve."

" 'Nuther mystery? I sho' hope y'all ain't aimin' to git in no mo' trouble," the old man said, reaching for a bag in the rig.

"It's about the bells in the church downtown, Uncle Cal," Mandie explained. "They're ringing the wrong time."

"Ev'rybody know dat, Missy 'Manda. De whole town mad 'bout it. Cain't set no clock by dem bells no mo'." Uncle Cal turned to go up the front steps and Ben and the girls followed.

Celia laid her hand on Mandie's arm, and stopped her on the porch for a moment. Uncle Cal and Ben went inside with the luggage. "Mandie, I just remembered something," she said. "Remember what April Snow told us when we left school for the Thanksgiving holidays?"

"She said, 'Enjoy your holidays because you might not enjoy coming back,' wasn't that it?" Mandie asked.

"Her exact words," Celia confirmed. "What do you think she's planning to stir up now?"

"I have no idea, but we'll be on the lookout for her this time," Mandie assured her friend. "We'll be prepared."

They went on through the double doors into the long center hallway. They stopped and looked around the wainscoted, wallpapered hallway. It was empty. Their eyes traveled up the curved staircase leading to a second-story balcony, which ran near a huge crystal chandelier. The place seemed to be deserted.

They walked on. A tall, elderly lady with faded reddish-blonde hair, wearing a simple black dress, came out of the office off the hallway.

"Hello, Miss Hope," Mandie said, hurrying to greet the lady.

"I hope you girls had a nice holiday," Miss Hope Heathwood replied, putting an arm around each girl.

"We did, Miss Hope. I know y'all did, too, with all of us noisy girls gone," Celia said, laughing.

"Oh, but we missed you lively young ladies," Miss Hope said. "You know we only had three girls here over the holidays—just the ones who lived too far away to go home. But we hardly saw them. They would show up for meal time and then disappear for the rest of the day."

"April Snow didn't go home, did she?" Mandie asked.

"No. She's around somewhere," Miss Hope said. "Now y'all get upstairs and get unpacked before time for supper." She turned back toward the office.

"Yes, ma'am," the girls replied together.

Mandie and Celia hurried upstairs to their room. They had been lucky enough to get a small bedroom together near the stairs to the attic and the servants' stairway going down. The other girls lived in rooms with four double beds and eight girls in each. Even though Mandie and Celia's room was hardly more than a large closet that could barely accommodate the necessary furniture, they were happy there.

A fire in the small fireplace warmed the room. Uncle Cal and Ben had brought up their luggage. The girls hurriedly began unpacking their trunks.

"I want to make sure that whoever wrote on the church walls is punished to the limits of the law. No one should be allowed to treat the Lord's house that way," Mandie said. "It must have been done recently because Grandmother didn't know about it until we told her. And she always knows everything first."

"It was probably done while we were inside the church," Celia said.

"Maybe." Mandie shook out her dresses from the trunk and prepared to hang them in the huge chifforobe. With her hands full of clothes, she opened the door to the chifforobe.

A small mouse quickly jumped out, landing on her boot and causing her to drop everything.

"A mouse! Look out!" Mandie screamed.

The mouse frantically ran around in circles on the carpet, apparently looking for a way to hide.

"I'll get Uncle Cal!" Celia yelled. She almost knocked down Aunt Phoebe as she ran out the door.

The old Negro woman appeared in the doorway with a broom, and found Mandie standing up on the bed, too frightened to move.

"I wuz jes' sweepin' de hall when I hears Missy scream," Aunt Phoebe said. "Lawsy mercy, whut be de matter?"

"A mouse, Aunt Phoebe!" Mandie cried.

"It c-came out of the ch-chifforobe," Celia stuttered, watching the floor around her feet for the creature.

"I don't see no mouse, Missy. Where it be?" Aunt Phoebe asked, sweeping the broom around the room. "I don't see none. It must be done gone and hid now."

"I d-don't know, Aunt Phoebe," Mandie said, collapsing on the bed.

Aunt Phoebe picked up the clothes Mandie had dropped in a pile and laid them on a chair. She examined the chifforobe. "I don't see how no mouse could git in there," she said. "Ain't no holes or cracks in it." She closed the door to see how it fit. "Somebody musta—"

"Put it in there," Mandie interrupted. Sliding off the bed, she stood up and looked at Celia. "You know who."

"Right," Celia agreed.

"Now, who dat be wantin' to put a mouse in yo' chifforobe?" Aunt Phoebe asked.

"Can't you even guess?" Mandie asked.

"You mean dat tall, black-headed, black-eyed gal wid a Yankee mama—whut's her name?"

"April Snow," Mandie answered. "You see, she told us when we left that we'd better enjoy our holidays because we might not enjoy coming back."

"But, Mandie, we don't know for sure that it was April," Celia reminded her.

"No, we don't. So, Aunt Phoebe, please don't tell anyone we thought it might be her," Mandie requested.

"I won't mention huh name, Missy 'Manda, but I will tell Miz Prudence dat a mouse got in yo' room," the Negro woman promised. "I'se gwine hafta put some rat poison out to git rid of it."

"Thanks, Aunt Phoebe," Mandie said with relief.

After helping the girls hang up the rest of their clothes, Aunt Phoebe hurried back into the hallway to finish her sweeping.

Mandie and Celia put their stockings and underthings in the drawers of the bureau and placed their bonnets in hat boxes on top of the chifforobe. Leaving personal belongings such as jewelry and letters in the trays of their trunks, they locked the lids.

Mandie stood up with the trunk key in her hand. "I think I'd feel safer about my trunk if I put this key on a ribbon around my neck," she said. "I can slip it under my dress. What do you think, Celia?"

"That's a good idea. I have some odd pieces of ribbon." Celia walked over to the bureau and pulled a handful of ribbons out of one of the drawers. "What color do you want?"

"Any color," Mandie said. "I think I have some extra ribbons, too."

"I have plenty here," Celia insisted. "I think you ought to take the blue one. It matches your eyes."

"But it won't show, so it doesn't matter what color it is," Mandie said, taking the blue ribbon.

"Well, you'll know what color it is anyway. I'll use the green one." Celia pulled out a bright green ribbon and carefully threaded it through the hole in her key as Mandie fixed hers. They tied the ends together, hung the ribbons around their necks, and dropped the keys out of sight inside their dresses.

"If somebody put that mouse in our chifforobe, it had to be April Snow," Mandie said, still nervously looking around on the floor.

"I think so, too, but we can't prove it," Celia agreed. "I just feel like I'm going to step on it any minute."

"Aunt Phoebe will get rid of it for us," Mandie assured her. "Let's sit down."

Sitting on the window seat, the two girls looked out at the bare limbs of the magnolia trees standing on the brown grass below.

"I'll be glad when Saturday comes," Mandie said. "Joe will be here then, and we can go back to the church."

"We can't unless we spend the weekend with your grandmother," Celia reminded her. "Miss Prudence would never let us go that far away from school."

"I thought you knew," Mandie said with a smile. "Grandmother promised to send Ben for us Friday after classes, and we won't have to come back here until Sunday afternoon."

"Oh, great!" Celia said excitedly. "We'll have all that time to work on the mystery."

The big bell in the backyard began ringing, beckoning the students to supper.

"Let's go," Mandie said, leading the way. The two girls hurried downstairs to wait in line outside the dining room door.

When Aunt Phoebe opened the French doors, the girls streamed into the dining room and took their assigned places, standing behind their chairs. No one was allowed to talk in the dining room, so they waited silently until all the girls were in. Then Miss Prudence Heathwood, the school's headmistress and sister of Miss Hope, entered from the other side of the room and took her place behind the chair at the head of the table.

As they stood there waiting, Mandie and Celia noticed that Etrulia had taken April Snow's place beside Mandie and April stood behind the chair directly across the table from them—where Etrulia ordinarily sat. They must have had permission to swap seats Mandie reasoned, because when Miss Prudence looked around the table, she did not mention the switch.

Miss Prudence picked up the little silver bell by her plate and shook it. All eyes turned in her direction.

"Young ladies, welcome back to all of you," Miss Prudence said. "I have an announcement to make. Our school is investing in those modern lights that work on electricity."

The students glanced at one another, not daring to say a word.

Miss Prudence continued. "A socket with a light bulb in it will be installed in each room. Hanging down from this socket will be a chain which you will pull to turn the light on and off. You have all seen this kind of light downtown at Edwards' Dry Goods Store, haven't you?"

"Yes, ma'am," the girls replied almost in unison.

"Good. Then you understand what I'm talking about," she said. "Now, there will be workmen coming in tomorrow, but y'all do not have permission to carry on conversations with these men. You will stay out of whatever room they are working on until they've finished. Do you understand?"

"Yes, Miss Prudence," the girls responded all around the table.

"After the lights are installed," the headmistress continued, "there will be more workmen coming to put in one of those large furnaces in the basement. This will be connected by metal ducts to what they call a radiator in each room. The house will be heated this way, and we will discontinue fires in the fireplaces except for emergencies and special occasions. You are not to talk to these workmen either. Are there any questions?"

"No, Miss Prudence," the girls said, again quickly exchanging glances.

Although the girls were curious about these modernization efforts, they dared not question Miss Prudence. The headmistress had a way of making a person look dumb. They'd find out about all this from someone else.

"Now, young ladies," Miss Prudence said, "we will return our thanks." After waiting for the girls to bow their heads, she spoke, "Our gracious Heavenly Father, we thank Thee for this food of which we are about to partake, and we ask Thy blessings on it and on all who are present. Amen. Young ladies, you may be seated now."

With the noise of scraping chairs, the girls sat down. The dining room held only half of the students. Mandie and Celia were in the first sitting.

Mandie kept an eye on April Snow throughout the entire meal, but the girl never once looked across the table. April completely ignored Mandie and Celia, quickly disappearing as soon as the girls were dismissed.

Mandie and Celia joined the other girls in the parlor after the meal.

Mandie looked around. "April Snow isn't in here," she said quietly to Celia.

"Maybe we should go back to our room," Celia suggested. "She might be up to something."

"You're right. Let's go."

They cautiously entered their room, fearing that the mouse might be there or that April might be lurking nearby. But the room was empty.

As Mandie looked around the floor for the mouse, she noticed white powder along the mopboard. "Aunt Phoebe must have put something on the floor to kill the mouse," she remarked.

"She said she was going to put out something," Celia agreed.

The girls sat down on the window seat and looked out into the early winter darkness. The wind blew hard against the windowpane, but the fire in their fireplace kept the room cozy and warm.

"I wonder how April got Miss Prudence's permission to swap seats at the table," Mandie mused. "You know she has never allowed that before."

"At least not while we've been going to school here," Celia added.

"April must have finagled that while we were gone home for Thanksgiving," Mandie decided. "I just know she must have been the one who put the mouse in our chifforobe."

"But how would she catch the mouse in the first place?" Celia wondered aloud.

"I sure wouldn't want to catch a mouse. Ugh!" Mandie shivered at the thought. She changed the subject. "What did you think of Miss Prudence's announcement at supper?"

"It'll be nice to have lights overhead, won't it?" Celia replied. "We have that kind at home, and it makes a big difference. We'll be able to see to read better at night."

"I suppose so," Mandie answered. "We don't have electricity or radiators, you know. My Uncle John has enough money to afford it. I don't know why he doesn't get all those things done. It would be less work for everybody. Even the church downtown here in Asheville has lights run by electricity, you know."

"But they don't have heat with radiators. Remember all those iron stoves sitting around the sanctuary?" Celia said.

"I know. Maybe Grandmother would donate enough money to put in the heat someday," Mandie speculated. "I suppose sooner or later everybody will have all these new lights and heat."

"Talking about the church, do you think we'll ever find

out who that man and woman in the church were?"

"Probably. If we just keep working on the mystery of the bells, I think we can solve the mystery of the strangers, too," Mandie replied, thoughtfully leaning her elbow against the window. "I'm still puzzled about that loud thumping noise and whatever made the belfry shake while we were up there. I believe everything that has happened is all connected."

"I think so, too," Celia agreed, watching her feet for any sign of the mouse.

There was a knock at the door and Aunt Phoebe came in and looked around. "Y'all ain't seen no sign of dat mouse no mo', has y'all?"

"No, Aunt Phoebe," Mandie replied. "Maybe the stuff you put around the mopboard got him."

"Stuff 'round de mopboard?" the Negro woman asked. "I ain't put nothin' 'round de mopboard. Where?"

"That white stuff down there." Celia pointed to some of it by the bureau.

"Lawsy mercy, Missies. I ain't put dat on de flo'," the old woman said, bending to look closely at the white powder.

"Then I wonder who did and what it is," Mandie said, stooping down beside her.

Aunt Phoebe stuck her finger in the white powder and smelled it. Straightening up, she looked on top of the bureau, picked up Mandie's powder jar and opened it. "Heah be whut dat is," she said. "Somebody done dumped all yo' bath powder on de flo'."

"Oh, for goodness' sakes!" Mandie exclaimed. "What is going to happen next?"

"I comes to tell y'all I be up heah fust thing after y'all goes to yo' schoolrooms in de mawnin'," Aunt Phoebe informed them. "I be gwine to put some liquid stuff dat you cain't see 'round de flo'. But it stink good, so I waits fo' y'all to leave yo' room. And jes' y'all 'member. Dis liquid stuff deadly poison."

"We'll be careful about dropping anything on the floor," Mandie promised.

"Dis stuff be dried up in no time after I puts it 'round," Aunt Phoebe told them. "Jes' leave dis white powder, and I'll clean it up in de mawnin'."

"Thank you, Aunt Phoebe," Mandie said. "April Snow probably did it, but we don't know for sure."

"I he'p you watch out fo' dat girl," the old woman said, shaking her head as she walked out the door. "She gwine hafta stop dis nonsense."

"Maybe we ought to talk to Miss Hope about the things that are going on," Celia suggested.

"What could we say?" Mandie asked. "We don't have any proof. Let's go find April and follow her around to see what she's doing."

"That's a good idea," Celia agreed.

The two girls left their room, walking slowly down the hallways, looking about for April Snow. She was nowhere to be seen. They returned to the parlor. There she was, sitting alone in a corner, reading the newspaper while the other students sat around talking.

Mandie and Celia looked at each other, then took a seat in two vacant chairs near Etrulia and Dorothy, a girl they didn't know very well.

Etrulia turned to them and said, "We've all been reading the newspaper. They say the whole town is angry about the bells in the church downtown. And now, because the bells are ringing thirteen times, they claim something bad is about to happen."

"That's just superstition," Mandie said. "The bells couldn't cause something bad to happen just because they're ringing wrong."

"I know that," Etrulia conceded, "but you know this town is full of superstitious people. They can really get everyone wound up about something like this."

"What else does the newspaper say?" Celia asked.

"Oh, there are several articles about it," Etrulia replied. "When April finishes reading it, y'all ought to look it over. Someone has even been writing on the back wall of the church."

Mandie and Celia looked at each other.

"When does this newspaper come out? What time of day?" Mandie asked.

Etrulia looked puzzled. "I suppose it comes out in the afternoon," she replied. "At least that's when the school gets it. You know it takes hours and hours to set up the presses and print it and then deliver it. I imagine they work on it all morning and then deliver it in the afternoon. That's what my father does. He owns the newspaper back home."

"You mean whatever news the paper has in it would have been collected early in the morning in order to be out in the afternoon?" Mandie questioned her.

"As far as I know, all the news has to be in by eight o'clock in the morning in order to be printed for the afternoon," Etrulia answered. "Why are you asking all this?"

"I was just curious about when the writing on the church wall was discovered," Mandie replied. "It must have been early this morning or last night, then."

"Yes," Etrulia agreed. "I sure hope they catch whoever is doing such disgraceful things."

Mandie nodded. "I do, too," she said.

Etrulia moved on across the room with some of the other girls while Mandie and Celia talked quietly.

"So we know the writing wasn't done while we were in the church," Mandie said hardly above a whisper.

"That's right," Celia agreed. "It would have had to be a lot earlier."

"Maybe someone did it in the dark when no one could

see them," Mandie suggested. "I'm just itching to solve this mystery."

"Well," Celia said with a sigh, "as soon as Friday comes, we can get started."

April laid the newspaper down and walked over to the piano as one of the girls began playing.

Mandie picked up the paper. The front page was full of news stories about the town's reactions to the bells ringing the wrong hour and the vandalism at the church. The only other news item on the front page was a story of a bank robbery in Charlotte the week before, which officials were still investigating.

So many things are happening, Mandie thought, *and they don't seem to be related at all.*

Chapter 4 / Concern for Hilda

Aunt Phoebe used the rat poison in Mandie and Celia's room the next morning. As she promised, it soon dried up, and the odor went away. There was no sign of the mouse, alive or dead.

As the week dragged by, April Snow seemed to avoid Mandie and Celia, and they didn't go out of their way looking for her, either. They did, however, stay alert for any mischief she might do.

Finally, Friday came.

Mandie and Celia, with their bags nearby, sat waiting in the alcove near the center hallway of the school. They watched through the floor-length windows for Ben to come in Mrs. Taft's rig.

Mandie sprang from her chair. "I hear him coming!" she cried, grabbing her bag. "I know Ben's driving. He's just aflying."

As the rig came within sight, the girls hurried outside onto the veranda. They were so excited about leaving school for the weekend that they didn't even feel the cold north wind blowing around them. The sky was cloudy with a promise of rain or possibly snow.

Ben halted the rig in the curved driveway, and the girls ran down the steps. Joe Woodard was with him.

"Joe!" Mandie exclaimed. "I didn't think you'd be in town until tomorrow."

Joe, tall and lanky for his fourteen years, jumped down from the rig and held out Snowball, Mandie's white kitten. "Well, I could go home and take Snowball with me, and come back tomorrow," he teased.

Mandie snatched the kitten from him and cuddled it. "Now, Joe," she said, "you know I'm glad you could come today. We're just snowed under with mysteries."

Joe ran his long, thin fingers through his unruly brown hair. "Fixing to get into trouble again, are you?" he teased.

Ben put the girls' bags in the rig and everyone climbed aboard.

"No, we aren't," Mandie argued.

"Not if we can help it," Celia added.

Ben held the reins loosely in his hands and waited for a lull in the conversation. "Is y'all ready to proceed now?" he asked. "Miz Taft, she say hurry back. We better git a move on."

"Of course, Ben. Let's go," Joe said.

With a slap of the reins, the horses took off at a fast trot down the cobblestoned streets toward Grandmother Taft's house.

Joe listened as the girls related what had happened since they returned to school. "And I suppose y'all want me to help solve this problem of the bells ringing wrong," he said.

Ben drew the rig up in Mrs. Taft's driveway.

Mandie smiled sweetly. "Of course," she replied, jumping down from the vehicle.

"Yes," Celia agreed, following Mandie. "Three heads are better than two."

Joe's long strides caught up with the girls as Ella, the Negro maid, opened the front door.

"Miz Taft, she be in de parlor," Ella informed them.

"Ben, you take dem bags on upstairs. Miz Taft, she be in a hurry to see dese girls."

"Yes, ma'am, Miz Housekeeper," Ben replied sarcastically. He took the other bag from Joe and headed for the stairs.

Joe's father, Dr. Woodard, waited in the parlor with Mrs. Taft. After exchanging greetings, the young people sat down together on a nearby settee.

Mandie cuddled Snowball in her lap. "I'm glad y'all could come a day early, Dr. Woodard," she said.

The doctor cleared his throat. "Well, you see, your grandmother sent for me." He looked to Mrs. Taft to explain.

"Sent for you?" Mandie looked at her grandmother, puzzled.

"Now, don't get excited, Amanda," Mrs. Taft said. "But Hilda is sick. She—"

"Hilda? Sick?" Mandie interrupted. "Is it bad?"

"Amanda," Mrs. Taft reprimanded. "Please wait until I have finished talking before you get excited. Yes, Hilda is sick. She has pneumonia—"

"Pneumonia!" Mandie cried. "That's what took my father out of this world. Oh, is it bad, Dr. Woodard?" She dropped Snowball in Joe's lap and ran to stoop at Dr. Woodard's knee.

Dr. Woodard smoothed her blonde hair. "I'm afraid it could get bad," he said. He had been Jim Shaw's doctor back in the spring in Swain County.

Mandie jumped up. "Where is she?" she demanded. "Where is Hilda?"

"She's upstairs in her bedroom, dear," Dr. Woodard replied. "We've got a special nurse staying with her."

"I want to go see her," Mandie said, turning to leave the room.

"No, Amanda!" Mrs. Taft called sharply. "Hilda is not allowed to have any visitors. We don't want everyone else to catch this and come down sick, too."

With tears in her blue eyes, Mandie turned back and dropped onto the settee.

Joe reached for her hand and held it tight. "I know you're thinking about your father, Mandie," he said softly. "But don't. It won't help. It will only make it worse."

Snowball stepped over into his mistress's lap, curled up again, and began purring.

"Mrs. Taft, we were just here this past Tuesday, and Hilda was visiting with the Smiths. Did she get sick all of a sudden?" Celia asked.

"Yes, they brought her home that night, and she was running a high fever," Mrs. Taft replied. "When she didn't seem to get any better, I sent for Dr. Woodard, and he got here this afternoon."

"We've done all we can do right now," Dr. Woodard told Mandie. "We just have to pray that the Lord will heal her."

As a tear rolled down her cheek, Mandie lifted her head and began to pray softly. "Oh, dear God," she said, "please heal Hilda. She has been through so much, and now that things are getting better for her, please let her live to enjoy it."

The others joined in with their prayers. When they were finished, Mandie took Joe's handkerchief and dried her eyes.

"I remember how Hilda looked when we found her in the attic," Celia said. "She was so scared of us, and so starved-looking. Then she found out we were her friends, and she started getting better."

"The poor girl had never had any friends," Joe added. "Imagine her parents keeping her shut up in a room just because she wouldn't—or couldn't—talk."

"But she *can* talk," Mandie said firmly. "She is beginning to say a lot of words. She just never had a chance to learn because her parents thought she was demented."

"Well, she is not real bright, but she has more sense than people give her credit for," Dr. Woodard said. "And I can see that with the proper care and attention, like Mrs. Taft has been giving her, she could eventually lead an almost normal life."

"You'll keep watch over her, won't you, Dr. Woodard?" Mandie begged.

"I'll be here for the weekend. Then I have to go back to Swain County to see some sick folks there," the doctor replied. "But the nurse we have up there now knows what she's doing, and another nurse will relieve her at bedtime. Hilda won't be left alone."

"Thank you, Dr. Woodard," Mandie said. "Thanks to you and the Lord, she's going to pull through. I just know it."

After a short silence, Celia changed the subject. "Mrs. Taft, has anything else happened at the church since Mandie and I were there?" she asked, pushing back her long auburn hair.

"The church keeps having different people investigate, but they can't find anything wrong," Mrs. Taft replied.

"That's because there is nothing wrong with the clock or the bells," Mandie declared, straightening her shoulders. "It's just some person doing something that no one can catch them doing."

"But, Mandie, we were there when the bells rang thirteen times for twelve noon, remember? And there was no one there at all except us," Celia reminded her.

"They were just too quick for us, but we'll catch them sooner or later," Mandie predicted. "Just you wait and see."

"What about the man and the woman we saw in the church, Mrs. Taft?" Celia asked. "Did you find out anything about them?"

"No, dear," Mrs. Taft replied. "I've asked about them everywhere, but no one seems to have seen them enter or leave the church. And, according to the description y'all gave me of them, I don't believe they are people I know."

"Why didn't y'all follow them when they left the church?" Joe asked. "Or at least watch from the door when they went outside?"

"Because that was when the bells started ringing," Mandie explained, "and we had to go up to the belfry to see if anyone was up there."

"Hmm, I might as well ask," Joe said. "When do we visit the church to look for clues?"

Mandie and Celia both looked at Mrs. Taft.

"I suppose you young people could go some time in the morning after it warms up a little," she said.

"Thanks, Grandmother," Mandie said. She turned to Joe. "We'll go early enough so we'll be back in time for dinner, Joe," she added.

"Oh, good. I absolutely refuse to miss a meal, especially from your grandmother's table," Joe teased.

"I sure hope there's not any more shaking and thumping in that belfry," Celia remarked. "I don't know how we're ever going to figure out what that was. It must have been something awfully strong to shake the belfry that way."

"Either the shaking caused the thumping, or the thumping caused the shaking," Mandie figured. "It was all so fast and so close together, it must have been connected."

"That has me puzzled, Amanda," Mrs. Taft said. "That church is well built, and I can't imagine anything shaking any part of it unless it was an earthquake. But it seems no one else in town felt anything, so it couldn't have been an earthquake."

"Don't worry about it, Mrs. Taft. We'll figure it all out," Joe assured her.

Mandie gasped. "Oh, goodness!" she cried. "I just remembered something. The full moon is tomorrow, and that's when Uncle Ned promised to come to see me. He won't know I'm here and not at the school."

"Well, you could go to Aunt Phoebe's house tomorrow night and watch for him," Mrs. Taft said, "provided Joe and Celia go with you. Since Aunt Phoebe's house is right there in the backyard of the school, it ought to be safe enough, don't you think, Dr. Woodard?"

"I'm sure they'll be safe with Aunt Phoebe and Uncle Cal," the doctor answered. "They're good people."

"But Grandmother, Uncle Ned doesn't come to visit until after curfew at ten o'clock so that no one at the school will see him," Mandie explained. "He always waits under the huge magnolia tree right down below our bedroom window."

Uncle Ned was an old Cherokee friend of Mandie's father. When Jim Shaw had died, Uncle Ned had promised him he would watch over Mandie. And he kept his word. He regularly visited her and knew everything that was going on where she was concerned.

"If it's going to be late, I'll send Ben with y'all. He'll have to take y'all over there anyway. I'll tell him to wait for y'all," Mrs. Taft said.

"Grandmother, could we leave here in time to go by the church and check it out again tomorrow night before we go to Aunt Phoebe's?" Mandie begged. "Please?"

"Why, Amanda, I thought you were all going to the church tomorrow morning," Mrs. Taft replied.

"We are, but we should go to the church as many times as possible because you never know when we might find something to solve the mystery," Mandie insisted.

"Let's have one thing understood here and now, Amanda," Mrs. Taft said firmly. "You are not to go to the church without Ben or another adult with you at any time.

And that applies to you, Celia. Don't you agree, Dr. Wood-ard?"

"Yes, ma'am," the doctor said. "There's no telling who or what you might run into at the church, and I certainly don't want Joe going there without an adult. In fact, I forbid it. Remember that, Joe."

"Yes, sir," Joe answered quickly. "I'd like to have an adult along anyway to back me up in case of trouble. These two girls wouldn't be much help if something un-expected happened."

Mandie glared at Joe. "I can remember a few times when *you* needed *our* help, Joe Woodard," she said. "Celia and I are both twelve years old, and you are only two years older."

Snowball jumped down to the floor and scampered out of the room. "I know. I know," Joe agreed. "Time about is fair enough."

"Remember the time the Catawbas kidnapped you, and—" Mandie began.

"I said, all right," Joe interrupted.

"Well, then," Mandie said, and turning to her grand-mother asked, "Is it all right then for us to go to the church before we go to Aunt Phoebe's house since Ben will be with us?"

"Amanda, you know it will be dark then," Mrs. Taft reminded her. "It gets dark early now."

"But the church has those electric lights in it," Mandie persisted.

"If we can find the strings in the dark to pull them on," Celia said.

"If we light up the church, everyone in town will know it," Joe objected. "And if there's anyone messing around there, they'll run away fast."

Mandie thought for a moment. "Could we take a lan-tern with us, Grandmother?" she asked.

"I suppose so," Mrs. Taft agreed reluctantly. "Just

don't stay out too late. Keep your visit with Uncle Ned short. And be sure you stay within sight of Ben at all times."

"Thanks, Grandmother," Mandie said. "We will. I promise."

Little did Mandie know how impossible that promise would be to keep.

Chapter 5 / Trapped!

"You are not taking that white cat, are you?" Joe asked Mandie as the three young people put on their coats the next morning.

Mandie looked down at Snowball, who was sitting on the arm of hall tree watching. "No, I guess not," she said. "He might get away from me and—"

"And get lost." Joe finished her sentence. "And then we'd have to go looking for him."

"All right," Mandie agreed. She turned to Celia. "Are you ready?"

"All ready," Celia replied, tying her bonnet under her chin.

Mandie stooped to look into the eyes of her kitten. "Now, Snowball, you stay here in the house," she cautioned. "Don't you dare go outside."

Snowball meowed in response and sat watching as the three young people opened the front door and went outside.

They all climbed aboard the waiting rig, Ben shook the reins, and they were off.

"Tell me again about that shaking in the belfry," Joe said.

"I think it was the floor up there," Mandie replied.

"Or was it the whole belfry trembling?" Celia asked.

"It could have been, but it seems like I felt my feet shaking," Mandie said.

Celia laughed. "I was shaking all over. That's for sure."

"You two are a big help," Joe said, exasperated. "How can I find out what caused something when I don't even know what it was?"

"We certainly don't know what it was," Mandie said.

"But if you could remember exactly *what* was shaking, it might help me figure out what was going on," Joe urged.

Ben pulled the rig up sharply in front of the church, and Mandie jumped down. "Anyway, here we are," she announced. "You can go up there yourself and look around."

"Yo' grandma, she say fo' me to wait right heah fo' y'all," Ben told Mandie.

"Please do, Ben," Mandie said. "If you get cold, come inside the church."

"It nice and warm under dis heah lap robe," Ben said. "I jes' wait heah."

The young people hurried inside the church and looked around the sanctuary. There was no one in sight.

Mandie led the way. "The door and steps to the gallery are right over here," she told Joe, taking off her coat. "Let's leave our coats down here. It's not that cold now, and they'll just get in the way."

After taking off their coats and leaving them on a back pew, Joe and Celia followed her up the stairs and across the balcony.

"Then this door here leads to the belfry," Mandie said, opening the door and showing Joe the bells overhead.

"And this must be the rope ladder." Joe grasped it and quickly skimmed upward.

As he swung off at the top, Mandie started climbing. Celia stayed where she was.

"Aren't you coming, Celia?" Mandie called down to her.

"I think I'll just stay down here and watch out for y'all," she replied nervously.

Mandie and Joe explored the belfry. They examined the floor and walls as well as the support the bells were anchored to. There was nothing loose.

"I know something was shaking when we were up here," Mandie declared. "I didn't imagine it."

"As far as I can tell, though, there is not even a loose board up here," Joe told her. "Could it have been the vibration of the bells ringing?"

"No, the bells weren't ringing when this happened," Mandie explained. "And don't forget, there was also a thumping noise, like something had fallen."

Joe inspected the wires to the bells. "How far away did the noise sound?" he asked.

"I suppose it could have come from downstairs in the sanctuary," Mandie reasoned. "But it sounded all muffled—a thick kind of noise. It wasn't a sharp sound."

"I think we should go back down and examine the whole church as we go," Joe suggested. "Maybe we can find something that has fallen."

"We thought the shaking and the noise must have been connected because everything happened so close together," Mandie explained, heading for the ladder. "I'm coming down, Celia," she called to her friend below. "Stay out of the way."

"All right," Celia answered. "Just don't come down too fast. You might fall."

Mandie quickly descended the rope ladder and jumped off the last rung. Joe followed.

"Did you find out anything up there?" Celia asked. She seemed relieved that she didn't have to climb the swinging ladder.

"No," Mandie replied, "but we're going to search the whole church now."

Joe looked around the balcony. "Let's begin here,"

he said. "Go up and down each row of benches and look for anything that might be loose or anything that might have fallen."

The three young people quickly covered the gallery and found nothing of interest.

"I guess we can go down to the sanctuary, then," Joe said, leading the way downstairs.

"Why don't we leave the sanctuary to the last and work our way through the basement first," Mandie suggested. "Then we can come back through here on the way out."

"That's a good idea," Joe agreed. "Do y'all know how to get into the basement?"

"Sure," Celia answered. "We have our Sunday school classes in the basement."

"Through this doorway here by the choir loft," Mandie said, pointing.

She opened a door to a hallway with Sunday school rooms opening off the sides and a stairway at the far end. The windows in the rooms shed a little light into the hallway.

Joe looked around. "This sure is a big church," he remarked. "They have classrooms back here and more in the basement?"

Mandie laughed. "There are a lot of good people in Asheville, so it takes a huge church to hold them," she said. "Besides, most of the people who belong to this church have a lot of money."

Joe headed down the stairs and the girls followed. At the bottom, they came to a door that opened into a hallway much darker than the one above. Since the basement was half sunk into the ground, the rooms off the hallway only had small windows near the ceiling.

"It's so dark down here I think we should all stay together," Celia suggested. There was a little quiver in her voice. "Someone could be hiding in this basement."

"You're right, Celia," Joe agreed. "Let's start on this side over here."

Starting with the first classroom on the right, they searched each room up and down the hallway.

"The only things in these rooms are a few chairs and a table," Joe observed, "so there isn't really any place for anyone to hide."

"That thumping noise could have been caused by almost anything, though," Mandie said.

They all shook a few of the chairs and tables along the way to see if any of them were wobbly. In one room they found an easel, but it seemed to be standing on strong legs. On the easel stood a piece of cardboard with a map roughly drawn on it in various colors. Nearby were several small cans of water-color paint.

"What's down there at the end of the hall?" Joe asked, heading in that direction.

"It's the room where all the classes gather for a song every Sunday before we go upstairs for the preacher's sermon," Mandie replied.

Joe surveyed the room. In the front there was a piano with a swivel stool on claw feet. Numerous chairs filled the rest of the room. "I think we've cleared the basement," he said. "Let's see what we can find in the classrooms upstairs."

The girls followed Joe back upstairs, searching each room that opened off the hallway. At the far end they came to the pastor's study.

Joe tried the door, but it wouldn't open. He looked puzzled. "I wonder why the preacher locked his office," he said.

"He farms way out in the country," Mandie explained, "so he probably does all his pastor work in his house. As far as I know, he comes to the church only when there's a service."

"Well, he still didn't have to lock the door," Joe said in exasperation.

"Joe, this isn't Swain County where everyone leaves their doors open and unlocked," Mandie reminded him. "This is a big city. There are all kinds of people in this town. The church doors are unlocked all day. Anyone could come in."

"Yes, even strangers, like the man and woman we saw here the other day," Celia added.

"Oh, well," Joe said with a sigh, "if we can't get inside that locked room, then neither can anyone else."

"Unless they have a key," Mandie said. "And I imagine the only people who have keys are the pastor, and the sexton, and maybe some of the deacons."

"All right, let's go," Joe said.

Inside the sanctuary they wandered toward the back. Then suddenly all three of them noticed something down at the altar.

"There's a flag or something there," Celia said, pointing.

"Or a banner." Mandie hurried forward.

Joe said nothing but took quick strides down the center aisle.

There, tied around the altar, was something that looked like a large piece of a white bed sheet with big red letters painted on it—just one word—*HELP!* The three young people stood there for several seconds just staring at it.

Mandie walked closer to inspect the cloth. "I'd say this is a piece of one of the choir robes," she said, feeling the material.

Joe bent to look at the lettering. "And the red paint came from the water colors we saw by the easel in one of the rooms downstairs," he said.

"Where do they keep the choir robes?" Celia asked. "Don't the choir members take their robes home with them?"

Mandie thought for a moment. "I imagine they do

most of the time, but someone could have left one in the church," she said. "Or maybe it was an extra one that no one was using."

"Should we take this thing down?" Joe asked.

"First, let's look for the rest of the robe," Mandie suggested. "It looks like that's only half of it."

"But, Mandie, we've been all over the church," Celia protested.

"I know we've been everywhere, but I don't believe this was here when we came in," Mandie argued. "We would have noticed it."

"You mean someone is here in the church?" Celia's voice was barely a whisper.

Joe puzzled over the matter. "Why would anyone put the word *help* on half a choir robe and hang it on the altar?"

"If we could find whoever did it, then we'd know," Mandie replied. "So I think we ought to look for that person."

"Let's stay together," Celia warned, "now that we know someone else is in the church."

The three young people again went through the entire church, finding nothing and no one.

As they returned to the sanctuary Joe spoke up. "I suppose we might as well remove that thing from the altar," he said.

But as they started down the aisle, Mandie caught her breath. "Look!" She rushed forward. "It's gone!"

Joe and Celia ran after her. Sure enough, the piece of cloth was gone. They looked all around, but there was no sign of it anywhere. Then the bells started ringing.

The young people stood still to silently count the rings. It was twelve noon, but how many times would the bells toll?

"Eleven, twelve," Mandie finished her count aloud. "It was right this time."

"We'd better go," Joe said. "Your grandmother will have dinner ready by now."

"I feel like having a good meal, myself," Mandie replied.

"Me, too," Celia agreed.

When the three returned to the rig, Ben was fast asleep under the lap robe, and they had to wake him.

The Negro driver sat up and yawned. "Y'all gone so long I jes' had to take me a nap," he said.

"Well, it's time to eat, Ben," Joe told him as the three piled into the rig.

When they got back to the house, they related their morning's adventures to Mrs. Taft and Dr. Woodard. No one had any explanations.

The conversation turned to other matters, and Dr. Woodard assured the young people that Hilda was resting comfortably—no worse, but no better than when they had left that morning.

Caught up in the excitement of their adventure, the young people counted the hours until they could return to the church that night.

When the time finally came to leave, Mrs. Taft gave the Negro driver strict instructions. "Now, Ben, you be sure you keep close tabs on these young people to see that no one harms them."

"Yessum, I will," Ben promised.

The young people didn't tell Mrs. Taft that Ben always stayed outside the church and that he even went to sleep.

It was dark when they reached the church, but the full moon shone brightly, and Joe had brought a lantern and plenty of matches to look around inside.

Ben stayed outside in the rig while the three noiselessly entered the church. Inside the vestibule, they looked around the sanctuary, which was dimly illuminated by the moonlight shining through the stained glass windows.

Joe took charge. "Let's not light the lantern until we have to," he suggested, heading for the stairs to the gallery.

"It'll be pitch dark on the stairways and in the basement," Celia said.

"And remember, we don't have very long if we're going to get to Aunt Phoebe's house in time to see Uncle Ned," Mandie reminded him.

"Y'all come on with me upstairs," Joe said, opening the door to the gallery. "I'll run up in the belfry and check it out."

Once upstairs, the three crossed the gallery in the dim light.

Joe opened the door to the belfry. "Wait right here," he told the girls, handing Mandie the lantern.

After disappearing up the rope ladder for a few minutes, he called softly to them, telling them he was coming back down. Landing with a jump, he said, "There's nothing going on up there. Let's look through the classrooms." He took the lantern from Mandie and headed down the stairs.

They hurriedly inspected the classrooms behind the altar, then turned to go down to the basement.

Mandie stopped at the head of the stairs. "It's too dark to see, Joe," she said. "We're going to have to light the lantern."

"I guess we'd better," Joe agreed. "We don't want to fall." Taking a match from his pocket and striking it on the sole of his shoe, he lit the lantern.

The light seemed bright after their eyes had become accustomed to the darkness of the church. Joe descended the stairs first, holding the lantern high so the girls could see. At the bottom of the stairs, the hallway was even darker. Thick shrubbery outside the small, high windows in the classrooms blocked the moonlight, and the lantern light threw weird shadows.

"It's spooky down here," Celia said.

Neither Joe nor Mandie responded, but the young people stayed close together as they crept from room to room, searching for clues. They ended up at the far end of the hallway.

"Nothing," Joe said with a sigh.

Just then there was a loud banging noise overhead. The three young people froze.

Celia grabbed Mandie's hand. "W-what was th-that?" she stuttered.

"Let's go find out," Joe whispered. Leading the way back down the hallway, he pushed on the door to the stairs. It wouldn't budge. "I'm afraid someone has locked this door," he said softly.

"Oh, goodness!" Celia cried. "What are we going to do?"

Mandie tried the door, too. It was definitely locked.

"Now we *know* someone is in the church," Joe said, pushing hard against the door again. "And that someone has locked us in here."

Mandie's heart pounded. "What are we going to do, Joe?" she asked. "We've got to get out of here and go to Aunt Phoebe's house."

Just as Joe was about to say something, the lantern dimmed and went out. Everyone gasped.

"Don't worry," Joe said. "I have some more matches." He struck a match to relight the lantern and touched the match to the wick. The lantern sputtered and went out. He tried another match. When it did the same thing, he lit another match to examine the lantern by its light. "Oh, no!" he exclaimed. "The lantern is out of oil! I'm sorry. It's my fault. I just grabbed a lantern out of your grandmother's pantry, Mandie, and I didn't bother to see how much oil there was in it."

"Oh, Joe, we really are in trouble!" Mandie cried.

"We could try the windows," Joe suggested, turning back to a classroom.

"They have bars on the outside," Mandie explained. "And they're awfully small, anyway."

Again the banging noises began overhead. The young people huddled together in the darkness. Mandie's heart pounded so loudly that she was sure the others could hear it. Her legs buckled beneath her. All three of them plopped down on the floor by the locked door.

Then there was complete silence upstairs.

"We've got to get out of here!" Mandie cried. "There may be someone dangerous up there."

"It must be someone who has some keys," Joe said. "Otherwise, how could they lock that door?"

"These locks have a thumb latch," Mandie said nervously, "and the thumb latch on that door happens to be on the other side, so all they had to do was flip the latch to lock us in here."

Celia squeezed Mandie's hand tightly. "Oh, Mandie, whatever are we going to do?"

"Let's say our verse that always helps when we get in trouble," Mandie said.

The three young people joined hands and repeated the Bible verse that always gave them strength. "What time I am afraid," they recited, "I will put my faith in Thee."

Mandie took a deep breath and rose to her feet. "Now I won't be afraid because I know God will help us get out of this predicament somehow," she said. "He always does."

"I wish I knew what was going on upstairs," Joe said.

"Me, too," Celia agreed. "Whoever is up there could be a dangerous character."

The three walked about, softly discussing possibilities. Mrs. Taft would be worried when they didn't return, and Uncle Ned would be waiting under the magnolia tree in the cold for nothing.

Somehow they had to get out!

Chapter 6 / No Way to Escape?

"I wish I hadn't suggested we leave our coats in the sanctuary," Mandie said, briskly rubbing her arms to warm herself. "Too bad there's nothing down here to build a fire in that big stove in the hallway."

"I'm cold, too," Celia complained, "and it's so spooky down here. What are we going to do?"

"We can't stay here all night," Joe said. "We've got to get out somehow."

Celia shivered as she paced back and forth on the cold concrete floor. "I wonder why Ben hasn't come looking for us."

"He probably fell asleep in the rig again," Mandie answered.

"Well, we've got to do something," Joe announced. "Let's try the windows. We might find some loose bars on one of them or something."

Celia looked up at the high windows. "I don't think we can reach them," she said.

"You're right, Celia," Mandie agreed. "I don't believe Joe can reach that high, either."

"I can always get taller," Joe said with a grin. He carried a chair over to the window and stood on it. "Like this," he added.

"You can just barely reach the window, Joe," Mandie

71

argued. "Celia and I would never be able to."

"Never mind. I'll check the windows myself," Joe answered.

The windows, which were locked by spring hooks, consisted of only one small pane, and they pulled out and down from the top like a door opening sideways.

Joe pulled the first one open and reached through to the bars outside. "No luck," he said. Shaking his head, he stepped down and moved the chair below the next window.

"I wish we could find something to knock the bars loose," Mandie said, looking around in the darkness.

"There's nothing here we can use," Joe reminded her as he opened the second window. "Remember, we checked the whole place."

Celia watched Joe trying to loosen the bars. "It'd probably be easier to break the door down than to knock out any of those iron bars," she commented.

"Let's try it, Celia," Mandie said. "We can work on the door while Joe works on the windows." The girls hurried out into the hallway.

"Hey, don't go hurting yourselves now," Joe cautioned. "That's an awfully strong door."

"We'll just see what we can do," Mandie called back to him. She felt her way through the darkness to the door at the end of the hallway. Celia clutched Mandie's shoulder and followed.

When they got to the door, Mandie ran her hands around the doorknob. "Oh, shucks!" she exclaimed. "The lock is on the other side, and the door opens into the hall this way. That means we have to pull on it instead of pushing."

Celia laid her hands on top of Mandie's on the doorknob. "Maybe it'll work," she said.

The girls tried to pull together on the door, but four hands wouldn't fit. Celia let go.

Mandie grasped the doorknob tightly. "I'll have to pull by myself," she said. She pulled as hard as she could, but the door didn't even rattle. The lock held fast. As Mandie shook her aching hands in the air, Celia stepped up for a try. Nothing happened.

"Maybe Joe could pull harder on it," Mandie said. "Come on. I'm going back there to see where he is."

The girls felt their way back down the dark hallway until they came to the end room where Joe was examining a window.

"Nothing yet," Joe said to them, running his hands over the bars outside. "As far as I can tell, all these bars are bolted into the brick and cement."

"And there's no way to get one loose," Mandie added. "Celia and I couldn't budge the door, either."

"What are we going to do?" Celia fretted.

"Now, Celia, don't forget. We're going to trust in God," Mandie reminded her friend. "Remember our verse?"

"I know," Celia whispered. "I just wish we could hurry up and get out of this place."

"Joe, why don't you stop working on those windows for a minute and see if you can do anything with that door?" Mandie suggested.

Joe stepped down, preparing to go on to the next window. "I only have these two left," he said, motioning to the ones on the end. "I've examined all the windows in the other rooms. I'll see what I can do with the door as soon as I'm finished here." Stepping up onto the chair, he inspected the bars on the window above him. "Just like the rest—solid," he said, stepping down and moving to the last window.

The girls watched silently as he climbed up, opened the window, and reached out to touch the iron bars.

He turned and grinned at them. "One corner is loose," he said excitedly. "If I can manage to get another corner free, we might be able to squeeze out."

Grabbing the bars with both hands, he shook them with all his strength. The loose corner wiggled a little, but the rest of the bars stayed firmly in place.

Finally Joe gave up. "Looks like we're in here to stay unless I can get the door open," he said. Closing the window, he stepped down from the chair.

"Maybe Ben will wake up and come looking for us," Mandie said hopefully.

"I don't imagine Ben will come inside the church when there aren't any lights on up there," Joe argued. "Let me try the door."

The three felt their way through the dark hallway to the door again. Joe took hold of the doorknob with both hands and pulled with all his might. Nothing happened. He released it, took a deep breath, braced his long legs, and yanked hard. Suddenly, he fell backward, knocking the girls behind him onto the floor.

"Land sakes!" Mandie cried, getting up from the hard floor. "What happened?"

"The blasted doorknob came off," Joe said, holding the knob in his hand. He stood up. "Maybe I can put it back on."

He felt around on the door for the place where the doorknob belonged. "The spindle that holds the knobs is gone!" he exclaimed. "So the other side of the knob is gone, too."

"How are we ever going to get out of here?" Celia asked.

"This is the back of the church, and Ben is parked on the road in front, but do you suppose if we yelled loud enough he might hear us?" Mandie asked.

"We could try," Joe said.

"If we could all get up there and open a window and yell, it might work." Celia sounded hopeful.

"The room where you found the loose bar has a big table in it, remember?" Mandie reminded Joe. "We could pull it over to the window and then put chairs on top of it. Celia and I ought to be able to stand on the chairs and reach the window."

"You might be able to if the chairs are steady enough," Joe said.

The three returned to the room where the table was. They pushed the table under the window with the loose iron bar, and set two chairs on top of it.

"Are y'all sure you won't fall?" Joe asked. "You could get hurt pretty bad, you know, on this concrete floor."

"At this point we just have to take chances," Mandie said. "But we'll be careful." She raised her long skirt and jumped up onto the table. Then swinging her legs around, she scrambled to her feet. Joe held the chair while she stepped up onto the seat. She looked up. Her head almost touched the ceiling in front of the window. "Come on up, Celia."

Celia copied Mandie's antics to get up on the other chair. Joe stood between the girls to support them and opened the window.

"Well, now that we're up here, what do we yell?" Joe asked.

"Let's just call Ben," Mandie said. Raising her voice, she started yelling. "Ben! Ben! Come to the back of the church!"

Celia and Joe joined in, and the three together hollered loud enough to wake the whole neighborhood.

Joe stopped to catch his breath. "He must be able to hear all the noise we're making," he said.

"Maybe he left," Celia suggested.

"No, Grandmother gave him strict orders not to leave us," Mandie said.

"Well, he's either gone off somewhere or he's deaf," Joe decided.

All three stood quietly for a minute as they tried to

look out through the thick shrubbery in front of the window.

Suddenly Mandie touched Joe's arm. "Did you see something move out there?" she whispered.

"I did!" Celia said quietly.

"Where?" Joe whispered back.

"There!" Mandie pointed through the shrubbery off to the left. "Do you suppose it's Ben?"

"I saw something move," Joe whispered.

Then the bushes quit shaking.

It must be Ben, Mandie thought. *Besides, if it were someone bad, he couldn't get in any more than we can get out*, she reasoned. She raised her voice again. "Ben! Ben!" she shouted. "We're in here!"

There was a quick movement in the shrubbery outside, then a familiar voice answered, "Papoose! Where Papoose?"

"Uncle Ned!" Mandie exclaimed as tears came to her eyes. "We're down here in the basement, Uncle Ned!"

Joe and Celia breathed sighs of relief along with Mandie as the old Indian moved between the bushes to the window and looked in through the iron bars.

"Papoose, Doctor Son, Papoose See," Uncle Ned called to them. (He called Celia *Papoose See* because he couldn't pronounce her name.) "How you get in there?" he demanded.

"Somebody locked the door, and we can't get out," Mandie explained. "Oh, Uncle Ned, you're the answer to our prayers."

"Please get us out, Uncle Ned!" Celia cried.

"Do you know where Ben is?" Joe queried.

"How did you know we were here?" Mandie asked.

"One time for each question," Uncle Ned replied. "First, must get out. Ben sleep. I get Ben." The old Indian turned to go.

"Wait, Uncle Ned," Mandie called to him. "The front

door is supposed to be unlocked. We came in that way. But somebody else has been in the church. Whoever it is locked the door at the bottom of the stairs."

"I go see," Uncle Ned nodded and hurried off.

"Oh, what a relief!" Celia climbed down from the chair and sat on the table.

Mandie and Joe sat down beside her.

"I guess Ben was asleep," Joe said in exasperation. "A lot of good it did to bring him with us!"

"Let's don't make trouble for him," Mandie suggested.

"We have to tell your grandmother the truth, Mandie," Joe said.

"But we don't have to go into detail," Mandie replied. "If she knows Ben went to sleep outside and we got locked in here alone, she might not let him go with us anywhere anymore, and then we might not be able to solve the mystery."

"If he goes with us anywhere else, he should stay right along with us and not take a nap outside," Joe said.

"You're right," Mandie agreed. "Next time we'll insist on that."

In a few minutes Uncle Ned reappeared at the basement window with Ben beside him. The girls quickly took their places on the chairs with Joe steadying them.

"Door locked," Uncle Ned announced. "Must think. Other way out?"

"Lawsy mercy, Missies, how y'all git in dat place all locked up like dat?" Ben called to them.

"We don't know, Ben," Mandie told him. "Someone locked the door to the basement while we were down here."

Joe reached out to touch the iron bars on the window. "These bars are loose in this one corner," he said, pointing. "I tried to get it loose enough for us to crawl out, but I didn't have any tools."

Uncle Ned examined the bars.

Ben watched as the old Indian shook the bars and thought for a minute. "I think I got a claw hammer in de rig," Ben said. "I go see."

"Please be sure you come right back, Ben," Mandie called after him.

"Yessum, Missy. I be back in a minute," the Negro replied.

Uncle Ned looked up from his examination of the bars. "Bars stuck good in cement. Hammer break cement. Much damage."

"I think my grandmother would pay for any damage we do, Uncle Ned—I hope," Mandie answered.

Ben returned with a large claw hammer. Everyone watched as the strong old Indian banged on the iron bars. The young people shielded their eyes as bits of cement flew through the air.

Uncle Ned shook the bars and hammered again. Then he turned to Ben. "You pull. I pull," he said.

Ben understood and braced himself to yank on the bars at the same time the old Indian did.

"Away!" Uncle Ned told the young people. "Bar come loose and cement hit papooses."

The three scrambled down and crouched on the table beneath the window, waiting.

"Pull!" Uncle Ned shouted.

There was a sudden, loud, cracking noise.

"One end loose," Uncle Ned announced.

The young people stood up to look.

"Must break other end," the old Indian fussed. He picked up the hammer from the ground. "Away!" he told the young people again.

Again they sat down, waiting and listening as Uncle Ned pounded and the wall vibrated with the hard blows. Cement flew everywhere. Mandie and Celia bent their heads to keep it from getting into their eyes. Joe moved away from the window to watch, and the girls followed.

Uncle Ned dropped the hammer. "Now!" he called to Ben.

Together the two men pulled and grunted. The bars wouldn't give. Uncle Ned picked up the hammer again and gave the bars a few more hard blows. Ben helped him pull again. Suddenly the bars gave way, and the two men fell backward into the shrubbery.

Mandie jumped back up on the chair to look out the now unbarred window. "Oh, thank you, Uncle Ned!" she cried.

The old Indian stood up and came over to the window. "Small to crawl through," he said, measuring the opening with his old wrinkled hands.

"I think it might be large enough," Joe said. "I can help the girls from in here if you can help them out up there."

"I help," Uncle Ned agreed.

The three young people happily chattered about who would be the first one out; then Mandie stopped suddenly. "I just remembered something!" she exclaimed. "Our coats—they're upstairs!"

"That's right!" Celia said.

"Well, I don't know how we're going to get up there with the basement door still locked," Joe told them. "And Uncle Ned said the front door was locked, too."

"We come in," Uncle Ned offered. "We open door down there."

"But Uncle Ned," Mandie said, "the doorknob is gone on both sides, and even the spindle dropped off."

"Me see." Uncle Ned turned to Ben. "We go down there. Me go first."

"Don't get stuck, Uncle Ned," Mandie called from below.

Taking his sling of arrows and his bow from his shoul-

der, he pushed them through the window. "Take," he told
Joe.

Joe took them and moved out of the way.

Uncle Ned squatted down and stuck his long legs
through the open window. As he slid in, his broad shoulders just barely made it through the opening. Ben, whose
frame was even bigger than Uncle Ned's had a harder
time, but when he finally landed on the table, both men
sighed with relief and looked around.

"No light?" the Indian asked.

"No, Uncle Ned," Mandie replied. "Our lantern is out
of oil."

Celia touched Mandie's arm. "Aren't there any of
those new electric lights down here like there are upstairs?" she asked.

"I don't know," Mandie said, looking around. "If there
are, there would be a string hanging from a fixture on the
ceiling."

The group searched each room for any indication of
electric lights, but they found none.

"Now, why would they have electric lights upstairs and
none down here?" Joe wondered.

"They haven't had the lights upstairs very long," Celia
replied. "They put them in since we came to school here
in Asheville, and I seem to remember something about
having to raise more money to wire the basement."

Mandie sighed in disappointment. "You're right, Celia," she said. "I remember now, too."

"What do you use for light when you're in the basement at night, then?" Joe asked.

"I don't think it's ever used at night," Mandie answered. "There are so many rooms upstairs that they
don't really need it."

Uncle Ned spoke up. "Where door?" he asked, putting
his sling of arrows over his shoulder again.

When they showed the door to him and Ben, Uncle

Ned felt around in the darkness. "Here knob hole," he said. "Notches inside."

"You see, there's no way to open it," Celia said.

"Never say no way anything," Uncle Ned replied. "Always way." He took one of his arrows from his sling, felt for the hole, and carefully inserted the tip of the arrow into it.

The young people and Ben hovered around, trying to see in the darkness. Uncle Ned slowly twisted the arrow, and they heard the click of the latch withdrawing in the lock. Carefully pulling on the door by the arrow in the lock, the old Indian gradually eased the door open.

Everyone gasped.

"But that door was locked!" Mandie exclaimed. "We couldn't turn the lock, remember?"

"It certainly was," Joe agreed. "And all Uncle Ned did was turn the latch and it opened. Someone has been playing tricks on us."

"You mean somebody locked it and then later unlocked the thumb latch on the other side?" Celia asked in disbelief.

"I guess so," Joe replied.

"Get coats," Uncle Ned urged. "Ben lock window."

Ben hurriedly latched the window as the young people started up the stairs.

Joe's foot kicked something, and he bent to pick it up. "Here's the other doorknob," he said, holding it out to Uncle Ned.

"Leave here. Must hurry," Uncle Ned urged.

When they all got upstairs, they found their coats just where they had left them in the last pew at the back of the sanctuary.

Celia hurriedly slipped into hers. "Thank goodness no one took our coats while we were trapped down there!" she exclaimed. "Oh, this feels nice and warm."

"Wait a minute," Mandie cried as Joe helped her into

her coat. "If the front door is locked, how are we going to get out of here?"

They all stopped and looked at each other, realizing Mandie was right.

Joe ran to try the front door. "It's locked, all right," he said, shaking his head.

"Is door in back?" Uncle Ned asked.

"You mean a back door?" Mandie replied. "I don't know. I don't think I've ever noticed. Let's go see."

They hurried to the back.

"I know where it is," Celia suddenly remembered. "It's in the back of the pastor's study. I remember seeing it once when the door to the study was open."

"And the pastor keeps his study locked," Joe reminded them. "Why would the back door be in the pastor's study?"

"His study was probably made out of the end of the hall. See?" Mandie pointed to the room down the hall. "And the door was probably already there."

"Oh, give me a country church anytime. These city churches are made too complicated," Joe moaned.

"Must go down, out window," Uncle Ned decided.

"Now, how's we gwine do dat?" Ben asked. "I almost didn't fit through dat window a-comin' in."

Mandie smiled. "Ben, if you fit coming in, you'll fit going out," she teased.

Uncle Ned led the way back down to the basement room where he and Ben had come in. "I go first," he said. "Then Ben. Be up there, help papooses get out. Doctor son last. Help papooses up. Take coats off and push through window."

They understood his plan. The old Indian gave Joe his bow and arrows and quickly scooted through the window. Joe handed the Indian's things back to him; then Ben started through. It took some squirming and twisting, but he made it all right. The young people removed their coats and pushed them through the window to the men above.

"Mandie, you go first," Joe suggested. "Then you can help Celia get out."

"All right," Mandie agreed, climbing onto the chair to reach the windowsill.

"When I get hold of your feet and push, you grab Uncle Ned's hands up there," Joe instructed.

Mandie did as she was told and soon found her feet firmly planted on the ground outside the window. She breathed a great sigh of relief.

Celia climbed through with no problem and then Joe followed, handing Uncle Ned the worthless empty lantern. He reached back inside to slam the window shut, hoping the latch would catch. It did.

Hastily putting on their coats in the bright moonlight, the young people ran out to the rig with Uncle Ned and Ben.

Mandie looked up into the old Indian's face. "How did you know we were here, Uncle Ned?" she asked.

"I go to school. Aunt Phoebe see, tell me Papoose at Grandmother house. I tell her I go to Grandmother. Aunt Phoebe not wait for Papoose now," the Indian explained. "On way to Grandmother, I see rig in front of church. Ben sleep. I know about bells. I know Papoose near."

"Then you heard us hollering our heads off," Mandie said with a nervous laugh.

Uncle Ned reached out and took her small hand in his old wrinkled one. "Papoose, what been doing?" he asked.

Mandie and the others related the night's events to Uncle Ned as they stood around the rig. They told him about all the strange things that had been happening to them since they started investigating.

"Papooses must be careful," Uncle Ned cautioned. "Sometimes bad people 'round."

"We'll be careful," Mandie promised. "Are you coming on to my grandmother's with us now?"

"No, Papoose. Must go. Horse wait under tree." He waved his hand toward a horse tethered under a bare tree across the cobblestoned street. "I come again. Remember—Papoose must think," he said. "Always think first, then do things."

"I'll try to remember that, Uncle Ned," Mandie promised.

"I promise Jim Shaw when he go to Happy Hunting Ground that I watch over Papoose, but Papoose must learn to watch, too," the old Indian reminded her.

"I love you, Uncle Ned," Mandie said, rising on her tiptoes to give him a quick hug. "I'll be careful."

Uncle Ned hugged Mandie in return, then hurried across the street to his waiting horse.

The young people piled into the rig. Ben picked up the reins, and they waved to the old Indian as he mounted his horse and rode away.

When the rig started off, Celia looked up at the clock in the steeple. "It's twenty minutes till eleven!" she exclaimed.

Mandie frowned at Joe. "I don't remember hearing the bells ring while we were in the church," she said, "but I know we got there before ten o'clock."

"You're right. They didn't ring," Joe said with a puzzled look on his face.

"No, they didn't," Celia agreed.

"More and more mystery," Mandie said. "We've just got to solve this thing before forty-'leven hundred more things happen."

"Well, right now I imagine your grandmother and my father are beginning to wonder where we are," Joe told her.

"I know," Mandie said. She was more worried about going back to face the adults than she was about all that had happened to them that night.

Chapter 7 / Back to School

Mrs. Taft and Dr. Woodard sat waiting in the parlor when the young people returned from the church.

Hurriedly hanging their coats on the hall tree, the three went to sit on stools near the blazing fire. They were cold from the weather and the fright they had just had as well as from the ordeal of now relating their adventure to the adults. Mandie picked up Snowball, who was curled up asleep on the hearth rug, and began to pet him.

Mrs. Taft had Ella serve hot cocoa. She and Dr. Woodard listened without interrupting as the three told of the events of the night. They raised eyebrows and gasped at some parts of the story but waited until the young people had finished. Then Mrs. Taft scolded them.

"I'm sorry, Grandmother," Mandie said, "but we didn't intentionally get locked in."

"No, I don't suppose you did," Mrs. Taft answered. "However, I shall have to speak to Ben. He should have stayed right with you all."

Dr. Woodard cleared his throat. "That could have been an unsavory character who locked you in," he said. He turned to Mrs. Taft. "Do you think they should just stop all this investigating business?"

"Oh no, please!" Mandie pleaded. "We have to find out what's going on."

Mrs. Taft thought for a moment. "I suppose it would be all right if they only go in the daytime—and if Ben stays right with them. But no more night adventures."

The three young people looked at each other.

"I won't be here tomorrow night anyway," Joe conceded. "We have to go home after church tomorrow."

"And we have to go back to school tomorrow afternoon," Celia added.

"We may not have time to do anything else about the mystery now, anyway," Mandie said with a sigh.

"It's late now," Mrs. Taft said. "You all get upstairs to bed. Tomorrow is Sunday, and we all have to get up early and go to church."

The young people started to leave the room and Snowball followed.

Mandie turned quickly and ran back to Dr. Woodard. "We've been so wrapped up in what happened to us that we forgot to ask about Hilda," she said. "How is she, Doctor Woodard?"

"About the same. No better. No worse," he replied.

"Is she going to just stay that way?" Mandie asked. "Isn't she ever going to get better?"

"We hope she will, Amanda," Dr. Woodard replied. "Like I said before, it's up to the Lord."

Mandie turned to the others. "Don't forget Hilda in your prayers tonight," she said.

Early the next morning, everyone was up, rushing around to get ready for church. At breakfast, Dr. Woodard announced that there was still no change in Hilda's condition. The nurses remained at her bedside around the clock, but Mandie felt frustrated that no visitors were allowed.

As they all piled into the rig to go to church, Mrs. Taft spoke quietly to the driver. "Ben, I need to have a little talk with you some time this afternoon," she said.

"Yessum, Miz Taft." Ben looked nervous.

Mandie leaned forward to whisper in his ear. "Don't get so worried," she said. "It's nothing really bad."

Without a reply, Ben picked up the reins and drove sedately to the church. He always left Mrs. Taft at her church and then drove on to his own down the road, picking up Mrs. Taft again after services were over.

As the group stepped down from the rig, Mrs. Taft looked back at her driver. "Now, please don't be late, Ben," she said. "We're in a hurry today."

"Yessum, Miz Taft," Ben answered, muttering to himself as he drove off.

Once inside the church, they all went to their Sunday school classes. Mrs. Taft's was at the rear of the main floor, and Dr. Woodard visited the men's class in a side room nearby. As the young people headed down to the basement for their classes, the first thing they noticed was the doorknob securely fastened to the door at the bottom of the stairs.

"I can't believe my eyes!" Mandie exclaimed in a whisper.

"It seems that whoever is doing these things around here comes back to reverse whatever happened," Joe remarked. "First the *Help!* banner and now this doorknob. . . ."

"Maybe the person is sorry afterward," Celia suggested.

"They're going to be sorry when we finally find them out," Mandie promised. "The house of the Lord is no place to play games like this."

Celia and Joe agreed.

After Sunday school, the young people went upstairs and joined Mrs. Taft and Dr. Woodard in the family pew for the preacher's message. Mandie was happy that the two big stoves in the sanctuary were roaring with fires to warm the whole room. *How different from last night*, she thought.

As soon as Reverend Tallant stepped up behind the pulpit, he mentioned the mysterious goings-on in the church. "We have not been able to remove the writing from the back wall of the church yet, but we should have that accomplished tomorrow," he began. "Now, however, we have another complaint. It seems that neighbors living nearby heard the organ playing here in the sanctuary along about midnight. Someone notified the sexton, Mr. Clark, and he came down, looked around, and found nothing."

The minister paused momentarily while latecomers were being seated. "Mr. Clark said he had gone through and locked the door at ten o'clock," Rev. Tallant continued. "Everything was all right then."

The three young people looked at each other.

"Ten o'clock?" Mandie whispered. "He certainly didn't check the basement then because we were locked in down there before ten, and it was twenty minutes to eleven when we got out."

Celia nodded.

"You don't know what time we got locked in," Joe whispered. "The bells didn't ring at ten o'clock, remember?"

Dr. Woodard nudged his son and shook his head.

The young people hushed.

The preacher continued speaking. ". . . and we want to ask for your prayers for little Hilda Edney, who is living with Mrs. Taft. She is very ill with pneumonia. Mrs. Tillinghast and her sister, Miss Rumler, also need our prayers at this time. They are both quite sick with the flu. Now let us pray."

Mandie bowed her head with the rest of the congregation and joined in the prayers, especially for Hilda. She was worried about her. Dr. Woodard had to leave for home after dinner, and although there were other doctors in Asheville, she trusted her friend Dr. Woodard more than them all.

At the conclusion of the service, Ben waited for them as they shook hands with the preacher at the door and stepped out onto the porch.

On the way home, the young people discussed the newest development in the church mysteries.

"So someone was playing the organ at midnight," Mandie said, trying to make some sense of it. "Well, I'd like to know how anybody got inside the church. It was all locked up when we left."

"Maybe they were able to open the window where Uncle Ned removed the bars," Joe reasoned. "Come to think of it, the preacher didn't mention that someone had torn the bars off that window."

Mrs. Taft spoke up. "That's because I spoke to him before he preached and told him what happened to y'all last night," she explained. "And I promised him I would pay for the damage."

"So, since he knew who did it, he didn't mention it," Mandie said. Suddenly she caught her breath in alarm. "I hope he doesn't think we've been doing all those other things."

"Of course not, Amanda," her grandmother assured her. "But I did tell him that y'all were trying to solve the puzzle for him."

"You told him what we were doing?" Mandie gulped.

"What else was I to say when the damage was there?" Mrs. Taft replied. "It had to be explained some way."

"You're right, Grandmother," Mandie agreed. "I hope he doesn't mind our getting involved."

Mrs. Taft smiled. "I'm sure no one will mind if y'all are able to solve this mystery," she said.

Ben pulled the rig up in front of Mrs. Taft's house and helped her from the vehicle.

As the others climbed down, Mrs. Taft spoke to the driver again. "Come to the back sitting room in about two hours, Ben," she instructed. "The doctor and Joe will be leaving as soon as we finish dinner, and then the girls have to return to school. I want to talk to you before you take them back."

"Yessum, Miz Taft," Ben replied, stepping back into the rig to move it from the front driveway. "I'll be dere."

Inside the house, Dr. Woodard headed upstairs to check on Hilda while everyone else sat in the parlor, waiting for dinner to be put on the table. Mrs. Taft was strict with her servants on Sunday. She insisted that they attend their churches, and all the cooking for Sunday was done on Saturday so that when the cook came home from church, all she had to do was warm everything and put it on the table.

Mrs. Taft sat in a big overstuffed chair in the parlor and looked lovingly at her granddaughter. "Do you and Celia have your things together to take back to school, dear?" she asked.

"Yes, ma'am," Mandie replied. "We're all ready. Are you going to send for us again next Friday?"

"If you and Celia want to come, of course, dear," Mrs. Taft answered. "You know I am always glad to have you girls here with me anytime."

"Thanks, Grandmother," Mandie said. "I'm always so happy to get out of that school, and I imagine Celia is, too."

Celia nodded.

"Especially when there's some kind of adventure going on," Joe teased.

Mandie pretended to look hurt. "You won't be able to come next weekend, will you?" she asked.

"Not unless my father has to come back," he said.

Dr. Woodard entered the room. "I still don't see any change in Hilda," he said. "I've changed the treatment a little, and I hope that will make a difference. But for now, she's just not making any progress."

"Oh, Dr. Woodard, couldn't I just open the door and peek in?" Mandie begged.

"No, I'm sorry, Amanda," he replied. "You will all have to stay away from her room for the time being."

"Will you be coming back next weekend to check on her?" Celia asked.

Mandie's eyes brightened as she looked at Joe, awaiting the answer.

"I'm not sure," Dr. Woodard said. "We'll see."

Mandie smiled at Joe. *At least he didn't say no*, she thought.

As soon as the noon meal was over, Dr. Woodard and Joe left in their buggy. Mrs. Taft retired to the back sitting room to talk to Ben.

Mrs. Taft told the Negro man to sit down. "Now, Ben, I want to know why you didn't stay right with Miss Amanda and her friends when you took them to the church last night," she began.

"I stayed in de rig, Miz Taft," Ben replied.

"But you fell asleep in the rig, and those young people were locked in the church," she scolded. "If Uncle Ned hadn't come along when he did, there's no telling when they would have gotten out."

"But, Miz Taft," Ben replied. The girls could hear him scuffing his feet nervously. "You see, it's like dis heah—I ain't s'posed to go in white folks' church."

"That's nonsense, Ben, and you know that," Mrs. Taft argued. "You know as well as I do that there's a gallery in that church where the colored people are all welcome to come and join in our services. There's no reason in this world why you can't go inside a white people's church."

"I don't go in dat gallery neither, ma'am," Ben replied. "You go to yo' church. I goes to mine. You white. I'se a Negro."

"You are not obligated to attend church with white

people, Ben, but you are obligated to carry out my instructions," Mrs. Taft said firmly. "That's what I pay you for—to do what I ask you to do. Now I don't want to hear any more nonsense. If you want to keep your job, you'll have to do whatever the job requires. Is that understood?"

"I understands, Miz Taft," Ben replied. "If you say dat's part of my job, den I does my job next time."

"Thank you, Ben. I knew I could depend on you," Mrs. Taft said. "You know it isn't long until Christmas, and I always give the pay raises at Christmas."

"Yessum, Miz Taft. You sho' does."

"You are not to let the girls out of your sight again when I have left them in your care," Mrs. Taft continued. "Not out of your sight for one minute. Can I depend on you next time they go somewhere?"

"Yessum. Yessum. You kin 'pend on me."

"Thank you. Now get the rig around to the front door," Mrs. Taft said. "It's about time for the girls to go back to school."

"Yessum."

Minutes later, the girls were reluctantly on their way back to school. When they arrived, Ben took their luggage to their room. The girls stopped to speak to Miss Hope, whom they met in the front hallway.

"I hope you young ladies had a nice weekend," Miss Hope said in greeting.

"Yes, ma'am, we did," the girls replied together. "Did you?"

"We've had a little sickness here this weekend," Miss Hope informed them. "Two of the girls came down with flu—Mamie Wright and Betty Blassingame. They both went home. Mamie just lives over in Hendersonville, and Betty lives out in the country near here, so their parents came and got them." Miss Hope looked worried. "I do hope we don't have an epidemic here in the school."

"Hilda has pneumonia. She's real bad off," Mandie told her.

"Oh, dear, I'm sorry," Miss Hope replied. "I'll be praying for her, and I'll pray that you two don't come down with it."

"Thank you, Miss Hope," the girls said.

"Hurry along, now, and get freshened up for supper," the schoolmistress told them as she continued down the hall.

As soon as the girls were sure she was out of sight, they took the steps, two at a time, up to their third-floor room.

"Well, I guess it's all lessons until Friday," Mandie said, pushing open the door to their room.

Celia followed, and both girls quickly removed their coats and bonnets and started to lay them on the bed. Instantly they jumped back and screamed.

There in the middle of the bed, on top of the counterpane, lay a dead mouse!

At the sound of their screams, Miss Prudence, who had been walking by, jerked the door open. "What are you—?" She saw the mouse, turned pale, and without a word slammed the door, running down the hallway, calling for Uncle Cal.

Mandie and Celia backed away from the bed and stood frozen there in terror.

"Sh-she's afraid of m-mice, too," Mandie managed to say.

Celia moved toward the door. "I'm g-g-getting out of here," she said, backing out of the room.

In seconds Uncle Cal appeared with a garbage bucket and a brush in his hand. "Where dat so-an'-so mouse, now, Missy?" the Negro man asked. He spotted it at once. Quickly turning the bucket sideways, he brushed the dead mouse inside. "All gone, now, Missy," he announced as he headed out the door.

Mandie's heart was pounding. "Oh, thank you, Uncle Cal," she said. "Thank you."

As he went out the door, Aunt Phoebe hurried in, carrying a clean bedspread. She quickly pulled off the one on the bed and replaced it with the one she had brought.

Mandie still trembled with fright. "Aunt Phoebe, do you suppose that's the mouse we found in the chifferobe?" she asked shakily.

Celia came back inside the room to hang up her coat.

"I don't be knowin', Missy," the old Negro woman said, smoothing the wrinkles out of the fresh counterpane. "But I tells you one thing. Miss Prudence, she be knowin' now dat mouse was real!"

"And Miss Prudence was afraid of it, too, just like us," Celia added.

"I hope she does something about it," Mandie said. "I think someone put that thing on our bed, and I hope we find out who did it."

"We find out," Aunt Phoebe promised.

Chapter 8 / More Trouble

Days passed slowly that week for Mandie and Celia at school. They longed for Friday to come so they could return to Grandmother Taft's and continue their investigation of the mystery.

The newspaper had declared a flu epidemic in the town of Asheville. Hundreds of people were ill, and the people in the town were blaming it on the mysterious happenings at the church. The bells continued ringing thirteen at midnight and the wrong number of rings at other hours during the day.

By Thursday of that week over half of the school had come down with the flu.

Miss Prudence addressed the students at breakfast on Thursday morning. "Young ladies," the headmistress began, looking around at the girls as they stood behind their chairs, "as you know, many of our students have contracted that dreadful flu that is going around town. We don't want it to spread any further here if possible. Therefore, classes will be dismissed until the epidemic is over."

The girls all looked at each other. It was unheard of for any of the students to speak out without being asked, but this particular morning Mandie forgot about the rules and dared asked a question. "Does that mean we can all go home, Miss Prudence?"

The headmistress looked sharply at Mandie, and Mandie cringed.

"Amanda, you have not asked permission to speak," the headmistress reprimanded. "However, since we want to get this settled as quickly as possible, I will answer your question. Yes, the girls who live near enough to come back at short notice may go home. We believe that you who are not sick are less likely to come down with this illness if you are in your own homes. Does that answer your question, Amanda?"

"Thank you, Miss Prudence," Mandie said. "Then I have permission to go to my grandmother's while classes are out?"

"That is correct," Miss Prudence replied. "But you girls who live a long distance away will have to stay here."

Celia looked at Mandie and without moving her lips, she whispered, "That means I don't get to go home. It's too far."

Mandie kept her gaze on Miss Prudence but muttered under her breath, "You can go to Grandmother's with me. We'll ask."

Miss Prudence continued, "You girls may leave the school as soon as you can make arrangements to go home. Beginning today, there will be no classes until further notice. Now let us give thanks for this food."

After breakfast Miss Prudence gave Celia permission to go with Mandie. The two girls could hardly wait for Uncle Cal to take them to Grandmother Taft's house. Hurrying to their room, they hastily threw things into bags and laid out their coats and bonnets.

"We don't know how long we'll be staying, so I guess we'd better take plenty of clothes," Mandie advised.

"Right," Celia agreed. "I'm sorry those girls are so sick, but this is good luck for us."

"I hope they all get well soon," Mandie said, dropping her school books into a bag. "I think I'll take some of my books so I can study a little now and then while we're at Grandmother's."

"That's a good idea. Then we won't get too far behind," Celia replied. She added some of her own books to her bag. "We'll be having our half-year examinations after Christmas holidays, and that's not very far away. It seems like we've had so many holidays—and now this unexpected time out."

"We're lucky Grandmother lives right here in town," Mandie said. "All we have to do is wait for Uncle Cal to take us. And just think, we'll have a little extra time to work on the mystery."

"We won't have Joe to help us, though," Celia reminded her.

Mandie flopped down on the bed. "Well," she said, "as long as Grandmother lets Ben go with us, we can try to solve something."

"Miss Prudence told us to take our things down to the front hall, remember?" Celia prompted.

Mandie jumped up and grabbed two bags. "We'll have to make two trips," she said.

"If we put our coats and bonnets on, we won't have to carry them, and we'll have two hands free to carry the bags," Celia suggested.

"You're right," Mandie laughed. "I'm in such a hurry, I'm not thinking right."

After putting on their coats and bonnets, the girls picked up two large bags each. They made their way down the stairs to the alcove in the front hallway. Just as they sat down to watch out the window for Uncle Cal, they saw him bringing the rig up the driveway. They grabbed their bags and went outside to meet him.

"Uncle Cal, I sure hope you and Aunt Phoebe don't get that flu," Mandie told the old man.

"I do, too, Missy Manda," he replied, putting the bags in the rig. "We'se too old to git dat kind of sickness. Might be bad. Old people die easier than you young ones."

"Please be real careful, and stay away from the sick ones as much as you can," she said, as she and Celia stepped into the rig.

"We has to he'p, Missy Manda," Uncle Cal said, picking up the reins. "Dat's whut we be heah fo'. Sick folks gotta have he'p, too."

"Maybe Dr. Woodard will come to town and help doctor the sick ones," Mandie said. "Hilda is real sick, according to the note I got from Grandmother yesterday, so he'll probably come back to see her."

True to her prediction, the next day, as Mandie and Celia sat looking out Mrs. Taft's parlor window, Dr. Woodard pulled his buggy up into the front driveway. The girls jumped up and ran to the front door to greet him.

Mandie opened the door. "Oh, Joe!" Mandie exclaimed. "How did you manage to come, too?"

Dr. Woodard followed his son into the front hallway as they exchanged greetings and removed their coats and hats.

"The Swain County schools closed today," Joe explained. "The flu hasn't reached that far yet, but they hope that by closing the schools it won't spread as far if someone comes down with it."

Mrs. Taft came into the hall to greet them. "Do come into the parlor to warm yourself before you go up to see Hilda," Mrs. Taft said to Dr. Woodard.

Joe followed the others into the parlor. Making his way with his father over to the hearth where the fire was blazing, he rubbed his hands together to warm up.

Snowball, curled up asleep on the rug, opened one eye to see who was invading his place at the hearth, then dozed off again.

Mandie sat on a stool near the hearth and looked up

at Dr. Woodard. "Our school is closed temporarily, too," she said. "About half of the girls have come down with the flu."

"I'm glad of that," the doctor replied, turning to warm his back in front of the fire. "Maybe it won't spread anymore."

Mrs. Taft sat down on the settee. "Did you know how bad the epidemic was here?" she asked.

"That's why I came to Asheville," the doctor replied. "To see what I could do to help the local doctors. We're lucky in Swain County. We don't have a single case yet."

"What about in Franklin?" Mandie asked, a little worried. "Is there any flu there?"

"Not that I know of, Amanda," Dr. Woodard replied. "I don't think you have to be concerned about your mother and your Uncle John. The flu all seems to be centered right here in Asheville."

"The newspaper says people are blaming it on the goings-on down at the church," Mrs. Taft told him, "as if that could bring on an epidemic."

"People can get some funny ideas sometimes when they can't figure out what's going on," Dr. Woodard said, sitting down in an armchair nearby.

"We're going to solve the mystery," Mandie announced. "Then they'll know how crazy their idea is."

Mrs. Taft looked at her granddaughter and smiled. "I certainly hope y'all can put an end to whatever's going on, Amanda," she said, "but I think it will take some doing."

Dr. Woodard went upstairs to see Hilda. He returned a short time later, shaking his head. "She's just about the same," he reported. "The nurse said she has been able to force a few spoonfuls of broth down Hilda's throat now and then, and she has been taking water, but she seems to just lie there, unaware of what's going on around her."

The young people planned to go to the church the

next morning. But it didn't work out that way.

Mandie and Celia woke early when Annie crept into the room. Trying not to disturb them, she started a fire in the fireplace. The girls, half asleep, lay there silently until Annie had left and the fire began to warm the room.

"Today's an important day," Mandie told her friend. "Let's get dressed and go downstairs. Joe may be already eating breakfast. He's always so hungry." Jumping out of bed, she reached for her clothes.

Celia stretched for a moment, then followed.

Snowball, who was curled up at the foot of the bed, leaped down to the floor to avoid being covered by the bedclothes the girls threw back. Finding a nice warm place by the fire, he curled up to go back to sleep.

Mandie laughed. "Look at Snowball," she said. "He doesn't want to get up."

"I didn't either," Celia remarked as she hastened into her clothes. "It was so warm in that bed."

When they finished dressing, the girls hurried quietly down the stairs to the breakfast room. Joe was already there, sitting at the table with a huge plate of food in front of him. But what caught their attention was the fact that the opened curtains displayed a heavy downfall of snow.

"Oh, no!" Mandie cried, rushing to look out the window.

"Oh, yes," Joe replied. "It's probably a foot deep out there already, and it just keeps coming."

Celia stood beside Mandie, surveying the white-blanketed outdoors. "We can't go out in that," she moaned.

Mandie turned away from the window to the sideboard where platters of food awaited them. "Maybe Grandmother will let us go out for a little while," she said, helping herself to the food.

"I'm pretty positive she won't," Joe disagreed, hastily eating his food. "She'll be afraid you'll get sick if you roam around in all that snow. Besides, the roads would have to be cleared off before Ben could get the rig through."

When the girls had filled their plates, they joined Joe at the table.

"What about your father?" Mandie asked. "Will he be able to get out to see the sick people?"

"He always does," Joe said. "With all the snow we have in Swain County, he knows how to manage. He leaves the buggy at home and rides his horse. That horse is used to snow, and it's easier to get around on horseback than it is to drive a buggy."

"That's an idea," Mandie said, looking up at the others. "Maybe we could ride some of Grandmother's horses to the church."

Joe looked doubtful. "I'd say that as long as it's snowing, you might as well be content to sit here in the house," he told her. "Your grandmother won't let you go out."

Joe was right. Mrs. Taft firmly told the young people there would be no traipsing around in the snow outside. She didn't want them to get sick. And they could fall and have an accident. She was responsible for Celia, too.

Dr. Woodard strapped his medical bag onto the saddle he borrowed from Mrs. Taft for his horse and carefully made his way around town visiting sick people.

The next day, which was Saturday, was still snowy and cold. The newspaper reported a long list of deaths caused by the flu epidemic. Complaints about the mysterious goings-on at the church filled the paper. People blamed the church for the town's bad luck—first the flu and now the terrible snowstorm. Some even dared suggest that the church be torn down if the members couldn't solve its troubles.

It continued to snow and snow. More and more people continued to fall ill. The young people sat in the house, fussing because they couldn't get at the mystery. Early Sunday, the snow quit, but it was almost waist-deep in places. People were out early trying to shovel the snow off the main streets in town because there were no city employees to do such a job.

One of the preacher's farmhands came by Mrs. Taft's house with the message that Rev. Tallant had come down with the flu, and there would be no service at the church that morning. The church would be unlocked, he said, for anyone wanting to go there and pray, but there would be no service. The young people stood in the kitchen listening as the man talked to Mrs. Taft and drank hot coffee.

As soon as the man left, Mandie asked her grand-mother, "Could we all just go to the church, anyway, this morning?"

"Amanda, you can pray here at the house as well as you can at the church," Mrs. Taft told her.

"It's a shame that we let the weather keep us away from the Lord's house," Mandie replied.

"Amanda!" Mrs. Taft scolded. "That's only your attempt to get at the mystery."

Dr. Woodard came through the back door, stomping his feet. He unbuttoned his heavy coat. "Cold out there!" he announced, removing his coat.

"Hurry on in to the fire in the parlor," Mrs. Taft invited, "and I'll get Ella to bring you some hot coffee."

"Did you get through the roads all right?" Mandie asked eagerly.

"Well, yes, the roads are pretty clear," Dr. Woodard said. "And I noticed Ben has even cleared the driveway here. But the snow is piled up higher than my head along the sides of the road. It really snowed!"

Mandie followed her grandmother and the doctor to the parlor as Celia and Joe tagged along behind.

As the adults took chairs by the fire, Mandie sat on a stool nearby. "Grandmother," she said, "Dr. Woodard says the roads are clear. Couldn't we go to the church for a little while? Please?"

"There's no service this morning," Dr. Woodard told her. "I've just been to Reverend Tallant's. He's a sick man."

"We got that message a little while ago," Mrs. Taft said. She looked over at Mandie. "I suppose you may go if Ben goes with you all and stays right by your side. But you must promise to be gone no longer than two hours. We'll be having dinner in a little over two hours."

"I promise," Mandie said quickly. "Thank you, Grandmother."

"Thank you, Mrs. Taft," Celia echoed.

Joe stood next to his father. "Do I have permission to go, too?" he asked.

Dr. Woodard looked at the young people's happy faces. "I suppose so," he said, "but remember what Mrs. Taft told you. Stay right with Ben, and be back within two hours."

The young people hastily grabbed their coats and hats and boots. They had no idea what they would do at the church, but they were eager to get there and look around.

This time Ben stayed with them. Inside the church, he stopped at the back of the sanctuary and looked around.

There was nobody else in the church. Evidently no one had come to pray. The young people searched the church. Ben held his breath as Mandie and Joe scaled the rope ladder to the belfry.

"Lawsy, Missy!" Ben gasped. "Miz Taft'll skin you alive if she ketch you a-doin' dat."

Halfway up the ladder, Mandie called down to him. "She probably did the same thing when she was young."

When they came back down, Ben followed them back into the sanctuary.

"Let's go down into the basement," Mandie suggested.

Ben took a seat in the back pew. "I stays right heah

and watch de front do'," he said. "I lets you know if'n somebody come in dis time."

"That's a good idea, Ben," Mandie called back to the Negro driver as she and the others headed for the basement.

There was no disturbance of any kind down there and no sign of anyone else being around.

The bells started ringing. The young people stopped to count, then ran through the church and up to the belfry. As they got there, the bells gave one last ring.

"It's eleven o'clock," Celia said, following Joe and Mandie to the rope ladder. "And the bells rang twelve."

They again went up into the belfry but could find no sign of anyone having been there.

"Guess we might as well go back to your grandmother's house," Joe said.

"I suppose so," Mandie agreed. "I was hoping we'd find something else here."

In the meantime, Ben, sitting on the back pew, stretched out his long legs to get comfortable and maybe take a nap. The toe of his boot caught in a loose thread in the edge of the carpet runner that ran the length of the pew. The rug was tacked to the floor and he reached down to disentangle his shoe.

"Now whutdat?" the Negro man mumbled to himself, as he felt a lump under the carpet where it had come loose.

He withdrew his boot from the thread and felt along the carpet. Poking under it with one finger he pushed out an old dirty key. Picking it up, he examined it, but he didn't know how to read and there was some kind of writing on the key.

"Oh, well," he said to himself, tossing the key in the air and then putting it in his pocket.

He stretched his legs back out, careful not to disturb the loose carpet. But the young people were there before he had a chance to take a nap.

"We're ready to go, Ben," Mandie told him as they picked up their coats and hats. "We haven't found a thing."

Ben stood up. "Dem bars on dat window, is dey still pulled off?" he asked.

"They're still off," Mandie replied. "Grandmother promised to pay for the damages we did, but she hasn't had time yet to get them fixed, I suppose."

"I s'pose somebody could be comin' and goin' through dat window whilst dem bars ain't on it," Ben told them.

The young people looked at each other.

"You're right, Ben," Joe agreed. "It would be easy to open that spring latch on the window with a knife and then close it back. No one would know it was ever open."

"Well, we can't just sit down there by that window waiting for someone to come in," Celia argued.

"We'll do that later," Mandie said. "Right now, we have to keep our promise to Grandmother and get back."

When the young people returned to Mrs. Taft's house, the place was in an uproar.

Hilda was missing! The house was being searched thoroughly for the girl.

"What happened, Grandmother?" Mandie asked anxiously.

"It seems that the nurse dozed off because she had been on duty since Friday night. The nurse who was to relieve her was unable to get through the snow," Mrs. Taft explained. "When the nurse woke up a while ago, Hilda was gone."

"How long has she been missing?" Joe asked.

"We don't know," Mrs. Taft replied. "The nurse said she must have dozed off some time before daylight, and she didn't wake up until a few minutes ago."

"Oh, please don't let any harm come to Hilda!" Mandie prayed, looking upward as she talked to God.

The young people quickly joined in the search. Every crack and corner of the huge mansion was looked into. Every inch of the grounds and the outbuildings was searched. Hilda was nowhere to be found.

"I don't understand how she got away in the weak condition she's in," Dr. Woodard declared as they all gathered in the parlor. "This could be serious for her, I'm afraid."

The townspeople quickly heard about the missing girl and came to join the search. Hours passed. There was no trace of Hilda anywhere!

Chapter 9 / Discovery in the Belfry

After going over Mrs. Taft's entire estate without finding Hilda, the search party fanned out all across town.

It was not snowing, but the high drifts, bitter cold temperatures, and strong north wind made things more difficult. Everyone was worried about the condition of Hilda's health.

Mrs. Taft allowed Mandie, Celia, and Joe to go with Ben in the rig to help look for Hilda. They knocked on doors and got permission to search people's yards and outbuildings. As they worked their way through the streets, they found themselves near the church about dusk.

"Ben, let's go look around the church and the grounds while we're this close," Mandie suggested.

"Whatever you says, Missy," Ben agreed, turning the horses in that direction.

"Do you think she could have got this far away from your grandmother's house?" Joe asked.

"Maybe," Mandie replied. "Somebody could have given her a ride in their rig or something."

"If she got a ride, there's no telling where in the world she could be by now," Celia reasoned.

Ben stopped the rig in front of the church. "I jes' stay right heah and waits fo' y'all," he said.

"Oh, no, Ben," Mandie protested as she and the others stepped down from the rig. "Grandmother told you that you were to stay right along with us wherever we go, remember?"

"Yessum," Ben grumbled, as he reluctantly followed them up the steps.

As soon as Joe opened the door, they all felt a great warmth from inside the church. They looked around. Someone had built roaring fires in both the big stoves in the sanctuary.

"I wonder why anyone would want to build fires in here today when there's no church service," Mandie said. "It couldn't have been the sexton. He knew Rev. Tallant wouldn't be here today."

Joe shrugged. "I'm not surprised at anything that goes on in this church now," he said.

"Maybe someone came here to pray, and got cold, and decided to build the fires," Celia suggested.

Ben plopped down in the back pew. "Now, y'all go ahaid and do whatever it is you gwine do," he said. "I sits right heah."

"Well, all right," Mandie said. "We're going to search the church for Hilda. If anyone comes in or goes out, yell for us."

"I will, Missy," Ben promised. He stretched his long legs out to get comfortable as he slid down a little in the seat.

"Upstairs first," Joe suggested, leading the way to the gallery.

They looked carefully in every place where someone could possibly hide. By this time they knew every nook and cranny of the building.

Joe skimmed the ladder into the belfry. "Nothing up here," he called down to the girls.

"It seems that we never find anyone here, but we always find signs of someone having been here," Celia remarked.

"We'll catch up with someone sometime. We've got to," Mandie said. "It's impossible for anyone to keep on doing things here and not be caught."

Joe slid down the ladder, and they went back downstairs. Making their way down the side aisle, they went through the door to the classrooms.

"We can go faster if we split up," Joe told them. "You girls take the rooms on that side, and I'll go down this side."

When they found nothing there, they went on downstairs to the basement. But a quick search of all the classrooms there revealed nothing.

"I guess we'd better get going," Joe said, looking around the hallway. "We've covered the whole church except for the pastor's study, and it's still locked."

"Let's go outside and look around the grounds," Mandie suggested.

When they got back to the sanctuary, Ben had nodded off. They all laughed.

Suddenly Mandie heard something. "What was that?" she whispered, looking around quickly.

"Sounded like something moving," Joe said softly.

"It wasn't very loud, whatever it was," Celia observed.

Moving over to the center aisle, they looked around and then started up the aisle. The two big stoves standing in the middle aisle still roared away with their fires.

As they started to walk by the first stove, Mandie glanced down to the right. "Look!" she exclaimed, stooping between the pews.

Joe and Celia huddled behind her to see. There lay Hilda, all wrapped up in choir robes and a small rug.

"Hilda! Hilda!" Mandie cried, smoothing back the girl's tangled dark brown hair.

Hilda didn't move. She looked as though she were soundly asleep.

"Is she—is she—all right?" Celia asked nervously.

Joe bent down and reached for the girl's wrist. "She's alive, but just barely, I believe," he said. "And she does have a terrible fever."

"Ben! Come quick!" Mandie yelled.

Startled, Ben jumped to his feet. "Yessum, yessum, Missy," he answered. Rubbing his eyes, he quickly looked around.

"Down here, Ben," Joe called to him.

Ben hurriedly joined them and gasped when he saw Hilda lying there, so flushed and motionless.

"Quick, Ben," Joe said. "Help me get Hilda into the rig. We've got to get her back to Mrs. Taft's house and into bed fast!"

"Oh, dear Lord," Mandie prayed, "please let Dr. Woodard be there when we get back."

As Joe and Ben picked up Hilda—robes, rug, and all—the girl started mumbling with her eyes closed. "God has come," she said in a whisper. "God has come!"

Tears came to Mandie's eyes. "She's still able to speak," she cried.

The girls followed as Ben and Joe carried Hilda outside and carefully tucked her into the rig.

"This time I give you permission to drive as fast as you can," Mandie told Ben.

"Cain't go too fast, Missy," Ben replied, picking up the reins. "It be slicky on de road 'cause of de snow."

In spite of the roads, however, Ben did manage to get up some speed, and soon pulled up in Mrs. Taft's driveway.

Mandie jumped down and ran to the house. "Grandmother!" she yelled, pounding on the door.

Ella quickly opened the door, and Mandie ran right past her. "Grandmother!" she screamed. "Dr. Woodard! Come quick. We've found Hilda!"

Mrs. Taft and Dr. Woodard hurried into the hall from the parlor just as Ben and Joe were carrying Hilda into the house. Dr. Woodard directed them upstairs, and the nurse who was still there tucked the girl into bed. The young people excitedly explained where they had found her.

Mrs. Taft and Dr. Woodard listened in amazement. Then Dr. Woodard sent everyone out of the room so that he and the nurse could tend to Hilda.

"We might as well go downstairs to the parlor by the fire," Mrs. Taft told the young people. "And you still haven't even taken off your coats and hats."

The young people followed Mrs. Taft down the stairs, unbuttoning as they went. In the front hallway, they hung their coats on the hall tree, then headed into the parlor.

"At least one trip to the church did some good," Mandie remarked as they pulled stools up in front of the fire.

Snowball, who was sleeping on the rug, stretched, stood up, and jumped into his mistress's lap.

Mrs. Taft sat down in an armchair. "I can't imagine how Hilda got there," she said. "And who could have built those fires and wrapped her up in all those things?"

"Someone must have," Mandie answered. "I don't think she could have."

"I hope she's going to be all right," Celia said.

"My father will do all he can. You know that," Joe assured her. "Maybe that warm fire and all those things covering her helped."

"Grandmother," Mandie said. "Hilda kept whispering, 'God has come. God has come.' She didn't open her eyes, and she didn't even seem to know she was being moved."

"She's running a high fever, and I'm sure she's delirious, dear," Mrs. Taft explained. "We'll just have to wait for Dr. Woodard to come back down and tell us how she is."

After a while the doctor joined them in the parlor.

"She's really sick," he said. "She seems to be out of her head completely."

"Let's pray for her," Mandie suggested. "God can heal her."

After they had all prayed for Hilda's recovery, they sat talking in the parlor. Dr. Woodard made repeated trips upstairs to check on the girl.

Mrs. Taft asked Annie, the upstairs maid, to relieve the nurse if she had to leave Hilda's room for any reason. She also instructed the nurse to check all the windows in Hilda's room to be sure they were locked and all the draperies drawn.

The young people talked with Mandie's grandmother long into the night. They still had no real clues in the bell mystery, and now they had Hilda to worry about. They even wondered if there could be any connection between Hilda's running away and the mysterious goings-on in the church, though it didn't seem possible.

There was no change in Hilda's condition that evening. Everybody finally got so sleepy that Mrs. Taft ordered them all to bed. Dr. Woodard promised to sleep in the room across the hall from Hilda's so he would be close in case of an emergency.

Mandie felt as though she had just gone to bed when she heard Annie steal softly into the room where she and Celia were sleeping.

As Annie knelt at the fireplace arranging the kindling for the fire, Mandie sat up and pulled the covers around her. "How is Hilda, Annie?" she asked.

Celia woke and accidentally kicked Snowball, who was sleeping at their feet on top of the quilt.

"Still de same," Annie replied. "I'se jes' been in de room to tend to de fire, and she jes' layin' still. Ain't movin' at all."

Celia sat up beside Mandie in the bed. "At least she isn't any worse then," she said.

Annie moved backward a little and fanned the fire with her big white apron to get it going.

Snowball stretched and yawned, then jumped down to take his place by the warm hearth.

Annie started to leave the room. "Yo' grandma and de doctuh, dey be in de breakfus' room," Annie informed them.

"Joe isn't up yet?" Mandie asked.

"Ain't seen him," Annie replied. "I gotta git his fire goin' now." She went out the door.

Mandie jumped out of bed. "Come on. Let's get dressed," she said. Celia followed.

The two girls shivered a little in the cold room. They quickly grabbed their clothes and stood in front of the fire to get dressed.

Snowball followed them downstairs to the breakfast room. Joe was already there.

As they went to the sideboard, Mandie whispered to Celia, "It takes a girl longer to get dressed than it does a boy."

Celia smiled.

The girls were glad to see the sun shining brightly through the windows where the curtains were pulled back. After exchanging morning greetings with Joe and the adults, Mandie and Celia filled their plates and joined the others at the table.

"I was just in to see Hilda before I came downstairs," Dr. Woodard reported, "and I'm afraid she's still not doing well at all."

The conversation turned to how the young people had found her at the church and questions about the whole puzzling situation.

"Grandmother, could we go back to the church this morning?" Mandie asked. "I'd like to see if the fire's burned out and if there's any sign of anyone there."

Mrs. Taft smiled at her granddaughter. "Amanda, you

visit that church more than you visit with me," she said. "But then, I was the one who got you started in all this tomfoolery. I guess it would be all right for you to go as long as Ben goes with you."

"Thanks, Grandmother," Mandie replied.

"I suppose your school will send someone to let us know when they open back up," Mrs. Taft said.

"I don't believe they'll open up again any time soon. All the girls who didn't go home are sick in bed now," Dr. Woodard said. "I was there yesterday, and the only ones walking around were Miss Hope and Miss Prudence."

"What about Uncle Cal and Aunt Phoebe?" Mandie asked quickly.

"Oh, yes, they're all right," the doctor said.

"Well, I guess we'll have a little longer, then," Celia said.

"But we'd better use what time we have, or we'll never get this mystery solved," Joe reminded them. "You know, I have to leave when my father does."

"That won't be for some time yet son," Dr. Woodard said. "I'd say about two-thirds of the town is down with the flu."

"You young people be sure to wrap up good and wear your boots," Mrs. Taft cautioned them. "I don't want y'all getting sick."

As soon as they finished their breakfast, the young people hurried to the front hallway and put on their coats and hats. Snowball followed them and sat on the arm of the coat tree, watching.

Mandie picked him up. "I'm going to take Snowball with me this time," she decided. "He needs some fresh air."

"I sure hope he doesn't run away," Joe said warily.

Snowball seemed to be thankful to his mistress for allowing him to go. He stayed on her lap in the rig and then clung to her shoulder when they got to the church.

Inside the sanctuary, both stoves were cold. The fires had long since gone out.

Ben dropped into the back pew for his usual nap while the young people looked around. They left their coats and hats on a pew near him.

They checked all the basement classrooms and found nothing there. Then they went up into the gallery and opened the door to the belfry.

"I have an idea," Mandie said, balancing Snowball on her shoulder. "Why don't we all go up into the belfry and just stay there a while? If we're real quiet, we'll be able to hear anything that goes on, and we can watch out the windows up there for anyone coming in or out of the church."

"That's a good idea," Joe said, reaching for the rope ladder. "I'll go first. Then you come next, Celia, so I can help you off at the top. Mandie has done it so much, I don't think she needs any help."

"Well—" Celia hesitated. "I suppose I can go up if that ladder doesn't swing too much."

"I'll hold on to it by the last rung down here to steady it," Mandie promised.

Celia nodded, and Joe scrambled up the ladder, waiting at the top while Celia slowly and cautiously made her way up and Mandie held the bottom rung.

"Just don't look down, Celia," Mandie reminded her. "Keep looking up at Joe."

Celia was shaking so badly that she didn't answer. When she finally got to the top rung, Joe took her hands and swung her up into the belfry. She sat down on the floor quickly. "Oh, my legs feel weak," she gasped.

Mandie hurried after her with Snowball clinging to her shoulder. About halfway up, the kitten looked down and dug his claws into the shoulder of Mandie's heavy dress. Suddenly, he jumped off her shoulder onto the rope ladder and clawed his way up by himself. At the top, he jumped into the belfry and landed at Celia's feet.

Celia laughed nervously. "I guess I'm not the only one who is afraid of that ladder," she said, cuddling the kitten.

"Let's walk around and look outside," Mandie said as she reached the top.

Just then the bells began ringing. The three young people instantly covered their ears at the deafening sound and began counting the rings. Snowball darted about in fear.

"Eleven rings," Mandie said, uncovering her ears. "But it's ten o'clock." She reached down to pick up Snowball.

"And we stood right here watching," Joe said with a puzzled look on his face. "We know that no one else was up here ringing those bells."

Celia made her way over to the walkway around the belfry. "I thought we were going to watch outside," she said.

"We are," Mandie agreed. "I'll go over on this side, and Joe, you take that side over there. There are only three of us, and there are four sides to the steeple, but we can all watch the side where the ladder is."

They did as Mandie suggested. As Joe made his way to the other side, Snowball ran ahead of him and into an almost invisible thread of some kind. It broke.

"Look!" Joe cried, stooping to inspect the thread.

Mandie and Celia watched as he traced the piece of thread to the mechanism of the huge clock. He pulled at it, and it came free, holding a tiny magnet on the end. The girls joined him and all three excitedly examined it. At last they had a clue!

"Someone must have put that magnet on the clock to mess up the mechanism, but where did the string go from there?" Mandie asked, looking around for the other end.

They searched and searched but could not find the

other piece of thread. Nor could they figure out where it had been attached. Finally they sat down on the floor, and Snowball curled up in Mandie's lap.

"Let's just have a quiet thinking session for a few minutes," Mandie suggested.

They all became silent and did not move. Even Snowball sat quietly, content in his mistress's company.

"Why didn't we find this thread before when we were up here, and why didn't all those people who examined the clock mechanism find the magnet before?" Celia asked.

"Maybe whoever put it there took it down whenever they heard somebody coming," Mandie reasoned. "But where could they be hiding?"

They were silent again.

Mandie's sharp eyes caught the slight movement of a panel in the wall. At first she thought she was seeing things, but as the panel moved, she got a quick glimpse of a pair of eyes staring right at her. She caught her breath and froze.

Joe and Celia looked toward the wall to see what had startled her.

Instantly, Joe jumped up and grabbed the moving panel. "Come on out, whoever you are!" he demanded, yanking at the piece of wood.

The girls jumped up to help. Snowball scrambled onto the floor. Joe reached behind the panel and grabbed hold of someone's shoulder.

At first the person struggled, but then he gave up. "I'm coming out," said a man's voice.

"All right. Then get out fast," Joe ordered, still holding on to the panel of wood to keep it from being pushed back into place.

Slowly, from behind the paneling, a little, old, gray-looking man appeared. He fell on his knees in front of the three young people. "I'm sorry, so sorry!" he muttered.

Chapter 10 / Phineas Prattworthy

The three young people stared in amazement at the gray-haired man before them. He was clean and neatly dressed, but his coat was threadbare.

"Who are you?" Joe demanded.

"Are you the one who has been making the bells ring wrong and doing all those other things around this church?" Mandie asked, putting her hands on her hips.

The old man cowered in front of them.

"Get up," Joe demanded. "We're not going to hurt you."

The man didn't obey. Joe got hold of his shoulders and pushed him backwards so they could see his face. The man was frightened.

He had bushy gray hair, bushy gray eyebrows, a long, thin face, a long nose and a wide mouth with thin lips. His ears stuck out instead of being flat against his head. He looked to be very old and very starved. He blinked at the three of them as tears came into his gray eyes.

"How did you get behind that paneling?" Mandie asked.

"I think you'd better give us some explanations real fast," Joe told the man.

The man's lips quivered as he tried to speak.

Mandie began to feel sorry for him. "Why don't we all sit down and talk," she suggested.

The young people sat down on the floor in front of the stranger who was still on his knees.

"I-I need someone to help me," the man said uncertainly.

"Help you do what?" Mandie asked as Snowball climbed into her lap.

"I am in great trouble that is not my fault," the man replied, clasping his hands tightly.

"I'll say you're in trouble," Joe said. "Just wait until the town gets hold of you."

Mandie looked at Joe with a frown. Then she looked back at the stranger. "Why have you been messing with the bells and doing all those other things?" she asked. "You *are* the one responsible for the *help* banner on the altar, and the writing on the church wall, aren't you?"

"And tearing up the paneling to hide behind," Celia added.

"I'm sorry. I'm sorry," the man said, hanging his head. "What else can I say?"

"Who are you, and where do you live?" Joe asked.

"My name is Phineas Prattworthy," the stranger replied, choking back the tears. "I live way out yonder over the mountain."

"Then why are you hanging around the church? What are you trying to do?" Joe sounded exasperated.

"I can only explain if you promise to help me," Phineas replied.

"We can't promise to help you until we know what you've done," Mandie said.

"But I didn't do what they think I did," Phineas told them, his eyes still wet with tears. "I have been wrongly accused."

Mandie leaned forward and asked, "Accused of what?"

"The grocer down on Main Street thinks I stole some groceries from him," Phineas replied. "But I didn't. I saw the man who did it, though. He came out of the store so fast that he dropped an apple. I picked it up, and when the grocer saw me with it in my hand, he thought I was the man who stole it, but I got away before he could catch me."

"That wasn't very smart," Joe said, shaking his head. "Why didn't you just explain to the grocer what happened?"

"I tried to, but he wouldn't listen. He didn't believe a thing I said," Phineas explained.

"So you came here to this church and started doing all these crazy things?" Joe asked. "Why?"

"I was only trying to get help," Phineas said. "I waited and waited, hoping to attract someone who looked like they would help me, but no one came along who looked trustworthy." He sniffed. "This church is the only place I could find to hide in, out of the cold."

Mandie's heart went out to the man at the thought of him being so hungry and cold. "If you live over on the mountain, why didn't you just go back home?" she asked.

"I lived with my son, and he died last month," Phineas explained. "I don't have any way to make a living. We don't own the house, and with my son gone, there was no one to pay the rent or buy groceries." Nervously, he rubbed the side of his long, thin face. "I'm not begging, mind you. I'd starve to death before I'd beg for something to eat. I'm only asking for someone to help me straighten out this matter with the grocer."

Mandie reached out and took the man's hand. "Mr. Phineas, we'll help you," she promised. "I believe what you've told us. We'll see that you have a warm place to stay and some food to eat."

"Mandie!" Joe exclaimed. "You can't make promises like that. We don't know this man. We'll have to check out his story."

"But he's hungry, Joe," Celia defended Mandie's decision.

"We can at least take him home to Grandmother and let her help us decide what should be done," Mandie said.

"All right. If you insist," Joe said. "But I've still got a lot of questions." He looked directly at Phineas. "How did you get behind that paneling?"

"I worked a piece loose one day and then found that I could slide down through the wall opening into the attic," the man explained.

"Attic?" Mandie's eyes grew wide. "Does this church have an attic?"

"It certainly does," Phineas replied. "That's where I left my bag."

"We didn't find any attic," Celia remarked.

"The only other way you can get into it is through the scuttle hole in the ceiling of the gallery," Phineas told them.

"So that's why we could never catch up with you," Mandie reasoned. "You hid in the attic."

The man nodded. "I saw and heard you three come into the church several times. One time I was in such a hurry to get through the paneling I fell all the way through to the attic. It made such a noise and everything shook so, I just knew you girls would find me that day."

The three people quickly looked at each other.

"So that solves that mystery," Mandie said, with a sigh. "And I suppose you wrote on the wall at the back of the church, too."

"I used whitewash which was supposed to be removable but I couldn't wash it off. It just got all blurred instead," Phineas said.

"And you put the magnet on the clock, too, I suppose," Joe said.

"You see, I used to be in the clock business long years ago. I knew I could control the mechanism with a magnet and I could withdraw it whenever I wanted to. I figured someone would come investigating the bells ringing and maybe they could help me but, like I said, I haven't seen anyone who looked trustworthy," Phineas explained with a sigh.

"And you locked us in the basement and then unlocked the door later. And you put that 'Help' banner on the altar and then took it away. Why did you do things and then reverse what you did?" Mandie asked.

"I guess I just had a guilty conscience," the old man said. "I needed help but I decided the altar was not the place to put such a thing so I took it away. And I had been outside the church and didn't realize y'all were in the basement when I locked that door. Then I heard you down there and had to come back and unlock it."

"Well, why were you locking the basement door anyhow?" Celia asked.

"I had thought I could sleep in the pastor's study on his settee that night and I wanted to be sure the basement was locked off in case anyone came prowling around. Then I found out the pastor's door was locked after all," Phineas said. "I hope you will all forgive me."

"But if you've been here hiding all this time, how could you live without any food?" Joe asked.

"Well, to begin with, I had the apple that man dropped, and then I had to look in trash cans," he told them.

Mandie and Celia cringed.

"The restaurant down on Patton Avenue throws out a lot of good food," he explained. "When I discovered that, I just went behind their building whenever I got hungry and helped myself. I don't eat much anyway."

Tears clouded Mandie's eyes to think of this poor man having to eat out of trash cans! She jumped up, dumping Snowball onto the floor, and grabbed the man's hand to help him up. "Come on," she said. "We're going to my grandmother's."

Joe looked at her with concern. "If you say so," he said.

Phineas seemed to have a bad leg. He was limping.

"Can you get down the rope ladder?" Mandie asked.

"Oh, sure," he answered. "All I have to do is slide."

"I'll go first," Joe offered. He still didn't trust the stranger.

Celia went down next, then Phineas.

As Mandie followed, Snowball fought against going down the ladder. He kept jumping off Mandie's shoulder into the belfry. After three tries, Mandie gave him a little swat and said, "Now you look here, Snowball! We are going down that ladder, and you might as well behave!"

Joe, watching the scene from below, climbed halfway up the ladder and reached for the kitten. "Give him to me," he told Mandie. "I can slide down with one hand."

Snowball squealed with anger as Joe grabbed him and held him tightly in one hand while he made his way down with the other. The kitten squirmed and tried to scratch as Joe landed below.

Mandie jumped off at the bottom and reached for the kitten. "Thanks, Joe," she said.

"Watch out," he warned her. "This cat is mad, and he's trying to scratch."

Mandie held the kitten tightly in both hands. He hushed his loud meowing and cuddled in her arms.

Joe shook his head in disgust, and the young people and Phineas headed downstairs.

As they approached Ben in the sanctuary, the Negro man stood up, looked at the stranger and asked, "Who dat be whut y'all got dere?"

"This is who we've been looking for all this time," Joe answered. "He's the answer to the mystery."

Ben just stood there with his mouth open.

"Come on, Ben," Mandie said. "We're taking him home to Grandmother."

After they were all in the rig, Ben flicked the reins and coaxed the horses to a fast pace. When the Negro driver pulled the rig into Mrs. Taft's driveway, Phineas Prattworthy looked amazed.

"Your grandmother lives here?" he asked.

Mandie climbed down from the rig. "Yes, my grandmother is Mrs. Taft," Mandie explained. "Come on."

Phineas stepped down beside her. "I know who Mrs. Taft is," he said. "I had no idea you were talking about her when you mentioned your grandmother."

"You know her?" Mandie asked, petting Snowball.

The others got down from the rig and stood around, listening.

"I knew your grandfather, Mr. Taft," Phineas told her.

Joe urged them all to go into the house. "I'm cold and hungry," he complained.

Inside, they left their coats in the hallway and ushered Phineas into the parlor where Mrs. Taft sat reading by the fire. Snowball jumped down and ran off down the hallway. Mrs. Taft rose quickly and stared at the man.

Phineas spoke first. "How are you, Mrs. Taft?" he asked, nervously.

"Phineas!" Mrs. Taft exclaimed, hurrying over to greet the man. "It is Phineas, isn't it?"

"Yes, ma'am. I'm Phineas Prattworthy," he replied.

"Where in the world have you been all these years, and where did these young people meet up with you?" Mrs. Taft asked. "Please come and sit down."

Mandie and her friends sat down, speechless, on low stools in front of the fireplace.

Phineas took the chair opposite Mrs. Taft. "Well, I fell on some hard times after y'all left Franklin, and I came over to the mountains to live," he said. "The tax man took all my property."

"You mean you lost that great big beautiful home?" Mrs. Taft looked deeply concerned. "Oh, Phineas, how sad."

"My wife died suddenly with the fever right before we

had to vacate the property," Phineas continued.

"Phineas, I'm so sorry," Mrs. Taft said.

The man fidgeted nervously. "I just had one son, Paul, you know, so he and I rented a small farm up in the Nantahala Mountains. We couldn't make much of a living out of it, but we didn't starve," he said with a weak smile. "Then I had a stroke and was helpless for a long while. I'm not much good anymore. About the time I was beginning to walk again, Paul came down with the flu and died."

"I'm so sorry," Mrs. Taft said again. "But just saying I'm sorry won't help. What can I do for you?"

"Grandmother," Mandie jumped into the conversation, "we found Mr. Phineas hiding in the church. He's the one who has been messing up the bells and everything."

Mrs. Taft looked shocked. "Phineas! You were doing that?"

"Yes, ma'am," he replied. "I'm afraid I'm guilty."

As he retold the story, Mrs. Taft sat staring at him in amazement.

"I can't explain why I did all those strange things at the church," he said. "I just almost went crazy not knowing what to do to get somebody to help me."

"I just can't believe that anyone could accuse you of such a thing," Mrs. Taft exclaimed. "Well, we'll just have to get this all straightened out. I'm well acquainted with Mr. Simpson, the grocer, and I think he'll understand when we tell him the story."

Dr. Woodard joined the others in the parlor after having made rounds in town and checking on Hilda. "Phineas!" he exclaimed in surprise. "How did you get here? The last time I saw you was when I doctored you for that stroke—about a year ago, wasn't it?"

The story had to be told again, and Dr. Woodard listened attentively. When Phineas told the doctor that he didn't know why he did such strange things in the church,

Dr. Woodard looked thoughtful.

"There are a lot of things that can cause a person to behave abnormally," the doctor told him. "Losing your wife, your son, and your house, and having that stroke all in such a short period of time was a lot for a person to bear. And then being unjustly accused and malnourished and living without any heat in that church most of the time—it's no wonder something snapped."

"Then I'm not crazy?" Phineas asked.

"Not likely," Dr. Woodard replied. "I think once we get this thing cleared up and get you well fed and cared for, you'll be back to your old self again."

Mandie smiled at Joe and Celia, satisfied that she had done the right thing in bringing Phineas to see her grandmother.

"That grocer may give you a fight, though," Dr. Woodard added.

Mrs. Taft spoke. "I told Phineas we would get this all straightened out for him. We'll just go talk to Mr. Simpson."

"I'm afraid that won't work, Mrs. Taft," Phineas said. "I tried to talk to him, and he wouldn't listen at all. He has his mind made up and won't change it."

"We'll see that he changes it, won't we, Grandmother?" Mandie said.

"Yes, we will," Mrs. Taft said confidently. "We'll have something to eat in a little while, and then we'll just go visit Mr. Simpson."

Mandie turned to Dr. Woodard. "How is Hilda this morning, Doctor?" she asked.

"I was just upstairs when y'all came in," Dr. Woodard replied. "She is still just lying there. That bout in the snow and the church certainly didn't help her condition."

Mandie explained to Phineas. "Our friend Hilda ran away from here yesterday," she said. "She's a girl my grandmother has living with her. Hilda has been real sick with pneumonia, and then suddenly she disappeared out of her bed. We finally found her in the church late yesterday afternoon. Did you happen to see her?"

"That must be the girl I saw come into the church in her nightclothes," Phineas replied quickly. "She was mumbling something to herself and then lay down on the floor. I thought she went to sleep. I found some old choir robes in a box in the attic and a little rug that was behind the altar, and I tried to wrap her up."

"Are you the one who started the fires in the stoves, then?" Mandie asked.

"Yes," Phineas answered. "It was so cold in the church I was afraid she would die. Then I remembered seeing the woodpile out behind the church, so I just gathered in enough wood and got the stoves going to keep her warm."

"Oh, how can we thank you, Mr. Phineas! You probably saved Hilda's life," Mandie told him.

"Hilda's not right mentally, Phineas," he explained. "And she's always running off somewhere."

"I had no idea who she was, but she looked like she needed help," Phineas agreed.

"The Lord will bless you for your kindness, Phineas," Mrs. Taft said.

"Imagine that," Joe said with a little laugh. "He was the one who covered up Hilda and started the stoves. One more piece of the mystery solved."

Ella came in to announce that the noon meal was on the table.

After a leisurely meal, Mrs. Taft announced that she was going to visit Mr. Simpson, the grocer, and the young people could go with her if they wished.

Mandie, Celia, and Joe excitedly put on their wraps in the front hall.

"After a busy morning tending to the sick, I think I need a couple hours of rest," the doctor said. "And Phineas ought to stay here out of sight until we're sure Mr. Simpson won't cause trouble."

"I'll stay here and soak up some of that warmth from the fireplace if it's all right with you, Mrs. Taft," Phineas added.

Mrs. Taft agreed.

Ben drove the rig sedately down the streets of Asheville. With one hand he kept flipping the key he had found in the church. He had no idea as to what it unlocked, or who had lost it, but somehow the key fascinated him. When he got a chance he would ask Missy Manda to tell him what the writing on it said.

He pulled the rig up in front of Mr. Simpson's grocery store. Mrs. Taft asked him to wait there for them.

Inside the grocery store Mr. Simpson, an overweight, bald-headed man in his middle forties, came forward to greet Mrs. Taft.

"This is a pleasure, Mrs. Taft," he said. "What can I do for you today?"

"We seem to have a problem that I think you can help us with," she replied. Then she explained the situation with Phineas Prattworthy. "He isn't guilty," she concluded.

"Oh, Mrs. Taft, I beg your pardon, but he is," the grocer protested. "Why, he was in here not more than ten minutes ago, stealing canned beans. I saw him."

"Ten minutes ago?" Mandie spoke up. "Mr. Simpson, it couldn't have been Mr. Phineas. He has been with us at my grandmother's house for the last three hours at least."

"That's right," Mrs. Taft confirmed. "We just left him there with Dr. Woodard."

"Please tell me, what does this Phineas Prattworthy look like?" the grocer asked.

"He has a bad leg from a stroke about a year ago, and—" Mrs. Taft began.

"That's the one. He limped," the grocer interrupted.

"I'm sorry, Mrs. Taft, but if you don't bring him in, I'll have to ask the sheriff to come out to your house and get him."

"Oh no, you won't," Mrs. Taft replied angrily. "You are not going to have Phineas Prattworthy arrested—not while he's in my house."

Joe stepped forward. "Mr. Simpson, there is definitely a mistake here," he told the grocer. "Mr. Prattworthy did not steal from you. It must be someone who looks like him."

"I don't have to identify him," Mr. Simpson argued. "I know him by his limp, and he's a stranger in this town."

Several other customers in the store edged closer to listen to the conversation.

"You have caused Mr. Prattworthy much distress by your false accusations. Why, he had to hide in the church to keep you from putting him in jail," Mrs. Taft said.

"Yes, you told me he had been doing all that damage at the church—ringing the bells wrong and writing all over the walls," Mr. Simpson shot back. "That proves that the man is deranged."

The other customers gasped.

"Phineas Prattworthy is not deranged any more than you are, Mr. Simpson," Mrs. Taft snapped. "You drove him to do all those things."

"I can only say that unless you bring him down here first thing in the morning, I'll ask the sheriff to go to your house after him," Mr. Simpson threatened. "Now, I'm sorry, but I have customers to wait on."

"I'll get the best lawyer in the state and sue you for false accusations if you press any charges against Mr. Prattworthy," Mrs. Taft promised. She turned to go. "Just be sure you remember that, Mr. Simpson."

The young people followed Mrs. Taft back out to the rig. Mandie took her grandmother's hand. "You were great in there, Grandmother," she said with admiration. "You handled it just the way I'd have done."

Mrs. Taft smiled and patted Mandie's hand. "I know, Amanda, dear," she said, stepping up into the rig. "You're so much like I was when I was your age."

The young people climbed into the rig.

"Now what are we going to do?" Joe asked as Ben picked up the reins.

"We're going to find the *real* crook," Mrs. Taft replied.

"But how?" Celia asked.

"It was probably some poor farmer around here who didn't have any money to buy food," Mrs. Taft reasoned. "I don't know any other reason a person would steal food from a grocer. I'm not sure how we'll find him, but we will."

When they returned to Mrs. Taft's house, they found Dr. Woodard asleep on the settee in the parlor, but there was no sign of Phineas Prattworthy.

"Sh-h-h!" Mrs. Taft whispered. "The doctor needs his rest. Don't wake him."

After quickly checking the front part of the house, they still couldn't find Phineas.

Annie met them in the hallway and told them what had happened. "Dat man whut was heah," Annie began, "he say tell you, Miz Taft, he have to go find de crook. He say you unnerstand."

Mrs. Taft let out a big sigh. "Thank you, Annie," she said. "I know what he meant." Looking at the young people in disappointment, she said, "Now, why did he do that? The law may very well catch him if Mr. Simpson tells the sheriff who he thinks has been stealing from him. Oh, dear!"

"We'll just have to go find Phineas," Mandie said.

"I doubt that we could find him," Joe remarked. "He's pretty good at hiding."

Annie spoke up again. "Miz Taft," she said, "dat Injun man whut Missy know, he be in de sun room."

"Uncle Ned!" Mandie cried, hurrying to the sun room. "He'll help us find Phineas."

Chapter 11 / The Robber!

Uncle Ned, as always, agreed to help Mandie and her friends. He knew Phineas Prattworthy and he listened carefully as Mrs. Taft explained the whole story with occasional interruptions from Mandie, Joe, and Celia.

"Must help find," Uncle Ned said as Dr. Woodard came into the sun room.

"Yes, I agree," said Dr. Woodard. "After all, Hilda might have died from the cold if Phineas hadn't done what he did for her."

"But, Dr. Woodard, I don't think he's guilty anyway," Mandie remarked. "We can't let an innocent man be prosecuted."

"Of course not, Amanda," Dr. Woodard replied.

"We find," Uncle Ned assured them. "Go now."

"I know we will find him with you helping us, Uncle Ned," Mandie told the old Indian, as they sat in the warmth from the fireplace. "Grandmother, may we go with Uncle Ned?"

"Amanda I just don't know," Mrs. Taft replied. "Evidently there is a robber involved in this, and he could be dangerous."

"Please, Grandmother," Mandie begged. "We'll stay right with Uncle Ned," she promised.

"Well, I suppose so," Mrs. Taft said uncertainly.

"Thanks," Mandie said.

"May I go, too?" Joe asked his father.

"I suppose if you stay right with Uncle Ned, it'll be all right," Dr. Woodard agreed.

"Thanks Dad," Joe said, grinning.

Mrs. Taft looked at the old Indian. "I'll send Ben with y'all, too," she said. "He can help see that the young people don't get into any trouble."

Uncle Ned nodded in agreement.

"And be back before dark," Mrs. Taft said to the young people.

They all nodded as Uncle Ned motioned for them to go. "Must go while trail fresh," he said.

The young people bundled up and followed the old Indian through the snow with Ben bringing up the rear. Ben didn't seem very happy to be involved in the hunt.

Uncle Ned traced Phineas's tracks in the snow through the yard, into the back, across the surrounding property, and into the main road. There, the tracks disappeared. The snow had been shoveled from the dirt road, and dozens of wagon wheels, horses, and footprints had marked the road.

"Maybe he went back to the church," Mandie suggested.

"He could have," Joe agreed. "We didn't tell Mr. Simpson that he had been hiding in the church—just that he had been ringing the bells and doing all that other crazy stuff. I don't believe Mr. Simpson would look for him there."

Uncle Ned nodded. "We look," he said.

Inside the church, the young people led the way, explaining to Uncle Ned what had happened there. They took him up to the gallery and showed him the rope ladder to the belfry. The old Indian was as agile as the young people as he scaled the rope ladder. Ben refused to go up.

In the belfry, Joe showed Uncle Ned the loose paneling.

"He said he hid in the attic, remember?" Mandie reminded Celia and Joe. "We never did go into the attic. Maybe he's there now."

"How can we get into the attic?" Celia asked nervously.

"He told us he could slide down through the wall behind this loose paneling into the attic," Joe said, shaking the panel in the wall.

Uncle Ned stood there looking and listening. "No other way?" he asked.

"Well, yes. He said there's a scuttle hole in the ceiling of the gallery," Mandie recalled.

"We see." Uncle Ned went back down the rope ladder, and the young people followed.

When they reached the gallery, they found Ben stretched out on one of the benches.

"Big help he is," Joe teased.

Ben got up sheepishly and joined the others.

Uncle Ned immediately spotted the trapdoor in the ceiling, but it was too high for them to reach.

"Need ladder," Uncle Ned said, looking around.

"There isn't a ladder in the building," Joe told him. "We've been through the whole church several times, and I don't remember seeing one anywhere."

"Then we get table, stack, reach," Uncle Ned decided.

The young people understood what the old Indian meant. If they brought the table and chairs up from the basement that they had used to open the basement window, they could probably reach the ceiling.

Ben was put to work helping. It was a job to get the big table up the stairs from the basement and then on up the narrow stairs to the gallery but they finally made it.

Straddling the table over the bench directly under the

scuttle hole, they put a chair on top of the table. The ceiling in the gallery was low. Joe and Uncle Ned could both reach the trap door by standing on the chair.

"I'll go up there," Joe volunteered.

Uncle Ned nodded and stood holding the chair for the boy to step on. The girls held their breaths as they watched. Ben stood back, watching as he flipped the key in his hand.

Joe had trouble trying to slide the trap door open. It refused to budge.

"Get chair. I help push," Uncle Ned told them.

Joe jumped down and hurried to the basement to bring up another chair. He placed it beside the other chair on top of the table.

"Ben, you'll have to hold the chairs this time. Uncle Ned is going to stand up on one and me on the other," Joe told the Negro man.

"All right," Ben agreed. He started to put the key in his pocket as he stepped forward to help. The key slipped out of his hand and went flying between the benches, making a loud rattling noise.

Ben stooped to look around. "I jes' lost day key whut I found in dis chouch de other day."

Mandie quickly asked, "You found a key? In this church? When?"

Ben, down on his knees, looking under the benches, raised his head to answer. "Missy, I find dat key de day y'all make me come inside de church, de fust time. It be on de flo' right under my foot where I set."

Mandie said, "Come on, let's help Ben find his key. He found it here in this church and you remember the man and woman were looking for something they had lost."

The young people quickly covered the floor. Uncle Ned, watching, bent to pick up something at his foot.

"Key," he told the young people, and he handed the key to Mandie.

Mandie squinted to read the faint printing on the key while the others crowded around to see.

"It says *Property of National* something or other, *Charlotte, North Carolina*, I think," Mandie said. "What's that other word there?"

"That's a *k* on the end of the word," Celia determined.

Joe looked closer. "Bank!" he exclaimed. "*Property of National Bank of Charlotte, North Carolina.*"

The girls gasped. Uncle Ned nodded in understanding, but Ben looked confused.

"If dat key be de property of de bank, den I'll jes' send it back to 'em," he said innocently.

"Ben, don't you know what you've found?" Mandie asked. "This must be what the man and woman were looking for here that day we hid behind the curtains."

Celia's eyes grew wide. "And if this is what they lost—"

"Those people must be connected with that bank robbery in Charlotte," Joe interrupted.

"You mean they were bank robbers?" Celia asked.

Mandie looked up at Ben. "Can I keep this key?" she asked.

"Sho', Missy," he replied. "Don't belong to me."

Mandie put the key in her pocket. "Uncle Ned, we need to get in touch with this bank in Charlotte," she said.

"We see, Papoose," the Indian agreed. "Now we go in attic. Be dark soon."

"You're right, Uncle Ned," Joe said, climbing up on one of the chairs. "We have to hurry."

Uncle Ned stepped up on the other chair. Ben held the chairs steady while Uncle Ned and Joe pushed on the trapdoor overhead. After several hard blows, it finally moved, and they were able to slide it back, uncovering a square hole in the ceiling.

Joe swung up inside the hole, and they could hear

him walking around in the attic. "The place is pretty empty," he called down to them. "I see Mr. Prattworthy's bag over there and some odds and ends, but there's nobody up here."

"Come," Uncle Ned called to him. "We go." Joe came back down, and they closed the trapdoor and returned the table and chairs to the basement.

As they left the church, Uncle Ned asked Ben to drive them out of town toward the mountains. "Robber not stay in town. Phinny he go, too," the old Indian decided.

They all nodded. The robber wouldn't want to be seen around town, so he would most likely hide out in the country somewhere. Phineas knew that, too.

As they rode along the bumpy, snow-covered country road, they kept watch for anything unusual. There were very few buildings on the road, a few tumbled-down barns, some rough country houses, an old deserted church building, and a school. They stopped at all these places and quickly searched them.

"Uncle Ned, it's going to be dark soon," Celia reminded him.

"One more place. Then go back," Uncle Ned replied.

"Oh, I do hope we can find him," Mandie said.

"Just hope the robber doesn't find him first," Joe cautioned. "The robber must know what's going on in town."

They came to a narrow dirt road branching off the one they were traveling on. Uncle Ned motioned for Ben to pull up on the side road. "Stop there," he said.

Ben did what he was told and brought the rig to a stop. The side road was too narrow, and the snow was too deep for the rig to go down it anyway.

"Come. We walk," Uncle Ned ordered.

They all piled out of the rig onto the frozen snow.

"What's down this road?" Mandie asked.

"Old ground camp for church," the Indian replied, leading the way.

Mandie laughed. "Oh, you mean a campground for the church."

"No more. Church no more use." Uncle Ned adjusted his bow and sling of arrows on his shoulder.

The young people walked carefully on the frozen snow to keep from sliding down.

Ben trudged along behind them, mumbling to himself. "Dem hosses dey gwine be froze to death 'fo' we gits back," he fussed.

"You put their blankets on them," Joe said. "They'll be all right."

"Not fo' long," Ben argued.

In a little while Uncle Ned stopped for the others to catch up with him. He held up his hand. "Quiet," he said softly. "Not far."

Everyone hushed and cautiously followed the old Indian.

As they came around a curve, a large, old dilapidated building came in sight. Several smaller structures sagged nearby, but no one seemed to be anywhere around.

Again Uncle Ned held up his hand for them to stop. He motioned for them to hide behind a cluster of huge tree trunks nearby, then sniffed the air. "Smoke," he whispered.

There was a loud scuffling noise from somewhere behind the big building. Uncle Ned motioned for them to creep forward and stay out of sight. He slipped around the corner of the building. The noise got louder.

They heard a man's loud voice. "That's what you're going to get for snooping in other people's business," he yelled.

There was a loud crack of a whip.

Uncle Ned took an arrow from his sling and softly crept toward the back of the building. The young people stayed right behind him, and Ben brought up the rear.

As they reached the corner, they saw Phineas. He was sitting, tied up, on the snow-covered ground, and a strange man with a gun strapped to his waist raised a horse whip, ready to strike.

Uncle Ned quickly pulled back his bowstring and let his arrow fly. The arrow whizzed overhead and stuck in the tree trunk just over the stranger's head. The man whirled quickly and reached for his gun, unable to see them hiding around the corner. He looked at the arrow embedded in the tree.

"Indians!" the stranger shrieked.

"These woods are full of Indians, mister," Phineas told him as he wiggled to get free of the ropes. "Great big, strong Cherokee Indians."

"Then we'd better leave," the stranger said anxiously.

In the meantime, Uncle Ned had raced around the building to the opposite corner, and at that moment he shot another arrow above the man's head.

"Looks like they've got us surrounded," Phineas warned. "No way we can get out of here."

"We have to leave," the man insisted, nervously eyeing the second arrow. "Those Cherokee Indians are dangerous."

"You leave. I'll stay right here," Phineas offered. "Those Cherokees are my friends."

"If I leave, you're going with me," the stranger ordered. "And if they're your friends, you can see that no harm comes to us when we leave. Otherwise, you are going to be greatly harmed by me."

Uncle Ned raced back to the corner where the others were watching through the bushes.

The stranger stepped toward Phineas. He had a limp! *So this is the man who stole from the grocer,* Mandie thought. Phineas had found him!

The old Indian motioned for the others to come near.

"I go behind man. Shoot arrow," he whispered. "He turn that way. I run fast. Shoot arrow again other way. Man get all confused."

"What can we do, Uncle Ned?" Joe asked in a low voice.

"You go that way. Get help," Uncle Ned motioned toward a slight path off to the right. "Mumblehead live that way. Two minutes."

Joe understood and nodded his head. Uncle Ned slipped around the building. Joe turned to the path and spoke quietly to Ben on his way. "Stay close to the girls," he whispered. "See that they don't get hurt. I'm going for help."

Ben nodded and moved closer to the girls. Together, they watched the stranger and Phineas through the bushes while Uncle Ned moved all around, shooting arrows from different directions.

The stranger seemed more and more frightened, apparently convinced he was surrounded by a whole tribe of Indians. "Hey, you!" he shouted at Phineas. "Call off these confounded Indians. Tell them we want to leave."

Phineas wiggled on the cold snowy ground to free himself from the ropes that bound him. "Do you think they're going to let us leave when they can see you're my enemy and that you've tied me up like this?" he scoffed. "Don't forget. They're my friends. If you don't release me, they'll come and get you in a few minutes."

The stranger limped around in circles for a while, evidently trying to think of some way out of his predicament. Without a word, he pulled a knife from his belt and slashed the ropes that bound Phineas.

Limbering up his wrists and ankles, Phineas finally managed to stand up. But just then, another arrow whizzed through the air and lodged in the tree behind the stranger, clipping his hat.

"Tell them to let us leave!" the stranger yelled, stomping around on his bad leg.

Phineas looked around and then let out a loud Indian yell as Uncle Ned grabbed the stranger from behind. Suddenly scores of Indians came out of the bushes and surrounded the stranger, taking his gun and knife away from him.

"Thank the Lord!" Phineas shouted. "And thank you, Uncle Ned!"

The girls ran forward and met Joe coming from the other side.

"Go!" an Indian's voice shouted.

The young people looked up to see Ben walking toward them, his eyes wide with fright, and a young Indian brave pushing him forward with an arrow poised at his back.

Ben's legs buckled beneath him, and he fell to the ground, begging for his life. "Please, I ain't done nothin'," he pleaded. "Please!"

Uncle Ned ran to Ben's rescue. "Redbird, leave," he commanded. "Ben friend of Papoose."

Redbird smiled and reached down to help Ben up. Ben rolled away from the young Indian, and managing to get to his feet, he ran to where Mandie and Celia were standing.

Mandie glared at the stranger. "You are the man who stole food from the grocer and caused Mr. Phineas to be blamed for it, aren't you?" she asked as Uncle Ned tied the stranger's hands behind him.

"What are you white folk doing with these Indians?" the stranger asked.

"I'm part Cherokee myself," Mandie answered, "and these Indians are my friends."

Joe stepped forward to help Uncle Ned. "Come on, mister," said in a deep, important-sounding voice. "We've got a rig not far from here. We're taking you to town."

The stranger protested. "I've got a bad leg," he complained. "I can't walk. Besides, my horse is in that old barn over there."

"You're not riding a horse," Joe ordered. "You'd only run away. You're going in the rig with us."

Uncle Ned called to the oldest Indian there, the head of the group. "Mumblehead, get horse. Tie to rig," he ordered. "Redbird, get braves. Carry bad man to rig. Hurry!"

Mumblehead disappeared while two young Indians stepped forward and picked up the stranger, carrying him to the rig as the others followed. Soon Mumblehead returned with the horse.

"Mr. Phineas, thank goodness we found you in time," Mandie said as they walked along. "Uncle Ned always knows what to do."

"How did you find the man?" Joe asked.

"I watched the store and sure enough, he came back to steal more," Phineas replied. "He stole a bag of beans and escaped before the grocer could catch him, but I followed him. His horse had thrown a shoe, so he was trying to walk," he explained. "He couldn't go very fast. Then when he turned in here off the road, he happened to look back and see me. There weren't enough bushes for me to hide in."

"Weren't you afraid of him?" Celia asked.

"I suppose so, but I was mad, too," Phineas said, "because he was committing crimes I was being blamed for."

"I can see why Mr. Simpson thought y'all were the same person," Mandie commented. "He's short like you, and he has a bad leg."

"Well, we don't exactly look alike," Phineas protested.

They got the stranger safely secured in the rig and tied the horse behind it. Uncle Ned thanked his Indian friends and told them goodbye as he and the others drove off.

The stranger moaned and groaned all the way, and

the young people kept a close watch on him.

Finally Mandie spoke up. "What's wrong with you?" she asked.

"There's lots wrong with me," the stranger replied. "This here leg has got a bullet in it, for one thing."

Mandie gasped. "A bullet?"

"Who shot you?" Joe demanded.

"I guess I might as well come clean, or I'll die from this leg," the stranger said. "My name is Kent Stagrene. I robbed that bank in Charlotte, and the guard shot me," he confessed, beginning to moan again. He bent down to hold his leg; then he looked up. "I got away with the money, though."

Mandie did some quick thinking. Taking the key Ben found out of her pocket, she showed it to the stranger. "Is this the bank?" she asked.

He reached for the key, but she held it back.

"Where did you get that?" Kent Stagrene asked angrily. "That's the key to the strongbox I took."

"Then where is the money?" Joe asked.

"I don't have it anymore," he said, turning pale. "Someone else stole it from me." Within seconds he passed out.

Uncle Ned tapped Ben on the shoulder. "We take stranger to doctor man," he said.

Ben headed for Mrs. Taft's house.

Chapter 12 / An Angry Mob

By the time Ben pulled the rig into Mrs. Taft's drive-way, it was pitch dark.

Ella greeted them at the front door and ran to the parlor. "They's home, Miz Taft, and they's got some man wid 'em," she reported. "Looks like he's hurt."

"Go tell Dr. Woodard," Mrs. Taft ordered, hurrying to the front hallway. "He's up in his room, getting his coat. It's so late that he was about to go out looking for them."

Uncle Ned and Ben carried the still-unconscious man through the doorway. Mrs. Taft stepped back. "Who is that?" she asked shakily. "What's wrong with him?"

"He's been shot," Joe volunteered.

Mrs. Taft began to sway slightly as though she were about to faint.

"We didn't shoot him, Miz Taft," Ben assured her. "Dis de man whut rob de bank in Charlotte. De bank guard done shot him."

Ben and Uncle Ned laid the man on the floor in the hallway.

"A bank robber!" Mrs. Taft cried.

"He need doctor man," Uncle Ned said.

Phineas and the girls gathered around Mrs. Taft.

"Thank goodness, you're back, Phineas," Mrs. Taft said.

Dr. Woodard came hurrying into the hallway, followed by Ella who stayed to see what was going on.

"Dr. Woodard, this is the bank robber and Mr. Simpson's thief all rolled into one," Mandie explained. "He confessed everything to us."

The doctor quickly knelt down to examine the stranger's leg. "It's pretty bad," he said, looking up at Mrs. Taft. "Do you have anywhere we can put this man? Even though he is a criminal he needs medical attention fast."

"Why, yes, I suppose he can be put in an empty room in the servants' quarters. Can you get him upstairs that far? The rooms are on the third floor," Mrs. Taft answered. "He'll be away from us up there."

"We can manage," Dr. Woodard said, standing up.

"We take," Uncle Ned said and motioned for Ben to help him pick up the unconscious man.

They moved slowly up the stairs carrying the criminal. Everyone stood watching. Dr. Woodard followed, giving directions.

"Ella, show them an empty room up there and then bring some coffee and cocoa to the parlor," Mrs. Taft told the maid.

The Negro girl hurried to pass the group on the stairs to direct them to a room.

The young people and Phineas removed their outerwear and left it in the hall and followed Mrs. Taft into the parlor.

Seated by the roaring fire in the parlor the young people related their adventures and Phineas filled in with his as Mrs. Taft listened. Ella brought in hot coffee and hot cocoa and served it.

"The man said his name was Kent Stagrene," Mandie said, pulling the key from her pocket. "I showed him this key that Ben found in the church. He said it belongs to the strongbox he stole from the bank. Then he said somebody else stole the strongbox from him. So I think the man and woman we saw in the church that day must be the ones who robbed him."

Everyone agreed.

Suddenly Mandie caught her breath. "Mr. Phineas!" she said excitedly. "I just happened to remember something. I'm pretty sure the newspaper said there was a reward for the capture of the robber. You can get that money!"

"I didn't capture the robber," Phineas objected. "He captured me. Y'all captured the robber."

Mrs. Taft spoke up quickly. "They're right, Phineas," she said. "You found the man and went after him. Besides, these young people don't need the money. And I'm sure you could use it to get back on your feet."

"Thank you, Mrs. Taft, but I still think they are the ones who actually captured the man," Phineas replied.

"We'll see about that," Mrs. Taft said with a twinkle in her eye.

After a while Dr. Woodard and Uncle Ned joined the others in the parlor.

"Is the robber going to live?" Mandie asked as the two men sat down.

"I think so," the doctor replied. "But he has a bad wound. He should have got medical help right away after it happened. Uncle Ned and Ben filled me in on all the details."

"What are we going to do with him, Dr. Woodard?" Mrs. Taft said uneasily.

"Well, we left Ben watching him for now to make sure he doesn't try to get away if he regains consciousness," the doctor replied. "But we'll have to notify the sheriff that he's here."

"Will the sheriff take him away and put him in jail?" Joe asked.

"I don't think so—not in the condition he's in," his father explained. "I imagine the sheriff will just let him stay here until he is out of danger. Then he'll move him."

"What will they do to him?" Celia inquired.

"That will be up to the bank in Charlotte," Dr. Woodard told her. "Our sheriff will probably send him back to the sheriff in Mecklenburg County."

"I never dreamed there would be so much danger," Mrs. Taft said wearily, "or I never would have agreed for these young people to go looking for Mr. Simpson's thief."

Before long, Ella appeared in the doorway to announce that supper was on the table.

In the dining room, they continued discussing the matter as they ate. The young people hardly ate anything, however, because they were too excited. Mrs. Taft said she was too nervous to eat, knowing she had a bank robber in the house. But Phineas, Dr. Woodard, and Uncle Ned made good headway into the delicious food set before them.

Mrs. Taft changed the subject. "How was Hilda when you were up there a while ago?" she asked Dr. Woodard.

"She's just not doing any good," he said, shaking his head.

"Is she conscious?" Mandie asked.

"No, I don't think so," the doctor replied. "She just lies there—doesn't open her eyes or respond in any way."

Ella rushed into the dining room and ran to Mrs. Taft. "De sheriff man he be here," she said. "He want to see you and de doctuh in de parlor."

Mrs. Taft glanced at Dr. Woodard in alarm.

The doctor took charge. "Ella, please tell him we'll be there in a few minutes."

Ella quickly left the room.

"What does he want?" Mrs. Taft asked. "Phineas, you'd better get out of sight. Mr. Simpson may have sent him for you."

Dr. Woodard laid down his napkin and stood up.

"That won't be necessary, Phineas," he said. "We'll just tell him the truth. We have the man upstairs that he's looking for."

Mrs. Taft followed Dr. Woodard out of the room into the parlor. Sheriff Jones was sitting by the fire. He rose to greet them. They all sat down to talk while the young people hid outside the parlor door, watching and listening. Phineas stayed in the dining room.

The sheriff started the conversation. "Sorry to bother you, Mrs. Taft, but—"

"Did that Mr. Simpson send you here?" Mrs. Taft interrupted.

"Well, yes, ma'am, he did," the sheriff admitted. "He told me you have the man who robbed his store, right here in your house."

"Of all the nerve!" Mrs. Taft exclaimed.

"I think I can explain, Sheriff," Dr. Woodard said. "You see, Mr. Simpson thought the man stealing food from his store was a man who is a friend of ours, whom we've known for years. This man's name is Phineas Prattworthy, and he has been living over on the Nantahala Mountain. But it so happens that we know for sure that Phineas is not guilty because we found the man who really stole from Mr. Simpson. He's upstairs. I've just removed a bullet from his leg."

The sheriff looked startled. "A bullet from his leg?" he asked. "Who is this man? Did Mr. Simpson shoot him?"

"No, Mr. Simpson didn't shoot him," the doctor said. "It seems this man also robbed a bank in Charlotte and was shot by a guard."

"That bank robbery last week in Charlotte?" the sheriff asked in disbelief. "You have the man who did it right here in this house?"

"Yes, we do. That's what I've just been telling you," the doctor insisted. "And he's the same man who stole Mr. Simpson's groceries."

The sheriff jumped up. "Where is he? I need to see about moving him to the jail!" he said excitedly.

"It's impossible to move him," the doctor warned. "He let that leg get infected, and right now he's barely hanging on. But if you want to see him, I'll be glad to show you where he is."

"All right," the sheriff agreed.

When the two men made their way up the stairs, the young people came back into the parlor and sat down. Dr. Woodard and the sheriff returned a short time later.

"Are you taking that terrible man out of my house, Sheriff?" Mrs. Taft asked.

The sheriff rubbed his chin thoughtfully. "No, I'm afraid I agree with Dr. Woodard that he shouldn't be moved right now," he said. "Unless you insist that I remove him from the premises, I'll leave him here."

"He can stay here provided someone guards him at all times," Mrs. Taft decided. "I don't want him wandering all over my house."

"He's not able to do any wandering around," Dr. Woodard assured her.

"Well, I can't leave Ben in there to watch him all the time," Mrs. Taft argued. "I need Ben for other things."

"If you'll allow it, I'll send a deputy over to guard him," the sheriff offered.

Mrs. Taft looked relieved. "That will be fine," she said. "Just get him out of my house as soon as it is possible."

At that moment, they heard loud noises outside the house. Everyone looked at each other.

Mandie ran to the window and peeked through the drawn draperies. "Grandmother!" she cried. "There must be a hundred people out in your front yard!"

Mrs. Taft and the sheriff quickly joined her at the window, followed by the others.

"What do they want, Sheriff?" Mrs. Taft asked nervously.

Everyone stared out the window at the sight of people everywhere. Some had lanterns, and they were all screaming something.

The sheriff took charge. "I'll go see what's going on," he said. Heading for the hallway, he opened the front door, and the others followed, staying behind him.

As soon as the door opened, the people on the lawn surged forward. "We want him! We want him!" they cried.

The sheriff took his pistol from its holster and fired a shot into the air. The crowd hushed. His face was in full view in the lamplight from the hallway.

"This is the sheriff here," he told them. "Now, what do you people want?"

"We want that man who desecrated the house of the Lord!" one man cried.

"We want the man who brought all that bad luck to this town with all that bell ringing and writing on the church wall!" a woman yelled.

"Send him out, Sheriff. We're gonna try him here and now!" another man shouted.

"He brung the flu down on this town and caused people to die!" a woman yelled.

The sheriff stepped forward. "Now you wait just a minute!" he hollered. "I'm the law in this town, and we're going to do things by the law as long as I'm sheriff. Now go home—every one of you!"

"We ain't going home till we git that man!" a man insisted.

The angry mob grew louder and louder, pressing closer and closer toward the house. The sheriff raised his gun and fired into the air again.

His shot was answered by another shot from the crowd. "We got guns, too, Sheriff," someone called out. "And we know how to shoot 'em!"

"I'm going to arrest all you troublemakers if you don't move on," the sheriff threatened.

"There ain't a jail big enough to hold us all," a woman yelled.

"Give us that man and we'll leave!" cried a man in front.

"We know you've got him," another bellowed. "Mr. Simpson said so."

Mandie pursed her lips at hearing this. *So Mr. Simpson was the cause of this*, she thought angrily.

"I'm going back inside now," the sheriff called back to the crowd. "We're having supper, and I don't want you moving any closer to this house. I'll discuss the matter with the lady of the house and let you know what she has to say." He quickly closed the door.

Before anyone could say anything, the sheriff turned to Mrs. Taft and explained. "Of course I didn't mean what I told them," he said. "I'm going for help. I left my horse in the backyard. I'll be back as fast as I can. Just don't open the door under any circumstances."

Rushing through the hallway, he headed for the back door. Everyone else looked at each other nervously.

"Let's sit in the parlor," Dr. Woodard suggested, leading the way. "The draperies are all drawn, so they can't see in."

"What are we going to do?" Mrs. Taft asked as they took seats around the room.

"Nothing," Dr. Woodard replied. "We'll just wait for the sheriff to come back."

Everyone sat silently for a few seconds and then Dr. Woodard spoke again. "I need to check on Hilda and our prisoner," he decided. "I won't be long." He stood up and left.

Mrs. Taft also rose. "I think I'll talk to Phineas," she said. "He must still be in the dining room."

"He probably is," Mandie agreed. "We told him to stay there."

When Mrs. Taft left the parlor, Uncle Ned moved

nearer to Mandie. All three young people sat in silence as the noise from the crowd grew stronger.

"They judge," Uncle Ned commented. "Big Book say not judge."

Mandie could feel her anger rising. "That's right, Uncle Ned," she agreed. Suddenly she jumped up and ran to the hallway. "I'm going to tell them what I think of them."

Before anyone could stop her, she opened the door, and the angry mob became very quiet as they saw the door open.

"Please listen to me," Mandie called to the crowd from the front porch. The lamps in the hallway illuminated the area where she stood.

Joe joined her while Uncle Ned and Celia stood back, just inside the house.

When the crowd saw that it was just Mandie, they laughed at her. "Where is the woman of the house?" they yelled. "We don't talk to no young'un!"

Mandie strode to the top of the steps. "Please listen to me!" she yelled at the top of her voice. "I know a lot of you are from our church, and you claim to be Christians. Well, you're not acting Christlike tonight!"

The people nearest the house hushed to listen, and gradually the whole crowd quieted.

"The Bible says, 'Blessed are the merciful; for they shall obtain mercy,'" she reminded them. "You are not showing mercy tonight. You are not behaving at all like Christians."

"Just give us that man," a man yelled. "He's the one who brought all this trouble on our town."

"No, he didn't!" Mandie yelled back. "No human being has the power to bring curses on people, or to cause illness or anything else. You people who are Christians should know that. That's plain old superstition, and there's no place for such thinking in the minds of Christians."

"Just give us that man!" the same man hollered again.

"I want to tell you about the man who was hiding in the church," Mandie continued.

The crowd immediately hushed.

"That man is so poor and disabled that he had to eat out of trash cans," she said. "He had no one left to care whether he lived or died—no one to take care of him." She took a deep breath and went on. "He happened to see a man rush out of Mr. Simpson's store and drop an apple. When he picked it up, Mr. Simpson falsely accused him of stealing. He had done nothing wrong, but he was afraid because he had no one to turn to. He hid in the church, hoping someone would come along who would help him."

"Why didn't he ask somebody to help him?" a woman yelled.

"Because he didn't think he knew anyone in this town," Mandie answered. "He didn't know anyone he could trust. You see, he was living in the Nantahala Mountains with his son. Then his son died, and the man had a stroke and was unable to work. Besides, he's very old."

"Well, Mr. Simpson said he stole from him," a man insisted.

"Tell Mr. Simpson to step forward if he's out there with you," Mandie ordered. "We'll straighten that out right now. Where is Mr. Simpson?"

"He ain't here," a woman said.

"He can't even fight his own battles, is that it?" Mandie mocked. "He has to get the town in an uproar to fight for him?"

"Where is that man who was hiding in the church?" a woman asked.

"He's right here in this house," Mandie replied. "My

grandmother has taken him into her home. Most of you know my grandmother. She would never protect a criminal. You know that."

"How do we know you're telling the truth?" someone yelled.

"Because we also have in this house, and under arrest by the sheriff, the man who *did* steal from Mr. Simpson. He is the same man who robbed the bank in Charlotte. He—"

The crowd went wild. "A bank robber!" they yelled. "In this house?"

Joe moved closer to Mandie and gave her a little pat on the shoulder for encouragement.

"Please let me explain! Please!" Mandie pleaded with the angry crowd.

Finally the people calmed down enough to listen.

"The bank robber was shot at the bank in Charlotte, and we found him out in the woods," Mandie explained. "Dr. Woodard is looking after him, and the sheriff's men are guarding him. As soon as he is able to be moved, he will be put in jail."

An old man stepped forward within the range of the light from the hallway and spoke. "I believe you, little lady. But the man did damage to the house of the Lord, and he ought to be punished for that."

The crowd waited silently for Mandie's reply.

"But that's not for an angry mob to decide," she reminded them. "That's the business of the church members, not the whole town. And not like this."

"I guess you're right, little lady," the old man said. He turned to the crowd. "It's time we'se all in our own homes," he yelled. "Let's go!"

A loud murmuring rippled through the crowd.

"Please go home," Mandie begged. "If you're the Christians you claim to be, you'll go on home. 'Blessed are the merciful; for they shall obtain mercy.' "

One by one, the crowd turned slowly to leave. Mandie's heart was suddenly thumping wildly as she realized what she had done, standing up to this crowd. "Good night, everyone," she called with a slight quiver in her voice. "God bless you."

Several in the crowd repeated her words back to her.

Without turning around, Mandie whispered to Joe, "Joe, I can't move!" she said. "I just realized what I did! They could have mobbed us!"

Joe put his arm around her, gently turning her toward the door. "You sure had me scared to death," he said as they entered the house. "I just knew they were all going to come on into the house!"

Joe closed the door behind them.

Uncle Ned stepped forward, put his arm around Mandie, and led her into the parlor. "Papoose, I proud of you," he said. "Jim Shaw would be proud of Papoose."

Mandie collapsed on the sofa. "Thank you, Uncle Ned," she replied. "Something just came over me, and I had to speak up for Mr. Phineas. I don't know what made me do it."

When Mrs. Taft returned to the parlor with Dr. Woodard and Phineas, they were astounded to hear what had happened.

Mrs. Taft started shaking. "You could have been killed, Amanda!" she exclaimed.

"But she wasn't," Dr. Woodard reminded her. "And she has cleared Phineas's reputation." He smiled at Mandie. "I think you'd make a good lawyer, Amanda—if we had such things as women lawyers."

"No, thank you," Mandie said. "Joe is going to be the lawyer."

Celia stared at her friend in amazement. "I could never have done what you did, Mandie," she said.

By the time the sheriff returned with reinforcements, the crowd had completely dispersed, and all he had to do was leave one deputy to guard the still-unconscious prisoner.

There was no more trouble in the town and Uncle Ned went home.

By the end of the week, Kent Stagrene, the bank robber, had regained consciousness and was well enough to be moved to the jail.

Mandie had kept the key, after showing it to the sheriff.

"I'll just keep it, Sheriff Jones," Mandie told him the day he moved Kent Stagrene from her grandmother's house. "Who knows, I might just find the box it goes to." They were alone in the front hallway.

"What if we find those people? We may need the key," the sheriff said. "Besides, that key belongs to the bank and I think we ought to return it."

"I'll bring it to you in a day or two," she said.

"Miss Amanda, I don't want you getting into any trouble with that key," Sheriff Jones said. "If word got around that you had the key, those gangsters with the strongbox might just come after it."

"But nobody knows I have it except you and my family here," Mandie said. "I promise. I'll bring it to you in a day or two. Please."

The sheriff looked into those blue eyes, so much like those of her mother whom he had once known, and finally smiled and said, "All right. Just a day or two now. Remember, no longer."

As soon as the sheriff left, Mandie hurried to find Joe and Celia. They gathered in the sun room to talk.

"I'm going to have to give up this key," Mandie told them. "What can we do about finding that strongbox before I let the sheriff have this key?"

"Now, Mandie, you are dealing with real gangsters when you try to get involved in this," Joe warned.

"Just tell me where you think they would hide the box," Mandie insisted, ignoring Joe's warning.

Celia spoke up. "Those people may not even be in this town any longer."

"That's right," Joe agreed. "There's no way we could find that box."

"We'll see," Mandie said.

The next morning the sheriff came knocking on the door, asking for Mandie. The adults were all gone and the young people were in the parlor. Ella ushered Sheriff Jones into the room.

"Well, Miss Amanda, I guess I need that key, if you don't mind," the sheriff told her.

"Did you find the box?" Mandie asked eagerly.

"We not only found the box. We also found that man and woman who had stolen it from Kent Stagrene," Sheriff Jones explained.

"Where are they? Can we see them?" Mandie wanted to know.

"Mandie, what do you want to see those people for?" Joe asked impatiently.

"I'd like to see if they're the same people we saw in the church," Mandie said.

"They were," the sheriff confirmed. "They followed Kent Stagrene to his hiding place after he robbed the bank and were able to take the box away from him. They came on into town here with the box with the intentions of staying at the hotel. When they went to register, the hotel clerk saw the box and recognized it as a bank box."

"Why didn't the clerk have them arrested?" Mandie asked.

"Well, instead of notifying my office the clerk thought he could get a reward for himself and he asked the strangers if they wanted to put their money box in the safe. The people suddenly decided they didn't want to register and left. The clerk followed them. The man and woman split up. The clerk tried to keep up with the man but the man was too smart for him. And the woman completely disappeared."

"You still haven't said how you know they were in the church," Mandie insisted.

"When we caught them they said they had lost the key in the church," the sheriff explained.

"Now we know," Celia said with a sigh.

"Where were they from, Sheriff Jones?" Mandie asked.

"No place in particular," the sheriff said. "They are professional gamblers and they travel from place to place, wherever they can set up games. They just happened to be in the bank when Kent Stagrene robbed it."

"Thanks for letting me know, Sheriff," Mandie said. "And, Sheriff, would you please do me a favor? Would you give the bank Mr. Phineas Prattworthy's name as the one who captured the robber? I understand the reward offered was for capture of the robber. And Mr. Phineas needs the reward money real bad."

"There are two rewards offered, one for the man and another one for the money," the sheriff explained. "As officers of the law we can't collect rewards so we'll just turn in his name for both rewards. I'm sure he'll be hearing from the bank."

"What about the hotel clerk?" Joe asked.

"He didn't capture the money," the sheriff said. "My deputy happened to be right there when it happened and he took the money box from the people."

"Thank you, Sheriff Jones. The rewards will mean so much to Mr. Phineas," Mandie said, smiling at the law officer.

And in a few days the bank in Charlotte sent a special messenger to see Phineas Prattworthy, bringing a letter of thanks and an enormous reward.

"I still don't feel I deserve it," the old man declared as they all sat in the parlor after the messenger left. "But I do owe the church for damages because of my bad conduct."

"You'll have plenty for that and plenty left over to live on," Mrs. Taft replied.

"Thank the Lord," Mandie said softly.

Mrs. Taft offered Phineas a house and farm that she owned near Asheville. He could make a good living off it with the help of a few hired hands which he could now afford. He was thankful for her kindness.

The next Saturday Uncle Cal came by Mrs. Taft's house with the message that classes would resume on the following Monday.

"I'm glad to see you, Uncle Cal," Mandie told the old Negro as she and Celia stood talking to him in the front hallway, "but I was hoping we'd have a little longer out of school."

"But, Missy, all dem girls done got well now, and you gotta keep on wid dat book learnin' so you won't be ignorant," he teased.

"Aren't you coming in?" Celia invited.

"No, Missy. I got lots of calls to make to git the girls all back to school," he replied, thanking her. "But me and Phoebe, we see y'all come Monday." And with that he left.

Mandie closed the door and turned toward the parlor. "Oh, shucks!" she said.

"But, Mandie, we knew everyone was better when Dr. Woodard told us he and Joe were going home yesterday," Celia reminded her.

They both sat down near the fireplace in the parlor.

"I know," Mandie said with a sigh. "Oh, well, the house seems so empty with everyone else gone that I suppose we might as well go back to school. And we do still have a mystery back there to solve. Remember our little problems with a certain mouse?" she asked.

Celia nodded. "Oh, yes," she said. "We never did get that cleared up, did we?"

Mandie sat silently for a minute. "I just wish Hilda would get well." She sighed again.

"At least when Dr. Woodard went home, he said she was no worse," Celia reminded her. "And he has those nurses staying with her around the clock. Maybe she'll change for the better soon."

Just then there was a knock on the door, and Mandie rushed to answer it.

When she opened the door, there stood Uncle Ned, smiling down at her. "Uncle Ned, come on in," Mandie greeted the old Indian, ushering him into the parlor. "I didn't know you were coming back so soon."

"I bring message from mother of Papoose," he said, sitting by the fire to warm his hands. He smiled broadly.

Snowball, who was curled up on the rug nearby, opened one eye to look at him and then went back to sleep.

"Good news?" Mandie asked excitedly.

"Yes. Good News," the Indian replied. "Mother of Papoose say she have big surprise for Papoose for Christmas."

"Surprise for Christmas?" Mandie puzzled over the message. "Tell me what it is, Uncle Ned. Please?"

"Not know, Papoose," Uncle Ned told her. "Mother of Papoose say she not tell me so I not tell Papoose."

"You mean Mother sent you all the way over here to tell me she had a big surprise for me for Christmas, and she didn't even tell you what it is?" Mandie frowned.

"I not know surprise, Papoose," the Indian repeated.

"Not even a little teeny bit?" Mandie teased.

Uncle Ned reached over to her and patted her blonde head. "Papoose, I not know surprise. Must wait for Christmas," he said with a smile.

"Oh, no," Mandie moaned. "I'll be wondering from now until Christmas holidays what this is all about."

"So will I," Celia added.

"It must be something awfully important for her to send you, Uncle Ned," Mandie reasoned.

The old Indian grinned. "Papoose see," he said. "Wait for Christmas."

After Uncle Ned left that afternoon, Mandie paced up and down in the parlor talking through this newest mystery. Celia sat patiently by the fire, petting Snowball.

What surprise could her mother have for her that was important enough to send Uncle Ned with the message? Mandie wondered. And why didn't her mother just wait until Mandie came home for the holidays and tell her about the surprise then?

Mandie could hardly wait.